Lara Bliss Loves Rose Madder Genuine

LARA BLISS LOVES ROSE MADDER GENUINE

By GJ Babb

Copyright © 2019 GJ Babb

gjbabb.com

The moral right of the author has been asserted.

Apart from any fair dealing for the purposes of research or private study, or criticism or review, as permitted under the Copyright, Designs and Patents Act 1988, this publication may only be reproduced, stored or transmitted, in any form or by any means, with the prior permission in writing of the publishers, or in the case of reprographic reproduction in accordance with the terms of licences issued by the Copyright Licensing Agency. Enquiries concerning reproduction outside those terms should be sent to the publishers.

This is a work of fiction. Names, characters, businesses, places, events and incidents are either the products of the author's imagination or used in a fictitious manner. Any resemblance to actual persons, living or dead, or actual events is purely coincidental.

Matador
9 Priory Business Park,
Wistow Road, Kibworth Beauchamp,
Leicestershire, LE8 0RX
Tel: 0116 279 2299
Email: books@troubador.co.uk
Web: www.troubador.co.uk/matador
Twitter: @matadorbooks

ISBN 978 1838590 147

British Library Cataloguing in Publication Data.
A catalogue record for this book is available from the British Library.

Printed and bound in Great Britain by 4edge Limited
Typeset in 11pt Sabon MT by Troubador Publishing Ltd, Leicester, UK

Matador is an imprint of Troubador Publishing Ltd

*Although you enter an imaginary land,
this book is for the real Laras.*

ONE

Emsbury, situated on the estuary of the river Em, the West Country. The summer season, 2009.

Jack Palanga, The Celebrities' Confidant, was seen first lurking outside the gates of Terpsichore Manor. Unlike most journalists, he did not file a story about Meade Daguerre's luxurious bolthole in the country and disappear. The next day he was in Emsbury where he bought drinks in the Crown and made himself agreeable to the regulars – at any rate to those who would talk. He said he was staying at the King's Reach, Emsbury's best hotel. It began to be told that he was interested in yachts and was seen with a camera, nosing around the marina and the boatyards upstream from the town. When Lara Bliss heard he had been enquiring about whether Meade Daguerre kept a yacht on the estuary she decided she ought to run him to ground and have a chat with him. She reckoned somebody enquiring about a fellow artist in Emsbury was trespassing on her patch, and if a journalist was tramping the streets and boatyards trying to concoct some summertime scandal she meant to find out what it was.

Standing at the bow of the foot passenger ferry, impatient to arrive, Bliss crossed the estuary from Seaview to Emsbury. She surveyed the scene with an affectionate, yet not uncritical, eye. True, she regarded the estuary – from the silver and umber swell carried ever inland on the southwesterly winds, to the steeply wooded slopes that enclosed the river Em as it made its way down to the sea – as a perfection. But she could not ignore the human intrusions on the scene, both good and bad. Immediately ahead and climbing the slopes towards the crest of the hillside that enclosed it, lay Emsbury. She saw in its serried rows of fishmen's cottages close to the shore, its churches – one Saxon, one Victorian gothic – it's jumble of business premises, shops and pubs that from the quay snaked up the steady climb out of the town, and its handsome seaside villas perched amongst the pines on every eminence and buttressed terrace, the sum of human striving, ingenuity, constancy and misplaced folly. She made a fine figurehead: commanding and almost (one may wish to say) *statuesque*: a woman of middling years who was clearly nobody's fool. Her frank expression and a handsome profile spoke of clear thoughts, a tolerant understanding of others and an intuitive grasp of the good life. She found Palanga in the Trawlerman Inn, halfway up the High Street.

'Hello, I'm Lara Bliss.' She found herself looking into the face of a tall, athletic young man wearing a cheerful smile. 'Jack Palanga, isn't it?' She had been expecting an older man with more of a hard-bitten, man-of-the-world appearance. He looked her up and down without speaking.

'Mr Daguerre seems to be bringing London ways to our little town,' she observed. She sat down on the bench opposite him and placed her gin and tonic between them on the table.

Palanga smiled. 'Meade Daguerre is always newsworthy.'

'Jack Palanga. That's an unusual name.'

'It travels well.'

'I seem to think you write celebrity gossip for a red top, do you not?'

'Do I?'

'And are practised at deflecting questions you care not to answer.'

He continued to smile pleasantly, but offered no comment.

'You're interested in Mr Daguerre?'

He laughed. 'I'm a journalist, so I'm interested in everything.' He looked at her confidingly. 'You're a famous local artist, aren't you? Everybody hereabouts seems to know you.'

'They do? Well, I'm president of the Emsbury League of Artists. I paint mermaids – emancipated mermaids, mind!'

'I'm sure they are, *very*. So, are you a fan of Mr Daguerre?'

'I imagine we have our ideological differences. I'm a romantic naturalist, he a neo-conceptualist.'

The distinction – offered without a trace of irony – caused Palanga to laugh out loud.

'So, why are you here?' she continued, not about to be put out by a smart Alec from London. 'As president of the League, I consider all artists in Emsbury are my business.'

He put on a serious face and leant forward. 'I'm looking for a spinnaker with a sunburst pattern. I hear Daguerre has a yacht with a spinnaker like that. Least ways, that's what a man in Poole told me.'

'What about it?'

'Can't say, just following my nose. Five-minute wonder, most likely.' With mock weariness he traced several loops in the air with his finger. 'Celebrities at play... The devil's always in the detail... Yet hope springs eternal!'

'Amen,' agreed Bliss. She shook with silent mirth. 'Mr Palanga, you work for a scurrilous rag. I am a local. I know this estuary and its inhabitants – the ones who, unlike you, aren't passing through. I also know all there is to know about its geography, its politics, its commerce. I insist you call on my expertise to dispel whatever dreadful tissue of lies you are concocting for your newspaper. I see nothing but ruinous libel for your proprietor unless you treat Emsbury and its inhabitants with scrupulous fairness.'

'I will,' he said warmly, '*I will!* Mind you, I don't shake off easily. I'm also interested in a dead Chinese man. Was *he* in your care?'

She looked at him soberly. 'Ah!' She knew the story: a body had turned up in a lay-by on the road between the higgledy-piggledy hamlet of Edwardian villas known as Seaview, across the estuary from Emsbury, and Totteringham. The man's ethnicity had been quickly established. The nearest Chinese community was over twenty miles away in the county town. Police enquiries there failed to turn up anyone missing, and a story had done the rounds that the victim had been brought from further afield and dumped from the boot of a car. In this quiet corner of the West Country the incident had been sufficiently... well, "alien" was a word some had used; sufficient to merit it being regarded with a certain dispassion. As a consequence, disquiet at the murder had become non-specific, generalised; it had spread over everything like a stain. And in the process the disquiet had lost its sense of having a source in a perpetrator and a victim.

'You mean the one they found in the lay-by on the road to Totteringham?'

'Yes, him. You know how he died?'

She took a sip of her drink. 'No, I don't.'

'He drowned in the sea.'

She thought about that for a while. 'Then it's extraordinary he should have been found in a lay-by!'

He nodded meaningfully. 'I'm just looking for a story.' He examined her with his stubborn smile.

'Yes, that was sad. Dumped far from home. The story didn't merit much attention, even in the Emsbury & District Advertiser. My offer still stands,' she decided, brightening. 'I know this town, and the district up and down the estuary. I'll save you from chasing after mysteries that aren't really mysteries at all.'

'Then you and I shall compare notes,' he laughed, 'when I have some to compare!'

TWO

Lara Bliss's niece, Cornelia – she was tall and angular and of somewhat advanced views for her thirteen years – had arrived in Seaview from boarding school to find that Lovage was being put up at the house. 'I've loaned him my studio,' her aunt explained. 'He's here on a rather important archaeological mission.'

Cornelia had a habit of looking anywhere but at the person speaking to her. It gave an impression not of shyness but of vagueness, a far-away look that suited the soft, pleasing contours of her face. It could have been the self-possessed look of a prodigy, even if it was impossible to say what particular talent she might have. But appearances were deceptive; when provoked there was a righteous prophet ready to erupt and judge harshly the world of flabby ideas and polite nothings. Lovage she had met; Lovage, she conceded, was *a good thing*: when it came to things dug out of the ground he had a streak of the fanatic. 'I know Lovage,' she said to Bliss as though divulging a secret. 'He works for the British Museum.'

'How on earth do you know him?'

'Oh, he used to work for Uncle Stan, before they gave him a proper job.'

'I knew he worked for Stan, but I'd no idea you'd met him. Small world!'

Cornelia found him in the studio, the largest of the range of ramshackled buildings that ran along the garden wall. She canvassed him determinedly to be taken to see what he was doing. So it was that Lovage found himself waiting for her, his forehead rested on the steering wheel of his Renault, a passably good-looking young man with a liking for corduroy and an extensive grasp of the scholarly aspects of his trade.

'*Cornelia, do come on!*' he said to himself. 'If you want to come, *come now*!' He looked at his watch. 'Time I was back.'

When finally she did arrive – throwing herself violently into the passenger seat – he took the road to Totteringham out of Seaview. Little more than a lane, it wound up through woodland, the trees canting inwards as though to engulf them. They cleared the trees suddenly, as the sun clears the clouds on a blustery day, and the wooded slopes that fringed the valley of the Em were below them. Out of the corner of his eye Lovage could see Cornelia gazing out blankly across the estuary towards Emsbury.

'How are things?' he asked. 'School a success?'

She squinted at him intently. 'Not really. It's a bit of a bore. Latin and all that.' It was quite obvious that on this subject she had no intention of humouring him with details.

Their climb continued and soon there came into view, beyond the estuary, the sea and the coastline stretching away westwards to the dunes of Foreland. As the road began to level off they turned through a gate. They bumped along a track running beside a stunted hedge. A rising vista of grassland, recently mown, opened up before them. Soon both the hedge and the track gave out and they drove on across the expanses of the field towards the horizon. When they breasted the ridge the hillside fell away into a natural amphitheatre. The bowl of the amphitheatre, hanging above the steep slopes of the Em valley, was enclosed by woodland on all sides, except in the direction from which they were approaching. Cornelia leaned forward, suddenly alert as she took in the rectangles of bare earth, fringed with blue plastic sheeting, where several trenches had already been opened up on the floor of the bowl.

Highest up the hillside was a trailer that had brought the equipment for the dig and beyond it a line of parked vehicles. As they freewheeled towards them, Lovage pointed out the main features of the dig.

'The archaeology unit of the county's Heritage Services is supposedly running things in consultation with a couple of archaeologists from the university. The university bods are the sticklers. That's the HQ: the marquee on the slope just above the excavation, and the tents above the marquee belong to the diggers camping here. There are some paying diggers as well; they stay at B & Bs somewhere; the university has roped them in as part of its summer school programme.'

Cornelia could see the activity in the trenches quite clearly now.

'Then there are the English Heritage people: they're helping out and keeping an eye on whether the site turns out to be important. And that's what I'm here for too, but on behalf of the British Museum. "Observing" they call it. To be frank,' he confided, 'I'm a bit of a spare part. The county archaeologists think it's their territory and the university people think the dig's being done in too much haste. There's a push on because of nighthawks.'

'Nighthawks?'

'That's what we call thieving treasure hunters. Anywhere there's a scent of treasure they hunt by night and call themselves nighthawks.'

'What, *gold*?'

'Yes, precious metals, coins. They use metal detectors.'

'Oh!' It may have been all Cornelia uttered but her interest had been thoroughly stirred. By the time they came to a halt next to a minibus with "County Heritage Services" written along its side she was transformed: the romance of digging history out of the ground had taken a grip on her, and here was an opportunity to see a crime scene at first hand. She set out at such a speed Lovage had to jog to catch her up. They made their way down past one end of the encampment. The interior of the marquee – the canvas walls were rolled up – was laid out with rows of tables and several people were sorting finds. Cornelia did not stop to see but pressed on towards the trenches where a dozen or more people were at work, scraping back the rich loam with conscientious restraint. Every so often a box of spoil would come out of a trench and be dumped on one of the sheets of plastic.

One of the diggers – a burly man in shorts with a crosspatch face – detached himself from a group examining something out of sight on the floor of the closest trench and came towards them.

'I was wondering if you'd come back,' he said by way of a greeting to Lovage. 'Who's this?'

Lovage gave a grunt, as if to say his comings and goings were his own affair. 'This is Cornelia; she's going to scrub pot shards.'

'Fair enough. All hands to the pumps, I suppose. You'll give her a tour?'

Lovage indicated he would and the man drifted away.

'Who's that?' asked Cornelia, regarding him with faint distaste.

'That's Bolshoi Bertie, from the county's Heritage Services,' he said in a low voice. 'He thinks he's running things; member of the Comintern.'

Cornelia didn't understand "Comintern" but suspected – rightly – adult facetiousness of some kind.

'There's a geo-physical survey in the marquee,' Lovage explained as they continued towards the centre of the dig. 'I'll show it to you later. It looks as though what we have here is buildings with rectangular rooms – Roman – intermingled with what might be circular enclosures with postholes. They would be earlier. We're putting in trenches across some of the biggest anomalies to try and see what's what. And over there – that's the lowest part of the site – there's a midden and ditch, full of pottery and other rubbish.'

'I want to see where they were digging for gold,' said Cornelia.

Lovage laughed and directed her towards the furthest trench, close to the eaves of the wood, where a young woman was excavating.

'Hello,' said the woman when she caught sight of them. She had stopped scraping with her trowel and was resting on her haunches, gazing up at them from the bottom of the trench. 'Come to see my rubbish dump?'

'Hello,' said Cornelia, instantly at ease with the woman. 'I'm Cornelia.'

'Hello, Cornelia, I'm Judith. Hello, Lovage. Brought any supplies? I could do with a fresh croissant and a cappuccino.'

'No such luck, I'm afraid.'

There was a tray full of fragments of pottery on the lip of the trench.

'They're Roman,' said Judith when she saw Cornelia looking at them. 'Imported from Germany – some things never change! This was a ditch and they filled it with rubbish. You can see the edges of the ditch where the soil changes colour.' She indicated the subtle division that marked the layer of earth she had exposed.

Cornelia was not to be deflected. 'But where were they searching for gold?'

'Ah, it's gold you're interested in! Well, before we started digging there was a hell of a mess back there, where the other trenches are, and another hole right here that went through to undisturbed soil.' Judith stood up and turned in the other direction to indicate the stretch of grass beyond the end of the trench. 'Over there you can still see where they've dug lots of little holes. And there's a serious bit of digging closer to the hedge where that pile of earth is, and another pit in the wood.'

'Can I go and look?' Cornelia asked.

'Sure, by all means,' said Judith agreeably.

Cornelia crossed the divoted grass to the large hole and stared into it as if she were trying to divine the identity of the person who had dug it. Lovage had trailed after her and watched with some amusement. 'It's only a rumour that they found anything,' he reminded her. 'We haven't recovered any actual finds.'

'They found gold – that's definite – and they would have dug this whole site to blazes if you hadn't interrupted them,' said Cornelia.

'Well, there's something in that,' he agreed. 'Once treasure hunters get a scent of something they won't stop until they've turned over the whole site. I've seen that elsewhere. But if they'd found nothing – which is most probable – they would have soon packed in. We can't even be sure how recent these holes are. Maybe as much as a month.'

'There's no weeds growing where they've dug.'

'True,' Lovage conceded, 'but this one is under the trees; the grass is thin and not much else grows.'

She looked up and saw that he was right: the hole was beneath the canopy of one of the oak trees that fringed the site. 'Well, what do *you* think?' she asked, shading her eyes to interrogate him.

He pointed back to where Judith had returned to her excavating. 'Everything coming out of Judith's ditch is fourth century AD. Nothing later. The amount of pottery suggests domestic activity on some scale, like a large homestead or a villa of some kind, and then it's probable the site was abandoned fairly suddenly. I suppose somebody could have buried a stash of gold coins or jewellery for safekeeping, and never came back for it, but that's just—'

'Slain!' exclaimed Cornelia, with bloodthirsty relish.

He laughed. 'Not unknown,' he agreed. 'End of empire and all that. You see these small excavations?' he pointed to the divot-like holes in the grass. 'That's where someone was being guided by a metal detector. There were a lot of bits of metal in the ground, close to the surface; probably from an animal pen.' He went over to the hedge and cast about on the ground for a while. Several times he stooped to pick up something and when he was satisfied he brought back his finds to show her. 'These are what he dug up.' He held out some small soil-encrusted objects in his palm. 'Galvanised nails rotted out of some sort of wooden structure. When the nighthawk gets a signal from his metal detector he digs to find its source. These nails were close to the surface because they're relatively recent. When he saw what they were he chucked them over there so they wouldn't trouble him again.'

Cornelia looked down into the large hole. 'But here it was a different story,' she said. 'Here he went on digging for some time.'

'Yes,' he admitted, 'but it doesn't mean he found gold.'

'Did he take away what he found?'

He looked puzzled. 'Take away?'

'Well,' she reasoned, 'if he chucked the nails over there to get them out of his way, wouldn't he have done the same with what he found here? Where is it? Large signal, large hole, large find, and if he took it away it was gold.'

Lovage laughed. 'Logical, I suppose.' He grew thoughtful. 'You know, I wonder if anyone looked.' He kicked the pile of spoil that had come from the hole and gazed towards the marquee. 'Maybe someone did.'

'What he found must have been metal and if it was rubbish he wouldn't have chucked it very far.' She scanned the grass in the vicinity to ensure she had not missed anything, but no, there was no sign of something a frustrated nighthawk might have thrown aside. Then she looked towards the hedge. 'It's quite a way to the wood. Could he have thrown it that far?'

'You make an interesting point,' Lovage admitted. 'Judith!'

She looked up from the trench.

'Did you find any scrap metal dug out of this hole?'

'No, but I've only been excavating here for the past couple of days. What are you thinking?'

'Cornelia's wondering what the nighthawk dug out of this hole. I think I might ask in the marquee.' He turned back to Cornelia. 'You want to come?'

'I'll stay here.'

He hesitated. 'Don't you want to see where all the recording and cleaning's done?'

'Later,' she insisted, making her way towards the hedge.

Lovage saluted and went off to consult.

Left to herself, Cornelia began to examine the ground beneath the length of hedge adjacent to the hole. She soon found several more of the corroded nails that Lovage had shown her. When she could find no more she walked back the other way, looking for a place where she could get into the wood. A length of three-rail fence filling a gap in the hedge offered her an easy climb. Almost immediately the grass on the other side gave way to drifts of last year's leaves. She walked the stretch of hedge she had already searched from the other side but couldn't find any metal. She turned into the woodland. The further she went the darker the shade, the more muffled became the chinking and scraping from the dig. She searched the area for anything that might have been thrown from the field by the nighthawk, but found nothing. She walked on further, taking a meandering path to avoid the fallen branches that were strewn everywhere. At last she came to the other hole that Judith had mentioned. This one was bigger than the one in the field but not so deep. She cast around and under a bush found a soil-encrusted lump that was clearly metal. She banged it several times on the trunk of a tree. The soil fell way and she saw it was a crushed piece of corrugated sheeting riddled with rust. She bore it out of the wood in triumph.

When she regained the edge of the field Lovage was descending the slope between the encampment and the trenches. Judging he was close enough to hear, she held up the piece of metal and shouted, 'Look what I found: *archaeology*!'

Abruptly the chinkings and scrapings stopped; heads turned to look. Judith leapt out of her trench and hurried over. A jubilant Cornelia held out the lump of metal for her to see, overcome with embarrassment at the stir she was causing. Judith laughed. Bolshoi Bertie came bustling up and when he saw what Cornelia was holding he was inclined to find the matter not the least bit amusing.

'What's this tommyrot? This is a place of work, young lady, not a sandcastle contest.'

'It shows…' stammered Cornelia. 'It shows they didn't find any gold in that—'

Bolshoi Bertie brushed aside her explanation. 'Never mind, never mind. Time for a cuppa anyway.' And with that he turned on his heels. Cornelia could see he had a terse exchange with Lovage when their paths crossed and as they parted she heard him say, 'Keep that child under control!'

'Oh dear!' observed Lovage when he reached her. 'Bertie's a trifle put out. Never mind, let's have a break.' He looked at her shrewdly and held out his hand for the lump of corroded metal. 'It hasn't occurred to anyone that the absence of scrap metal might indicate that somebody has made off with something of value,' he said in a non-committal voice. 'Fairly simple deduction, I suppose, but no one has actually made it.'

'Isn't this some farmer's field?' Cornelia asked. 'Doesn't *he* know what's been going on here?'

'Ah, yes! Well, there's a point: the land's part of an estate belonging to someone from London. It's let for grazing to a local farmer called Bennett.'

'Bennett! We should go and talk to him.'

Lovage looked doubtful. 'He was here yesterday: a grim-faced sort of bloke.'

'So what? Farmers look after land, don't they?'

THREE

As evening came on, Lovage drove Cornelia back to Bliss's house in Seaview. Cornelia had to concede that he had made himself very comfortable in her aunt's studio. A space had been cleared for a bed and he had put up his suitcase on an old wooden chest. Several shirts and a jacket hung from an easel as an extemporised wardrobe. Otherwise the studio was pretty much unchanged. Across from the bed stood a second easel that still held a small unfinished painting: a still life of marine hardware, the carefully rendered arrangement of objects glowing in sultry colours against a dark, mysterious sea and a placid evening sky. A Lara Bliss picture always included her signature figure of a mermaid, either "in the flesh", or, as here, carved on the stock of an anchor. When asked about her mermaids, she would reply in the following terms: 'They are the golden sea sprites of the Em estuary. On some moonlit nights I've heard them singing on the rocks beyond Chancellor Island. How divine that was! I was young, of course, a mere girl. I never hear them now.' And for a moment her cheerful countenance would cloud over as if a sudden regret had welled up from somewhere deep inside, momentarily devastating her sunny nature. It was an alarming sight, for Lara Bliss was not given to introspection, nor to moping about the state of the world.

She was blessed with campaigning energy and an interest for every day of the month, yet in the matter of the Em estuary and its sea sprites she had a romantic attachment that had deepened with the years, almost in step with her estrangement from the follies of love of her youth.

Cornelia took a bite out of one of Lovage's apples and gazed out of the window. 'So, why are they so jumpy,' she asked finally, 'up at the field?'

Lovage gave a sigh of resignation. 'There's politics in archaeology, same as everything else, and a rescue dig always attracts the big beasts of archaeology politics.' He paced about distractedly. 'I'm still not sure the site warrants the fuss. You've seen it. It looks like a very plain Roman farmstead to me. But nighthawks are something else! We all detest them because they destroy the archaeology. Everything they take away is treasure trove: gold or silver coins, jewellery, plate. It's all supposed to be reported.'

'What's that about nighthawks?'

They both started at the question. Lara Bliss, president of the Emsbury League of Artists, widowed aunt of Cornelia Grace Hyndman, was standing in the open doorway, gazing with a dissatisfied frown at the unfinished painting on the easel. She made an impressive sight, set against the bright sunlight in the splendour of her floral dress.

'Come in Lara, please,' said Lovage meekly, as befits someone about to undergo an inspection by his landlady.

'Discussing nighthawks, eh?' Reluctantly Bliss shifted her gaze from the painting to Lovage. 'I've heard there's mischief afoot.'

'Cornelia thinks the nighthawks have found gold up there.'

'I've heard that too. I've also heard a dealer came down from London trying to buy it.'

'It can't be true!' exclaimed Lovage, dismayed to have her give substance to Cornelia's imaginings.

'Apparently,' she continued, lowering her voice, 'he stayed at a pub in Totteringham, up the estuary. He's put out the word, and the word is he's coming back and he'll have cash for anyone who's got treasure to sell.' She winked at Cornelia. 'Can't promise it's true. It's what my cleaner told me over tea this morning. She's an awful old gossip. I pay her for four hours cleaning and she'd gossip the entire four if I let her.'

'I want to find out who *he* is – it's sure to be a man – and make him return what he's stolen,' declared Cornelia in her fiercest and most spiky manner.

Bliss nodded understandingly. 'Lovely idea! Brimming with natural justice! How are you going to do that?'

'Go and see Mr Bennett. He farms the land; he must know something.'

'Ah, the Bennett clan!' said Bliss with the air of a weary magistrate. 'Is that Barnstable Bennett or his father, Silas Bennett?'

'I don't know which one it is, but he's a grim old codger,' said Lovage.

'Ah! That's Silas. He's a bad lot: used to bake porkpies till the Food Safety Officer put a stop to it. That man wouldn't care if he poisoned the whole county.' She gave a cheery snort of laughter at the thought of the county laid low by porkpie poisoning.

'You could charm him!' said Cornelia rather hopefully.

Bliss laughed again. '"*Have you been digging, Silas?*" Is that what we should ask him?'

'No!' said Cornelia, once again showing her unquenchable sense of conviction. 'No, he didn't do it, but he knows who did.'

'Does he? Divination!' Her aunt looked impressed. 'Very well, I buy my Christmas tree from Silas; have done these past ten years. I'll take you to see him. Beard him in his den. How about that?' She leant towards Cornelia with a conspiratorial cock of her head. 'Make him squirm.'

FOUR

Another of Lara Bliss's estimable qualities was to act immediately on any decision: no pause for reconsideration, no backtracking, no second thoughts. The morning was beginning to luxuriate as she led Cornelia and Lovage past the herbaceous border on their way to the carport where her Vauxhall Astra was parked. Unlike her, Lovage was a reluctant party to Cornelia's unshakable conviction that Silas Bennett should be questioned about the raid on the archaeological site. Lovage was a young man with impeccable academic credentials but otherwise unworldly and scarcely one for a confrontation of the sort they were planning. Bliss opened the car door for him and into the back he clambered. The Astra was old and its bodywork remodelled by Bliss's careless manoeuvring at low speed; it had become the automotive equivalent of a worn gardening glove and the seat fabric felt like perished suede to the touch. Cornelia leapt in beside her aunt, who bullied the engine into life and launched the car into an untidy three-point turn that sent the gravel flying.

Being a grockle, Lovage had only the haziest sense of the geography of the Em estuary and surrounding countryside. 'Which way are we going?' he asked as the Astra shot up the lane.

'Don't be daft, man,' Bliss replied cheerfully, very much *not* a grockle, 'there's only the one way out of Seaview: inland towards Totteringham.'

They climbed the hill and soon they had passed the turning that led to the archaeological dig. Reaching the open heights, the road meandered inland in a series of serpentine bends, following ancient field boundaries. Banks on either side, topped with hedge, obscured the view of the surrounding countryside. Eventually they came to a broken junction sign indicating a turning to the right. Without slackening speed Bliss swung the steering wheel. As they crossed the centre of the road any big city driver would have decided that the Astra was far too wide for the gap it was heading for. Not Bliss. The car thrashed through the bracken growing on either bank, releasing showers of rainwater from the previous night's storm. The lane, which was really no more than two parallel metalled tracks, dropped.

'Is this…? Does this go back down to the estuary?' wondered Lovage.

'No, not to the Em. This goes down to Smeltertown. There's an inlet goes out to the sea from there, but it's pretty silted up.'

'Smeltertown. It's a town then?'

Bliss laughed. 'No, a few farms, a house or two hidden away, some industrial ruins. There used to be quite a lot of mining inland and once they smelted tin here in a small way, but that was long ago. There's not much left to see now; its all gone back to nature.'

The lane continued its steep descent and they re-entered the woodland typical of the district's coastal valleys. Great masses of foliage gathered above their heads, forming a tunnel pinpricked by shafts of brightness. Soon they had descended so far the effect under the trees was more like moonlight than sunlight. A stony ramp appeared to the right, cutting off from the lane at an angle. Bliss set the car at the ramp in her impetuous manner, clashing the gears to find first. The car went grinding up the slope, the uncertain grip of its front wheels making it skip left and right. They rounded a derelict stone building and came into a farmyard, quite buried under the trees. Bliss brought the car to a halt with a metallic rip of the handbrake. She glanced round at Lovage and saw the very picture of someone who wished he were elsewhere. A figure was already studying the Astra from the shadowy interior of one of the lean-to buildings enclosing the far side of the yard. Bliss pushed open her door, lowered her feet to the ground and surveyed the sea of mud and muck. She could hear the gentle grunting of contented pigs from the buildings and their stink was heavy in the air.

'Haven't the faintest idea about clearing up or hygiene, have you, Silas?' she said loudly.

The figure – a man – hobbled into the open with the aid of a stick and stared at them pie-eyed from under a shaggy brow. He wore a mossy overall belted with sisal.

'Morning, Mr Bennett.'

'How do, Lara,' he barked. 'What brings you out here?'

'Simple matter, we're looking for local insight, Silas. And you're the man.'

'Oh, am I?' he wondered with infinite scepticism.

'Yes indeed, you are,' she replied, appraising him from top to toe. 'You farm the field where the archaeologists are digging. Who's been up there doing a bit of treasure hunting?'

He gave a wheeze of laughter. 'Now there's a blunt question!' he said.

'You're a canny sort, and nobody would go digging for treasure on your land without your say-so.'

He gave a snort and scowled. 'Ah, well here's the thing: that Mr Daguerre artist chappie may rent out the grazing to me but he's still the owner.'

'Ah, so it's Meade Daguerre's land is it? I didn't realise.'

'He, and his, go traipsing about on the land, driving their four-by-fours as they will.'

'Excuse me,' enquired Cornelia, leaning out of the car window, 'but has anybody shown you gold they've found anywhere around here? I'd love to see it, if they have.'

'Only gold I've seen is here,' he retorted, holding up his wedding ring finger.

Cornelia drooped with disappointment.

'Now Silas, I really can't believe you've not heard the stories,' objected Bliss. 'You'd know if someone were wandering about up there with a metal detector, even if it were in the dead of night.'

'I have heard it said that someone's been digging at night, it's true. But it's only been surmised by chaps like me as have seen the signs of digging. If I don't know who, it means it's *grockles*, and my bet is it's those grockles up at Terpsichore Manor. I'd go and ask Mr Daguerre what those lads working up at his pile do of an evening. I've heard they're rowdies, getting drunk.' He leaned forward to emphasis his sense of scandal. 'I've heard tales about nudified girls on his boat.'

'Hmm! Surely you don't believe scurrilous tosh about a celebrity like him, do you?'

'Well, that's what I hear. They sail out and anchor off Chancellor Island. Wild shindigs, I hear.'

'Local girls?'

'Loose types most likely.'

'Perhaps partying with mermaids,' decided Bliss wistfully.

'And what's for sure is the devils go drinking over Totteringham way.'

'Meaning what?'

'Meaning that's where some chappie from London's been enquiring after finds.' He fixed Cornelia with his eye. 'Go there if it's gold you're after.'

Bliss nodded. 'You heard that story, then?'

'It's a pack of grockles.'

'Is it so? At the dig they think it's locals, not grockles.'

'No, never! I'm telling you, it's grockles. But chaps are looking out for 'em now, so they'll be lying low.'

'Are there any of that sort down here?' asked Cornelia suddenly.

'Meaning what?' said Silas, in a voice that had been getting more and more prickly.

'Oh, I don't know,' she replied airily. 'Pirates? What about smugglers?'

'No such thing,' he retorted. 'Not to my knowledge, not in Smeltertown.'

Bliss gave Cornelia a look, as if to say, *there's no more to be gained from this conversation.* 'Thank you, Silas,' she said, tugging at the waist of her jodhpurs and inhaling the air as though questing an elusive scent. 'I've enjoyed our little talk. I think I'll follow up on your suspicions and have a word with Mr Daguerre. Not met him yet and as he's a fellow artist I have, I confess, been negligent in my duties as president of the League. I should have exchanged fraternal greetings with him before now. Is he down from London?'

'Been abroad. Came down from London yesterday afternoon, apparently, according to Barney.'

'Barney's out, then, is he? Banged up on some trumped-up police rigmarole, wasn't he?'

'Possession of stolen goods – a technicality. Lobsters grow free in the sea, don't they? Mr Daguerre is a great one for lobster at his restaurant.'

'I'm partial myself. Well, see you around, Silas, and remember we're in the market for old coins if any come your way, aren't we, Cornelia?'

Again Cornelia poked her head out of her window. 'Yes, please think of us if you hear of anything!'

Bliss cautiously turned the car in the mud and muck, and Silas gave them the benefit of a scowl as they departed.

'You hit a raw spot with that question about pirates and smugglers, Cornelia,' said Bliss, as they ground up the hillside. 'Something fishy going on in Smeltertown, I wonder?' Another thought came to her as the Astra cleared the last of the trees. She caught Lovage's eye. 'A gin and tonic refresher? How about following Silas's advice and having a spot of lunch in Totteringham?'

FIVE

The approach to Totteringham lay in a deep cutting beneath the trees. At the bottom lay the High Street, which straggled out across the valley with a single sharp angle in the centre where it swung left to cross the Em on a low-slung stone bridge that marked the highest reach of the tidal waters. This was the main road westwards, the lowest crossing of the river, a route continually clogged with holiday traffic during the summer months.

'Which one should we try?' said Bliss as she crawled away from the junction, turning left into the High Street. 'There's the Cart & Ford, the Hampson Arms and the Feathers?'

'Do we know where this coin dealer set up?' Lovage wanted to know.

'If, as Silas says, it was grockles doing the nighthawking it must have been the Hampson. The other two are strictly for the locals – death metal or rockabilly, take your pick!'

Bliss parked in the Hampson's car park and she and Lovage escorted Cornelia into the lounge bar, which was a scene of noise and animation, the carvery being in full spate serving the mid-week pensioners' luncheon special.

Bliss bought a round of drinks. A casual enquiry about old coins from the young man who dispensed them met a shrug.

'Do Meade Daguerre's people come here?' she asked.

'Yeah, sometimes,' he said begrudgingly.'

'They're a pretty fast crowd, aren't they?'

He shrugged again.

'Are they here now?'

'No, not in the day, but those girls hang out with them.' He pointed to two young blondes sitting at the far end of the bar engrossed in their mobiles. They wore shorts and tee shirts. The expensive sunglasses perched in their hair said they were grockles.

Bliss nodded her thanks and took her drinks over to the corner table where Lovage and Cornelia had established themselves. It was near the carvery and a group of elderly women was eating at the next table. She eyed them speculatively while she sampled her gin and tonic. When she put down her glass she leaned over towards them.

'Excuse me, may I have a word?'

Three bespectacled faces turned towards her.

'Are you girls often here?'

'We're regulars, aren't we?' said the nearest, a rosy-cheeked pensioner.

'Have you seen any sign of coins being bought or sold?'

'Trinkets?'

'No, coins.'

Lovage caught the pensioner's drift and intervened. 'What kind of trinkets were they?'

'We all saw them, didn't we?' said her blue-rinse companion, pushing aside her plate. 'She was talking to a man, at that table over there, but I don't know if they were for sale. She had a handkerchief and three or four little gold objects, like charms – figures. Maybe an animal like a dog, and they were laid out on the handkerchief on that table. And when someone walked by she flipped the edge of the handkerchief over them, quick like.'

Her mates nodded.

'Not coins then?' said Cornelia, faintly disappointed.

'No, dearie, not coins. They were little gold figures.'

'She? A woman?' asked Lovage.

'Yes, a young woman with flaxen hair. In braids it was, tied up.'

Bliss and Lovage gaped at one another, as if to say, 'There's a thing! *Flaxen hair in braids!*'

'Could you describe her in more detail?'

'Well, she weren't well dressed. Might have been a London type down here for the sea air.'

'Thin, she was; needed feeding up,' said her companion. 'There's a lot of her type get in here. Grockles, the lot of them.'

SIX

'Now look here, you two,' said Bliss, stirring uneasily on the sofa, 'there's no way a famous model would be openly selling treasure trove to some dealer from London in a pub, is there?'

Lovage shrugged and tapped the photograph he had found in July's edition of Vogue. 'Here she is: "*Gitta Jensson, the Danish model, her hair in braids – her signature look for the season – escorted by husband Meade Daguerre to the opening party for the summer exhibition at the Royal Academy. Evening dress by Dior*". I rest my case.'

Bliss took the proffered magazine and scrutinised the photograph. They were caught in motion, swinging past the camera, perhaps emerging from a doorway, although only of portion of frame was in the shot. She was slightly behind his shoulder, her gaze lowered demurely, her cool Nordic beauty caressed by the lens. He was altogether a more assertive figure, solid, resourceful, well-built. A year or two into his forties, Bliss guessed, looking straight into the flash with a combative certainty, confident in his celebrity and the rightness that it was he who was being captured for posterity by the photographer. There must be – so she thought – some quality decipherable in his unremarkable face that explained his extraordinary success. She looked from feature to feature, trying to detect what it was, without success.

'Must be a gift from the Gods,' she decided.

Cornelia wanted to see the photograph close to. 'She's lots better looking than him and he's been plundering his own archaeological site!' she said in a scandalised voice.

'And sent her to a pub in Totteringham to flog the finds? I beg to differ!' Bliss got to her feet and paced the room, amidst the chintz, in an unruly state of mind. 'They said she was badly dressed. Gitta Jensson is a model for crickey's sake!' She stabbed a finger in the direction of the photograph. 'That's Dior!'

'Look,' objected Lovage, 'those pensioners' idea of well dressed would not be the same as Gitta Jensson's. They were dressed in Crimplene! They also said she was thin-looking and from London.'

'First it was coins, now it's gold charms, without the slightest bit of evidence. And you're accusing the last two people in the whole neighbourhood to have a motive for stooping to cultural vandalism. They're wealthy, successful and he's an artist, for heaven's sake!'

Lovage looked at her with glassy eyes. 'It doesn't make much sense,' he said, 'but there's strong circumstantial, don't you think? And if he isn't a nighthawk, what about his assistants? Remember what Silas Bennett said?'

'Okay,' she conceded, 'I have heard they're a pretty wild bunch. *Artists, dearies!* They've a reputation to uphold! Doesn't mean they'd stoop to that.'

'I say we should go back to the pub, find those old ladies and show them her photograph – see if they recognise her!' said Cornelia.

'Not a bad idea,' agreed Bliss, 'but what about a more direct approach? How about lunch at The Estuary with Meade Daguerre?'

Lovage looked horrified at the thought. 'Lara, I'd rather not. The last thing I fancy is sucking up to celebrities. Anyway, I have to be at the dig. If I don't turn up and dig like everyone else the people from the county's Heritage Services think I'm only here to spy on them for the Museum.'

'I see – politics, politics!'

'Don't talk about it!'

'How about you, Cornelia?'

Cornelia wrinkled her nose in distaste at the idea of wasting half the day sitting in a restaurant and shook her head violently.

'Fine, I'll take Miles Sleight. He's always keen on an outing. I'm going to get the measure of Meade Daguerre… and his menagerie!' She dismissed Lovage and Cornelia, and once she was alone she picked up the telephone.

'Miles, dear, it's Lara. How are you?

'Very fair, Bliss,' a reedy voice assured her from the other end of the line, 'very fair. Been pickin' me dwarf beans. How are you?'

'Topping, Miles. How about joining me for a spot of lunch?'

'Interesting proposal. Anything particular in mind?'

'The Estuary.'

'Oh, very fair! Hear they have very good seafood and a decent cellar. Some London artist-wallah set it up.'

'Come on, Miles, you know it's Meade Daguerre's. Don't pretend. We're going to have lunch with him and offering him our warmest welcome on behalf of the League.'

'It's strictly for yachters; it'll be dead from October to May. Used to be a bank, you know. Martin's Bank, it was. A very proper sort of bank that was… in it's day.'

'Stop going on, Miles; it's all ancient history. I want you to be distinguished and diplomatic. We're going to be welcoming, and make sure you bring a topic!'

A hoarse cackle came from the phone. 'Fair enough, fair enough! Any idea when?'

'Next week. I'll let you know which day when I've spoken to him.'

SEVEN

Cornelia could charm when it suited her purposes, but in the main she was suspicious, disregarding of social niceties and fiercely inquisitive: a cheerful sceptic in the making. Hers may not have been a sweet personality, but it was not one you could ignore, and one that her aunt indulged, for she saw a divine spark in her gawky, loose-limbed niece. For her part Cornelia saw Lara as a force of nature, like tides and the seasons. Unlike those children uncertain of their place in the world she did not yearn for conventionality, for that anonymous, proper, faintly puritanical parent-figure. She thrived on explosions, disgraces at tea and the clash of gears – things that were unwelcome to not a few girls of her age. The archaeological dig, Lovage camping in her aunt's studio and plundering nighthawks were her kind of entertainments. Since Thursday's visit to the archaeological dig Lovage had been unresponsive to her unspoken wish to be taken again. She had no intention of pleading and was waiting for the chance to corner him. When he came back unexpectedly at lunchtime on Saturday she saw her opportunity and ten minutes later, having rapped on the half-open door, she found him ironing a shirt. Silently she watched as he threaded the shirt onto a hanger.

'Where are you going?' she asked.

'There's a barbeque tonight, at the dig.'

'Oh! Are we…?'

'No, just me.'

'My aunt's given me her dinghy.'

'Allowed you to borrow her dinghy,' he corrected.

She ignored his correction. 'Do you row?'

'Better than I dance.'

'The tide's about right for a row across to Emsbury. You really can row, can't you?'

He looked at his watch as though he was calculating his timetable for the rest of the day. 'Why are you going?'

'Fish. Fish for supper.'

'You weren't expecting to go to the barbeque, were you?'

'Just asking.'

He looked at her, uncertain whether she was disappointed or being deliberately obtuse. He sighed, realising he'd been manoeuvred into doing something for her. 'Well, straight there and back.'

They went down through the long grass to the water's edge where there was a tangle of bushes and a clearing that led to a stretch of stony beach. The dinghy was stranded alongside a small wooden jetty. A mooring rope was tied to one of the bushes. Cornelia untied the rope and together they slid the boat down to the water's edge and scrambled in.

'I've seen an outboard motor in one of the sheds,' he said as he fitted the oars to the rowlocks and prepared to row. 'You should get Lara to let you have it. You could explore the estuary.'

'She won't unless I promise to wear one of these,' she said, looking for sympathy as she struggled into her life jacket.

'Fair enough, you might have to swim for it. Anyway, it suits you.'

As Lovage spoke, the dinghy was thrown about by the wake of a cabin cruiser, driving home the prudence of his remark. He put his back into his rowing and soon they were well clear of the shore, although Emsbury still had the look of a toy town on the other side. There was a lot of traffic on the estuary: yachts, inflatables, speedboats – pleasure craft of every conceivable kind – criss-crossed its wide expanse. The sea proper was still some distance to the south, where the long low outcrop of Chancellor Island was visible. The island guarded the entrance to the estuary, taming the might of Atlantic rollers as they entered its mouth.

'Well, you certainly *can* row!' Cornelia conceded. 'But aren't you too grand to be digging?'

He gave a modest shake of his head. 'I'm just the office boy. Some suspicious gold coins come on to the market in London. The county's Heritage Services starts squawking and it seems they might have come from here. Next thing I know the Museum's decided to send me to take a look. Anyway, I like digging.'

'And how's it going? Find any gold yet?'

'It's chaotic; everybody's got something to say about everything. They're arguing about where next to dig. There's a lot of local interest in what we're doing and that always means trouble.' He pulled at his collar uneasily. 'We're all wondering if your nighthawks are still about.'

'They're not *mine*,' she said indignantly. 'Anyway... can't have them digging wherever they like, stealing stuff.'

'Always good humoured – digs – but there's an atmosphere up there like we're being watched.' He shrugged, as though shouldering away a sense of apprehension. 'Why don't you come and scrub pottery on Monday? We're getting bucketfuls.'

'Okay.' She allowed herself a smug grin, gratified to have succeeded in getting what she wanted without wheedling it out of him.

When they reached the centre of the estuary Lovage shortened oars to take in the scene for a moment. The sky was cloudless, a vast expanse of blue, but for two aircraft contrails that went almost from horizon to horizon – one south-north, one east-west – marking out a great cross.

'What are expenses?' asked Cornelia. She was staring up at the contrails with a frown on her face. 'Somebody told me they travel on expenses.'

'Expenses?' repeated Lovage, not quite sure what she was driving at.

'Yes, expenses. People fly on them, don't they?'

'Yes, lots do, I suppose.'

'It's like free money, isn't it?'

'Free? No, it's money set aside to pay for things people aren't expected—'

She wasn't interested in some long-winded rigmarole. 'People that should know better fly on expenses all the time, don't they?'

'Well, people have to fly.'

'Why? You don't have expenses, do you?'

'Not to fly.'

'Who gives them expenses to fly round the world all the time?'

'Companies… governments… organisations.'

'I think they should stop it, it's filthy pollution and the people doing it on expenses should know better.

Ordinary people don't get expenses. I haven't got expenses.'

'No, well you're not important enough.'

'If I were important, I wouldn't fly. I would get them to come to me.'

'Then it would be all the same as far as your filthy pollution's concerned.'

Cornelia looked at him as though he had committed a traitorous act. 'That's the second time you've done that, you know! It's not *my* filthy pollution.' She tossed back her hair. 'I wouldn't want to talk to people with expenses anyway. If I was the Prime Minister I'd tax expenses at one hundred percent... or more!'

Her disapproval had little effect because Lovage's attention had switched to matters maritime. Amidst the bustle of boats he had picked out an unusual craft heading upstream towards them. It was – as much as he could tell from his foreshortened view – a small boat of elegant design, and forward of the raised bridge was a smokestack emitting a plume of smoke.

'Isn't that something!' he exclaimed. 'It's a steam launch!'

Cornelia looked, but the river was too densely populated to see what he meant. A flotilla of sailing boats had come round their stern and they blocked the view downstream as they tacked back towards the Emsbury side of the estuary, sails clattering as their booms swung to catch the breeze. Two motorboats that had chased one another out from the opposite shore now decided to turn downstream through the flotilla, their wakes rocking the dinghy. Then the steam launch came back into view, maintaining its steady progress upstream. Lovage was suddenly alive to the possibility that it might run by them very close if they stayed where they were, and he decided to row on, although perhaps a little late to have any great effect on the outcome. The launch deviated not a degree, nor slackened its pace, carving through the sailing boats as though no one on board had the slightest thought of keeping a lookout. It passed close behind the dinghy, the wake lifted its stern and slapping it down again, causing it to take in bucketfuls of water. As it swept on up river Cornelia glimpsed three silhouetted figures seated beneath the awning shading the length of deck to the rear of the little bridge. Taking the swamping as a personal affront, she fixed them with her annihilating stare. They did not move or seem to register either her or the pleasure craft all around them, but remained steadfastly gazing upstream, unheeding, as though their eyes were transfixed by some enchantment.

'Uncaring brutes,' she yelled, the launch still scattering craft in its wake. She shook her fist, vowing vengeance would be hers.

'Egregious!' declared Lovage. 'And inconsiderate! *Some people!*'

EIGHT

On Monday morning there was a blustery wind from the west, bringing changeable skies filled with cotton ball clouds and a feeling of rain coming soon. After breakfast, Lovage, in the company of Cornelia, left Seaview for the dig. When they arrived he went to collect his implements from the marquee, and she made her way straight to the trench where, on her previous visit, Judith had been working.

Where was Judith? she wondered, finding it empty. She scanned the other trenches and finally spotted her under the canopy of the marquee, absorbed in the scrutiny of something lying on one of the tables. Now that she had the trench to herself she felt tempted to do a little independent excavating. She looked around and saw that Judith had left a trowel lying on the ground close to the lip of the trench. She picked it up and tried to decide where to apply her energies. The broad, shallow trench did not strike her as a particularly fruitful prospect. After all, she reasoned, it was only a rubbish dump; she was more interested in the holes made by the nighthawks. She sauntered over to where the first of the large holes lay in the shadow of the oak. No, she reasoned, not this one; this one was clearly dug out. She climbed over the fence and made her way to the second hole where she had found the piece of scrap metal. What had happened here? Had a nighthawk been in the field and pushed out in this direction, led by the signals coming from his metal detector? Or had he been going in the opposite direction, sneaking up through the wood, on his way to the site of the dig? Something had led him to search well away from where the archaeologists had decided it was worth digging. Did he know something about the extent of the site they did not? Or had he just been prospecting in random fashion? It seemed plain enough to her that the size of the hole meant he had picked up a strong signal, but equally it appeared that he had abandoned the hole when he had struck the piece of scrap metal. What had he done next? In which direction had he gone: towards the field, or deeper into the wood? Cornelia peered into the shadowy half-light ahead of her. She was not sure, but she thought she could see another pile of earth at the very limits of her sight. She made her way towards it through the tangle of undergrowth, eager to pursue the slightest clue the nighthawk might have left, but as she got closer she saw it was only where some animal had been burrowing. She kicked the loose spoil disconsolately, but when she looked ahead again she saw another mound of freshly dug earth in a clearing between two ancient trees. Instantly she could see it was more promising. She went towards it at a lope. As she drew close one thing grabbed her complete attention: the staring eye sockets of a cracked and stained skull.

She gaped. *'What the hell?'*

She circled round the mound, suddenly very alert and more than a little alarmed. There was no doubt about it: several bones, as well as the skull, were protruding from the spoil. And now she could see the pit from which they had been excavated.

'Grave robbers!' she breathed, shaking her head wonderingly.

She peered into the pit. A good deal of the spoil had trickled back in, but in several places she could make out the sides of what looked like a coffin. It suddenly seemed very quiet in the clearing and a craving for sunlight and human company overwhelmed her. She backed away and turned and ran, her clothes snagging repeatedly on the undergrowth as she forced her way towards the edge of the field.

'Hi, Lovage! Over here!' she yelled as she climbed the fence. 'Lovage, come here! I've found something!'

He rushed over from the trench where he was talking to one of the diggers, putting his finger to his lips as he approached, thinking she was about to cause a scene, like Thursday's incident with the piece of scrap metal.

'It's human remains,' she said melodramatically from her perch on the top bar of the fence. 'It's much better than I could have ever hoped for! Much better than gold!'

NINE

At precisely one o'clock Lara Bliss climbed the steps that led to the terrace fronting The Estuary, Meade Daguerre's restaurant. Miles Sleight had been there some time sitting on the wall. He was gazing out across the sweep of the estuary, smoking a cigarette.

'Hello, Miles,' she said cheerfully, interrupting his reverie.

He turned towards her, raising his cigarette in a salute. 'Hello Bliss. Days of windsurfing definitely over,' he wheezed.

Bliss laughed. There was something leathery about Miles's complexion that suggested a smoked sausage. Indeed, he was widely credited by the members of the League to be so pickled by tobacco smoke that he was immune to disease, or any other frailty of the flesh. By no stretch of the imagination could he be thought of as sporty and the image of him in a wetsuit, wrestling with the sail of a windsurfer, struck her as delightfully absurd.

'Come, Miles, a glass of something white will do us both the world of good!' she decided, inspecting with an appreciative eye his bohemian ensemble of crisp white shirt held at the throat with a gold stud, black linen waistcoat and jacket over pale cream trousers and co-respondent shoes.

Miles tossed away the butt of his cigarette and, with a little bow, held open the restaurant door for her. She entered, the courtly attentions of her companion turning her arrival into something quite regal, the old banking hall making a splendid background to their arrival.

'Marvellous day; the quayside looks so carefree!' she said as Terence, the maitre d', approached.

'Good morning, madam,' he replied, primed to expect her. 'It is, as you say, quite marvellous. Mr Daguerre is already here. Won't you join him at his table?'

Bliss swelled magnificently. 'Delighted. What a pleasant room this is! Isn't that a Richter over there?' She pointed to the large photo-realist painting of a foggy, November river bank on the far wall.

'Yes, madam, it is. And next to it, a suite of pictures by Tulip McGruff, a fellow-student of Mr Daguerre's at the Royal College.'

He led them across the restaurant to the corner table between the bar and the window, where Daguerre was already seated.

'Hello,' said Daguerre, rising to his feet as they approached. 'Very pleased to meet you, Lara.'

'And I you.'

They shook hands.

'And you're Miles? Glad to meet you, Miles. Admired your sculpture outside the British Telecom building in Brighton when I was on my Foundation Course there.'

'Ah, my Sixties period. Youthful indiscretion!'

'I thought it was hot stuff at the time. You went figurative in the Eighties, didn't you?'

Miles was eyeing the open bottle of champagne standing in its cooler amidst the table setting. 'Fibreglass is evil stuff so I dropped it,' he wheezed, lowering himself into his chair. 'And I've become a humanist in the fullness of my years.'

'Well, let's drink to that!' laughed Daguerre, pulling out a chair for Bliss.

'This is delightful!' she said, once she was seated. She beamed at Daguerre enthusiastically. 'I am so happy you've come to settle in the district. You add such breadth to our little community of artists!' From the several photographs she had seen of him, she had thought him rather ordinary looking, but in life that impression was completely overturned by the sense of vigour he exuded; the air of animation and purposefulness.

Terence had been pouring champagne while they had been running through these pleasantries and now he placed the glasses before them.

'Here's to humanism,' proposed Daguerre, raising his. 'I'm glad to see you here, Lara. Very nice. And you, Miles.' He wasn't looking at them as he spoke, but gazing off into the distance as though something there fascinated him. 'It's a nice part of the country, and a nice change for me.'

'As I was saying to you on the phone,' Bliss replied, 'in my capacity as the president of the Emsbury League of Artists I felt I should welcome you to Emsbury at the earliest possible opportunity.' She half raised her glass. 'Hence my invitation, which you have so utterly subverted!' She looked at him chidingly.

'My pleasure, Lara. What's the point of having a restaurant if you can't treat friends? "League" sounds very grand. How many members do you have?'

'Forty-six strong, we are, including associate members. We have open studios in the spring and an annual exhibition in the town hall every October. It's quite a social event in these parts.'

'Impressive!'

'I shall make it my business to have you elected.'

Daguerre laughed. 'I'll put myself up.'

'I shall propose you, and Miles will second your nomination. Coming from the president, the proposal will carry a lot of weight.'

Daguerre laughed again, this time a little uneasily. 'There'll be opposition to me joining?'

Bliss looked apologetic. 'There are reactionary forces everywhere; you know how it is!'

'Damned rampant partisanship,' sniggered Miles into his champagne.

Daguerre was taken aback. 'They'll vote me down? Why, because they don't think I'm an artist?'

Bliss was feeling distinctly uncomfortable at the direction the conversation had taken. She suspected it might be fuelled by some undeclared rivalry on Miles's part that she had not anticipated. 'As Miles says—'

'What do they think I am?' The affront seemed to amuse him.

Bliss was unsure – something of a rarity, this – how to steer the conversation back to safe ground. She was determined to intervene before Miles could reply. 'Oh, I don't think…'

'Interior decorator… Manufacturer of corporate *décor*… designer museum fodder.' Miles rolled his eyes gleefully.

'Good God! I'm humiliated!' Daguerre laughed. He took up his champagne. 'Here's to the naysayers! I suppose they paint Impressionist views of the estuary.'

For a moment or two, Bliss stared out of the window while her irritation at Miles's little provocations subsided. It occurred to her, although she didn't remark on it, that the view over the estuary had the sparkling generalities of an Impressionist painting. She wondered if Daguerre was having the same thought. He, she noticed, seemed to be taking Miles's digs in his stride and it struck her that he was used to disparagement from other artists, which all too easily he could dismiss as professional jealousy. Her gaze wandered to Miles, who was absorbed in buttering a fragment of bread roll. She was thinking his verbal barbs had been very ready to hand, and wondered if, left to his own devices, he numbered amongst those who would blackball Daguerre.

'I consider myself a straightforward figurative artist,' said Daguerre at last.

'Do you?' Miles looked up sharply from his task. 'I think of you as a latter-day Duchampian conceptualist.'

'Now, Miles,' chided Bliss, 'let's not bandy labels, or I'll have to admit to being a maritime romantic!'

'Ah yes!' said Daguerre, 'I've done my research; you're a painter of marine subjects, aren't you?'

'Mermaids, Meade, mermaids. That's my theme. They reflect my experience of this lovely estuary; they personify the magic of the place. You understand?'

Daguerre nodded, seemingly beguiled by her earnest, enquiring gaze. 'And you know the district to its fingertips?' he said finally.

'Every crack and crevice!'

Daguerre laughed. 'Then you're the girl for me!'

'We all have to have a theme,' said Miles suddenly. 'It's a rule of the League that you must have a theme. I suspect yours, Meade, will be discontinuity.'

Bliss glared at him, daggers drawn. 'Miles always did harbour a waspish nature,' she said, wondering whether she might reach to kick him under the table.

Terence's arrival with the luncheon menus saved Daguerre from having to respond. He had already concluded that Miles was a little senile and gave him a genial wink.

'Ah, thank you most kindly, most welcome,' Miles murmured to Terence, fetching out his reading glasses as he took refuge behind his copy of the menu.

'Talking of local,' said Lara confidingly to Daguerre, 'there's a story doing the rounds about the archaeological dig on your land.'

'Oh, yeah, yeah! They started digging while I was in Germany. It's not much of a story, is it? Don't tell me they found something!'

'Didn't you know, the site's been raided by treasure hunters; its been declared a rescue dig? The British Museum's sent down an observer. He's staying with me.'

'Rescue dig?' Daguerre looked put out. 'Nobody's mentioned this to me! What sort of treasure?'

'Oh, Roman coins, gold.'

'A hoard?'

'Something of the sort, yes.'

'Well, I never! I must go and take a look. Why wasn't I told?'

'I suppose they're trying to keep it hush-hush. Some are saying it's not locals, its grockles.'

'Grockles? What's that?'

'Oh, you know,' chuckled Miles, giving Daguerre a humorous twinkle over the top of his glasses, 'people like yourself. Outsiders passing through.'

Daguerre looked pained.

Bliss intervened. 'Some say your people at Terpsichore Manor are behind it. Seen any of your studio assistants with a metal detector?'

He shook his head. 'That's nonsense! This is all news to me. Not the kind of thing any of my crew would do, I'm sure.'

Bliss was watching Daguerre carefully and had the impression he was genuinely taken aback.

'What about your wife? She might have seen something, perhaps?'

Daguerre shook his head. 'Gitta? No, she's not here; she's in Denmark, working: modelling assignment for Vogue.'

Bliss sat back and smiled. 'Well,' she decided soothingly, 'this is *delicious* champagne!'

'It's a crime without a victim,' decided Miles, ruminating on nighthawks. 'Who cares about stuff abandoned in the ground millennia ago? It's another modern fetish, that's all. I say strength to their arms!' And he gulped down a good half of his champagne. 'I think I'll try the oysters.'

Daguerre raised his glass but didn't drink. 'Look, Lara,' he said, suddenly earnest, 'they call me one of Thatcher's children. Quite right! Grand old lady. I don't come from anywhere, might have amounted to nothing, but times have been good to me, particularly the last ten years. Made a mint of money from the Russian oligarchs, bless 'em. Now they're gone and I'm here. I've put certain things behind me, if you know what I mean, and I want to make a place for me, a proper roost for me and my family.' He leant forward. 'I don't care to think of myself as a grockle – *bloody horrible word*! I will do what it takes to become part of the community. I know what it means: it means *participating*... and I intend to!'

Bliss had shuddered inwardly at the mention of Thatcher. Now she sat back and sipped her champagne with downcast eyes, sensing, with a tiny sexual frisson, that she was on the verge of being bought by a man she had scarcely met.

'I'd like to do something meaningful for the League, and I'd very much like to come and see your paintings.'

'Then you shall,' said Bliss demurely. 'Why not come tomorrow? I've a cracker just finished.'

'Fair enough,' smiled Daguerre, 'let me ask Carrie what I'm doing tomorrow.' He picked up his mobile from the table, but before he could make the call Terence hovered up to his shoulder with watery eyes.

'Excuse me, boss,' he said in a strained voice, 'but Baltasar's heard you're here and he's asked me to give you a message.'

'Go on.'

'Sorry to have to tell you this, but he says if you're intending to eat here he's going to poison your meal.' He took a breath before continuing. 'He doesn't mean it but I thought I'd better tell you... just in case.'

Daguerre's smile had taken on a certain fixity of expression. 'Lara... a bit of advice: the Puy lentils with poached quail's eggs are not to be missed. But if you'll excuse me a moment, there seems to be a little dissent in the kitchen and I think I should have to have a word with the chef. You go ahead and order.' He rose to his feet.

TEN

Lara Bliss gave Lovage a penetrating look over her raised cup of tea. 'She found... *a skeleton?*'

He nodded.

'*Good grief!* The Child Sleuth strikes again! Trouble follows that girl wherever she goes!'

Lovage paced about and then sat down. 'It's perfectly obvious the nighthawks are still actively interested in the site,' he said vehemently. 'It's bloody annoying and it pains me to think they were digging in the wood after we started the rescue dig. They must have been there over the weekend. Our people were asleep in their tents two minutes away and didn't hear a thing. Cornelia was on the right track the first time she went up there.'

'Atta girl!'

'I think she's lost interest in treasure, now human remains have turned up.'

'Constancy is *not* her thing. Where is she now?'

'On the prowl. She's taken the dinghy out on the estuary.'

'She loves that dinghy.'

'Maybe she's taken it across to Emsbury.'

'I had lunch there today.'

'Oh yes, your meeting with Meade Daguerre!'

'Typical celebrity: too busy to relax for more than two minutes, but he's coming to see my work tomorrow so I'm going to have to reclaim my studio for the day.'

'Fine.'

'I'm not sure it was a good idea taking Miles. He was rather sharp with him. I don't think he cares very much for an in-comer like Meade.'

'Did you ask about the nighthawks?'

'Seemed shocked. And his wife's been away, so it can't have been her in the pub, flaxen braids or not.'

'Oh! What about his people?'

'Didn't pursue it; not politic. If they did it, he doesn't know. God knows how many grockles he's got working up there. Bit of a boys' club by all accounts.'

'Drew a blank, then.'

'I suppose so.'

'Whoever they are,' Lovage decided ruefully, 'they know what they're doing, that's for sure.'

'What do you think they stole?'

'Well, it's a grave: lead coffin, about two feet below the ground. Roman. Everything thrown about, any old how. Besides the coffin all that's left is bits of skeleton and a badly corroded silver statue base. It's probable there were more grave goods; the coffin's high status. You can only imagine what's been taken. It's right outside where we're digging and it's possible there's more graves there. The county people think we're excavating a temple. If it is there could be lots more grave goods, votive offerings, which would explain the gold trinkets those old ladies saw in the pub. Myself, I think there's still a possibility it's just a simple farmstead.'

'When will you know which?'

'Soon. They're going to open two new trenches.'

'Well, you lumpkins wouldn't have found the grave but for Cornelia.'

'That's what's so galling,' agreed Lovage.

Bliss laughed.

'The thing is both the new trenches will be in the field. The National Trust owns the woodland all along that side of the estuary as far inland as Totteringham. What with English Heritage and the county's Heritage Services also involved the restrictions on how and where we can dig are ridiculous. The National Trust says we can excavate the grave but the rest is out of bounds. They're not going to let us dig in their woodland until we've done enough in the field to show what we're dealing with. Cornelia's great virtue is not being susceptible to politics.'

Bliss laughed again. 'True, and good for her!'

'And we have to put a guard on the grave tonight.'

'Really?'

'I've sort of volunteered to sleep up there. How long can that go on? Turn our backs and the nighthawks'll be back.'

Bliss shifted in her seat; she had more to say about Meade Daguerre. 'I have to admit, despite the ants in his pants, I was pleasantly surprised by how down to earth he was.'

'Oh? How do you mean?'

'Not what I was expecting, though I suppose he's been spoilt by money and fame, same as the rest. You know, he wasn't conceited or toffee-nosed. Seems he genuinely wants to fit into our little community. I suspect he might try to ingratiate himself with me by buying one of my paintings when he comes here tomorrow. How much should I ask?'

Lovage looked askance. 'Pah! Don't sell, Lara, it's too humiliating. It doesn't mean a thing to be bought by him. Tell him they're not for sale.'

'I thought twenty thousand would given him pause.'

'Oh well,' he laughed, 'that does seem suitably steep.'

'Oh?' She feigned effrontery for a moment. 'That's not steep for a genuine Bliss! And only last month he made two and a half million from that arts centre deal in Dubai – so I read in my daily rag. Anyway, if I'm to help you find out who the nighthawks are I might need to keep our little flirtation going.'

Hardly had she finished speaking when the telephone rang. It was Carrie, Daguerre's PA, calling with profuse apologies on his behalf, saying he would have to cancel tomorrow's visit as something unavoidable had turned up. She would re-schedule his visit as soon as possible. 'So sorry... Sends his apologies... Very keen to come to your studio...'

Bliss put down the phone and pulled a face. 'Damn, he's stood me up! Maybe that's a guilty conscience talking after all!' She looked up and saw that Lovage was preparing to leave. 'You off?'

'Those of us spending the night doing guard duty are meeting for drinks in Totteringham first.'

'The Hampson Arms?'

'Yes.'

'Have fun. Keep an eye out for gold trinkets.'

ELEVEN

The archaeologists not already in their tents were preparing to turn in. A health & safety-sanctioned campfire was burning in an extemporised hearth. Bolshoi Bertie was worrying about the arrangements for the night's vigil. Lovage, who had just turned up after a pleasant evening in the pub in Totteringham, stared down at him pityingly.

'Can I put a woman on as a watchman?' Bolshoi Bertie asked of no one in particular.

Monica, his aide-de-camp, gave a snort of derision. 'Of course you can! I'm going to do it, whatever you say. And its "watchperson", if you must!'

Lovage, who found Monica's independence of spirit perversely seductive, giggled. 'I'll be there to protect you,' he said fondly.

She huffed and looked away into the night.

'The trouble with you, my good friend,' began Bolshoi Bertie, very much on the pomp, 'is that you don't understand the necessity to keep the excavation a zone of professional practice... *at all times*!'

Lovage stared at him contemptuously. 'I don't this, and I don't that! What are you talking about? Broken pots, a few bits of foundation is all *you've* dug up so far. Where's the harm in a little entertainment of an evening?'

'Where's Judith, then?' he demanded accusingly.

'I don't know.'

'You left her in Totteringham! She called on her mobile five minutes ago.'

Lovage looked nonplussed. 'I thought she'd already gone with one of the others.'

'She stayed to make sure you didn't get into trouble. You shouldn't have been driving.'

'I didn't see her.' He sat down suddenly and held his head in his hands. 'Why didn't she make herself known to me?'

'You slipped away while she was in the loo, you cretin!'

Lovage pulled a face of remorse. 'The last I saw of her... she went to the bar to get a Coke... with a slice and no ice!'

Monica laughed at him and got to her feet, 'Come on, big man, you're coming with me to guard a hole in the ground.' She kicked him dispassionately, as though testing a tyre. 'You're no use for anything else.'

Lovage staggered upright with as much dignity as he could muster. 'Fine, I promised I'd pull my weight.' He looked down severely at Bolshoi Bertie. 'Don't call me 'til seven thirty.'

Bolshoi Bertie dismissed him with a scornful flick of the wrist.

Monica had picked up two sleeping bags and she pushed one into Lovage's arms. They went down the slope together, Lovage stumbling wildly at times. They came to the piles of spoil from the trenches and then the trenches themselves. The night was still and quiet. Lovage looked back to the faint lights of the encampment on the hillside.

He uttered the one word, '*Picturesque!*' and weaved after Monica towards the black mass of the wood.

When they reached the fence Monica switched on her torch and they proceeded through the tangled undergrowth, with much swearing from Lovage, until they arrived at the clearing where the looted Roman grave lay. Here they spread out their sleeping bags in an impromptu bivouac. Lovage went off into the night to relieve himself. He could only see the vaguest of shapes in the dark, but he could feel the ground went downwards at a slight incline. When he stood still he could hear – he didn't know how – the soft night-time sounds of the silent, wooded slopes dropping away steeply to the estuary. He listened hard, stretching for the sound of lapping water – a ridiculous endeavour, he decided. He felt thoroughly drunk and liberated out there in the wilds, no mortgage, no attachments, nothing but archaeology to hold him down to the ground.

'*Archaeology!*' he howled. 'Arch-*AE*-ology!'

The echo surprised him with its joyfulness. And then he heard Monica shout something in reply, but didn't catch the words. Were the nighthawks coming up through the woods below him? He listened for the little chinks and scratchings they would make as they forced their way through the underbrush. Did they use night vision glasses? Might they be watching him now? How determined and resourceful were they? Had the treasure they had already found told them what the stakes were, something he had no idea of? If there was a hoard of gold somewhere in the stretch of woodland between the fence and the slope down to the river, what might they be prepared to do to steal it?

'No good worrying about that!' he yelled. 'Not going to worry about it!'

'Come in, boat seventeen!' he thought he heard Monica shout back. Then came a muffled shriek, scuffling and a crack as though a rotten branch had snapped.

He turned and tacked wildly in the direction of the clearing. When finally he reached it there was no sign of Monica.

'Moni-ca!' he hissed. '*They're here!*'

He criss-crossed the clearing several times until he stumbled over his sleeping bag still lying where he had left it, but of Monica and her sleeping bag he could find nothing.

'MON–IC–A!' he shouted.

He stood still and listened intently. There was silence and – worse – he felt a compulsion to cavort about in the impenetrable blackness, waking every shade of night lurking there. He heard the crackle of snapping twigs as if something heavy was being dragged. He tried to head in that direction, hardly feeling the whiplash of branches as he crashed recklessly forward.

'Come out, come out, wherever you are!' he challenged, going first this way, then that, without any real sense of where his adversary – if he had one – might be. Then from the direction of the dig he heard a loud bang followed by the crackle of firecrackers. For a moment a lurid rosy glow lit up the woodland canopy. The sound of fireworks went on a little longer and then there was silence. He found himself clinging to a tree trunk, waiting for something to happen. He thought he heard more movement and rushed forward. Then someone, or something, was behind him and he twisted round, but before he had a chance to regain his equilibrium he was laid low by a blow to his upper right arm. He tried to calculate how hard he had been struck and decided he could still get up and run. He rose to his knees and found himself staggering forward, the ground giving way beneath his feet. He was falling, skidding headlong, and then abruptly he came to a halt. His ears had ceased to work. He was lying on his side, his head lower than his feet. Loose flakes of soil were flowing through his fingers. He could make out nothing of his surroundings. In another minute, he decided, he'd pull himself upright and orientate himself, but he was comfortable where he was and a warm muzziness overcame him. He was weak-willed, very weak, he chided and, without making the least attempt to extricate himself, he drifted into a dreamless sleep, shaken by his fall and unreasonably intoxicated.

TWELVE

Some time later Lovage awoke. The first light of dawn was breaking through the tree canopy and a terrific dawn chorus was already in full spate. He was cradled by the extensive root system of an ancient tree clinging to the slope. *God, was he stiff!* He tried to move and began to appreciate that if he disentangled himself too energetically he risked a much greater fall than the one he had already taken. His memory was not altogether clear, but he had the impression that an unseen assailant had attacked him after he had lost touch with Monica. He elevated his head sufficiently to see his feet and was relieved to find he still had both shoes on.

'MON–IC–A!' he yelled experimentally. It was an experiment he was not inclined to repeat since it set a roaring pain loose in his temples. He groaned and began to haul himself into a sitting position. The previous evening's indulgences had thoroughly poisoned his system and getting upright was painful work. By the time he was reasonably straight he had decided he was bruised all over.

'Oh, shite!' he said to himself, thinking what a ridiculous figure he must have cut, blundering around in the trees. 'Bloody nighthawks! Bloody hell!'

He contemplated the climb up the slope. It was very steep, but down looked worse: he could make out the feathery tops of trees some way below him. Gingerly he began to reach out for any root on which he could get a purchase. Fortunately, leftwards, where the slope gave promise of moderating, there was a ready supply of handholds. He scrabbled in that direction, his feet sending down cascades of shale flakes. It was with an immense sense of relief that he made it to safety. He lay on his back, laughing, his head thrumming with booze poison.

'Get me out of here!' he demanded, ordering his legs into action, and painfully he retraced his steps through the wood, until he was leaning over the length of fence in the hedge dividing the woodland from the dig. The scene before him was dewy and unpopulated, an early morning mist still obscuring the upper stretches of the field. He remembered Monica was supposed to be guarding the rifled grave and he doubled back to find her. The clearing bore no sign of her presence, but his sleeping bag was still where he had left it. He felt thoroughly sorry for himself, too sorry to be unduly worried about Monica's whereabouts. More concerning was the question of whether Judith had managed to get back from the pub, and how annoyed would she be at having been abandoned there. Was she the reason he had drunk so much? Had he developed a passion for her? Wasn't she inconsolably beautiful over the rim of his fifth whisky? He shook his head, despairing at his behaviour, and made his way back to the fence. It was then that he became aware of the smell of burnt rubber hanging in the air. He squinted towards the campsite and saw, haloed by the sun breaking through the mist, the charred skeleton of the Heritage Services' minibus, the grass surrounding it scorched black.

Some of the archaeologists were already stirring when he reached the campsite and his arrival brought several more, amongst them Bolshoi Bertie, out of their tents. All the talk was of arson, someone having torched the minibus. No one seemed interested in what had happened to him. He was hearing for the third time how the minibus had gone up in flames while everyone's attention was fixed on him crashing about in the wood when Monica emerged bleary-eyed from her tent. He was surprised. Of course, he was relieved to find her safe, but he was perplexed as to why she had abandoned the grave and what she had been doing in the moments before he was laid low by the blow to his arm.

'Am I glad to see *you*! I thought you'd been kidnapped!'

She looked him up and down, in the grip of mixed emotions herself. 'What happened to you? You had the whole camp in uproar.'

'It was nighthawks. They attacked me.'

'Did they? Some fucking hooligan was tossing fireworks about. They set fire to the minibus.'

'What the hell?'

'It was unlocked and full of people's clobber. Seems like one or more fireworks were thrown into it.'

'That's crazy!'

'Yes, and it seemed like you were creating a diversion for them. We didn't know what to think. There were all these fireworks and then you disappeared.'

'Oh, really? You don't think I was involved, do you?'

'No, I suppose not,' she said without much conviction.

'Well, I got myself tangled up in a tree. I had to wait until it grew light to climb back up.'

'Climb back up? More like you passed out.'

'Look, someone hit me pretty hard!' He rubbed his arm where he had been struck. 'What were you doing anyway?'

'Nothing. I tried to follow you and then saw there was a fire, that's all.'

'*That's all?*'

'Yeah. I came up here and tried to help put it out.'

'Well, I'm blowed! And nobody stayed to guard the grave?'

'No. Bertie wouldn't let anyone stay.'

He looked at her intently until she looked away, and wondered whether there was more to it than that. Yet again he experienced the feeling of being an outsider, of not really knowing what was going on, but the idea that she was lying to him seemed preposterous, so he swallowed his suspicion and raked his hand through his hair, suddenly desperate for coffee and a shower.

'Fuck it! Blame the booze! Better apologise to Judith.'

Monica glanced towards her tent. 'She must be still asleep. One of the paying guests went out of his way to bring her back last night. She'll forgive you.' She eyed him boldly and added, in her most disparaging voice. 'You poor little mutt!'

That incensed him; of course he had reason to be angry with himself, but mostly he was angry with her for dismissing the attack on him as a drunken fantasy. He stalked off up the hillside. First he went to take a closer look at the blackened shell of the minibus. Nearby he picked up the cardboard husk of a firework. The label read: "Astral Starburst". He was about to throw it away when he realised it might be evidence and he placed it back where he had found it. Judith's tent was lower down the hill and he headed back that way.

When he arrived, 'Er... Judith!' he began, addressing himself to the green canvas. 'Hate to disturb you, but I want to apologise for last night. Leaving you behind like that was completely unacceptable, raging headache my punishment, truly sorry.'

'Stop posturing, Lovage! And get out of my light, I'm reading,' came a voice from inside the tent.

He sidled round the tent so that his shadow no longer fell on the canvas. 'Sorry.' He lowered his voice. 'What did you see when you got back here last night?'

'What *do* you mean?' was the furious retort, the canvas quivering suggestively.

'Were you here when we were attacked by nighthawks? I think they were trying to scare us off.'

'There was a right hullabaloo going on when I got here. You were out of your mind and had disappeared, and the minibus was in flames!'

'I wasn't out of my mind,' said Lovage in a hurt voice. 'This is an exaggeration! I thought the nighthawks were attacking Monica. Someone punched me, or hit me with a branch or something. Laid me flat! I was merry, I admit, but by no means out of my mind.'

Judith's head suddenly appeared between the flaps at the tent's entrance. 'Well, I don't know, Lovage. Go figure it out for yourself. Were they yobs having a laugh or was it nighthawks trying to make us abandon the dig? Were they digging in the wood last night?'

'Good point. I suppose I should have noticed, but I'm telling you it was definitely nighthawks. Come with me?' He said the latter in such a beseeching voice that she laughed.

'All right,' she said wearily. 'Give me a minute to get decent.' She ducked back into the tent, and after what seemed like a titanic struggling with garments and bedding, she emerged.

It struck him there was something majestic about the way she stepped out into the morning air. 'You look… look… Look, I really am sorry!' he gabbled, failing utterly to do justice to his feelings.

'*Can it!*' she said brusquely. She began the descent of the hillside, leaving him to trail after her.

'Are we going there now?'

She threw a single, 'Yes' over her shoulder.

They passed brewing coffee and newly ignited health & safety-sanctioned campfires where bacon was beginning to fry. Lovage felt weak with hunger, but he had put himself in Judith's hands and now it was too late to change his mind. She led him down the hillside and across the site of the dig and over the fence into the wood.

'Where were you?' she asked when they reached the clearing with the despoiled grave.

'We were right here. Or at least, I was. I went in that direction to have a pee.' He pointed. 'I heard Monica yell. I came back here and she was gone. I raced about a bit – you know, concerned – and someone hit me. And I fell!'

'Where?'

'I don't know. Somewhere over there.' He gestured vaguely. 'I slid down a way. I was lucky; it was steep.'

'Well, this grave's not been disturbed again, has it? No nighthawks here.'

'Well, no, but…'

'No buts, Lovage, it was hooligans.'

'Then what's that?'

She picked up what he was pointing to. 'It's a green sock.'

He came over to get a closer look. 'Perfectly good green sock. Size ten shoe, I should think.'

'Never mind about that, where did it come from?'

'Somebody from the camp?'

'Odd! Not from the camp. Who'd drop a sock like that? And why?'

'Not an archaeologist's sock, then?'

She was adamant. 'Not that kind of green.'

He looked at her as though she were a speculative abstraction. 'As you say.'

'What?'

'Odd. Very *odd*!'

'Maybe. Coffee?'

'Definitely.'

THIRTEEN

The uncomfortable jolt of a fall wakened Lovage. This time the fall was purely psychosomatic – a myoclonic jerk – since he was securely wedged between the bags of spare tents and the side of the trailer where gratefully he had lain down to have a nap. As he stretched drowsily a voice began to intone in a gleeful whisper.

'Suck-a-lick-a-lolly! Give me that taut young body on a spit!'

Lovage sat up with a jerk. 'Whhh-at?'

Lying in the grass close to the trailer was a scruffy young man in khaki shorts and a tee shirt. He had a pair of binoculars trained on the dig.

'Oh lovely, lovely indiscretions while digging the unyielding earth!' he groaned.

'What the hell?' swore Lovage. 'Who are you, anyway?'

The voyeur seemed not in the least put out at having been discovered. In fact, he seemed to think Lovage a fellow connoisseur. 'The girls are letting it all hang out while they dig, aren't they?' he gloated.

'Take off, or I'll have you barred from the site.'

The man looked aggrieved. '*Only looking!*' he snarled with such savagery that Lovage was momentarily taken aback.

'That's bracing physical work,' Lovage pointed out indignantly, 'not a pulchritudinous spectacle for your entertainment. Clear off, and stop being a pervert.' He returned his shoes to his feet and hauled himself out of the trailer as the unrepentant peeping Tom sloped off with a disgruntled backward look.

'What a jerk!' Lovage exclaimed under his breath, wondering to which team of archaeologists the man belonged. He felt refreshed by his nap but his throat was parched. At a distance he followed the peeping Tom towards the encampment. Apart from several people scrubbing finds in the marquee, the tented village was empty. Everyone else was excavating or supporting the diggers down at the trenches. He searched for a bottle of mineral water in the supplies tent and when he looked up the peeping Tom had disappeared. He scanned the dig for him and, when he didn't see him, assumed he had slunk away to his tent. Cornelia had appeared at his side. She was eating a large Chelsea bun.

'Where did you get that?' he asked enviously.

'Just got it.' She danced out of his reach.

He looked her up and down. She was dressed in some fashion designer's idea of a scouting uniform, complete with hiking boots topped by thick, rolled down socks. Over the uniform she was wearing a life jacket.

'You've got red streaks in your hair.'

'It's an experiment.'

'Really? It looks like a chemistry experiment. How did you get here?'

'Hitched a ride.'

'From?'

'A baker's van.'

'Hence the bun?'

Cornelia was guarded. 'Possibly.'

'Well, perhaps you should get a ride back. I'm going to be busy.'

Cornelia looked at him critically. 'You look dragged up. Catch a nighthawk? Or one been chasing you?'

'Something like that.' He gestured to where the burnt-out hulk of the minibus stood on the hillside. 'I'm not going to be intimidated into giving up. They're going to say it was hooligans when the police get here; I say it was nighthawks and I'm going to find out how they *got* here, so why don't you…'

They had reached a trench where Bolshoi Bertie was scraping round a patch of recently uncovered stonework. They watched him attentively for a while in the hope that something wonderful would materialise. Eventually Bertie stopped his scraping and looked up at them with a scowl. Lovage spoke before he could.

'There's a dirty sod up on the hillside watching the girl diggers with binoculars. Is he one of yours?'

'Where?'

Lovage scanned the hillside. 'He's disappeared.'

'What, Tony or Roy?'

'No, not them. Younger. More of a roughneck.'

'There aren't any other men in my team. They're all women.'

'That's strange. He must be one of the English Heritage people.'

'No, the Heritage people are all old, retired. One of the university people?'

'No.'

'A helper from the archaeological society?'

'No.'

'I know, he was the Portable Antiquities Scheme Funds Liaison Officer.'

'Ha, ha! Forget it. I'll ask Judith, she'll know.' Lovage gave him a dismissive salute and walked on, somewhat puzzled.

Cornelia followed. 'He wasn't a nighthawk, was he? Your dirty sod, I mean.'

'Sorry, you didn't hear that.'

'Well, who was he?'

'I don't know.' He turned round and looked back towards the encampment. He was wondering whether Cornelia had a point. 'He didn't behave like an archaeologist. Archaeologists definitely don't ogle co-workers... *No*, no nighthawk would be so stupid!'

By this time they had reached the eaves of the wood and Lovage was peering into the trees, his hands resting on the top rail of the length of fence.

Cornelia finished the last of the bun and licked her fingers. 'Go on then, I won't follow you.'

'Yes you will, I know.'

'All right then, I will.'

'Fine!' He stepped onto the middle rail and threw a leg over the fence. 'Don't say I didn't warn you when you're miles from anywhere.'

She stooped, slid between the middle and top rails and stood waiting for him to make his way down from the fence, her face a picture of forbearance.

'Yes, all right, smart Alec,' he conceded irritably, 'let's go.'

They followed what had, by now, become a well-beaten track to the looted grave.

'Somebody was here and he hit me,' Lovage announced, picking up a chunk of fallen branch and hefting it. 'With something like this.'

She gave the branch a cursory once-over. 'He came through the forest,' she decided.

He dropped the branch with a sigh of resignation. 'Did he? Which way?'

'Up.'

He took the green sock from his pocket and showed it to her. 'I found this sock here.'

She looked at it distastefully. 'That's interesting; it's a man's sock. Probably stinks.'

'No.' He raised it to his noise. 'Perfumed actually.'

'We should find its pair.'

Lovage tossed her the sock and she pushed it into her pocket. 'I want to see where I fell,' he continued, 'but watch out, it gets steep suddenly.'

They walked on, him scanning the ground in the hope of finding the other sock, or some indication of the nighthawk's approach. After a while he stopped. 'It must have been here. See how the ground drops away.'

Together they went towards the edge. The slope was almost vertical and only held together by a covering of holm oak.

'You fell down *there*?' exclaimed Cornelia, impressed.

'Somewhere here, yes.' He pointed. 'I think I ended up caught on that tree.'

She leant out to see more clearly. 'Lucky you!'

Now he could see by daylight how steep the slope was, he could only agree. But for the numb obstinacy that had taken hold of him, he would have been appalled at the narrowness of his escape.

They turned right along the ridge, heading inland. After a while they came to a place where the slope grew less steep and they were able to descend, continuing in the same general direction. As they progressed the trees became larger, the light beneath them shone green. Soon they came to a rock face that blocked their way and they turned back towards the sea, still descending. There was silence, apart from the lumps of shale they kicked loose, always running downwards before them. For a while the tree cover thinned and they came upon great clumps of fern. Then they were forced to turn upstream again and, after a further descent, found themselves at the base of the rock face that had blocked their way higher up.

'There's a footpath,' said Cornelia, who was in the lead. She slithered down a bracken-covered bank onto a stretch of level ground and looked both ways.

'More of a lane than a footpath,' decided Lovage, examining the parallel ruts in the mud. 'Somebody comes this way in a vehicle. Which way shall we go?'

'That way.' She pointed to her left. 'That way goes to the estuary.'

He wheeled about to face in the other direction. 'And that way?'

She didn't know.

'We need a map,' he observed dryly. 'Let's do as you say. At least we'll get out of the trees and see where we are.'

She shrugged. 'Okay.'

They went on. The lane ran straight through the trees for a while, sometimes in a gulley, and always going down. Then, its rate of descent increasing, it made several hairpin turns, back and forth across the slope. The wheel ruts here were deep and full of standing water.

'I hear the river,' decided Cornelia.

She was right: through the trees they could see brightness. The tide was in and water lapped between tree roots that ran this way and that over the boulder-strewn shingle. Just then they came to an outcrop of rock. She clambered up and Lovage followed. They pushed through low-hanging branches and found themselves above the foreshore, emerging into an expansive view of the estuary.

'Look, isn't that the steam launch that nearly ran us down the other day?'

The launch was pulling away from a boathouse standing beside an outcrop of rock on the other side of the water. The boathouse was built rather grandly in stone, somewhat in the style of a Swiss chalet. The gable end facing the water had overhanging eaves and double green doors. On the first floor level, above the doors, there was an ornate wooden balcony. They watched until the launch, heading towards the sea, had dwindled to a shimmering blob.

'Whose boathouse is that?' wondered Cornelia.

Lovage shrugged. 'It's a pretty building.'

'It looks utterly sinister to me.'

'Could people be crossing the estuary here? If they come down in a vehicle they must have a reason.'

'Maybe that steam launch ferries them across.'

He thought for a moment and then made up his mind. 'Seems unlikely that nighthawks would come all this way. There has to be an easier way to get to the dig... perhaps from the other direction. Come on, let's walk back to your aunt's house; it can't be much further downstream to Seaview. We need a map and I bet Lara's got one.'

FOURTEEN

Lovage's and Cornelia's trek downstream to Seaview turned out to be nearly three miles, and hard going along the estuary foreshore. It was well over an hour before they reached the welcome refuge of Lara Bliss's lounge. She had been painting most of the morning and they found her reclined on the sofa, a gin and tonic close at hand. She greeted them with pleasure, although pleasure rapidly turned into a stern appraisal of her niece.

'Cornelia, I've been wondering where you were! That hair does *not* suit! What is it?'

Cornelia shrugged. 'I found it in the kitchen. Food dye.'

'Well, it makes your hair look diseased.' She regarded her niece critically, confronted by another aspect of her she had not fully contemplated before. 'And why are you wearing a life jacket?'

'It's fashionable.'

'Not all the time! The point *is* taken! If you want the outboard motor for the dinghy you don't have to make such a song and dance about it! Please *do* have it!'

'Thank you,' said Cornelia dutifully.

'And where did you get to this morning? I was worried about you.'

'She turned up at the dig with a bun,' said a footsore and hungover Lovage, sitting down on the arm of a chair.

'Did you indeed! I don't dare to ask how you got there, you careless creature!' Her exchange with her niece had so preoccupied her that only now did she notice Lovage's begrimed and dishevelled appearance. 'What on earth happened to you?'

'He was set upon by treasure seekers and slept under the stars,' said Cornelia, as if reciting a fairy tale.

Bliss ignored her.

'My night was not restful,' Lovage conceded, quite able to imagine how he must look. 'Declaration of war: Nighthawks firebombed the minibus!'

The last startled her. 'Firebombed!'

'They attacked me in the wood – I was guarding the robbed grave – and while everyone's backs were turned someone set fire to the minibus; threw fireworks into it. The county mob thinks I'm exaggerating blaming nighthawks. They think it was hooligans.'

Bliss looked impressed. 'I've never heard of such a thing. It's not the sort of trouble you expect in Emsbury, that's for sure. And they attacked you?'

'Yeah, swiped me with a branch or something and I fell down a steep slope. Lay there all night.'

'What an adventure! Sounds positively picaresque!' She was beginning to read between the lines. 'Confess! Were you one over the odds? You spent the entire evening in the pub in Totteringham!'

He looked forlorn. 'I don't know what happened.'

'It wasn't about that woman you've met at the dig, was it?'

'Judith,' prompted Cornelia. 'L-l-l-l-ove.' She gave a gurgle of delight at the sight of his displeasure and hardly bothered to evade the swipe he aimed at her.

Bliss laughed richly. 'Fancy some lunch? Shepherd's pie?'

'That would be wonderful.'

'No probs – won't be a minute. It's in the oven.'

'We need a map: large-scale. Got one?'

'Of the Em?' Bliss went over to bookcase at the end of the room and came back with an Ordinance Survey map. 'You really *must* give me the whole story over lunch. Pour yourself a drink. Cornelia, there's juice if you want it. Come through into the kitchen when you're ready.' She could not resist one final thought for her niece. 'Cornelia, that colour's a mistake! Get rid!'

When they had finished their drinks, Cornelia and Lovage trooped through, and Bliss provided a bland but plentiful meal, which they both relished heartily.

'My God, I was hungry!' said Lovage when he had finished. 'Lara, tell me, who in Emsbury has a steam launch?'

She looked up from her plate. 'Willy Basington – he has a steam launch. Also a traction engine called Gertrude. He's a steam engine buff. Goes in for renovating old cars as well.'

'Ah! So, does he have a boathouse on the estuary?' He pushed away his plate, clearing enough room to unfold the map.

'Picturesque?'

'Looks like a cuckoo clock,' said Cornelia.

'Yes, that's his. He lets the sea cadets keep a couple of sailing boats there. There was once a ferry at that point.'

'Ferrying nighthawks!' declared Cornelia with a told-you-so look.

Lovage had a pressing question on his mind. 'What's the background of someone who collects steam engines and has their own boathouse?'

'He's our other local celebrity! Haven't you heard of *Super Start-ups*?'

'No.'

'It's a TV show for budding entrepreneurs on one of the digital channels. Willy fronts it; he does a very good muck'n'brass Northerner, although actually he's a bit of a sweetie from around here. He puts entrepreneurs' business plans through Willy Basington's "Five Tests of True Entrepreneurship", and backs the winners with his own money. It's quite a cult thing.'

'A TV presenter, then?'

'Not only; extremely successful industrialist!'

'Huh!'

'A pillar, he is. County cricket supporter, very generous to the drama society, the church renovation fund, not to mention the League. He has a very nice estate and a rather grand house called High Pevrille. The estate comes down to the river upstream from Emsbury. It's famous for his asparagus beds and his collection of mechanical marvels.'

'High Pevrille. Ah, yes! It's marked on the map. Wealthy?'

'Very. And his father before him. Factories in the Midlands – Birmingham, I think. Engineering and electronics company doing work for the Ministry of Defence, so I've been told. He has an interest in a local business too, run by one of his discoveries. It markets speciality local produce to London restaurants. West of England delicacies: meat, cheeses, organic vegetables, seafood. Bit of a hobby but apparently it's quite the thing. Why the interest?'

'When we were crossing over to Emsbury at the weekend his steam launch nearly capsized our dinghy We saw it again today near the boathouse, didn't we, Cornelia? It was here,' he jabbed at the map, 'where this track comes down to the estuary. See?' He drew his finger across the map. 'We came down the hillside from the dig. In the other direction the track goes up through the woods,' he traced the route, 'and close to Terpsichore Manor. That's Meade Daguerre's place, isn't it?'

For a moment they gazed at the map in silence. What struck them all was the almost perfect symmetry with which High Pevrille and Terpsichore Manor were located on either side of the estuary,

He leaned closer. 'The track's marked "Pilgrim's Way". It crosses the road between here and Totteringham and then runs down to Smeltertown. And look,' he moved his finger in the other direction, 'there's a track on the other side of the estuary that starts at Willy Basington's boathouse. It skirts Emsbury and goes west towards Foreland. It's marked "Pilgrim's Way" too.' He gazed at Bliss, a look of surprise on his face. 'It's extraordinary! Did you know there were miles of tracks running through these woods?'

Bliss got up from her seat and came round to look over his shoulder. 'I've walked Pilgrim's Way. It's a coastal path pilgrims used to follow. It goes east beyond Smeltertown, and much further along the coast than that. Some of the other tracks probably date from when there was tin smelting down in Smeltertown.'

With his finger, Lovage pinpointed the location of the dig on the outer edge of the woodland that fringed the estuary. 'I don't think the nighthawks come across the estuary to raid the dig. Too difficult. You know who else this makes me think of?'

Bliss gave a hoot of laughter. 'Silas Bennett?'

'Yes.'

'He claims its grockles!'

'He would, wouldn't he? It looks like Pilgrim's Way runs close to his farm down in Smeltertown.'

Cornelia put her knees against the edge of the table and leant back with a sardonic smile. 'So he's the gimpy senior citizen who floored you with the hunk of tree!'

The jibe exasperated Lovage. 'It's all very well thinking it was just a big prank that went wrong, but they've got to be stopped, or it'll end with somebody getting hurt.'

'Come, help me with the washing-up,' Bliss decided, making to clear the plates from the table.

Lovage sighed wearily and began to fold the map. 'Tell me, didn't you say Silas had a son?'

'Yes, Barnstable. A bad lot. He was in prison for stealing lobsters. You remember Silas telling us? Not his first brush with the law by a long chalk. Why do you ask?'

'Before I left the dig I saw this odd thing: a man ogling the female diggers through a pair of binoculars. I thought he was somebody working at the dig, but I didn't check and now I wish I had.'

'Barnstable?'

He shrugged noncommittally.

'Tomorrow I'll walk Pilgrim's Way with you,' she promised soothingly. 'We'll walk the stretch down to Smeltertown and call in for another chat with Silas.' She tapped the folded map with her forefinger. 'I still think things point to Meade Daguerre's boys' club being the nighthawks. It has to be grockles to be so enterprising. Arson's a wee bit strong for Emsbury.'

Just then the telephone rang in the living room and she went to answer it. She came back in a while. 'That was a journalist called Jack Palanga. You heard of him?'

Lovage shook his head.

'He's another one with a bee in his bonnet about Meade Daguerre; he has some sort of celebrity gossip column in one of the rags. Wants to buy me a drink at the Hampson Arms in Totteringham this evening. Come and meet him; he's an entertaining mischief-maker and he'll love your story.'

Lovage sat back wearily. 'Why there?'

'Everyone goes there, apparently.'

'Yes, well, one night there's enough for me, Lara. I'll stay here and babysit Cornelia.'

'No you won't!' said Cornelia indignantly. 'I won't be here. I'm off out now.'

'Where are you going?' Bliss demanded.

'I'm going to take the dinghy. I'm after that steam launch.' She was defiant, daring either of them to interfere with her plans.

'All right, dear, you do that. And C—'

Cornelia was almost out of the room.

'Those red streaks: they must go!'

'Yes, a mistake. I'm going to try green.' Cornelia took the green sock out of her pocket and waved it at them. 'To match this.'

Bliss and Lovage looked at one another and shared an indulgent grimace.

'Not entirely a wasted morning,' said Lovage, putting away the map. 'Could you give me a lift back to the dig, Lara? The police will arrive eventually. I suppose they might want a statement.'

'Yes. Let's finish clearing up and I'll take you. I'm curious to see the crime scene.'

FIFTEEN

That evening, as Meade Daguerre drove up Totteringham's High Street in his Range Rover, he caught a glimpse of Jack Palanga entering the Hampson Arms. Without saying a word he turned round in the entrance to the Co-op car park and drove back towards the pub. Carrie, his PA who was sitting in the front passenger seat, looked at him enquiringly.

'Did you see who that was?' said Daguerre.

Daguerre's studio manager, Mortimer, was in the back of the car. He leant forward. 'Who d'you mean, Meade?'

'That bloody journo. He's the one who started the doubts about my bloody yacht.'

'The one you caught on the drive outside the house today?'

'Yes, the one I saw off. Perhaps *he* can tell us where the bloody thing is! Why the hell's he here?'

'Oh! Well, everybody comes here. It's the only halfway decent pub this side of the estuary.'

'Do they? Do you and the boys come here?'

Mortimer nodded.

'Let's go and have a chat, shall we? I want to ask him where he gets his bloody information!'

Daguerre led his passengers into the noisy pub. The bar was unpleasantly full of gabbling grockles. He glimpsed Palanga across the crowded room and went after him. When he caught up with him Daguerre was taken aback to find he was about to join Lara Bliss, who was sitting by herself at a table. He recovered his composure and hailed her. 'Lara!'

'Meade!' She signalled animatedly for him to join her. 'What a pleasure! Come and have a pew.'

'Love to,' said Daguerre evenly. He pulled up a stool and sat down. 'My PA, Carrie.'

'We spoke yesterday.' Bliss eyed her indulgently. 'This is Jack Palanga, who writes for some scurrilous rag.'

'We've met, haven't we, Mr Palanga?'

'Ah, yes, he's after you, isn't he?' said Bliss with a wink. 'You're too high profile not to have someone minding your business.'

'At the moment I'm definitely off duty,' said Palanga smoothly.

'Pity you couldn't come to the studio today, Meade.'

'Yes, sorry, but I've got a bit of a push on. This is Mortimer; he runs the studio at the Manor.'

Mortimer nodded and said, 'Drinks?'

'Thanks, Mortimer.' Daguerre rose to his feet, fished a wad of twenty-pound notes from his pocket and gave it to him.

Bliss indicated her fresh gin and tonic and shook her head. Palanga had already drained most of his half pint and he nodded. Mortimer left for the bar.

'We're on our way to Emsbury marina,' Daguerre said, addressing Bliss, although the words were meant for Palanga. He smiled bitterly at her. 'We're going to see if my bloody yacht is actually where it's supposed to be.'

Palanga finished his drink with a showy expression of relish. 'It is. At least, it was this morning.'

Daguerre bristled. 'So you've been keeping a watch on it?'

Carrie's mobile rang and she left the table to answer it.

Both Daguerre and Bliss were staring at Palanga expectantly, but he didn't respond.

'Actually, I have a question,' Daguerre said abruptly. 'Where did you get your information about my yacht?'

'Sources.'

'What the hell does that mean?'

'It means I never give them away.' Palanga gave the surface of the table a brisk flick with his hand. 'Self-evident, isn't it?'

Daguerre was nonplussed. 'Why are you fucking with me?'

'I'm not, Mr Daguerre, but you employ a lot of people and I don't think you really know what's going on in your own backyard. Doesn't mean it's my job to tell you.'

Daguerre leant towards Bliss. 'He thinks the crew of my yacht have been up to some unspecified hanky-panky.'

'I was merely asking questions,' said Palanga.

Bliss let out a peel of placatory laughter. 'Well! I think we should all act as though we're here to help one another!'

Daguerre and Palanga looked askance at her, the thread of their dispute momentarily lost.

'Look, Meade,' Bliss continued, determined to keep the peace, 'when you're in the public eye all sorts of rumours fly, don't they? Down here it's almost impossible for you not to be the subject of gossip.'

Daguerre gave a snort of exasperation. 'You're not going to bring up that bloody Tomb Raiders nonsense, are you?'

'Well,' she was conciliatory, 'nighthawks *have* been running rings—'

'Wait a minute!' interjected Palanga. '*Nighthawks?*'

'People with metal detectors robbing the archaeological site.'

Palanga's memory appeared to have been jogged because he nodded thoughtfully. 'Site? Where?'

'There's the remains of some sort of Roman settlement on the hill above the estuary,' Bliss explained. 'One of the archaeologists working at the dig is staying at my place, and he says nighthawks have raided it. Some sort of grave has been robbed under their noses.' He leant forward to give dramatic emphasis to what she was about to say. 'Last night they set fire to a minibus at the dig! *And* attacked my house guest!'

Palanga looked at her intently. 'Set fire…? Really?'

'Yes, really! And some dealer from London's been putting the word about that he'll give cash for what's been stolen. He's supposed to have stayed at this pub. His name's Selwyn, or some such, so I've been told.'

'Exactly where is this dig?' enquired Palanga, his nose for a good story aroused.

Bliss had to laugh. 'You've missed a trick there, haven't you? It's on Meade's land.'

Palanga's eyebrows shot up.

'It's on land I rent out for grazing,' Daguerre objected. 'I agreed to a reduction in the rent as a gesture – *as a gesture!* – while the dig is going on. I only just heard about this raid and – *I mean, setting fire to a minibus!* – it's absurd to think my people would have anything to do with something like that!'

At that point Mortimer returned to the table with a tray of drinks. He placed a brandy and coke in front of Daguerre and passed him the wad and change.

'Mortimer, have any of the fabricators at the Manor got a metal detector?' Daguerre demanded.

'I wouldn't be surprised,' said Mortimer cheerily, oblivious to the possibility that he might be committing an indiscretion.

Bliss sat back with a *who-knows-what-those-young-art-students-of-yours-get-up-to-while-you're-not-around* grunt. Palanga laughed to himself.

'Er, excuse me, Meade, but what's this about?' asked Mortimer, sensing he had said the wrong thing.

Daguerre ignored him. 'So, the local gossip is that my employees are plundering *and* terrorising an archaeological dig that's on my land, and my sailing crew is up to no good on my yacht. Is that about the strength of it?'

Palanga and Bliss looked at one another, in no haste, apparently, to contradict him.

'Look, they're high-spirited, that's all. The rest is bloody character assassination!'

'I hear they skinny-dip with girls off Chancellor Island,' said Bliss wistful.

'Lara,' Daguerre appealed to her, 'you heard what I said yesterday about fitting in. And I meant it. I don't want scandal.'

Bliss had been enjoying her little teasing conspiracy with Palanga, but Daguerre spoke so beseechingly she felt slightly ashamed. 'We don't mean it,' she laughed, 'do we Jack?'

Palanga looked non-committal. After a pause he said, 'Just let me talk to your crew, that's all I ask.'

'Meade—' Mortimer tried to intervene again, but Daguerre cut him off with a shake of his head.

There was an uncomfortable moment's silence and Daguerre fished in his pocket for his car keys. 'We're on our way to Emsbury to check on the yacht; how about joining us?'

'Why not?' agreed Palanga, taking a draught of his fresh half.

Carrie was back. 'Henry's mobile's still switched off,' she announced, too preoccupied to sense the awkwardness in the air. 'I called him at home. His father answered and said Henry hasn't been to see them all summer.'

'Very useful,' decided Daguerre. 'Did you get hold of anyone else?'

Carrie shook her head. 'I've tried everyone I can but only managed to get hold of Little Dave. He's studying for his re-takes in Dorking and hasn't been here all month.'

'Even better,' said Daguerre facetiously. He stuck his index finger in his left ear and jiggled it as if his hearing were defective. 'Try again. Someone must answer eventually.'

Carrie took a sip of her drink and was about to leave the table when Daguerre changed his mind.

'No, we're going.' He stood up. 'Make the calls in the car.'

She shrugged. 'I'm sure the yacht's where it should be.'

Daguerre ignored her.

Bliss drained the last of her gin and tonic. 'We'll follow,' she said, gathering herself to leave.

Even though it was growing dark by the time the convoy of cars reached Emsbury, the marina was still alive with activity. Most of the moored boats were still occupied, their crews enjoying the balmy evening. The largest boats were moored on the river side of a long jetty where the water was deep enough to keep them afloat, even at low tide. Daguerre led the others along the jetty. The *May Queen*, a big, broad-hulled racing yacht, all fresh paint and polished chrome fittings, was tied up at its furthest end.

When he reached her, Daguerre inspected her suspiciously, looking for any sign she had been taken out to sea recently, as Palanga claimed.

'Handsome boat, Meade,' said Bliss.

'We're planning to do the Fastnet next month,' he replied with a hint of pride.

The yacht was closed up and silent, but for the water slapping against her hull. She appeared very shipshape, everything carefully stowed. Followed by the others, Daguerre dropped into the cockpit. There was a low cabin forward and he put a key to the door. The door was not locked but it seemed reluctant to yield and when finally it did he was immediately met by the stench of coagulated blood. He stopped and covered his nose with his hand. Silently he signalled for Mortimer to join him. Together they pushed the door fully open, forcing back some obstacle. Meade felt for the light switch. Immediately a scene of absolute chaos confronted them. Everything loose had been upturned or smashed as though a violent struggle had taken place. There were smears of blood everywhere and sprinkled over everything were sheets of A4 that had cascaded from a ream packet. The remains of the packet lay in the centre of a pool of blood. The pool was so great it looked as though someone had bled out over the floor of the cabin. With some care, Daguerre took a step forward, avoiding the blood, dark as a tar trap.

'*What the hell!*' he exclaimed. 'Christ, this looks like a murder scene!'

'Oh my God!' groaned Mortimer, staying in the doorway. 'What's happened here? Seems like someone's bled to... How long has it been like this?'

Lara peered round him to see for herself what they were talking about. She was struck dumb by what she saw; it looked like the scene of an atrocity. Daguerre was deathly pale. Without a word he signalled they should back up. The three of them stood on the deck in a kind of daze. Palanga, who had been some way behind the others, made to enter the cabin but was held back by Daguerre.

Then they heard Carrie's voice from the jetty. She was trying to find out why the building contractor's workmen had not turned up to work at the Manor. 'Mr Daguerre can't wait... It doesn't matter; you're the one who has to juggle... Can you confirm you'll be there tomorrow then?'

'*Carrie!*' yelled Daguerre with such violence that Carrie stopped and guiltily shut off the mobile. 'We've got a crime scene here. Call the police and whatever.'

She looked transfixed with fright, her pretty, childish face a grotesque yellow. For a moment it seemed as though she might faint, then she came to and began to jab away at the keyboard like a thing possessed.

Bliss quit the yacht. She lowered herself into a sitting position on the edge of the jetty and gawped across the estuary. 'Bad business,' she muttered. 'Looks like murder. Emsbury will be shocked!'

'I think you should go,' murmured Mortimer to Daguerre. 'I'll deal with this.'

Daguerre looked at him incredulously. 'Don't be ridiculous! What would the police make of that? We all stay till they arrive.'

A local policeman came, but soon gave way to detectives from the county's Serious Crime Squad. A Chief Inspector Wriggley was in charge. He took Daguerre away to his car to quiz him about the yacht and its crew.

'Now, you say you employ a crew to look after the boat and crew for you when you feel like sailing. You've a man called Henry Balfour in charge. You're his employer?' Wriggley was a man of middling years and middling height. Everything else about him was sharp: sharp nose, sharp chin, sharp elbows, a sharp tongue and sharp-eyed. He had begun, as was his habit, by affecting a mild, even dreamy, manner as if he knew that in his line of business the appearance of sharpness was a disadvantage.

'Yes, I suppose so. We have an understanding, you know. He loves to sail.'

'Tell me about him.'

Daguerre was getting over the first numbness of his discovery; he was also beginning to wonder what really he knew about Henry Balfour.

'He's a student.'

'University?'

'Cambridge. I came to know him when his father bought a couple of things of mine. Henry learnt to sail on his father's yacht; his father races quite seriously. He wasn't doing anything this summer and I asked him if he wanted to skipper for me. He brought some of his chums to crew. I rent them a cottage in the town.'

'I'll have the address, if you don't mind.'

'Yes, sure. I pay them retainers. Their time's their own when I don't want to take the yacht out.'

'Sounds quite casual.'

'Yes, I suppose.' He spread out the fingers of both hands. 'I've got a push on in the studio.'

'Enemies? Fights? Anything like that?'

'No. They're good friends… affable… You've got to understand, they're well-set-up people. All of them.'

'Super! Well-to-do, good backgrounds, above reproach, blameless youth.' Wriggley sensed his attitude was running away with him and he pulled himself up. 'And when did you last see this Mr Balfour?'

'I haven't seen any of them since I went away. I've been in Germany. Must be two weeks and more. Carrie knows – she keeps my diary.'

Wriggley nodded absently, as though half his attention was fixed on something happening across the estuary. 'Your assistance will be invaluable in finding out what happened here, I'm sure.' He took a ring-bound notepad from his pocket. 'In the meantime I'm going to seal your boat. Forensics will take a look tomorrow, when it's light.'

Daguerre nodded. 'If he was here you'd know…'

'What?'

'You'd see this is inexplicable.'

Wriggley allowed himself a thin smile. 'Always the case.'

Wriggley and Daguerre returned to the jetty where Daguerre's party were standing about listlessly.

'My colleague taken everybody's details?' asked Wriggley.

There was a murmur of assent.

'Nobody leaving the area?'

They shook their heads.

'You touched nothing.'

They all nodded.

'Nothing untoward, unusual before you opened the door?'

They shook their heads a second time.

'Anybody know if the crew is at this address in Emsbury? Cider Cup Place? Number Eight?' He held up his notepad as though talking to a class of five-year-olds.

Carrie spoke up. 'I think they might be away. Last time I talked to Henry he said they might go to the north coast for some surfing, what with Meade being away.'

Wriggley made a note. 'We'll need to see to you all again tomorrow. In the meantime I suggest you don't talk about this to anyone. And I don't want any one of you to contact Mr Balfour or any of the others. Is that understood?'

They all indicated their assent.

'Mr Palanga, your reputation goes before you, sir.' He gave Palanga a look of pure poison. 'No premature disclosure in your rag!'

Palanga raising a placatory hand, seemingly surprised that Wriggley already knew of his business. 'I need a stiff one.' He looked at Bliss. 'Fancy a brandy?' He turned to the others. 'Boys and girls, I'm buying!' And with that he took the jetty back to the shore.

SIXTEEN

In the chintz splendour of the tiny study off her lounge, Lara Bliss was breakfasting: fruit, toast and Marmite, and a large cortado. The shock of last night's discovery had given her a troubled night but now she had a day of strenuous activity in mind and she needed fortifying. A heinous crime had been perpetrated in her backyard. It was an affront and she was determined it should be cleared up. As a preliminary she wanted to see the crime scene by the light of day. The foot passenger ferry crossed the estuary to Emsbury every hour during the summer months and she caught the first of the morning. Yachts already dotted the estuary's smooth waters. To her left the sun picked out the greys and greens of Chancellor Island. As the ferry chugged its way across she had time to revisit her nocturnal musings. So, why, she asked herself, had some grockle sailor-boys been fighting on board a yacht in Emsbury's marina? That much damage and that much blood, she reflected, meant that something dire had occurred. Meade Daguerre had said Henry Balfour was from a good family, well-connected, father something important. That made him an unlikely criminal, or victim. And was Daguerre an irrelevancy or was the incident in some way related to his extraordinary celebrity? Sex? Jealousy? Money? A dreadful accident? She could see into the marina and knew that the *May Queen* must be somewhere amongst the clutter of masts. What had Daguerre said Balfour was studying? Medicine, was it? She shook her head, a little pang of dismay brimming up. Still, she reflected, the sun still shone! And now they were past the marina entrance and approaching the quay where the ferry docked. One of the crew struck a bell to warn the quayside of their coming. It rang out sharp and clear across the lower town. And there was the terrace in front of Daguerre's restaurant, and standing on the terrace she could make out a tall figure, staring in her direction, a hand shielding his eyes.

'Damn me!' she said to herself with a chuckle. 'It's Jack Palanga. What's he doing there?'

The longer she watched the more certain she became that he was waiting for the ferry's arrival, almost as though he were expecting her.

By the time the ferry docked his vantage point was lost to sight. She made her way up the slipway to the square where the end of the high street arrived at the estuary's edge. The terrace fronting The Estuary restaurant occupied a high point to the left. She started up the steps to the terrace and as she climbed Palanga came back into view at the top, still standing where she had seen him from the ferry.

''Morning, Lara!'

'You schemer! How did you know I was coming?'

'I phoned and was told,' he said with a bow.

'Cornelia!' she huffed. 'I should have come incognito.'

'Hardly possible,' he replied with a broad grin.

The breeze seemed determined to make his point for him as it tugged at the hem of her dress, displaying to full effect the dress's pattern of large roses on a dappled cerise ground.

'Looked like a murder scene to me!'

'I wouldn't know,' she said, a little breathless from the climb. 'A grim evening though. What can I do for you, Mr Palanga?'

'Well, in the pub last night you were about to put to rights my suspicion that the good folk of Emsbury are criminals all,' he laughed. 'And now you've got a possible murder scene to explain away. Well, well, your metal is being tested and no mistake!'

'First, buy me a coffee. Second, Henry Balfour and the rest are not locals; they're grockles writ large. We see a lot of them down here in the summer months, goofing about in their yachts. We shall untangle this business, Mr Palanga, and if it is a crime – rather than the scene of some dreadful accident – you'll see it's not a local crime at all.'

He nodded, as though accepting her challenge. 'Then coffee it shall be! And time for a candid comparing of notes, perhaps!'

Some time later those citizens of Emsbury interested in the warp and weft of minor happenings noted that the president of the Emsbury League of Artists and the uppity journalist down from London were conferring in the rear of the Scolded Cat Tearooms. Pleasantries disposed of, Palanga addressed himself to the main item on the agenda.

'Meade Daguerre: the Wild Man of Contemporary Art.' He declaimed it as though reading a newspaper headline.

'That was a decade ago, Mr Palanga. He's reformed, married and middle-aged. That's why he's come to Emsbury.'

'What brought me to Emsbury was Meade Daguerre. You say he's reformed, no longer the wild man, but there's a lot of stories about him out there. Perhaps he can't escape his past. That would make good copy. Then there's the drowned Chinese man.'

Bliss sat back. 'Ah! You've mentioned him before. A bit of a stretch tying him to Daguerre, isn't it?'

'Maybe. A man with no identity, no papers, no possessions; undernourished, bad teeth and no dentistry: just a man from China in a cheap suit. Where did he come from, if it wasn't a boat?'

'Bristol,' shot back Bliss.

He shook his head. 'He's not the first this summer. There was another one in the sea off Lyme Regis.'

'Really?'

'Really! The one they found in the Totteridge lay-by fell off a boat and drowned before he could be pulled back on board.'

'So you say.'

'The issue is: why was he dumped away from the sea unless it was to mislead the authorities?'

'Lot of surmise. Nobody's even sure he was Chinese.'

'Oh, I'm sure of that!'

'Really? You're not saying it was Meade Daguerre's yacht he fell off, are you?'

'Well, let me put it this way: it was a yacht with a sunburst spinnaker that brought me here.'

'So you say.'

'A couple of months ago a friend of a friend was drinking in a bar in Rotterdam. He fell in with a crewman – a Basque – from a freighter that carries oak from Turkey. The Basque said on their next trip they had a rendezvous with a yacht with a sunburst spinnaker twenty miles due south of the mouth of the Em estuary. He was very precise.'

'Was he? And did he know why?'

Palanga leant forward, lowering his voice conspiratorially. His reply was bright with zeal. 'No, he did not – or wouldn't say – but Daguerre's yacht used to be berthed at Poole. There's some met the crew as they sailed along the coast – "layabout toffs", they said. Weren't in a hurry, rather conspicuous, stopping off anywhere there was nightlife. Some gained the impression they were involved in smuggling.'

'*Smuggling?*'

'Since they've been here they've been in the habit of taking the yacht out, haven't they? Some say they moor somewhere off Chancellor Island and stay out there over night. Some say local girls have been joining them, but I've not yet come across any who have.'

'Mermaids!' said Bliss, opening her eyes wide in mock horror. 'Seduced by mermaids!'

'Now the skipper and the rest of the crew are missing!'

'I can see the missing bit doesn't help matters.'

He laughed good-naturedly at Bliss's dismay.

'And it *is* a story!' she added reluctantly.

'Would you care if there were a scandal?'

She considered the question. 'You think Meade Daguerre's involved?'

He smiled wickedly. 'That's the story I want.'

She looked at him long and hard, and slowly relaxed. 'I have never heard such a farrago of conspiracy theory nonsense!' she laughed. '"*A friend of a friend*"! You've animated the damn thing out of nothing!'

'Oh, it's not blather, Ms Bliss.'

'I shall warn Daguerre what you're up to immediately!'

'No, you won't.'

'Oh? Why won't I?'

He laughed again. 'For the sake of the story, of course!'

He looked so eager and dashing that Bliss felt a sudden, overpowering desire to indulge him. 'Very well,' she conceded, 'let's follow your trail for the time being. But what about Henry Balfour? Handsome, intelligent, well-connected?'

'One of England's finest,' agreed Palanga. 'Older brother Rex is already MP for somewhere safely Tory. *Will go far!*'

'Privileged, then.'

'Enviable cultural capital.'

'So what went wrong? Who was fighting on that boat, and why was all that bloody chaos left behind? Whoever was involved must have known it would be discovered sooner or later.'

He shrugged. '*That's* the question!' He leaned forward conspiratorially. 'Why don't you and I find the crew and ask them? If anyone knows, they do.'

'Ah, yes, they're living in Doctor Needham's cottage in Cider Cup Place. I had it in mind to see if they were in.'

'No one there.'

'Didn't thinks so. That girl Carrie said they're on the north coast, surfing.'

'She did. But I think they're closer at hand. I think they've decamped to the beach at Foreland.'

'Why do you think that?'

'I've been climbing walls. One of the crew has an old VW campervan. The VW's gone but their surfboards are still in the backyard of their cottage. They've rented kites and landboards from Farley's boatyard. The beach at Foreland is the best place for landboarding for miles: broad empty beach and a steady wind from the west.'

'How do you—?'

'I know that,' he interrupted triumphantly, 'because I've studied the "Best Beaches For Landboarding" website.'

'Good for you! Top marks for sleuthing! I know Foreland. There's a wetland nature reserve there. To get a vehicle to the dunes at the far end you have to lift the gate off its hinges. Want me to take you?'

'Why not? How about now?'

She sat back with a look of satisfaction on her face. 'You'd have to come back to my side of the water.'

'Fine.'

'But first I want to take a peek at the crime scene, my second in as many days!'

Palanga drained his cup. 'Fair enough! And let's avoid that detective Wriggley; he looks an evil sod.'

SEVENTEEN

Detective Inspector Wriggley arrived on the sweep of gravel at Terpsichore Manor shortly before ten o'clock. His drive through the dewy landscape had been invigorating and the scene before him was altogether reassuring: a fine manor house, workmen climbing the scaffolding to begin their day's work, expensive cars parked in the driveway. The ignition off, he could hear birdsong and the distant drone of a mower. There was a tap on the window and he looked up from his notes to see Mortimer, Meade Daguerre's studio manager, gazing in at him through the side window. He shoved his door open, forcing Mortimer to step back in haste. At the same moment the rear door was thrown open, revealing a dwarfish, ill-favoured man who had been sitting there unnoticed.

'Good morning. Lovely day! It's Mr Mortimer, isn't it?' said Wriggley. He indicated the other man who was now getting out of the car. 'My colleague, Detective Sergeant Brisley.'

Mortimer's hand was thoroughly shaken. 'Morning,' he said.

The manner of the policemen's arrival was intended to unsettle his composure. They observed the niceties, but they did so brusquely. It created an air of apprehension, as if they were about to set loose some wilful force.

'The boss is in the house. You want to come in?'

'Thank you, Mr Mortimer,' said Detective Inspector Wriggley cheerfully. 'You lead on – we'll follow.'

Overnight a great deal of information about Meade Daguerre and the inhabitants of Terpsichore Manor had come Wriggley's way, coloured by their well-established reputation for bringing fast London living to the Em estuary. There had been little time for sleep. In the process he had formed an extremely jaundiced impression of Daguerre. "A man with a disreputable past, bought by The Establishment" was the way he saw it. As far as he was concerned, Daguerre's whole career smacked of charlatanism, which, coincidentally, he saw as the stock-in-trade of the smarter sort of swindler. Clever, very clever, ingenious, strategic. Gifted? He begged to doubt it, but then art, contemporary or not, was not much to his taste. Wriggley's business was unsettling others, but modern art was on the short list of things that unsettled *him*. There was something in it he missed, and that, he felt, was a vulnerability and it made him think he should be steely where Daguerre was concerned.

There might be something of an enigma about Daguerre, but Mortimer was a different matter. Mortimer he had summed up to his complete satisfaction: a man in his middle thirties, capable, with a good deal of experience of practical living. He had been in Daguerre's employment for more than ten years and managed many of his business affairs. In so far as Wriggley was capable of charitable thoughts, he recognised Mortimer as the sort of man who would be good in a complicated disaster with damaged engineering and dangerous chemicals. His keen sense of observation already told him that in other circumstances he was rather colourless, stolid, self-contained, not prone to anger and safely insulated from the wilder desires that troubled some of his fellows: a decent type but lacking imagination.

They entered the hall – a large, baronial space with a fine marble floor – through two sets of doors. On the left was a large morning room, unfurnished and freshly painted, with what could have been a late period Picasso in a heavy frame leaning against the wall. Meade Daguerre was sitting at a small chrome trolley in the centre of the room, staring at the screen of a laptop. He stood up when he saw the detectives.

'Sorry to barge in,' said Wriggley, sounding anxious and obliging. 'My colleague, Detective Sergeant Brisley.'

The dwarfish detective seemed not to realise he was being introduced and continued to gaze about with incurious malevolence.

'Morning,' said Daguerre, shifting his weight from one leg to the other, uncomfortable at finding himself caught up in a police enquiry.

Mortimer had followed the detectives in and now softly he closed the door.

'Deary, deary, deary me!' began Wriggley, as though talking to himself. 'Violent altercation in a confined space. Criminal damage. Somebody severely wounded and a great deal of blood lost… *at the very least*! No attempt to conceal events. Door not locked, nobody nearby heard anything.' While delivering this recitation

Wriggley fixed a wary eye on Mortimer even though he was addressing Daguerre.

'It seems so,' agreed Mortimer, somewhat abashed.

'No good beating about the bush. Clinically delivered, if a little obvious.'

Daguerre was perplexed. 'I'm sorry, are you describing your way of talking?'

'No, no,' Wriggley laughed, 'the crime! A struggle: crashing about, but most likely once, with a well-chosen blade. All we need to do is identify the man capable of such an act.'

'But there isn't a body... is there? We don't know anyone's been killed, do we?' Daguerre's voice had lost its strength and he coughed.

'No. No one's turned up at a hospital missing an armful of blood either.'

'You quite seem to relish the whole thing, inspector.'

'I do, I do! It's methodology, Mr Daguerre. I have mine; you – being a man of the arts – have yours... *I expect*.' At that he looked comically doubtful. 'I must get a picture of exactly what happened, second by second. Once I have a whole, continuous picture, with no jump cuts, I know I'm only one step from solving the crime! *Real-time video!* You understand such a concept, I take it... being a man of the arts?'

Daguerre gave a weak laugh. 'You're pulling my leg, right?'

Wriggley looked mystified. 'No, not at all. It's the challenge I enjoy, Mr Daguerre. Police work: it's everything.'

'I see.' Daguerre lowered the lid of his laptop and awkwardly thrust his hands into his pockets.

'This is a developing story, Mr Daguerre. We can have no idea where this investigation will take us.' Wriggley said this with a fair degree of menace. 'You should prepare to deal with the press; that marina is seething with rumours. The *Evening Standard* has been making enquiries. Expect a deluge!'

'Yes. I am. I'm going to ask my gallery to send someone.'

'*Your gallery?*' He gave Detective Sergeant Brisley a look, as if to say, 'Here's a novelty!'

'Yes, my gallery in London: someone to handle the PR.'

Wriggley laughed with apparent good nature. 'PR! Someone from London, eh? Probably wise to get in a foreigner. Virtue of distance! Are you aware the sport you were with last night – Jack Palanga – is of that unpleasant species of journalist that deals in the misfortunes of the famous?'

'Yes. Hack!'

Wriggley was suddenly grave. 'Has a beef, does he? Been pestering?'

'He was here yesterday. He's not welcome. A sensation-monger, isn't he?'

'But quite sincere, I thought.' Wriggley looked nonplussed, as though an unaccountable phenomenon had crossed his path. 'And Mr Balfour, the skipper?'

'Can't get over it, really. Shocked.'

Wriggley was solicitous. 'I have spoken with his family. They are inconsolable, but hope for the best. Not a sign of him at their end. Not surprising!'

Daguerre took his hands from his pockets and raised them as though in an act of surrender. 'Who knows why! I thought all of them perfectly decent…'

'We need to find him and his... What *are they*, exactly? Crew? Colleagues? Mates? My detectives went to their cottage in Emsbury very early this morning. We were hoping to catch them in their beds, roust 'em out, see if there were any victims, check a few alibis – that sort of thing. *No one at home!*'

'They sometimes go off to the north coast for the surfing. Somewhere near Rock, I believe. Campsite. Maybe this has nothing to do with them. I was out of the country so they knew I wouldn't be sailing. They're just ski-bums doing their summer thing.'

'*Are they?*' Wriggley marvelled at the description. 'I hear they're in the habit of inviting young women onto the boat and having parties out beyond Chancellor Island. Tales of nudity and lasciviousness.'

Daguerre gave an exasperated snort. 'You know how gossips exaggerate. Just high spirits, I expect.'

Brisley snorted back, derisively.

'I understand you're married,' Wriggley continued.

'Yes, my wife's in Denmark.'

The two detectives gave one another a look as though this was an admission of some significance.

'You've informed her?'

'I don't want her rushing back.'

'But have you told her?'

'No, not yet. You told me...' Daguerre looked uncomfortable. 'She's on an important modelling assignment.'

'Quite... So, who was here at the house the night before last?'

'The nanny – Consuela – was here with the kids. Mortimer. Several of my fabricators were here.'

'Fabricators?'

'Yes, that's my studio assistants. I employ quite a few, although some are on holiday at the moment. They have rooms at the back of the house.'

'I hear you have a bit of a zoo up here, pardon the expression. Did anyone from here have reason to go to the yacht at all?'

Daguerre sighed. 'Carrie, my PA, and Taz, one of the fabricators were there the night before last. They wanted a little privacy, if you know what I mean... so I've been told.'

'By whom?'

'Oh, them! They told me last night when we got back here.'

Wriggley's face had elongated in a parody of gravity. He consulted his notebook. 'So, that's Miss Crowthorne, I take it? She was with you at the marina. Is she here now?'

Daguerre nodded.

'And this... *Taz?*'

'Yes. Terence Rakusen. Henry Balfour turned up.'

'I see. Better wheel them in. Wouldn't want to think they were withholding, would we?' Wriggley cast about as though the revelation had exhausted him. There was a couch covered in dustsheets in front of the bay window and he threw himself down on it with such violence that his shoes squawked on the floor.

For a moment Daguerre gazed in surprise at the stricken detective and then signalled to Mortimer to fetch Carrie and her beau. 'Carrie is a poppet,' he said, by way of a plea for clemency.

Wriggley stared at him mildly, but made no response. Still he had said nothing when Mortimer returned with the two miscreants. There was a sudden flurry of activity as Brisley brought the room's single chair and placed it facing the couch. Wriggley hauled himself upright and smiled benignly at Carrie, who had the flinching demeanour of the guilty.

'By the way, girls and boys, for those that don't know, my name's Detective Inspector Wriggley and I'm in charge of this investigation. Please sit down, Miss Crowthorne.'

Brisley propelled the chair into the back of her knees and she sat down abruptly.

'The queen of tarts,' mused Wriggley with a faraway look in his eyes, 'did break some hearts.' Suddenly he lunged forward, bringing both feet down on the floor with a crack. In a moment he had collapsed back into his former languid pose. 'Random act of violence. You see, like what happened on Mr Daguerre's boat. Right?'

Daguerre began loudly. 'I don't see why—'

The detective threw up a hand. 'No? Sorry about that. Sorry about that, Miss Crowthorne.' He gave the three of them a surly look. 'Little enactment, for the purposes of edification. *You*,' he pointed accusingly at Carrie, 'could have been more forthcoming last night!' He passed a hand across his brow as though he had lost his train of thought. 'Now, where were we? Ah yes! Miss Crowthorne, please explain what happened at Emsbury marina the night before last.'

'I was there with Taz.' She indicated the blond fabricator.

'Good.' He was staring at her intently. 'I'm not interested in your actions, Miss Crowthorne, but do I believe rightly that you were disturbed whilst fornicating?'

Carrie features crumpled. 'Henry... and another man.'

'Did you recognise the other man?'

'I didn't really—'

'I was the one who saw him,' said Taz, deciding the bullying had gone far enough. Brisley jabbed an elbow into his side just below his ribs. He flinched and was silent.

'Calm, calm!' said Wriggley. 'Mr Daguerre, I appeal to you. Your people must understand, we need their help.'

'I think that's what they're doing: assisting the police with their enquiries.'

'Funny thing, that,' decided Wriggley with a dry chuckle, 'I could have sworn... Never mind. Let's start again, shall we? *Renounce the past and start again!*' He sank further into the couch. 'Miss Crowthorne, was Henry Balfour alive when you left the marina?'

'Yes.'

'What was he doing when you last saw him?'

'He was standing on the jetty, watching us leave.' There was a long silence and then Carrie continued. 'Henry chucked us off the yacht. Somebody was with him. He kept in the shadows. We came back here on Taz's motorbike.'

'What time was this?'

'Twelve-ish. About midnight.'

'And there was no trouble between you about him turfing you out?'

'Henry's the skipper. Everyone knows he treats the yacht like it's his.'

'This person with Mr Balfour… was he a member of the crew?'

'I didn't see who he was.'

'Was there anything else?'

'Last night the yacht was at a different mooring.'

'So, it was moved after you left?'

'Yes.'

Daguerre made a clucking sound with his tongue against the roof of his mouth. Wriggley shot him a glance – a warning to stay silent.

'Were you in the habit of joining the boat for parties?'

'No.'

'Never?'

She shrugged. 'I never sailed with them. They kept it to themselves – the yacht, I mean.'

'The cabin was normally locked, I presume.'

'Yes, Henry has a set of keys and a spare set is kept here in the office.'

'I see. And you had them locked away so nobody else from the house could get at them without you knowing?'

'Yes, I kept the key.'

Wriggley put his hand to his brow and looked pained. 'Thank you, Miss Crowthorne,' he decided, 'that's all for now.' He indicated she could go. 'Terence Rakusen.' He turned to Taz and watched as Detective Sergeant Brisley propelled him forward. 'Come and have a seat, Mr Rakusen.'

Taz sat warily. There was a moment of silence as they waited for Carrie to leave the room.

'I understand you were looking for a little privacy.'

'Yes.'

'You saw a man accompanying Mr Balfour?'

'Yes.'

'Not a member of the crew?'

'No, definitely not.'

'Never seen him before?'

'Never.'

'Description?'

'Young, tallish, boyish face, wearing a suit, dark. Could have been Chinese, you know?'

'Chinese! I see. You knew the members of the crew?'

'Yes, I was at school with two of them. Year ahead of me.'

'Did you see any of them as you left the marina?'

'No. I don't think any of them were in Emsbury.'

'Where did you think they were?'

He shrugged. 'They go all over, as they please.'

'But Mr Balfour turned up with this man and he wasn't one of the crew.'

'Yes, he did.'

'A man you didn't know… but who you might be able to identify if you saw him again?'

'Yes, I suppose.'

'Really?'

'Yes.'

'What distinguished him as Chinese?'

'Dark, lanky hair… His features, the shape of his face.'

'You sure of that?' Wriggley sounded sceptical.

'I think…'

'Did he speak to you?'

'No.'

'And Mr Balfour hadn't been stabbed when you left?'

'Absolutely not!'

Wriggley looked at him blandly and seemed to lose interest. 'Thank you, Mr Rakusen. Tell your... er... friend we'll need fingerprints, DNA sample from both of you... for the purpose of elimination.'

'Was all that really necessary?' demanded Daguerre, when Taz had gone.

Wriggley rose to his feet and approached him. 'The niceties, Mr Daguerre,' he chided gently, 'are for the convalescent home. I have a dozen or so detectives standing idle, awaiting instructions. I have expensive equipment and plant awaiting deployment. Mr and Mrs Taxpayer expect the efficient use of public resources. They expect me to solve crimes and bring miscreants to book. Time is a valuable commodity, of which I have insufficient. Detective Sergeant Brisley,' he gave a nod in his direction, 'is a very fair man and an excellent judge of character. His sort keeps us safe, though we may not know it. As you are Mr Balfour's friend and employer, I'm entitled, I believe, to ask for your full cooperation.'

Daguerre found himself weakening. 'You have it, of course.'

'Yes, of course. Thank you, Mr Daguerre. That's fine, then. But, if you'll excuse me saying so, celebrity sometimes creates an aura and inside that aura strange things occur. Celebrities can be a law unto themselves; theirs is a magical power, as I'm sure you're aware.'

Daguerre was now on the back foot. 'Yes, I suppose so.' A movement made him glance over his shoulder and he saw that Detective Sergeant Brisley was right behind him, intimidatingly close. Hastily he stepped aside and realised that the two detectives were preparing to leave.

'Thank you, Mr Daguerre,' said Wriggley. 'I'm glad we have a goo-goo understanding. We may not trouble you again today. But then again we might. May, might, which is right?' He shook Daguerre's hand heartily.

Brisley came forward and offered his hand in a similar demonstration of goodwill.

Daguerre walked the detectives to the front door. Wriggley had the satisfaction of knowing that he was sufficiently disconcerted by their thuggery to feel nothing but relief at their going. His last sight of Daguerre was as he turned to rejoin Mortimer in the hall. By that time he and Brisley were standing on the far side of the drive by their car.

Brisley was fuming. 'This here is like a bloody country house murder mystery.' He kicked at the turf, his mackintosh flapping at his heels. 'Mopsy-topsy twats!'

'Probably,' agreed Wriggley, scanning the sky with a meteorologist's eye. 'Anyway, your behaviour was a disgrace. You should have been shown out by the tradesman's entrance. Which of last night's people shall we pop in to see next? Bliss or Palanga?'

Brisley joined him in squinting up at the sky. 'I'm peckish,' he decided.

'Ah yes, the Hampson Arms in Totteringham. It might tell a story or two.'

'Then – speaking personally – I fancy a word or two with Mr Palanga, the thorn in our side. How I hate the species called "investigative journalist". We should wring his neck while we're about it. But what about the Bliss woman? She's nearest and it doesn't look like she terrorises easily. I'll have to try being nice.'

'Be yourself, Brisley, that always seems to work.' Wriggley checked Lara Bliss's address in his notebook. 'Yes, Seaview – that looks an efficient use of our time. A spot of early lunch and Ms Bliss it shall be. Mount the chariot!'

Brisley was navigator, providing directions from the back of the car, an ancient road atlas open on his knees. They went down the drive, through the gatehouse and turned right. Wriggley negotiated the winding lane at a stately crawl.

'Sir, at this rate,' complained Brisley after a while, 'we'll be stuck in these lanes all day! Insufficient bottle, is it?'

'Never mind about my bottle, Brisley,' replied Wriggley as he slowed into yet another blind corner. 'Are you strapped in? All we need is some cretinous dolt going too fast in the opposite direction to park your nose in the back of my neck!'

They continued in silence.

'Anyway, what happened on that boat?'

Brisley sniggered. 'Some nasty shit crawled out of the woodwork and bit poor Cock Robin. I hate these educated kids who won't grow up.'

'Could still be a storm in the proverbial. Whichever way, another day and the powers that be will want this thing sorted. We'd better work out who's involved pretty damn quick. Who stuck what knife in whom? And why?'

'A DNA match would help.'

Wriggley looked at his watch. 'Well, forensics will be crawling all over that cottage and the crime scene by now.'

'There's a surfeit of suspects, if you ask me. Mr Daguerre's out of it, isn't he?

'Yeah, wasn't him; head's full of fluff.'

'What about our pair of ardent lovers?'

'Jealousy rears its ugly head? Rivals falling out over that bint? Sexy piece, she is! No. He's as meek as a muffin. That isn't the scenario: too bloody lame!'

'Taz!' scoffed Brisley in disgust. 'What's wrong with Terence? Perfectly good name.'

'You're just jealous because nobody thought to call you Taz,' jeered Wriggley.

Brisley ignored him. 'What about the crew? Alcohol-fuelled falling out? Odd they should have gone off, isn't it?'

'Yes, they're prime, aren't they? They're in on this smuggling, if you ask me. They think they're anarchists… with drum and bass soundtrack. Somebody moved the boat according to that girlie. Why? To dump a body? Mind you, it could have been a stupid accident, playing with a knife, getting into an argument for no reason, flailing about. I can just imagine it.' Wriggley made a pitiful mewling sound. *'I didn't mean to do it. I didn't realise I had a knife in my hand.'*

'Ha! Ha! Ha!' they roared venomously.

'Then there's the Chinese muppet.'

'Chinese mafia seeped out here? They're getting very adventurous if they have.' Wriggley grew meditative. 'If they'd killed Balfour, or one of the other sailor boys, they'd certainly have had the sense to get rid of the body. Perhaps we should get some divers in and search round that jetty. If that's the story, the rest must have gone off before it happened, otherwise they'd be sitting around in shock, bleating. I don't like the way the boat was left trashed though. No attempt to clean up. Either it was one hell of a hasty business or somebody is making a point. Then there's that drowned Chinese soul we had some while ago. Our fraternal colleagues in Bristol say that was amateur; if so, it's unlikely there's a connection. Yes, the Chinese man complicates things; you don't get Chinamen in country house murders. I'll have to refer him back to Bristol, but we don't want them on our backs, do we? So let's try and keep our best ideas in our back pockets.'

EIGHTEEN

Lovage had slept in and almost made good the previous night's excesses. He prepared coffee and opened the door of the studio with the intention of drinking it sitting quietly on the garden seat on the shady side of the lawn, while he wrote a report to his line manager at the British Museum. Instead he was stopped in his tracks by the sight of Cornelia who was already occupying the bench, her limbs composed in an elegant sprawl, as though she had collapsed in a faint. She was quite still and he began to think she must be asleep. Her face was hidden behind a waterfall of blonde hair streaked with bottle green, making it impossible to tell from looking whether she was conscious or not. He glanced at his watch and speculated that she was unlikely to be sleeping in the garden in mid-morning, so he made his way over to her, all the time taking care not to slop his coffee. Still Cornelia did not move. He began to think she was truly asleep when suddenly she spoke.

'Murder most foul!'

He was so startled he spilt coffee on his canvas shoes. 'Damn it!' he swore. 'Why did you do that?'

She squinted up at him, unmoved by his outburst. 'Did you hear about the murder scene?'

'Murder?'

She tossed back her hair. 'On a yacht. Aunt Lara found the murder scene last night. You were snoring when she got back here.'

'Murder?' He was inclined to think she was making it up. 'Anyone we know?'

'I don't think they've found the body yet so I can't tell you his name – *obviously*!'

'Really? Or *her* name. How come Lara's involved?'

'She went to the marina in Emsbury... There was blood everywhere.' She said this with great relish. 'It was a bloody bloodbath.'

He gave her a beady look. It crossed his mind that, after all, she was telling the truth, but he suppressed the temptation to ask her the details, deciding he'd rather hear the story directly from Bliss, unembroidered. 'Where's Lara, anyway?'

'She went back to Emsbury.' She looked at him meaningfully. 'Crossed over to the other side. You know?'

He was mystified. 'No, I don't know! What for?'

'She's investigating; looking for clues. Actually, she's going to meet that journalist who's been snooping on the artist bloke who owns the yacht where they found the murder scene... though she doesn't know it.'

'You mean – what's his name? – Jack Palanga? On Meade Daguerre's yacht? Didn't know he had one. What's that about?'

She did not reply but made to get up. He thought she was about to do so gracefully, but she remembered herself just in time and rose to her feet with an ungainly jerk. He felt a pang of disappointment, as though he had been denied something lovely.

'You're still wearing the life jacket I see.'

She ignored the remark. 'When are we going to the dig?'

'We're not. We're going to walk Pilgrim's Way, remember?' He indicated his notepad. 'I have to finish my report to the Museum first. Let's hope Lara's back soon. We'll see then what she's got to say about your murder business.'

Cornelia gave a scornful huff and walked away.

NINETEEN

By the time Lara Bliss caught the ferry back from Emsbury with Jack Palanga it was nearly lunchtime. They met Lovage on the drive. He had long since finished his report to the Museum and had almost given up waiting.

'You're back, then,' he said dryly.

'Yes,' agreed Bliss. 'You hear about this business in Daguerre's yacht?'

'So it's true!'

'Yes, ghastly scene last night; that yacht was a total charnel house! This is Jack Palanga; he's the journalist I told you about. Jack, this is Dr Lovage of the British Museum.'

'You work up at the dig,' said Palanga, shaking his hand. 'You must tell me about the raid before I go.'

'Yes. Pleased to meet you.' Lovage turned back to Bliss. 'I was about to leave. I thought we were going to walk the Pilgrim's Way today, but if that's been shelved I'm going to the dig.'

'No, stay!' she urged. 'Come and have something to eat. I *have* to tell you about last night.'

Lovage listened silently while she made doorstep sandwiches and recounted the story of the discovery of the suspected murder scene. Palanga stayed in the garden and paced, Cornelia keeping an eye on him at a distance. When the sandwiches were ready the four of them made an impromptu picnic on the lawn. There was some kind of regatta underway on the estuary and the yachts made a pretty backdrop to their meal.

'So,' said Lovage, having heard everything Bliss had to say, 'who did it, and why?'

She laughed. 'That's what everyone is wondering! We're going to find the crew and ask them precisely that question. Jack thinks he knows where they are.'

Lovage felt a slight sense of grievance at her news, even though he had already given up on the hope that they were going to spend the day walking Pilgrim's Way. 'I thought we were going to track down nighthawks.'

'I know, but bloodshed in Emsbury! The character assassination of Meade Daguerre! We should protect his interests, don't you think?' She spoke earnestly, with a glance at Palanga.

Cornelia had been listening attentively and she had a gleam in her eye. 'Chasing murder suspects! That sounds exciting.'

'I thought you wanted to go to the dig,' said Lovage.

'No way!' She shook her head adamantly.

'Fine,' said Lovage, realising that the scent of something as dramatic as murder trumped archaeology, nighthawks and grave robbing.

'Jack thinks they've gone to Foreland. There's a chance we can get to them before the police do.'

'They *are* murder suspects, aren't they?' said Cornelia.

'Persons of interest,' her aunt corrected, using the term self-consciously.

'Material witnesses,' added Palanga.

Concluding that both Lara and Cornelia were for the moment only to be swayed by Palanga – expert on all matters homicidal – Lovage took himself off to the studio to gather his things. The others made their way towards Bliss's Astra. As they did so Detective Inspector Wriggley's BMW pulled into the drive, requiring Cornelia to make a rapid backward leap into the shrubbery. It came to a halt spitting gravel. Wriggley climbed out and for several moments, a kindly smile on his face, seemed fascinated by some obscurity in the mock orange several degrees above Cornelia's head. He turned his gaze on Bliss and Palanga with dramatic suddenness.

'Ms Bliss! Mr Palanga! How fortuitous! Not one but two of the very people we were hoping to see!'

'We're just leaving,' said Palanga, in a voice that suggested they could not delay.

'Now, now, let's not get ahead of ourselves, Mr Palanga! My colleague and I – this, incidentally, is Detective Sergeant Brisley – would be blessed if we could ask you a few questions about last night. It's been put to us – *rumour and innuendo being what it is* – that the assault, murder or whatever it was on that boat, had something to do with some illegal enterprise Mr Balfour and the crew of Mr Daguerre's boat...' He stopped abruptly and gazed at Palanga, appraising him up and down. 'We hear you've been sniffing out some such story for quite a while. We're intrigued to know why you went to the yacht with Mr Daguerre last night.'

'It was at his invitation,' replied Palanga. 'I'd told him I thought – like you – that the crew was up to no good. He wanted to question them.'

'Did you get the impression Mr Daguerre was aware of what you would find on the yacht?'

'Good God, no! I got the impression Mr Daguerre thought his yacht might not be there.'

'Why's that?'

'I think he thought Balfour and the others had made off in it. In fact, I think he'd forgotten he had the thing until I starting asking him about it. That was yesterday afternoon. Later we bumped into one another in the pub in Totteringham and I told him I'd seen it moored in the marina earlier in the day.'

'And?'

Palanga shrugged. 'He wanted to check for himself. Nobody there last night had anything to do with what happened on that yacht.'

Brisley greeted Palanga's avowal with a disbelieving tut.

'I went out of curiosity,' Bliss announced gravely. 'The only exploits of the *May Queen* I've heard about have come from the inventive mind of Mr Palanga.'

Palanga nodded and looked inscrutable. 'I have sources.'

'Your sources are the tittle-tattlers of the pubs of Emsbury,' jeered Brisley.

'I have to inform you, Mr Palanga,' said Wriggley, in the voice of one making a grave allegation, 'that contrary to the throw-away jibe of my colleague, I have reason to believe that you have an informant in the county's Serious Crime Squad.'

'And who would that be?' asked Palanga evenly.

'Would that I knew! *Would that I knew! Yes*, this incident is inconvenient, to say the *very* least! *Yes*, it has the potential to compromise an investigation that has been almost two years in the making! *Yes*, we are concerned that you are about to disclose prematurely that investigation! *No*, it is *not* a laughing matter!'

'*Really!*' scoffed Palanga. 'And what investigation is that? Perhaps now you're ready to admit that this yacht business is linked to the drowned Chinese!'

'No known connection!' retorted Wriggley heatedly. 'What happened on that boat is most likely a local matter. The dead Chinaman was drowned in a barrel meant for curing hams. Our colleagues in Bristol have arrested four of his ethnic persuasion.'

'That's bollocks!' said Palanga. 'He had seawater in his lungs. That man died in the sea.'

'There was more *nitrite* than *chloride* in that water! Mr Palanga, you and I are in need of a frank exchange of views.' His tone suggested his patience was wearing thin. 'I'm finding myself wondering how much more you know about what happened on that boat than you're letting on. Yes, indeedy! I think you'd better come down to the station for a proper chat… if you'd be so kind.'

'Purely for the purposes of eliminating you,' added Brisley, giving him a look of utter repugnance.

'Not in any absolute sense, I hope,' laughed Palanga. 'Happy to oblige, *really*! Be glad to pick your brains while I'm at it.'

Only the policemen expected what happened next. With a velvet display of force, Brisley propelled Palanga towards the car. The move was so rapid that Palanga had no chance to pull away. He hardly had enough time to give Bliss a sickly smile over his shoulder as Brisley thrust him into the rear of the car. As Brisley did so, in a mockery of solicitousness, he clamped his cupped hand down on the crown of his head to prevent it coming into contact with the doorframe.

'I want to come too,' Bliss demanded, alarmed by the suddenness with which Palanga was being taken away.

Wriggley placed himself between her and the car. 'A sentiment intended to be helpful, I'm sure.' He pursed his lips thoughtfully. 'We came here in the hope of a nice chat, but process takes precedence. Process dictates priorities, Ms Bliss. Concerning Mr Palanga, our preference is to speak with witnesses one by one. Saves time, prevents confusion. We all have our professional creeds. Mine is to follow my nose like a bloodhound, rounding up facts as I go. Tiresome sometimes – being so methodical – but I must have my method. Eliminate the inessential; follow the blasted branch to where the bolt struck earth! It's a fascinating life, isn't it Brisley?' (Brisley was having a terse exchange with Palanga and the question was addressed to his straining back.) 'But I don't expect citizens caught up in the wash of crime to fully comprehend.'

Bliss blinked at him, temporarily lost for words.

'Must be like art,' he continued blithely, preparing to close the car door as Brisley followed Palanga into the back of the BMW. 'I was only saying so to Mr Daguerre a couple of hours ago. Ah, the anointed ones! The museum, the hushed halls! Mind you, birds of the feather, artists are: zero morality, the irresponsible witnesses of our life and times. Look, you've got me all warmed up!' He flapped his arms in a grotesque pantomime of a fledgling exercising its wings. 'Such a pity we must be gone! It would give me the greatest pleasure to resume this conversation at a mutually convenient moment.' He slammed the door on Brisley, opened his own, bowed, and climbed behind the wheel. The BMW backed towards the road, wheels spinning, Bliss watching it go with a brow like thunder.

'Wow, that's some crazy, cock-eyed double act!' said Cornelia admiringly.

'Really! I think that was more than a bit high-handed!' Bliss steamed. 'You'd think they thought Palanga had murdered someone!' She wrapped her woollen cardigan tightly about her. 'It's too much!'

'He probably did!' decided Cornelia. 'Now you'll have to postpone your search for the crew, won't you?'

'No, of course not!' Concern clouded Bliss's face. 'But I fear he may be gone some time. Too many ideas for his own good has Jack Palanga! Cornelia, go and fetch Lovage. Tell him he can't go to the dig. We need a man with us to lift the gate and he'll do!'

TWENTY

The sky had turned a sombre grey and the afternoon had taken on a sullen, unwelcoming character. The track, which ran alongside the seaward shore of Foreland Water, the maze of waterways that lay behind the dunes of Foreland, was badly rutted. Bliss drove the Astra with caution. From the back seat Lovage saw the vehicle first.

'*Look, look!* That has to be their campervan.'

In the distance the distinctive shape of an old VW was visible, parked not far from the track and in the lee of one of the giant dunes that populated the extreme end of the Foreland peninsula.

Bliss pulled onto the verge with a jolt. The scrapes and bangs to the bottom of the car had become too much for her. 'I'm going to break my suspension!' she declared, turning to Lovage. She nodded towards the campervan. 'You sure that's it?'

'No,' said Lovage, 'but it's the right make.'

'In that case we walk from here.' She climbed out of the car and stood, waiting impatiently for the others to get out. 'I think I'd rather have left the car at the gate.'

They made their way towards the VW in single file. Closer to, they could see that an awning had been pitched along one side of the vehicle and beneath it was set out a picnic table with integral benches. Under the oppressive cloud cover the scene had a desolate air and the VW had the look of something abandoned by a vagrant.

'They're not here,' Lovage decided.

They circled the vehicle in silence.

'What d'you think's happened?' asked Cornelia with a shiver.

Lovage tried the doors and found they were all locked.

'They'll be landboarding,' decided Bliss uneasily.

'No,' said Lovage, his hands cupped to the window, 'their kit's in here.'

'They'll be doing *something* on the beach. Let's go and find them.' Bliss indicated the path disappearing into a cleft between two dunes, and without a moment's hesitation set off in that direction, taking the loose sand in her stride.

Their path skirted great mounds of sand topped with marram grass. Here and there pegged boarding had been used in an attempt to control the drifting. Once they reached the skyline they found themselves faced by a second range of dunes, lower than the one they had just crossed. From their vantage point they could see stretches of beach and the sea beyond.

'Je-sus!' muttered Lovage, overcome by a sense of dread about what they might find. 'I've got a bad feeling about this.'

'Nonsense!' insisted Bliss stoutly. '*Ahoy!*' she shouted.

They paused to listen, but heard only the distant sound of surf.

'They'll be out on the beach somewhere,' she assured the others stubbornly.

'Or in the sea,' Cornelia offered.

They pressed forward, Lovage in the lead.

'Perhaps they're resting somewhere,' said Bliss.

Cornelia looked incredulous. 'If they're here, they're dead,' she said, matter-of-factly.

'They *must* be around somewhere,' insisted Bliss for the third time.

'No, they've gone. They're not anywhere here,' said Cornelia, shaking her head.

Bliss gave her a stern look but said nothing.

'Did you see sleeping bags in the van?' said Lovage, inclined to agree with Cornelia. He cast around with a puzzled frown. 'I couldn't see any. Should we walk along the beach a bit?'

'Four young men don't come to harm easily,' Bliss insisted.

Cornelia gave her aunt a sceptical look. 'Let's find them, then.'

Foreland beach was always empty, even in high summer. The difficulties of reaching it saw to that. The Crown owned the land on the seaward side of Foreland Water, the National Trust the wetlands behind. The area was designated an endangered wildlife habitat, and keeping holidaymakers away, even the hardier sort of hiker, was the chief concern of both landowners. Bliss, Lovage and Cornelia trod the high water line, marked out by a jetsam of red carnations, dozens of them. Then they began to notice gelatinous domes of a delicate violet half buried in the sand.

'Jellyfish,' said Cornelia. 'What does it mean? Did they kill themselves?'

Lovage crouched down to inspect one lying with its tentacles uppermost. 'No, for some reason they're dying out there.' He nodded out to sea. 'And then they get washed up like this.'

'Never seen so many,' mused Bliss, gazing into the shallows where the waves were breaking. 'The wind must be bringing them in.'

'It's sinister, isn't it?' said Cornelia. 'A portent.'

'Don't be ridiculous!'

They walked on until Lovage stopped and put is hand to his forehead, mystified by what he could see ahead. 'What's that?'

'It's the island you can see it from my garden.'

'*Really?*' He was struck by unfamiliarity of the view; it was as though his sense of location had deserted him. He knew he must be looking towards Emsbury but from where they were standing not a single habitation was visible. The land rose up quite suddenly beyond Foreland and instead of dunes heavily-wooded slopes came down to the sea darkly. A little way out to sea was an outcrop of rock topped with stunted trees that guarded the mouth of the estuary. Lovage found the unfamiliarity disquieting; it occurred to him that they could be looking at the primeval coastline before the first settlers came to build on the high ground above the estuary.

'Yes, that's Chancellor Island,' said Bliss.

'It looks so different from here. It looks close. We must have walked a long way back towards the estuary.'

'Some, but it's still quite a step.'

'Can we go back to the car now?' Cornelia wanted to know.

'No point in going on, I suppose.'

Cornelia felt vindicated. She tried not to look smug, but could not resist reminding them of her prediction.

'I told you, they've gone. They haven't been here since yesterday.'

'It doesn't look good, first the cottage, then abandoning their vehicle and disappearing,' Bliss mused, stopping to scan the flat distance of the seashore as she had many times since they had begun their walk. 'Left in a hurry, judging by the way they've abandoned everything.'

'Not their sleeping bags,' Lovage reminded her.

'Perhaps they're porpoise hunting,' said Cornelia.

A gap in the dunes allowed Lovage a glimpse of Foreland Water. 'Maybe they've turned to water fowl twitching,' he suggested fatuously.

'I'm worried,' confessed Bliss. 'I wish Palanga hadn't got himself taken in for questioning. It was his idea they'd be out here and we've proved him right... sort of. But what does it mean that they've gone?'

'It's a wild place,' said Lovage, indulging his indefinable sense of apprehension as he took in the immensity of flat sand, the sea running in over the shallows to one side, the dunes rolling away to the other. 'I wouldn't have anything to do with Palanga if I were you. You've no idea what kind of scoop he's planning. He might turn you into some kind of caricature. All of us, for that matter! *Look there!* Those are police cars! Isn't that Detective Inspector Wriggley's BMW?'

In a gap in the dunes towards Foreland Water they just had time to register a convoy of police vehicles barrelling along the track, heading in the direction of the abandoned VW.

'Palanga ratted on us!' exclaimed Lovage in a told-you-so sort of voice.

'To be fair, he didn't know we'd still come even though those policemen had taken him in. I'm not sure I want to meet Wriggley again today. I think we might creep away,' decided Bliss.

'This whole adventure has been a complete waste of time,' Lovage grumbled. 'We should have spent the afternoon doing what we said we would, which was getting on the trail of the nighthawks by walking Pilgrim's Way.'

TWENTY ONE

Rita Carshalton brought her Maserati to a halt on the drive of Terpsichore Manor. The engine died with a comforting growl. She opened her door and put a pair of Jimmy Choo shoes out on the gravel. Easing herself out of the car, she slipped expertly into the shoes without her feet touching the ground. At this moment, statuesque, voguish – a woman of the world in a mature sort of way – she was the quintessential Rita, the dazzling embodiment of what it was to be Rita Carshalton, a work of art of greater refinement than some of her artists could ever hope to achieve. From dark glasses to shoes, every item of her ensemble was perfect, as was décor of her office, as was the detailing of her two Mayfair galleries and Holland Park house. She inspected the scaffolded front of the house with an approving eye: never before in her career had she represented an artist as successful as Meade Daguerre and largely on the back of his success she had, in fifteen short years, become one of the most important art dealers in London. It had helped that her husband – her third – was MD of Mittelstandbank-München, a venerable Bavarian institution through which she had gained access to some of the most important German collectors of contemporary art. Her entrée had ensured that their collections were well endowed with the landmark works of Daguerre's career.

Now it was time for the museums! My Meade, a blue-chip modern master, the wunderkind of the moment, the contemporary moment!

She swished to her left and to her right, wondering whether her arrival had been noted. She need not have worried; it was Daguerre himself who appeared breathless at the gate in the high wall that bounded the lawn on the far side of the house.

'Rita, darling!' he exclaimed. 'I heard there was Maserati on my drive. How come you're here?'

They made a little ritual of kissing. 'Hello, darling. Thought I'd surprise. I was going to send Jeremy, but he fucked up so badly on the Jewish Veterans' Memorial, I thought I'd handle things myself.'

He was impressed she had come in person to keep the press at bay. 'It's good to see you. With Gitta away I'm in need of reinforcements.'

'Don't want you out on a limb on some murder rap, do we?'

Daguerre ducked. 'Steady on!'

'Your gates are open. Must keep them shut from now on. I can't believe it's Jack Balfour's son. He must be devastated. Have you spoken to him?'

'He's not dead, you know. Well, I mean, until they find a body let's not…'

'Must do the proper thing. Mustn't look estranged from the family, it might be taken wrongly. Police got a culprit? Is there dirt to dish on the other boys?'

Daguerre shrugged. 'They've all bloody well disappeared. God knows why. They were supposed to be looking after the *May Queen*, you know? I trusted them.'

Rita looked at him sharply. 'Sounds dangerously *laissez-faire*, Meade.'

'Not a bit of it!' Daguerre cast around for some way to explain the situation. 'I can't be out sailing all the time. They're a good team and Henry ran them well. I didn't feel I had to watch them every minute. I'm not their keeper.'

She looked somewhat short of convinced. 'Tell me again.'

'Complete mess in the yacht. Every inch a murder scene. Blood. Everything smashed and no sign of who did it.'

She pulled a face. 'I see headlines, Meade. I see big headlines! Bad Boy of British Art headlines!'

'Don't tease! We're not going in that direction. *I'm trying to fit in!* Know what I mean?'

'Meade! Look, I've got a Freud working on the PR for your next show. This little West Country problem is going to cut across all that. I've been turning over the angles as I was driving down.' She saw the look on his face and flapped a hand at him. 'Oh, don't scold! I know it's not the right spirit and all that. Ghastly and calculating it may be, but we can't help what happens, when it happens, can we? They'll be ga-ga, gagging and agog over this story, believe you me! We'll play it down as much as you like but it won't make one bit of difference! Look, help me out with my things, will you? A lovely Fendi frock for evenings is getting wrinkled in the back of the car.'

'Rita, you need to understand the context. Down here it's different! Most people don't know what I do, even if they've heard of my name. Modern art is – *you know* – rubbish as far as they're concerned.'

Rita indicated he should stick out his forearms and she draped the clothes bag containing the Fendi over them for him to carry. '*And*, dear boy, they shop at Primark!'

'Look, Rita, in the evenings people change tee shirts and go to the pub. We don't have much of a dress code in the restaurant!'

Rita formed her lips in a little moue of distress. 'Darling! Poor you, no female flesh in fresh Fendi! No wonder people holiday abroad!'

'You are going to be serious about this, aren't you Rita? Things have been decidedly hairy since I got down here.'

'Of course, Meade, I'm cool! It's my job to protect your career; you can leave me to handle the press. I can see the newsrooms frothing at the mouth right now. All you have to do is keep up the good work in the studio.'

'Yeah, well, there's a journalist already on my tail. He was bugging me yesterday afternoon, and came to the marina last night. In no circumstances do I want him anywhere near me again. He's called Jack Palanga.'

'I've heard of him: writes some sort of celebrity column, doesn't he? Listen, is there anything about this business I should know? I mean, we may court controversy, but...' She hesitated. 'But you really are in the clear, aren't you?'

'Yes, of course.' He was appalled. 'I hadn't even thought about the yacht since I got back! Good God, you don't think...'

'No, I don't.' She gave him a reassuring pat on the arm. 'But, you know... In the country people go a little... *mad*!'

Daguerre signalled a halt. 'Look, here we're fine. Let's get you inside... We'll have dinner at the restaurant later. This Fendi dress will please the bloody celebrity-spotters.'

'Oh. I'm all for that. And a little drinky would *not* go amiss.'

He took her up to a guest bedroom at the front of the house. On the way she admired the scaffolding on the second floor of the staircase where new cabling was being installed for the lighting. Then she was eager to see what he was working on so they left the house and went through the garden wall into the yard of the home farm. The yard was enclosed on two sides by buildings the size of warehouses. They went straight to the west studio where Mortimer was distressing an oak bedstead, as part of Daguerre's latest work, for which he had coined the phrase "a stampede of furniture". When he saw them enter, Mortimer switched off the chainsaw and lifted the visor of his facemask. Daguerre wanted a word with him about the cut he was making, which gave Rita time to compose her answer to the inevitable question. She assumed a critical stance: her weight on one leg, arms folded. Soon enough he was back at her side.

'Well, what do you think?'

Rita always found this a difficult moment. She wanted to sound insightful, but more often than not the moment of truth like this found her mind drained of thought.

'Is that a sofa hippopotamus?'

'One shouldn't be too literal.'

'It reminds me of Noah's Ark: the animals coming in two-by-two.'

That disappointed him. 'It's meant to be more vigorous and bestial than bloody Noah's Ark!'

'It is! It really has a *bestial* demeanour; compositionally it's extremely dynamic. Overall the act of transformation rather reminds me of Picasso's bull's head, the one he made from the handlebars and saddle of a bicycle.' She was pleased to see Mortimer nod sagely in rhythm with her explanation.

'Good point, but Picasso never tried anything on this scale,' observed Daguerre.

She joined in with the head nodding. 'This is less domestic, more monumental than any transformation Picasso ever attempted.'

'As you'd expect. Anyway, comparisons with Picasso make me queasy. If it smacks of Picasso and Noah's Ark it's not really doing the business.'

To her alarm he was sounding increasingly despondent. The cares of competing for the contemporary moment with the giants of art had descended upon him and he stared at the assemblage of gimcrack second-hand furniture with an anguished expression.

'No, no, Picasso is irrelevant,' she decided, drawing on her reserves of diplomacy. 'Here you have wardrobes and tables and all kinds of stuffed furnishings, so the comparison is not at all appropriate. If anything it's surreal… Dali-esque.'

Daguerre was an admirer of Salvador Dali and at the suggestion of a kinship he brightened. 'A hint of the surreal, but not too theatrical,' he suggested.

She withheld her response while she scrutinised the furniture with furrowed brow and narrowed eyes. 'Operatic, yet not really theatrical. This is the sort of thing the Pompidou might go for, although they'll want Euros and Pounds to be treated at par, as per usual. Somewhere in the Far East, maybe? Seoul would love it, but that would be like burying it in a hole in the ground.'

Daguerre was not listening. He had gone over to Mortimer and was indicating one of the legs of a table. 'Hack off another couple of centimetres,' he said. 'See if you can't get it to rear up a bit more.' He made claws in the air with his two hands and mimed a snarl. 'The whole thing is still a tad too orderly. We've got to get it more animated and chaotic… *and bigger!*'

At that moment Seth came in from the other studio. 'Meade,' he began hesitantly, 'we've got a problem.'

Daguerre wheeled round. 'What?'

'Some of the figures from the Titanic piece have gone missing.'

'Ask Justin, he knows where they are.'

Mortimer overheard their exchange and intervened. 'You asked me to get rid of him while you were in Germany,' he reminded Daguerre.

'Oh God, yes, he was always staring at me and giving me that weird smile! I thought he was going at the end of August!'

'You said asap.'

Daguerre gave a baffled shake of the head. 'Well, I can't remember what I said. I'd better take a look.'

All four of them crossed the yard to the other studio. Seth led the way to the table in the printing area where Justin had been working. He gestured at the empty tabletop. 'They were here, and now they're not.'

Daguerre marched over to the other end of the studio where a three-metre long vitrine stood. It had been specially made in Milan and was bisected diagonally by the model of the deck of the Titanic. He drew back the dustsheet that partially covered the vitrine and inspected the model. Finally he spoke.

'There are supposed to be lifeboats suspended between the deck and the bottom of the vitrine. Where are they?'

'Justin had them out on the table,' Seth said.

'Fuck, there were nearly a quarter of the figures in those lifeboats! When did Justin go?'

'He cleared out last week, just before you got here,' said Mortimer.

'He left "Good riddance slavery" painted on the wall of his room,' added Seth. 'He made nearly all those figures; took him months.'

Daguerre closed his eyes and held his breath while he thought. 'Mortimer, I want you to get those figures back.'

Rita had her nose to the vitrine, examining the tableau. 'I love it!' she enthused. 'Don't negotiate; call the police!'

Daguerre ignored her.

'Can I pay him?' asked Mortimer with a doubtful expression.

'No, you bloody well can't!'

'Call the police,' Rita insisted.

'He'll destroy them,' Mortimer assured her.

'Just get the figures back,' decided Daguerre, 'and until you do make sure the bloody thing's covered with that dustsheet.'

TWENTY TWO

Foreland delighted Detective Inspector Wriggley. He revelled in its bleak simplicity. He saw purity in the vista of silica to which the scraps of marram grass clung for dear life. He had no doubt Brisley loathed it. Brisley always took against anything he found pleasing. It was one of his shortcomings as a colleague. The search for the crew of the *May Queen* was not going well. The campervan had not revealed any clues as to their whereabouts. He had their names now: besides Balfour they were Neville Quartermain, aged 19, Cosmo Fairweather, aged 22, John Dunwoody, aged 22 and Michael Ditzel, aged 20. *"The police wish to interview these men to assist them with their investigation of a serious crime."* That was the message being broadcast the length and breadth of the South West. He congratulated himself on his philosophical calm in the face of knowing that time was short and soon his superiors at Divisional Headquarters would be bearing down on him.

'What is the sum of our collective intelligence?' he enquired wistfully of Brisley.

Brisley scratched the top of his head with the cap of his ballpoint, his notebook at the ready. 'The VW campervan's registered in the name of Michael Ditzel. Food in a cold box. Two tents, various bits of kit.' He hunched his shoulders in exasperation. 'Looks like they just walked away.'

'When?'

'Wasn't today. The food left on the plates is rock hard. Yesterday.'

'Did they take anything with them?'

'Not much, by the look of it. Mind you, we don't know what they brought.'

'Any wallets or wristwatches lying about?'

'No.'

'Toothbrushes?'

'No.'

'Are they trying to run away from us, or has some evil befallen them?' Wriggley wondered.

Brisley cackled grimly. 'The Lord Almighty knows; I'm baffled! Maybe an envious God snatched them up.'

'Or maybe they went to the north coast, like Mr Daguerre suggested.'

'How?'

'Offered a lift by some kindred spirit?'

'More of them, are there?' Brisley looked as though the idea disgusted him. 'Shall we put up a roadblock going that way?'

'Bit late, Brisley, don't you think? No, I'm happy enough if the traffic cops keep a lookout.'

Brisley nodded his head, indicating Bliss's car parked up beside the way they had come. 'They got here before us.'

'Yes, they did, didn't they,' agreed Wriggley. 'Let's see if they're minded to share information with the police, or whether they sneak off to meet up with that berk Palanga. I'll wager you a fiver they can't wait to be gone. Let's look the other way.'

'We could waylay them.'

'No,' decided Wriggley, 'we can't be bothering with them just now. Look the other way.' He took hold of both his ears between thumbs and forefingers and pulled them out grotesquely. 'What if one of them sailor boys stuck a knife in another? They wouldn't all run, would they? Nah, doesn't make sense.'

'Not if he were dead. Perhaps he weren't and they bandaged him up.' Brisley pulled a face and consulted his notebook. 'Nobody's been to A&E; nobody's made a complaint. Perhaps they're hoping to keep it private.'

'Then they should have cleared up after themselves, shouldn't they?'

'According to our information all except Balfour left Emsbury Monday morning.' Brisley squinted at the sky. 'One of them could have sneaked back later in the day, easy as pie. They'll give one another alibis, that's for sure. A close lot they seem to be.'

Wriggley nodded. 'I don't like it, them disappearing.' He scuffed the sand with his toe. 'There's something going on we haven't caught a whiff of yet.'

'Well, chief, we'll squeeze it out of somebody hereabouts soon enough.'

'If you can find someone to squeeze.' He gave a snort of laughter as he scanned the forlorn dunes. 'I like it here, Brisley. I like the light and the space. There's a primal quality I find exhilarating, like the first landfall of a new continent.'

'You can keep it; it's alien and unproductive,' Brisley countered. 'I like cottages nestled in a dip, and a ford with a thatched pub, and a post office selling homemade jam.'

'You always was Home Counties, Brisley. You've a soft-centred, stay-at-home sort of sensibility!'

'I like what I like!' retorted Brisley with a grimace. 'I've no time for your existential tastes. Why are the short-listed buildings always modernist?'

'What?'

'Short-list buildings are always modernist!'

'What's that got to do w—?'

'It's the contemporary sensibility. It's all wrong, craving after horror and alienation.'

Reluctantly Wriggley put up a hand to stop him. 'Desist, Brisley, desist. Let's not let aesthetics divert us from the task at hand.' He would have happily bickered the afternoon away, but events demanded his attention. They had to return to Emsbury. Rex Balfour, Henry's MP brother, was due to make a conference call, seeking, on behalf of the family, an explanation for the strange circumstances of his brother's disappearance. It was Wriggley's duty to tell him what they knew; not a task he relished, given the state of their enquiries.

TWENTY THREE

It was late afternoon by the time Bliss, in the company of the others, arrived back at the house. It was with some relief that she saw Jack Palanga sprawled in the rose arbour across the lawn from the French windows of her sitting room. He looked a little worn.

'They let you go in one piece, then?' she said, examining him curiously, half expecting to see bruises and welts.

'They tweaked my nose a bit and tried hauling me around by the lapels,' he said, the blithe tone a little forced.

'Oh, did they! Any good questions?'

'They kept going round in circles, all the same old ground. They're half inclining towards the view the crew did it. Have you heard about the Chinese?'

'The one that drowned?'

'No, another. Apparently, according to Wriggley, a couple from Daguerre's studio were engaged in some hanky-panky on the yacht when Henry Balfour turned up with a Chinese-looking man. Balfour kicked them out.'

'Really? What happened then?'

'That's the question. Nobody knows.'

'The social scene round that yacht was quite murky, wasn't it? We've been to Foreland without you.'

Palanga heaved himself upright and looked from Bliss to Lovage with an air of expectancy. 'I wondered... And?'

'Drew a blank,' said Lovage, still rankled by what he considered to have been a waste of his time.

'Not that they haven't been there,' added Bliss. 'Their campervan is there, abandoned.' She waited for Palanga to ask her what she thought had happened to them, and when he didn't she stuck her hands to her hips. 'I'm wondering what the hell is going on, Jack, and what you know you're not telling us!' She looked at him accusingly.

He rose to his feet, swaying slightly as if teetering on the brink of a well-laid trap. 'Nothing, I assure you. I'm feeling a little drained. How about an invitation to a stiffener?' His voice had lost its bantering tone.

'Good idea!' She could see he was having a vulnerable moment and wondered what he was not saying about his experience at the hands of Wriggley and Brisley. It crossed her mind that if he was momentarily demoralised, and his newshound's code temporarily forgotten, there might be an opportunity to get him to share information that he had, up to now, kept to himself. She took his arm and led him towards the house.

Lovage and Cornelia exchanged looks behind their backs and followed.

'So, they've done a bunk,' Bliss prompted Palanga as she began the expert manufacture of three large gin and tonics. 'Left their campervan. It's like they've dropped everything and run. Not been kidnapped, have they?'

'They took their sleeping bags,' Lovage reminded her with a touch of exasperation.

'True, we couldn't see sleeping bags. Any idea where they might have gone?'

Palanga shook his head. 'I share your puzzlement.'

'Your tormentor, Chief Inspector Wriggley, arrived.'

'What did he say?'

'We scarpered.'

'I'm afraid I told him we were planning to go there.'

'We thought as much. No wonder he didn't bother to stop us.'

'He's what my mother would call "a Tartar".' Palanga rubbed the back of his head with a rueful grimace.

'Did he offer you violence?' Bliss wondered.

'He wants you to feel like you're in his power and he can make things happen to you if he takes a dislike.'

'Did anything?'

'I was warned off. "Robust" is the word that comes to mind. He didn't actually say it, but he wants me out of the county. He's developed this cock-and-bull story about me having a mole in the Serious Crime Squad. It's nonsense.'

Her face expressed a degree of solidarity with Wriggley. 'Course, you're a grockle and a journalist, that's more than enough for these county folk. But maybe he thought you've been less than frank. He's like me, in that respect.' She laid aside her drink. She had been nursing an intuition for some time and now was the time to air it. 'You're not really called Jack Palanga, are you? Racy name, but you don't look in the slightest bit like a Jack Palanga.'

He laughed like one caught out in a harmless deception. 'No. Well, in a manner of speaking, yes,' he confessed. 'Stage name, you might say: "Jack Palanga,

The Celebrities' Confidant". There's two of us, actually: me and Will Farthing. He's on paternity leave – twins – at the moment.'

'And you're—?'

'My name's Matt Fernyhaugh, but Jack Palanga's the name on my press card.'

Lovage gave a grunt of disapproval. 'No doubt who's real, then!'

Bliss judged it was time to loosen her ties of loyalty to Palanga and let Lovage in on the reason for his interest in the *May Queen*. 'Mr Palanga here is being such a persistent ass because he's been sent to investigate Meade Daguerre's involvement in the smuggling business in this part of the country.'

Lovage's eyes widened and he snorted incredulously. 'How does that work, then?'

It was clear to Bliss that Palanga had dropped his objection to her letting others in on his story because now he seemed determined to convince Lovage it was credible. He fixed him with his gaze. 'Think of this: there must be more than a hundred sea-going pleasure craft moored in this estuary at this time of year. Imagine them as a swarm of flies. They go out to sea every day; they sail up and down the coast; they sail out towards the shipping lanes. Who knows what they do once they're out of sight of land? Surveillance? Only for the very suspicious.'

Lovage was dubious. 'Do the kind of people who sail on the Em do that kind of thing, never mind Meade Daguerre?'

'Those kind of people are everywhere,' Palanga observed knowingly.

Bliss finished her drink and began to prepare a second. 'Mr Palanga has the makings of a half-decent scandal... if it's true.'

'There's more,' confided Palanga. 'I think they're smuggling illegal immigrants.'

His audience shifted uneasily; embarrassment filled the air. In the matter of "the illegal immigrant" both Bliss and Lovage shared a distaste – primarily aesthetic – for the populist rhetoric that clung to the issue, and preferred to pass it by in silence. Palanga had no such sensitivity, and was not to be deterred. He held up a hand. 'The drowned Chinese man.' He counted him off on a finger. 'The mysterious Chinese man with Balfour the evening he was killed.' He counted off another finger. 'And the unexplained journeys out to sea of the *May Queen* that Meade Daguerre says he didn't know about.' He flourished the hand as if this trumped the other points. 'Chinese illegals!'

Bliss gave a sceptical laugh. 'Yeah, *"Meade Daguerre says he didn't know about it"*: your words! Why would he get anywhere near something like that?'

Palanga shrugged. 'Some ideological garbage from his disreputable, lefty, anarchist past? I'm not saying he's the moving force; I'm saying he's facilitated it.'

'No one in their right minds would bring illegal immigrants ashore in these parts, not even the boys Meade employs on his yacht. They'd stick out like a sore thumb!'

'A container through Felixstowe or Dover is the way you'd bring them in,' said Lovage dourly.

'What, you think there aren't any illegals hereabouts?'

Bliss was dismissive. 'There's not even a kebab shop in Emsbury.'

'Oh yes, I forgot, this is still English England. Perhaps they're being brought in here precisely because it's unexpected. I don't know how the coming-in works, but here they are! All you've got to know is where to look!'

'Show me, then,' she challenged him.

'All right, I will.'

Bliss rose as if to fetch her car keys.

'No, no! They're not *that* easy to find!' Palanga protested. 'When the time's right.'

She sat down, sobered by their exchange. 'Okay, keep the mystery going, but why is all this happening here? That's what I'd like to know!'

'Don't take it personally; it could be anywhere.' He shrugged. 'It's part of a bigger story. Wriggley wants to ensure I keep it out of the papers, that's his beef.'

Bliss exchanged a despairing look with Lovage. 'And this *squalid business* is why someone was – what? – murdered on that boat?'

'As you say, Lara, there's a murky scene round that yacht and we'll only get the inside story when the crew turns up. Let's hope someone hasn't abducted them, eh?' Palanga shot out his arm and peered at his watch. 'I must go.' The gin had clearly revived his spirits and suddenly he was galvanised into action. 'I have to catch the ferry; I have a dinner engagement in Emsbury.'

'I don't suppose you'll tell us with whom?'

'Sorry, my proprietor forbids such disclosure.' He stooped and put on a fair imitation of Wriggley. '"*I follow my nose like a bloodhound, rounding up facts as I go!*"'

Wasn't it reasonable, thought Bliss, after he had gone, that Palanga should be left to pursue his scoop in his own, idiosyncratic way? After all, he was the one with an eye for a story and the ready access to the media. She understood now that what had happened on Daguerre's yacht was part of something she was not a party to. Palanga's account of his questioning by Wriggley had been curiously devoid of detail. Yet again, a veil had been drawn and she wondered what kind of understanding they had reached. She sensed a whiff of something else, but what it was, short of treachery, she could not tell.

TWENTY FOUR

The failing light of evening found Daguerre and Rita Carshalton in The Estuary, seated at Daguerre's table in the corner between the bar and the window. Terence, the front of house manager, was taking their orders.

'Baltasar has called in sick, boss,' he said softly. 'We're a bit shorthanded in the kitchen, but I think we'll handle it.'

Daguerre leaned back in his chair with a sigh. 'Bloody liability!'

Terence looked round the busy restaurant cautiously. 'Things will calm down when trade drops off a bit.' He drifted off to greet some newcomers.

'No fun being a restaurateur, is it?' said Rita sympathetically. 'If you need a new chef I can ask Harry Fielding. He'll send someone down to give you a hand.'

Daguerre looked at his glass moodily. 'Baltasar's great. The problem is the sauce. When he's on song he manages lots of covers, and he keeps the standard high.'

'I'll call Harry and have a word. Leave it to me.'

Terence had returned. He leant very close to Daguerre's ear so he could not be overheard. 'Perhaps, boss, an end-of-season bonus would salve his pride; keep him on the straight and narrow.'

Daguerre gave him an imperceptible nod as he explained to Rita. 'I bought this place when I first rented a house down here. It's my investment in the town, and it serves a need. It makes me feel like I'm making a contribution. Baltasar has his off days, but he's a find.'

She took them both in with an indulgent smile. 'You always were such a provincial boy!' She said this as though it were a lovable attribute, signalling Daguerre's rise above his antecedents, but she didn't linger on the point. Instead she leant towards him in a way that indicated she had something confidential to say, and Terence had the discretion to move away. 'Tell me, Meade, since I've come all this way, what's going to be the centrepiece for your retrospective at the KunstwerkenInstituten?' She traced a line in the condensation up the side of her glass with a crimson nail. It was of particular concern to her to know since the try-out of the centrepiece was going to be in the larger of her Mayfair galleries.

The grim discovery in the cabin of his yacht was still playing on Daguerre's mind; his guard was down and he felt immensely grateful that Rita had come in person in his hour of need. Lulled by a second glass of champagne he felt inclined to share a secret he had sworn to himself he would keep until the last possible moment. He leaned forward conspiratorially. 'Promise you'll keep it to yourself?'

She made a cross in the air with her wet finger.

'Do you remember I said it would be something *"monstrous"*?'

'I do, yes.'

'I'm planning to make an installation of Afghan refugees in a shipping container.'

'What?'

'Twenty asylum seekers – Afghan professionals – rag picking. They spend their time sorting through a shipping container of second-hand clothes looking for western gear to wear: Death Metal tee shirts, shell suits – that sort of thing. Over time they exchange their ethnic Afghan clothes for ones they find in the container; bit by bit they lose their identity as Afghans and they turn into – *you know* – Euro street trash.'

'*They* turn?'

'No, quite right, *we* turn *them*!'

'I see,' she said faintly, taking a fortifying pull at her champagne.

He could see that what he had described did not accord with her idea of "monstrous". He suspected that her most immediate concern was not to appear indifferent to the plight of the Afghan nation. 'I'm allowing the voiceless to give utterance,' he explained. 'It's all about vehiculating voicelessness.'

Rita looked lost. 'You mean *ventriloquising* voicelessness?'

'No, *vehiculating* – It's me,' he placed his hand on his heart, 'doing my bit to bring the global phenomenon of migrant exclusion to the attention of a wider... to a global public. There's a second stage...' Again he lowered his voice. 'To be effective we must take it out of the gallery. For the try-out in your gallery the second stage will be to confront Parliament by moving the container to the traffic island in Parliament Square. While encamped there the Afghans build a Tower of Babel out of cardboard tubing under the guidance of a Shigeru Ban architect. That's when they give utterance. We'll do the same in Berlin outside the Reichstag.'

'*Good God!* That's arranged?'

He nodded. 'They'll be squatting.'

'That *is* monstrous!' For a long moment she was struck dumb. 'They'll get moved on, I suppose.' She had a second thought. 'Possibly deported.'

'I said asylum seekers, not illegal immigrants.'

She shrugged as though the distinction was lost on her. 'Is this parody?'

'*No.* Well...' It was Daguerre's turn to hesitate. 'Well, at one level, I suppose could be seen as such.'

She looked relieved. 'Good. I think that's important.' She was beginning to get the hang of the idea. 'So, they're rag picking. That's menial labour. And they're professionals: doctors, engineers?'

'That sort of thing.'

'*Vehiculating voicelessness.* That has a ring to it! They're forced to choose – and dress in – worthless, crass clothing... and lose their voices. So, their finding of voices is...? Wait, *I see*! The Tower of Babel is a sort of Constructivist statement; their radicalisation. They come into *utterance*... and we see them for what they *are,* not what we have made them: a parody of us!'

'Well...' Daguerre was beginning to think she was getting carried away.

Rita nodded her head. 'There'll be logistics.' She was at ease with logistics.

'Yes. Loos and refreshments, I suppose.'

'Translators.'

'Quite. And an imam.'

'Um.' That was beyond her experience of logistical support. 'Muslims, then?'

'Rita, they're Afghans!'

She gave him a look of anxious enquiry. 'But no opium farmers?'

'*No!* Should there be women?'

She giggled, her critical faculties quite overwhelmed by the politics of the question. 'That's one for you.'

'I don't know, that's why I ask.'

Formalist aesthetics came to her rescue. 'They'd be more uniform if they were all men.'

'Good point. All men, then.'

Two young waitresses arrived at the table bearing their sautéed asparagus.

Rita's mind was racing. 'Sounds quite political, Meade. You'll have the shopping trolleys piece in the downstairs gallery?'

'Probably. You know... sculpture... Maybe the stampede of furniture... if it's resolved.'

'Quite a show!' She had divided her asparagus in two and now began to work her way through the first pile in tiny mouthfuls. 'What you need at this stage of your career is major statements.'

'No doubt about it!' There was a clatter. Daguerre had dropped his knife and fork. 'There's that bloody snooping journalist over there!'

'What?'

'Jack Palanga, The Celebrities' Confidant.'

Rita's eyes widened with surprise. 'Meade, I know that man he's dining with! That's Willy Basington!'

'*Willy Basington?*'

'Yes. Have you met him?'

'No, but I know about him – he's a friend of Gitta's. They did some charity thing together. Christ, I've caught his eye and he's coming over!'

Willy Basington, debonair, bronzed, was working his way across the room. He was wearing an immaculate linen suit and sporting an MCC tie.

'Greetings from the other side of the room!' he said as he reached the table, exuding charm. 'I had to come and make my obeisances.' He reached for Daguerre's hand and shook it warmly. It was as though he and Daguerre were the greatest of chums. 'You have an invitation to come and see my asparagus beds.'

Daguerre struggled to his feet, almost convinced he was mistaken to think they had never met. 'Yes, I have! Wednesday next week, isn't it?'

'Yes. Laying on a little drinks do. Lots of people eager to meet you.'

'You know Rita, my gallerist?'

'Yes, we've met. Hello. Wonderful.' He leant over and kissed her on both cheeks. 'You were at Glynbourne in Freddie's party. Wagner, I seem to remember?'

Rita engaged him with her professional smile. 'Yes, superb, wasn't it?'

'Yes, quite electrifying. If you're still here next Wednesday you'd be most welcome at High Pevrille.' He grew serious and concerned. 'Meade, I wanted to say how terribly upset I was to hear about your little problem with the yacht. One doesn't like to intrude, but awful, really awful! Can I do anything to help? Local people can be so obtuse in times of crisis.'

'Well... thanks! We're all a bit up in the air. The police seem a bit feral – *you know?* – and the yacht's crew's gone missing. Any news about where they might be would be extremely helpful. We're at a bit of a loss.'

Basington struck a thoughtful pose for a moment. 'Let me see what I can do. I'll ask around. Can I ask a favour?' He paused with a magnificent grasp of the dramatic. 'I've got a film crew following me around, off and on. They're shooting publicity stuff for my next TV series. Could they do a bit on your terrace in a while?'

Daguerre dismissed the need for him to ask with a wave of his hand, as though it were too little a thing to speak of. 'You know that's Jack Palanga you've got at your table, don't you?'

'I do. He's a bit pushy, isn't he? Tabloids, eh! But the world and his wife gobble up The Celebrities' Confidant column, and one must go with the tide.' He gave Rita the benefit of his rueful, sparky grin. 'He's got an idea or two about your yacht: Your Mr Balfour is just a crazy mixed-up kid!' He laughed richly. 'Well, must get in gear and shine for Madam Media. See you both next Wednesday.' And he was gone. As he reached his table Palanga waved cheerily.

Daguerre had a feeling he had been mugged in his own restaurant, although how exactly he could not fathom. And Rita, in some equally indefinable way, had been a party to the act. There was a whiff of subterfuge in the air, and it stung.

TWENTY FIVE

Thursday morning, and the sun shone; everything on the estuary was wearing the brightest of hues. Cornelia had disappeared early in the dinghy and Bliss was painting in her bedroom. Lovage was about to leave for the dig when the telephone rang. There was an extension in the studio but Lovage let it ring until Bliss yelled from the bedroom window that she couldn't take the call and he should.

'Hello,' he said loudly.

'Bliss?'

'No. She's upstairs.'

'Tell her Miles says another body's turned up.'

'Another body?'

'Yes, a proper corpse this time. Very dead. Name's Toby Griffin.'

'Oh dear! Lara know him?'

'Of course: a *dear* friend.' A pause. 'Who is that, if you don't mind me asking?'

'Sorry, name's Lovage.'

'Oh, you're the chap staying in Bliss's studio, aren't you? Must be inspiring, living with real art.'

Lovage thought he heard a titter.

'Tell her Miles Sleight called. I'm the ancient geezer she takes to lunch to exercise me mandibles. And tell her the Emsbury League of Artists has lost its treasurer to the death drive that's sweeping our dear little town.' Another titter. 'Can't wait to hear what the Stunner makes of it.'

'Stunner?'

'That's what we locals call the Emsbury & District Advertiser. Irony flourishes in our little town.'

'Oh?' Lovage was nonplussed. 'Should I fetch Lara?'

'Tell her yourself. And tell her a certain eminent sculptor will be putting himself up for treasurer.'

'Who's that?'

'Me, though I blush to mention the name. Goodbye.'

'Good—'

Slowly Lovage replaced the receiver and regarded the telephone as though it had revealed a talent for malevolence. He held his breath and waited, expecting it to show more of the same. Shortly his capacity for action revived and he stirred himself to leave the studio. He crossed the lawn and beneath Bliss's honeysuckle-embowered window, feeling thoroughly misused, he shouted up at the open leaded lights. 'Lara! Miles Sleight says Toby Griffin's *dead*!'

There was a muffled explosion from within and Bliss's head shot into view, two long-handled paint brushes clamped between her teeth. 'What *do* you mean?' she said, sweeping the brushes aside. 'Did you say *Miles*?'

'Yes. He sounded tipsy.' Lovage was exasperated, squinting up into the sun. 'He said something about a death drive sweeping Emsbury.'

'Toby, *dead*! Impossible! He's the life and soul... and not even fifty! How'd it happen?'

'I don't know. Murder?'

'Murder! Ha, ha! Ridiculous! Did he say it was murder?'

'No, he didn't.'

'*Don't be provoking, you alarmist!* I'll call him back. I rather hope it's one of his jokes!'

'Quite likely. I'm going to work. You sort it out.' Lovage rid himself of the whole business with a wave of his hand. 'By the way, Miles said he's going to put himself up for treasurer. And from now on,' he informed her with a sudden surge of resolve, 'I'm confining myself to archaeology!'

TWENTY SIX

Rita Carshalton had an unsettled night. Despite her best efforts, events had cast a pall over her evening with Daguerre and she had retired early, only to find sleep evading her. The more she had thought about his idea for the centrepiece of his exhibition at the KunstwerkenInstituten, the more fretful she had become. 'What if the Afghan thing flops?' was the question that haunted her insomnia and plagued her dreams. Multiculturalism might still be a bright, shining thing but the thought of Afghan asylum seekers weighed like lead on her spirits.

'They're the generative motif of an assisted readymade,' she told herself firmly, 'and that makes them art.' She also approved of the title: "*Vehiculating voicelessness*". Yes, she liked the sound of that; Daguerre never made a misstep when it came to titles. But, whatever she told herself, another thought followed: 'Is it a mistake, rigour-wise?'

Yes, the issue, she divined, was one of rigour. She fully appreciated that the assisted readymade was Meade's stock-in-trade but could Afghans, however "assisted", be a rigorous concept? Her difficulty was that she recognised rigour when it was pointed out to her but was never quite sure she could identify it when left to her own devices. Rigour was like backbone, she thought. No, she corrected herself, it was more like being in possession of a good argument, like rhetorical power. Or was it correct grammar? The more she had tossed and turned, trying to tease the matter out, the more indistinguishable from conventional good manners rigour had seemed to become, and that, she had decided, could *not* be right. What was rigour in this instance? Was it the status of the Afghanis: a depiction of cultural disenfranchisement? Was it the way it dramatised the politics that had made them refugees? It certainly could not be their status as men! She was pretty certain that choosing living human subjects as the material for a work of art was insufficient, given the precedents she could bring to mind. How did being Afghans make a difference? Was it enough?

Morning found Rita perched on a little boudoir chair in her bedroom. Outside the window another delightful day was unfolding, but she was too preoccupied to notice. Her mobile was clamped to her ear.

'Darling!' she began precipitously. 'Son-of-a-bitch-of-a-headache. How goes it with Mitsy?'

A confident laugh came from the other end of the line. 'Where are you, Rita? Sounds like the bottom of a well.'

'I'm at Meade's new place in the country.'

'Really! Rusticating, eh? I hear Meade's mislaid his strapping young stallions in a murder mystery. Courting controversy, as usual!'

'Where did you hear that?'

'A little bird. It's not hit the internet yet, but it soon will.'

'Worried about Meade. Not the yacht thing, but he's got an idea about installing some Afghans in the gallery, picking rags out of a shipping container.'

'How many?'

'Oh, lots! I'm not sure Meade understands the legal distinctions between asylum seekers, economic refugees and illegal immigrants. *What d'you think?*'

'Live Afghans?'

'Yes, the real thing.'

'Sounds fabulous.'

'*But Orlando*,' she demanded, in a sudden, immoderate rush of anxiety, 'is it enough; does it have *rigour*?'

'Rigour? Rigour's a bit passé, darling. Promiscuity is more the thing these days.'

'He's got all sorts of ideas about moving it to Parliament Square, where they're going to build.'

'That sounds promiscuous, don't you think?'

'I keep thinking it's a bit *déjà vu*.'

'I think it sounds *so-o-o-o-o* Meade. Meade's in total control of the exhibition thing; he knows how to look after himself. Look, it's got spectacle, performativity, abjection and post-colonial politics—'

'*Vehiculating voicelessness*,' she said faintly.

'There you go! What more could you want? Nice of you to worry, though. Wish I had you to worry about Mitsy Rothchild-Breitling for me. She's driving me crazy with her changes of mind. And, darling, her taste in art! It's all Soutines and tiny Klees with no presence at all. That villa of hers is a barn, and the pictures don't work with my massing, or the finishes. I'm in despair!'

'I *do* worry, Orlando, *I do*!' she gushed supportively. 'I've told you before: she needs to be bold; she has to go modern and get rid of the Klees to one of those nice Dutch museums. Then you'd have no problem at all with your massing... or your finishes. She needs Basilitz and Kieffer.'

'You're *so* right! But only Meade could persuade her to do that. You? Me? Forget it! The old witch wants that place to have an entirely new look without committing to any sort of personal revolution. A *total* impossibility! You know it, I know it, *but she, my dear, is impervious*!'

Rita was hesitant. 'Well, Meade might be persuaded. He likes to evangelise. I'll try and put it to him, when the moment's right.'

'Would you, darling? That would be so... so *right*!'

TWENTY SEVEN

Lovage arrived at the excavation, his spirits recovered from his disagreeable telephone conversation with Miles Sleight. More importantly, he had convinced himself that he was not in love with Judith. He was looking for her to prove himself right when he ran into Bolshoi Bertie in the lea of the documentation marquee.

'Good morning! Any developments?' said Lovage, in a begrudging concession to diplomacy.

'Ah, we were about to send out a search party!' replied Bertie with a facetious smile. 'Not possessed by the holiday mood, *I hope*!'

Lovage resisted the temptation to reply in similar vein. 'I've been trying to lay my hands on the nighthawks. It seemed rather important.'

Bertie looked sceptical. 'Well, *we've all* been digging. Would be nice if you lent a hand. We need to speed things up. They're furious about the minibus at County Hall.'

'They should be more worried about what's being spirited away from the site.'

'I suppose. So far there's only been one reporter wanting stories of lost hoards of gold. Soon there'll be more. What then?'

As he was speaking a movement on the hillside behind him caught Lovage's attention and he turned to see a car coming down the slope towards the site. As it grew nearer he could see it was a police BMW. The car came to a halt, drawing up next to the burnt-out minibus. Everyone stopped what they were doing to watch. The doors were thrown open and out stepped Detective Inspector Wriggley and Detective Sergeant Brisley. They surveyed the scene.

'*Doctor Lovage!*' Brisley bawled. '*Is there a Doctor Lovage here?*'

Lovage found himself putting up his hand like a third former. 'That's me!'

Wriggley indicated he should approach, which he did, hesitantly, with an indefinable sense of wrongdoing.

'I'm Detective Inspector Wriggley!' Wriggley announced. He held out a roll of khaki twill tied with a ribbon of the same material. 'Archaeology!'

'Yes,' agreed Lovage, unclear what was expected of him.

'I understand, sir, that this archaeological site may have been looted.'

'Yes, almost certainly.'

'Good.'

'Aren't you leading the investigation into the criminal damage to Meade Daguerre's yacht?' added Lovage wonderingly.

Wriggley smiled. 'Indeedy, I have that privilege. Do you know a Toby Griffin?'

'Yes. Well, *no*, but I had a call about him this morning. He's dead, isn't he?'

Wriggley looked grave. '*Deceased*. Yes, I'm afraid so.'

Lovage assumed the worst. 'I suppose it's linked to the yacht thing you're investigating.'

'No, no, not at all. Separate investigation. The county's a bit short-staffed, it being the holiday season. Besides, all human drama fascinates me; can't keep my nose out of a good mystery. It turns out Mr Griffin died of self-strangulation.'

'Oh!' He was taken by surprise. 'That's too bad!'

Wriggley was unmoved. 'We were called to his house at about quarter to nine last night. Apparently he had an accident while dressed in a cycling costume.' He pulled a face that suggested disapproval of Lycra and men with shaved legs. 'He had become entangled. He slipped and strangled himself. Misadventure.'

Lovage gulped.

'What we call asphyxiation,' Wriggley continued with grim relish. 'But, no matter! I came here to seek your advice because we found these.' He pulled at the ribbon securing the roll, allowing it to unroll a little way. The fabric was sewn into a number of pockets, and stowed in the first was a small golden effigy.

Lovage took a sharp intake of breath. 'My God! Would you mind?' He eased the effigy, which was of a wolf or perhaps a dog, out of the pocket and into the palm of his hand. 'It looks like a votive offering. It's gold! Roman! Are there more?'

Wriggley gave the roll to Lovage, who crouched down, placing it on the ground so he could examine its contents. In all there were five similar effigies.

'Where did they come from?'

Wriggley was exasperated by the question. 'That's what we're here to ask *you*! You're the expert... apparently... so we're told.' He applied his hands to a giant itch at the back of his head.

Lovage strove to correct the misunderstanding. 'I meant, where did *you* find them?'

'They were out of place – struck an incongruous note – in Mr Griffin's house. We also found a fair amount of jewellery and a drawer full of wristwatches. Bit of a magpie, apparently. You understand?'

'Er...' Lovage was slow to grasp the conclusion Wriggley was leading him towards. 'A thief?'

'Of that ilk... an artist certainly,' said Wriggley dourly.

'Huh! Any sign of a metal detector?'

'Doubtful. Can't remember.'

'Well,' Lovage's gaze was still fixed on the golden effigies, 'they're of exceptional quality. Roman... yes, Roman. You'd need more evidence to say they came from here. Nothing we've discovered is anything like these.'

Wriggley received his opinion with a sniff. 'Some gold coins too. I'm impounding the lot on behalf of the Crown. Perhaps you would inform the authorities at the British Museum so that a proper determination of their provenance can be supplied to my office. It is not in my nature to blacken the name of someone so recently deceased but it would appear that Mr Griffin was a receiver of stolen goods.'

Lovage was absorbed in his examination of the effigies. One by one he returned them to their pockets. 'You're absolutely right to have taken these into your care. If these are what I think they are they're important, in which case the British Museum might want to exercise a claim on its behalf. The main thing for the moment is that they should be properly secured – and any others this man might have had in his possession.' He hesitated before continuing, picking his words with care. 'I've been trying to find out who's been digging on this site. Someone in the bar of the Hampson Arms told me they'd seen a couple looking at something like these.'

Wriggley nodded thoughtfully. 'D'you know who?'

'No, I'm afraid I don't. It was something I was told by old lady. She said there was a man and a woman – a woman with blond braids – but I didn't follow it up.'

Wriggley looked at him askance. 'Indeed, indeedy! Hampson Arms – I know that place; bit of a scene by all accounts. I'll make further enquiries myself. We shall, in the fullness, lay our hands on Mr Griffin's accomplices. Now, who's the representative of the county's Heritage Services?'

Lovage pointed to Bolshoi Bertie, who had been watching their exchange from a distance.

Wriggley gave Lovage a curt nod and stalked off in Bertie's direction. Lovage trailed after him, shoulder to shoulder with Brisley, curious to see what Bertie would make of the effigies.

'Would need to consult colleagues about their identity,' said Bertie cautiously when he had examined the bundle of effigies. 'What d'you think, Lovage?'

Lovage shrugged. 'They look like the genuine thing to me. I suppose they might have come from the grave or one of the pits the nighthawks dug, but I'm still not sure that the buildings here are anything but a farmstead.'

'I think it's a more important site than that,' said Bertie. 'We need more time, that's all.'

'Then you've got a bit of a security issue, haven't you?' observed Wriggley dryly. He appraised the burnt-out minibus. 'Criminal damage as well! I've seen the report: fireworks!'

Bertie nodded.

'I hope you're not expecting my uniforms to camp out up here?'

'No, no,' he assured him, 'we can take care of it.'

'Good. I wouldn't want law-breaking condoned, even if this stuff's been lying about in the ground for God knows how long.' He looked around with an air of disapproval. 'If you'll excuse me, we have matters to attend to.'

Lovage watched the BMW leave with mixed emotions. The gold effigies, he reflected, could well be part of a hoard of national, even international, importance. The question was, was it buried where they were digging and, if it was, how much of it had the nighthawks already taken? The prospect of a major find thrilled him, but he rather dreaded the disputes that would follow. He was only too aware that Bolshoi Bertie's truculent attitude towards him reflected wider provincial sensitivities that would resist such a find being acquired by his bosses at the British Museum. He knew that the county's Heritage Services people would want the dig to proceed in all haste, those from the university would not. From his perspective it was more important to try and retrieve everything that had already been spirited away from the site, never mind that it was notoriously difficult to retrieve treasure trove once it had been stolen.

'Well,' said Bertie with a smirk, 'now we can leave it to the authorities to find the nighthawks, can't we? All hands to the pump here, sort of thing.'

Lovage shook his head stubbornly. 'Not yet. I'm going to have words with someone who knew Toby Griffin, see what she says.'

He walked up the hill to his car, feeling in his pockets for his car keys, conscious that Bertie's eyes were on his back. Now was the time for him to urge Lara Bliss to do her bit: she had known Toby Griffin, and she knew his friends and acquaintances. Amongst them there must surely be a clue as to the identity of the rest of the nighthawks.

TWENTY EIGHT

Still the sun shone and the grass was dappled with saffron. From the centre of the lawn Lovage considered the open window of Bliss's bedroom. 'Lara, LARA!' he called.

'What is it?'

'Come down. I need to talk to you about Toby Griffin.'

Eventually she appeared downstairs at the French windows. She wore a distracted air and her hands were daubed with oil paint.

'Half the League's phoned already,' she said wearily. 'Miles is behaving dreadfully badly. He thinks it's comical to put himself up for treasurer. He's positively gleeful.' She threw up her hands.

'"Misadventure", according to Detective Inspector Wriggley.'

'I'm in shock!'

'Yes, well, you're going to be even more shocked when you hear what kind of misadventure.'

'Miles says the police have been at Toby's house *in a swarm*.'

'Wriggley turned up at the dig with some things he'd found at Toby's studio.'

'Really? That man's everywhere! Like what?'

'Gold effigies. Votive offerings. Roman. He thinks they might have come from the dig so he's impounded them.' He screwed up his face. 'They *are* of exceptional quality. He also said they've found wristwatches and jewellery at Toby's place. Do you understand what I'm saying?'

She was startled. 'He stole them?'

'Seems he was a receiver… of stolen goods.'

She pulled a face of woe. 'I can't believe it! He's looked after the League's finances scrupulously for years. Now you're telling me he's some kind of Fagin!'

'What d'you know about him?'

Bliss thought. 'Bohemian type, a bit of a toucher. Does – did – freelance bookkeeping to make ends meet. Shows in the Royal Academy every summer, but never made an academician. Serious, modest landscapes. Old-fashioned, I suppose. Euston Road hangover; what they call dot-and-carry. Likes women. *Oh, my God!*' she exclaimed suddenly. 'Jayne Wilson, the potter! She knocks about with Toby *and she's blondish and sometimes wears her hair in braids*!' The spark of excitement intensified. She laughed. 'Didn't occur to me to think of her in the same breath as Gitta Jensson: rather tired and grubby-looking with a shrewish face. Settled here a couple of years ago. Refugee from Hackney. Could she be our woman with flaxen hair?'

'She a member of the League?'

'Of course: applied arts affiliate. Ghastly, lumpen pots!'

'We should pay her a visit… *now*! What about it?'

'Absolutely. Word of caution: one of our feminist firebrands. If we're going round there we'd better be diplomatic.'

'We can't worry about being polite while important archaeology is disappearing onto the black market.'

She raised a hand acknowledging he was right. 'Think you were knocked down by a woman the other night?' She raised an eyebrow. 'Could it have been Jayne who attack you?'

He was indignant. 'No, it wasn't any woman known to me; too much heft!'

'Didn't think so. Could it have been Toby, then?'

'Did he have heft?'

He laughed, as though at some recollection. 'No, not much. Scant pedal power too. He certainly wasn't a cat burglar, and I don't know anywhere around here you can buy fireworks at this time of year. Bound to be more people involved, don't you think?'

'That – *diplomatically* – is the question we need to put to… er…'

'…Jayne Wilson.' A frown furrowed her brow. 'Seems there were all sorts going on in the League I've been blind to. Thought I had the measure of Emsbury and Emsbury people. Apparently I don't.'

TWENTY NINE

It was nearly four o'clock; sub-editors were getting restless and their reporters were hungry for news. The gateway to Terpsichore Manor was a mock medieval affair with flanking turrets and an archway. The lane it let on to was narrow and hemmed in by dense thickets. For thirty yards in either direction the vegetation was held back by mown grass verges, and since news had got out of the strange occurrence on Meade Daguerre's yacht they had been occupied by an assortment of vehicles: mostly SUVs and large, anonymous-looking vans. They were all mud-spattered and had a lived-in air as if collecting news were a safari. Rita stood on the verge, next to the barred gates, facing a cluster of cameras.

'Good afternoon, I'm Rita Carshalton,' she announced. 'I'm a business associate of Meade Daguerre. He's asked me to make a short—'

'Love, look this way, and say the name again,' shouted a stout, middle-aged pig of a man.

The digital displays of cameras began to wink ominously. There was a whiff of anarchy in the air.

'I said *Rita Carshalton*! I'm going to read a short statement on behalf of Meade Daguerre. Please allow me to finish, and I'll be happy to take questions.'

She apprised her audience of a dozen or so journalists with a steely eye. They were a disconcerting collection of oddities; nearly every one was some kind of grotesque. Twenty seconds ago they had been gabbling like geese; now their eyes devoured her hungrily, quite a few with cigarettes jammed in their mouths. The snout of a video camera seemed terribly close to her face.

'Is Mr Daguerre here?' shouted a pimply youth with a red nose.

'And is it true Gitta's been in Denmark by herself for the past two weeks?' demanded another pest with a squint.

She ploughed on in a firm voice. 'I have been asked to read the following statement on behalf of Mr Daguerre concerning recent events relating to his yacht.'

'Speak up!' bellowed a cheeky chappy in a check car coat.

'This is the statement.' She lifted the single sheet of A4 into her line of vision. 'My wife and I are greatly distressed by a recent event that has resulted in considerable damage to our yacht. The police are currently investigating this event, and until they have completed their enquiries we are not at liberty to comment on them, or the wider investigation. The crew of the yacht, to whose keeping it was entrusted, are currently being sought by the police to aid them with those enquiries. Neither I, nor my wife, have been in contact with any member of the crew since the events in question. I am cooperating fully with the police and appeal to anyone who has information about the events that occurred on the yacht on the night of July sixteenth to come forward and assist them with their investigation. I intend to stay here until the matter is cleared up...' She paused. A restive tide of chatter seemed in danger of making her statement inaudible. She resolved to finish in a louder voice. '...And those responsible brought to justice. I would be glad if the press would respect our privacy, and the privacy of our family at this time.' Rita eyed her audience sternly. 'Thank you.'

'Ms Carshalton! Ms Carshalton! Rita! Rita!' was the cry that went up the instant she had finished reading.

'Is it true,' enquired a penetrating voice, 'that Meade means to set fire to a Ferrari in the doorway of the National Gallery as his next work of—'

'Are you aware of the close relationship Henry Balfour had with Mrs Daguerre?'

There was a sudden stilling in the milling and everyone looked at the questioner, a tall thin man with a lantern jaw and a pencil moustache. In one sentence he had articulated the two things that the newshounds had been circling with salacious sniffs since they had descended on Emsbury: a marital scandal and a motive for the disappearance of the skipper of the *May Queen* – a *crime passionnel*!

Rita stood open-mouthed. 'Gitta Jensson is in Denmark, on location for Danish Vogue,' she said finally. 'She is also taking the opportunity to visit her parents. I don't think you should read into—'

'Miss Carshalton, isn't it the case that—'

'Is the Ferrari burning a comment on the Glasgow airport car bombing?' insisted the penetrating voice.

'Was Gitta having a fling with Henry Balfour? Wasn't he seen leaving the Spotted Dick Club in her company last month?'

'Wasn't it her photographed with him eating a sandwich on a park bench?'

'Henry Balfour is currently missing,' insisted Rita, battling against the tidal wave of accusations. 'His disappearance is in no way connected with Meade Daguerre, his wife, or anyone in his employment. At the moment the damage to the yacht is inexplicable, possibly a robbery that went wrong or—'

'What was stolen? If it was a robbery, what was—'

'Nothing was stolen. I was going to say, "*or some other event we can only speculate about*". The police will have their own press conference in due course, but at the moment they're pursuing their enquiries.'

'We know that, duckie. Why doesn't Meade come and talk to us?'

'Yeah! What's he doing? If he's nothing to hide why isn't he here himself?'

'He is trying to concentrate on his work schedule. He has some very important commitments to fulfil and this crime has come at a very difficult time.'

'How difficult? Are these difficulties of a marital nature?'

A burly man who had been sitting in the driver's seat of a dark Shogun with the door wide open, got to his feet. 'Is there any truth in the rumour that Mrs Daguerre is in Denmark having a termination?'

Rita felt as though she were drowning. 'No, none at all! This is all unfounded tittle-tattle, and nothing whatsoever to do with this event.'

Her audience gave a groan as if some puritanical bore had just put a stop to their impromptu party.

'If we get any information overnight we'll share it with you immediately. Thank you.' Rita retreated through the gates, reflecting that now she knew what it felt like to escape a gathering of all the artists she had ever turned down for an exhibition.

THIRTY

From a great height: the estuary, the sea to the south, the river emerging from the deep wooded valley running inland, into high country. Closer to, upstream from Emsbury, a dinghy bobbed on a stretch of the river.

It was nearly high tide and for the moment the tide and the current of the river moiled restlessly. Next to an outcrop of rock at the crown of the bend – on the left-hand bank as Cornelia looked inland – stood Willy Basington's boathouse. She was spying. Why? Because she had neither forgotten nor forgiven that she had almost been run down by Willy Basington's steam launch. Some twenty minutes before, the steam launch had passed her going upstream. She had tried to follow but had gradually fallen behind until it had been lost to view. She was convinced it had been heading for the boathouse but now she had the building in sight she was not so sure.

As she sat there, the dinghy wallowing in the middle of the river, a sudden report rang out, and then a further two in quick succession. Her immediate thought was that they were gunshots and she was the target. She slid to the floor of the dinghy, crouching between the thwarts. It was some moments before she could bring herself to peep out over the gunwales to see what was happening.

The boathouse on its promontory was the only point of differentiation: downstream the sunlit vista of thickly wooded slopes broadened out as the bend of the river curved its way towards the sea; upstream the trees on either bank crowded in ever closer to one another. It was now more than a minute since the reports, and their echoes had long since died away. She thought she saw movement in the trees near the boathouse. Further upstream a water bird broke from the foliage with a clatter. The sound of an outboard motor started up and a skiff, low in the water and a good deal longer than her dinghy, came into view upstream from the boathouse. She could not be certain whether it had emerged from behind the promontory of rock beside which the boathouse stood, or had been concealed further away, amongst the trees overhanging the water's edge, but quickly it was in full view, making for the centre of the river, skimming effortlessly over the water. She was still taking this in as it began to show her its stern as it turned upstream.

No sooner was the turn completed than one of its occupants looked back in her direction. He raised his arm above his head. His face, Cornelia could have sworn, cracked with a malicious grin. She made out the shape of a pistol. He fired. She ducked, again thinking she might be the target. A luminous streak arced into the sky creating a path of greater light against the afternoon sky. A percussive crack rolled across the water.

Cornelia straightened up. 'A signal flare,' she breathed, 'but why signal?'

The flare glowed with great brilliance as it began its descent. Cornelia watched with the creeping realisation that it would land extremely close to the dinghy.

'Oh my God!' she exclaimed as she made a grab for the ignition of the outboard motor. 'It's Willy Basington's gang and they've been aiming for me all along!'

THIRTY ONE

Jayne Wilson lived in a dilapidated terraced cottage, one of five, all equally neglected. They were some way back from the estuary, their backs buried under the hillside that hemmed in Emsbury. At the rear they had tiny yards under a face of rock topped with vegetation, admitting no sunlight, damp and miserable in winter. Bliss parked outside the cottage's rickety front gate, and she and Lovage surveyed the scene. The garden gave onto a kind of sun lounge of corrugated plastic and glass that ran the width of the front. They walked up the path, which was edged with straggling geraniums, growing amongst the weeds.

'Mind on higher things,' confided Bliss. 'Widely read in a narrow sort of way.'

She tapped on the door, and after a few moments a tatty-looking woman in her late thirties with a dissatisfied look about her poked her head out of the inner part of the house. She did indeed have two rattail braids of grey-yellow hair, a far cry from Gitta's operatic Brunhilda-style look.

'It's me, Jayne,' announced Bliss, in her most ladylike voice.

Jayne Wilson's face lightened and she came to the sun lounge door with a smile.

'Hello Lara. Fancy you being here!'

'Always nice to call by,' Bliss cooed, scarcely able to disguise her deceitful intent. 'Hope it's not inconvenient. I've brought a friend to see your pots. This is Dr Lovage of the British Museum. He's here for a few weeks' fieldwork; supervising the archaeological dig on my side of the water. All things ceramic are very much his sort of thing, so I thought I'd take him round to see some of the highlights of the League's creative work while he's here.'

Jayne was evidently delighted. 'Oh, well, come in!'

Lovage shook her hand and murmured something suitable.

'Cup of tea, perhaps?' she asked, her head held coquettishly at an angle, the flattery of attention for her pots allaying any suspicions she might have about the real reason for their visit.

Bliss fixed Jayne with look of compassion. 'You've heard about Toby Griffin?'

Jayne's brow clouded. 'Ah, yes!' She shook her head disconsolately. 'Last night. Silly man! Always was.'

'Sad, though. Great loss; a stalwart of the League. Old friend, wasn't he?'

'Yes, tragic. One of my best clients for a time,' she reflected despondently.

Bliss's face took on the look of one dealing with an indiscretion.

'I gather his appetites got the better of him.'

'Appetites?' she looked puzzled.

'You know, being a client of yours was part of a bigger picture, so to speak.' Bliss glanced at Lovage and saw that he was avoiding her eyes.

'Lara, I'm not sure what you have in mind, but when I say he was a client, I mean that he has, for a number of years, been buying ceramic sculptures from me on an instalment plan, so much a month. I may misunderstand, but we're not referring to other... occupations, are we, which he pursued *without* my assistance?'

Bliss, very much on the back foot, looked appalled at the thought of a misunderstanding. 'No, not at all, but thank you for making that *so* clear! He must have an excellent collection.'

'He does.'

While this exchange had been going on Lovage had taken the opportunity to look around. The sun lounge was crammed full of bric-a-brac. On three shelves attached to the front wall of the cottage, between the window and the door, was a collection of ceramic objects that took the place of honour in the chaos. 'Are these your ceramic sculptures?' he asked gracefully. 'They're very interesting.'

Jayne cleared the way towards them as if she intended to launch into an impromptu introduction, but Bliss waylaid her.

'Tea first, Jayne,' she laughed. 'I know you when you get going. Otherwise we'll be dead of thirst before you're done.'

She pouted for a moment, but otherwise didn't seem to mind the delay. She took them into the dark interior and reminisced about Toby Griffin without much sentiment while the kettle boiled on the Calor gas burner. Then they went back into the sun lounge and Jayne cleared laundry off two rattan seats, and one of her cats off a chair, which she took for herself. When she judged that her guests were seated comfortably, with their teas to hand, she leant forward, addressing herself principally to Lovage.

'My ceramics are the epitome of women's work, but the spouts don't pour and the handles don't hold. I subvert the expectations of form and glaze. Don't expect utility from my ceramics, even if they refer to the everyday and look like jugs and vases. Historically, "everyday" signifies the drudgery of womankind. Of course,' she paused simperingly, *'you know this*, but it's a mantra that cannot be repeated often enough, even if it means I do wear my heart on my sleeve.'

Lovage depreciated the very idea, fully aware that he was out in the open and being bombarded from a prepared position.

'Tell me,' Bliss broke in, 'you said Toby was *one* of your best clients. Who else is?'

'Recently? I've sold some to Willy Basington.'

'Really!'

'Yes, he's a fan. My immediate bone of contention,' Jayne continued, unconscious of the stir her revelation had caused, 'is that the League only allows me to be an affiliated member because it classifies me as a craftsperson making objects of utility. The classification of my work by medium is precisely phallocentric patrimony at work in which the crafts are designated by medium and those mediums are the ones traditionally associated with women's work. Worse, they're classified as inferior to the fine arts, the preserve of men. Hence I remain an affiliate, only allowed to submit three works to the League's annual exhibition while full members can submit five!'

Bliss closed her eyes and spoke with restraint. 'Jayne, we have been over this a thousand times. The League's rules make the conditions for membership very clear and we need a two-thirds majority of the members to change the rules. You insist on your status as a ceramicist, and that means affiliated status!'

'*I do!*'

'There you are then,' said Bliss.

'Mine is a principled position,' Jayne explained waspishly to Lovage. 'The League's mostly men.'

'Tricky,' he sympathised. 'Can I ask you, Jayne,' he spoke in a drawl, 'whether you have come across any small Roman sculptures cast in yellow metal in your travels?' He felt her become especially attentive. 'I ask because it seems the police recovered a number from Toby's house after his death.'

She shook her head. 'No. I can't think of seeing anything like that.' There was a tinny edge to her voice that hadn't been there before. 'Mind you, there's all sorts going on between members of the League. Were they stolen or something?'

'In a manner of speaking. There's a suspicion they're treasure trove dug up from the site we're excavating. We think a dealer from London might have been down here trying to buy them. You haven't met anyone like that?'

'No, I haven't. Why are you asking me?'

'Oh, no reason. Because you knew Toby, that's all. I'm asking around because my work for the Museum is concerned with safeguarding our archaeological heritage.'

'The League,' added Bliss, rather too eagerly, 'needs to be seen to do the right thing when cultural artefacts of historical importance are at risk.'

'*Cultural artefacts!* Depends on your definition of culture… and history,' Jayne muttered.

'The police—' Lovage began.

'The police have no idea how many such things there might be. How can they? They can't chase after things they have no proof exist!' Jayne shrugged her shoulders. 'The summer season is short and while it lasts local people have to make money. I work in the kitchen at The Estuary at the moment and my shift is about to start.' She rose to her feet.

'Thank you, Jayne,' said Bliss brightly. 'Lovely tea.'

'Yes, and I genuinely admire your ceramics,' added Lovage. 'They're just the kind of thing the British Museum should be selling in its shop: original works that comment on history and culture, whatever our differing views on those terms. No doubt about it.'

Jayne's jaw grew less taut, wordless before the glittering prospect he was dangling before her.

'If you have any documentation I would be happy to take it back to London with me. Museum shops can be so dull and predictable.'

She nodded, not daring to speak.

'I'm staying with Lara. Call me.' He took her hand and shook it. 'Goodbye.'

Bliss went before him up the cracked garden path.

'The exit was rather well done,' she said, when she judged they were out of earshot. 'I didn't know you had such diplomatic skills.'

'Lara,' he replied modestly, 'I work for the British Museum!'

'Of course!'

'She practically admitted she's involved, did she?'

Bliss nodded. 'She's covering for someone and it's not just Toby Griffin. She doesn't even seem particularly bothered about his death.'

'I know, hard-hearted. I'd say there's a pretty good chance those figures came from the dig. And what about Willy Basington buying her things?'

'I never heard of anything so unlikely! I *cannot* see Jayne's ceramics on his mantelpiece!'

'Could buying her ceramics be some sort of cover for trading stolen artefacts?'

'What would be the point of that?'

'Oh, I don't know…' He paused for thought. 'What if she says Willy's bought her pots but really he's given her the money for archaeological finds? That way the money's washed clean. Maybe he's keeping half the League in tea and biscuits.'

She pulled an expression of bewilderment. 'Jayne's never sold a thing at our annual exhibitions, and in one afternoon I find she's got two collectors buying her work!'

Lovage was struck by an idea. 'Do you know if Willy's been buying from Toby as well?'

'I've been to High Pevrille and I've never seen anything by either of them.' She stopped in her tracks. 'But he has got a couple of early sculptures by Miles Sleight. Great big ones in the garden.' She looked as though the world of certainty was crumbling before her eyes. 'Surely Miles can't be involved!'

They had reached the car.

'He's the one I spoke to on the phone, isn't he?' said Lovage. 'What did Jayne say about all sorts going on between members of the League?'

'No, no, he's much too infirm to be dashing about in the middle of the night!'

'Keep an open mind.'

'Yes, I suppose so.'

'What next?' Lovage was reluctant to leave matters so unresolved. 'Who else have we got as a suspect? Are we still interested in Silas Bennett?'

She looked blank. 'I don't know. I wasn't expecting Jayne to be quite so defiant, conspiracy or not.'

'We're stumped, aren't we? We need more information, but where do we find it? Maybe we should break in and search Jayne's house while she's at work.'

Bliss gave a wry snort. 'Or Toby's.'

'What about Basington?'

'Grief, no: you don't see him unless he wants to see you!' Bliss was adamant. 'Too brazen! Not to mention the layer upon layer of assistants! Let's let the dust settle. Jayne will be round with her photographs, you can be sure of that. We'll try and waylay her then. Meanwhile, I'm going back to my painting; you should get back to your dig. The funeral is going to be a very interesting affair!'

THIRTY TWO

Avery Audley was a long-standing friend of Meade Daguerre's from his student days, when they had both been members of the same group of self-proclaimed radicals. Audley was by no means as successful as Daguerre. He had turned his hand to every medium of contemporary art – performance, video installation, sculpture, photography – and, following a period of intense application, all had petered out on him. During his enthusiasm for sculpture his lack of ability had been so obvious that his wife (now divorced) had hired him a walk-in skip as a birthday present. Inability was not the only reason for his failings as an artist; he was unstable in thought as well as in love, and prone to bouts of melancholia, during which he sank into inertia. In contrast, when unburdened by his condition, he was hyper-garrulous and an international conduit for art world gossip. He regarded Daguerre as one of his dearest friends, a point on which Daguerre indulged him. At about the same time that Bliss and Lovage left Jayne Wilson's house Daguerre received a call from him. After an exchange of greetings and a terse explanation from Daguerre about recent events the conversation developed as follows.

'You going to Tuscany this year?' asked Daguerre idly.

'Nah. I'm teaching summer school in Glasgow.'

'Should be fun.'

'Lovely girls, old son, lovely. I heard about the Afghan thing.'

'Heard *what?*' Daguerre was startled. 'What about it?'

'Edgy business, Afghanistan; a lot of antipathy to Afghans. It's a bloody fuck-up and's caused endless, pointless loss of life to British troops.'

'Avery, how did you get hold of that?' he said, dismayed. 'I've only told Rita about the Afghan thing, and in the strictest confidence... *and very recently*!'

'Orlando. Orlando told Siegfried and Siegfried told me. According to him she thinks you're making a mistake and wants you to switch to showing something else, or some such. That's the gist, anyway.'

'*Fuck!* Bloody gossips! What's Orlando's beef?'

'Mitsy Rothchild-Breitling's house conversion. Rita wants you to persuade Mitsy to sell the Klees and go contemporary.'

'*Me? Persuade!* Talk about divided loyalties! I'll kill Rita! You can't trust Orlando with anything! Bloody gay mafia gossiping across the fucking world!'

'That's not the point.' Audley sounded misunderstood. 'This is a confidence issue, Meade. You can't have your dealer going around undermining confidence in your bloody art. It's not done!'

'*Bloody hell!*'

'Tell her to fuck off.'

'Meaning?'

'I don't know. She needs to get in line.'

Daguerre was so aghast at Rita's disloyalty that he failed to grasp what Audley was saying. 'She should do *what?*'

'Get her fears out in the open. You need to find out what's going on.'

'Nothing's going on.'

'Plenty are yakking. You sure there's not another artist doing something similar, about to show in Cologne or somewhere?'

'What, with Afghan asylum seekers?' he scoffed.

'Or Syrians, or Ethiopians. I don't know.'

Daguerre tugged at a handful of his hair. 'Rita's staying here, Avery. She'd tell me if somebody was.'

'Staying?'

'Yeah. She's got her hands full. The press are here in force over the business on my yacht.'

'Not surprised.'

'She's keeping them at bay for me.'

'You're not in trouble, are you?'

'No! Of course not! Don't be bloody ridiculous! Why would you think…?'

'Oh, you know, people sometimes go mad in the sticks. Weird things happen.'

'You're not the first person to say that. What nonsense is doing the rounds, eh? We're all *completely* non-psycho people, for Christ's sake!'

'Oh, I know, of course I do. Yeah, sorry to mention it. I just had a feeling something was up. Wanted to offer my support.'

'It isn't. Nothing's up, but Henry and the rest of the crew have gone missing. It's totally *inexplicable*! And *unexpected*!'

'Yeah, well, tell the press that and they'll think you're responsible, one hundred percent.'

'How can you say that? I just used two adjectives that say the absolute opposite, didn't I? How could they sound remotely like I know where they are? You're not making sense!'

'Oh, yeah, I know... I suppose they think it's like those murderers – usually they're wives or boyfriends – who get on the telly making tearful public appeals for the murderer to give himself up. They don't even remember they did it themselves. They've blanked it. They even kill to get the attention of the police and the media. There's a name for that, but I can't remember...'

'*Really?*'

'Stockholm... No that's something else, isn't it? Munchausen's syndrome by proxy...?'

'Fuck! Many thanks for the ringing endorsement of my innocence!'

'All I'm saying, Meade, is don't bother proclaiming it. Keep out of the limelight. Let people speculate, fine. It'll blow over all the quicker.'

'Yeah, well, sage advice, Avery. I must go. Bye.'

He came off his mobile boiling with rage. He stormed out of the studio, saw Carrie about to enter the office and archive building and hurled his mobile at her. It missed narrowly, clattering off the cladding. She looked to him in disbelief, which he took for dumb insolence.

'That *fucking* Avery Audley! How come he has my personal mobile number? Did I tell you to give him my personal mobile number? *Did I?*'

'He's always had it,' she objected, in a frightened voice.

'I keep telling you I don't want my mobile number to go to all and sundry – and every other week I find some asshole has it 'cause you've given it them! Now *he's* calling me, giving me aggravation!'

Carrie started to answer back but Daguerre cut her off with a furious bark. 'Get rid of that number. *Fucking Avery Audley is banned!* Get me a new sim… No, get me a new mobile, and make sure no one knows the number.'

'Not even Gitta? How's she going to text?'

'I don't want anybody knowing; I don't even want me knowing! No one! Where are the others; where's Mortimer?'

Carrie knew that Mortimer and the fabricators made themselves scarce when he threw a tantrum. She shrugged her shoulders and stammered, her face flushed.

'Don't give me the fish face,' he stormed. 'Where are they?'

'Meade,' she pleaded, biting her lip, 'two curators have just arrived. Magnussen Olsen from Oslo and Mrs Ikeda from Japan.'

Daguerre froze. He stared through Carrie as though she weren't there. 'Here? *Now?* I can't have curators mincing about here now!'

'They've come down from London in a hire car.'

'Really! Did I invite them?'

'So Rita says.'

'Shit! Where are they?'

'In the house. Consuela's giving them coffee. Oh, she's here now!'

Daguerre turned to see Max, his son, running across the yard followed by Consuela. Consuela was carrying Fanny, who was trying to wriggle free. Behind her, looking somewhat sheepish, was a very tall, washed-out looking man with grey hair and a grey suit. Beside him was a squat Japanese woman of middling years wearing glasses and dressed from top to toe in plaid. She had the radiant smile of someone at her wits' end, for she was far from London and quite out of her depth.

'Daddy, where's the bonfire?' demanded Max, dodging through the door of the studio.

Daguerre tried to catch him but he was too slow. The child made for the pile of furniture Daguerre was trying to turn into an animalistic stampede.

'Look at the bonfire!' Max cried exultantly. '*Look!*'

'It's not a bonfire, Max; it's… it's an accumulation. And be careful it doesn't fall on you!' Daguerre wondered who had dubbed it "the bonfire"; it sounded like the wit of one of his fabricators, probably that weirdo he'd fired, Justin. He set off in pursuit of Max but quickly gave up, anxious to preserve an air of parental control. He turned back towards the door and saw that Consuela had entered – Fanny still in her arms – followed by the curators.

'AAArrr–ah!' screeched Fanny when she saw him and attempted to fling herself across the intervening space.

Daguerre skirted Consuela and Fanny's imploring arms, and made his way towards the curators, a fixed smile on his face. Behind him Max had almost completed his first lap of the furniture.

The grey man stepped forward. 'At last! We discover you at work!' He took hold of Daguerre's hand and shook it solemnly. 'Magnussen Olsen, director of the Post-Family Art Foundation in Oslo. I am afraid – ya! – we have sprung ourselves on you.'

'Yes, we come,' agreed the Japanese curator, her radiant smile undimmed. 'I am Ikeda from Municipal Museum and Art Gallery of Osaka.'

'You mustn't look at that,' Daguerre said, indicating the furniture as he shook her hand. 'It's a bit of a dog's dinner.'

The Japanese curator looked from Daguerre to the pile of furniture with a stricken expression.

Olsen gave a dry laugh. 'This is a most picturesque colloquialism. I have heard it before. In Norway we say—'

By now they were all well inside the studio. Behind the curators there was a commotion as Rita Carshalton rushed in, cutting off the end of Olsen's remark.

'Hello, I see you're *here*! *Magnussen, Mikko,* how nice!' Rita looked in a complete twist, having lost the race to warn Daguerre of the arrival of the curators. She had been delayed by a phone call – the information she had received *was not good* – but instead of being able to pass on the message to Daguerre she found herself compelled to welcome the visitors. 'Have you had some refreshments? I'm sure Meade would be glad of a few moments to compose himself.'

Daguerre gave a laugh at the thought of composing himself, his gaze returning to Max who was still running round the furniture. 'Max, come here,' he pleaded with a reasonableness he didn't feel. He tried giving Consuela the death stare but she was fully occupied with Fanny.

'We have a pleasant task to perform,' announced Olsen, quite oblivious to the strained atmosphere.

Mrs Ikeda nodded in agreement.

'The Organising Committee of the Bahrain Biennale – ya! – has afforded us the great privilege of presenting you with the International Peace and Reconciliation Medal, awarded to you unanimously by the jury for your contribution to art.'

Rita, who had been informed previously about the award, gave a cheer of approval. Daguerre gazed uneasily at the medal Olsen held out for him.

'They send their greetings and their regrets that you were unable to attend the Biennale in person, although your art made a stupendous impression!'

'Well, thank you, I am... touched! You know, I can't recall...' Daguerre wavered. He turned to Rita. 'What did the British Council send to Bahrain?'

She gave him a look that said he should be diplomatic, and she would brief him later.

He carried on regardless. 'The "Ten Cautionary Tales of Modernity", wasn't it?' He bashed his head to indicate the importance of remembering what he had exhibited in Bahrain.

'The committee considered the works reflect great commitment to reconciliation and world harmony,' said Mrs Ikeda, her eyes bright with zeal.

Daguerre laughed uneasily. 'If it was the Cautionary Tales, they're supposed to be about − I wonder if I recall correctly? − "angst and the alienation of the contemporary subject − specifically the artist − confronted by the art market in capitalist modernity". But what do I know?' He made a dash for Max and scooped him up before he could begin another circuit of the furniture. 'This studio is closed to visitors at the moment, I'm afraid,' he announced, with all the good grace he could muster. 'You've come a long way... and this work is still in progress... certainly not worthy of your appreciation! I thank you with all my heart for the award. The jury does me a great honour.'

'Great honour,' agreed Rita.

'If we go to the other studio I can show you some finished work.' He made for the door, holding Max aloft.

'It looks *most* exciting,' said Mrs Ikeda. 'Perhaps you finish this while we are here? Are those animals, you provocateur?'

'We'll see,' he replied with a grim smile.

'And where is your lovely wife?'

'She's in Denmark, on a photo-shoot.'

'Such talent! I hope we see her before we go.'

'Yes, she'll be back soon; you should stay until she comes. That would be nice.'

'Papa,' said Max, 'can we do some painting in the house?'

'Yes, of course. We can all do painting. Good idea.'

'With our fingers?'

'Finger painting! Why not?' Daguerre swung round to close the door behind him and clipped Max's head against the doorframe, causing him to wail uncontrollably.

'Meade,' hissed Rita with great urgency as they crossed the yard to the house, 'the police have just rung. They say the blood in the yacht is pig's blood.'

THIRTY THREE

It was Friday morning, the day following the revelation that it was pig's blood that had been liberally splashed about the interior of Meade Daguerre's yacht. Detective Inspector Wriggley, a figure of discontent, sat behind the scoutmaster's desk which had been moved to the centre of the platform at the head of Emsbury's Scout Hall. Before him sat his team of detectives, stalwarts of justice and fair play. Most would have not looked out of place in a reunion of rugby forwards. The course of events on the night of Henry Balfour's last known visit to the *May Queen* remained a source of conjecture.

'Anybody got any ideas?' said Wriggley at last.

'Someone slaughter a pig?' growled one detective.

'Hog roast,' said the team's joker.

'Somebody was putting a scare in them.'

'*All right!*' said Wriggley, who had already decided that this was the direction to go. 'Somebody wanted to frighten those sailor boys. At some point they were meant to go to the boat, see the mess, and take fright.'

There was a murmur of assent from the gathering.

'So who did that and why?'

There was a long silence before someone spoke up. A detective pointed out that they still didn't know the identity of the man who was with Balfour when he arrived at the jetty. Maybe, he suggested, he had had a disagreement with Balfour, gone back later and smashed the interior of the boat.

When the detective had finished Wriggley sat for a full minute, staring at his hands. The hall fell into an uneasy silence.

Finally he rose to his feet. 'Gentlemen,' he began gravely, 'we must remember The Bigger Picture. Was it sailor boys this act was directed at, or was it the famous artist chappy, Meade Daguerre? It is possible we are looking at a detail, an atypical detail, that misleads us as to The Bigger Picture! Surmise, surmise, surmise! Surmise and speculation dominate the landscape of our enquiries. Let us acknowledge that there are forces at work about which we lack *in-form-ation*. The field of our investigation is marred by asymmetrical flow; it remains a discontinuous terrain. So far our mapping tools have failed their purpose. Precious time has passed and we have lost the initiative. Indeed, *we never had it*!'

Brisley who was standing behind Wriggley's chair muttered, 'Bullshit!'

Wriggley ducked as though a tennis ball had bounced off his head. 'But *conjecture* can wait!' His voice grew more hopeful. 'From today our enquiries will benefit from a new *premise*. The officer at the back of the room is Detective Inspector Cardew from the West of England Organised Crime Squad based in Bristol. He has information concerning Balfour that will give new impetus to our enquiries.'

There was a stir in the room. A man with a goatee came forward, saluting the detectives like a minor celebrity on a TV panel game. He climbed the steps to the platform and stood by the desk Wriggley was seated at.

'Thank you, thank you,' Cardew began. His voice was as reedy as Wriggley's was forceful and penetrating. 'Mr Henry Balfour was, as you know, a student at Cambridge University. Some months ago he came to the attention of my colleagues of the East Anglian Force.' He took a wad of paper from his pocket and referred to the top sheet. 'Besides being a sportsman of some note, Mr Balfour took an interest in politics, radical left-wing politics of a subversive nature. In this he was somewhat at odds with the rest of his family. Not exactly a black sheep, but considered somewhat wayward, politically speaking. *Ah-hem!* In the debates of the Student Union he argued on more than one occasion for the dissolution of the state.' He paused to give his audience a beady look. 'He was a leading light in a student association called the Global Migration Paradigm. It espoused the free movement of people irrespective of borders or nationality. The Student Union was sufficiently ill-advised as to provide substantial funding for the GMP over a two-year period. Amongst other activities, the GMP raised money for appeals against deportation by illegal immigrants.'

Cardew paused again and regarded his audience. 'You may think this was just university pranks and the usual Socialist Worker nonsense, but his tutor was sufficiently concerned to report his activities to the authorities. He believed that Mr Balfour was either personally involved in assisting nationals of other countries to evade UK border controls, or aiding and abetting others in such intent.'

He extracted a piece of paper from the wad and studied it.

'Amongst the methods used to bring illegal immigrants ashore is the use of small, fast vessels for the last leg of their journey. We have obtained a number of emails between Mr Balfour and a,' he checked with the sheet, 'a Mr Cosmo Fairweather. In these emails Mr Balfour proposes that yachts of the sort that regularly race off the south coast during the summer months would provide an excellent cover for this activity. They can easily rendezvous with a merchant ship being used by people smugglers; in busy shipping lanes the momentary docking needed to transfer human cargo is practically undetectable, unless witnessed at close quarters. They are swift, silent, and can make landfall in any cove, or on any beach, to drop off their cargo. There are few or no checks on them when they return to their moorings. Their only drawback, Mr Balfour notes, is that they cannot land more than a handful of people on any one trip.'

Cardew looked up to check whether his audience was still with him.

'As we know, Mr Balfour was an expert sailor and working as the skipper of precisely this sort of vessel. We also know he was a young man of very independent views. Mr Fairweather was a member of the crew and Balfour, he and the others are now missing. It seems that some – or all – of these young men may have taken employment as crew of the *May Queen* precisely to put a plan of this nature into action, knowing that the owner was frequently away. Now, they may have been driven by high principle, however misguided, but these kind of illegal immigrants being trafficked into the UK habitually fall between the cracks of normal society. They are precisely *trafficked*, and their lot is to become the property of gangs that consider them a valuable commodity.'

'Prostitution,' said somebody out-loud from the body of the hall.

'Quite so,' he said indulgently. 'In the South West we have several such gangs under surveillance but it is not easy to pin them down to any wrong-doing and they're even harder to penetrate. These young men may have got in over their heads. Let's be clear, they are far from being typical members of this kind of operation.'

Again Cardew gave his audience a meaningful look while slowly he put away the wad of paper.

Wriggley rose to his feet. 'Thank you, Detective Inspector Cardew.' He waited while Cardew returned to his seat. 'There you have it, gentlemen, a possible reason why an expensive bit of tackle was trashed: something went wrong with the relationship between our sailor boys and people traffickers. Who are they? The Bigger Picture, gentlemen! As Detective Inspector Cardew has indicated, our colleagues have been watching a number of business premises and other addresses. It is highly likely we seek a gang with ties to foreign parts and so far our enquiries, in and around Emsbury, have come up with nothing of the kind. Have we missed something? We need to look harder, dig deeper! Mr Balfour was a young man of principle, however wrong-headed. He may not have been aware of what was happening to the people he was smuggling. Perhaps he found out. High principle meets the pragmatics of business, sometimes an explosive mixture!'

A gust of muttering swept round the scout hut. Wriggley motioned for quiet.

'Should this get out, media interest in what is, at the moment, little more than an unsavoury incident of vandalism will intensify; an unwelcome spotlight will be thrown on our investigation. It won't be a pretty sight to behold: brother of a Conservative MP, in the employment of one of the country's most newsworthy artists, involved in people trafficking! Strange goings-on in a charming seaside town in the middle of the holiday season! *Ugly!* What's more, undue media attention runs the risk of undermining our wider investigation into gang crime. We have already had occasion to warn off a journalist called Mr Palanga who has been pursuing enquiries in this direction, believing the foreign nationals come from China. We have been concerned he was intending to publish a scoop linking Mr Balfour and Mr Daguerre with that wider investigation.

'Then there is the worrisome disappearance of the crew. Let's not deceive ourselves, these sailor boys knew their stuff; they could sail that boat from here to Timbuktu if they wished. We're keeping a watch on all their known places of residence, but given their lifestyle, this may not be enough to reel them in. Until we question them we won't know the full part they've played in this story. Nor will we discover who else had knowledge of what was going on. All that's clear – as you have heard from Detective Inspector Cardew – is that one of their number, Mr Fairweather, is explicitly implicated in Mr Balfour's plan to smuggle people into the UK. We'll look like the back end of a pantomime donkey if we don't find them before the press.

'We also need to look for illegals in the hope they will lead us to the traffickers. We must move swiftly, but we – as public servants – cannot be seen to pursue our investigation on the basis of racial profiling, so I have been advised by our Community Liaison Supremo and the Diversity Office.'

A second wave of muttering swirled around the stage.

Wriggley held up his hands as though offering a blessing. 'Illegals call for sensitivity, gentlemen! Detective Sergeant Brisley has some guidance concerning the rules of engagement.'

Wriggley sat down. Brisley, clearly gratified to be in sole possession of the stage, marched to the front and came to smart halt. There was a smatter of ironic claps.

'Community Liaison Officer Singh could not be here today. Leave of absence on the grounds of religious observance...'

There was a communal groan and several raspberries were blown.

'Gentlemen!' admonished Wriggley from his seat, 'enough of the raillery!'

'...So apologies from him, and here is the gist of his advice: no racial profiling means what it says! It means no looking for the ethnics under the bed, savvy? It means no early morning raids on every broken-down dosshouse stuffed with a potpourri of humankind. If you want to raid said premises, then raid an even greater number that have no obvious link with the suspected ethnic persuasion. This is what we call contra-surveillance and half of you will be assigned to these duties. We must observe appropriate and proportionate – I say *"proportionate"* – policing procedures at all times. A member of the

Diversity Office must accompany any raid whether or not contact with an ethnic minority is a possibility. You will distribute *Police Action On Diversity* leaflets to surrounding properties after any such raid, especially if shouting and yelling, door and window breaking have accompanied said raid. The Compliance Office must be informed of any contravention of protocols and will want to see your Community Action Reports on all contacts with the public.'

A low rumble of rebellion went up from the hall. Brisley sniffed loudly and stepped back from the edge of the platform.

'There you have it, then,' declared Wriggley brightly, giving the detectives the benefit of his Glad Day, Love and Duty smile. 'We kick off first thing Monday morning. Detective Sergeant Brisley will be bringing round the straws. Short straws mean you're on early morning raids. At this time of year Emsbury has a large floating population, but a paucity of ethnics, so that will be the chief location for contra-surveillance. Since the raids'll be random, expect the unexpected!'

THIRTY FOUR

Lara Bliss had not heard from Jack Palanga since Wednesday when she had found him sitting on her lawn following his grilling by Detective Inspector Wriggley and Detective Sergeant Brisley. He had gone off to dinner in Emsbury and after that he had disappeared. She thought it likely he had decided to heed Wriggley's warnings and moved on. She was greatly surprised therefore when early on Sunday morning she received a call from him informing her he was in Emsbury and would be on his way over on the first crossing of the foot passenger ferry.

She rousted Cornelia out of her bed and went to tell Lovage.

'He wants us to go and find illegal immigrants,' she announced to them both. 'You remember, I bet him he couldn't show us any?'

Lovage groaned, but since it was Sunday he could hardly refuse the call.

Palanga arrived half an hour later. He was keen to be underway and hustled them into Bliss's Astra. Once they were on the road he relaxed, although to the irritation of the others, he remained vague about their destination. When Bliss insisted that, as the driver, she should know where they were going, he said, 'Tinmouth Farm'. She was satisfied for the moment, but Cornelia was not.

'Never heard of it! What happens there?'

'You'll see.'

Cornelia pouted silently at her own reflection in the window.

'Love the mystery!' laughed Bliss. 'Where have you been, anyway?'

'London,' Palanga replied shortly. 'Consulting sources... keeping up to date.'

'Any leads?'

He shrugged and smiled enigmatically.

She scrutinised him severely in the rear-view mirror, possessed of a sudden intuition. 'You've changed direction, haven't you? Did that rag of yours give you new orders?'

For a moment Palanga looked as though he had been caught out. 'Nonsense, I was simply working on other stories. I can't devote all my time to what goes on in this neck of the woods, you know.'

She was still sure she had hit on something. 'Meade's off the hook, isn't he?'

He sniggered. 'Oh, not a bit of it; he's firmly *on* the hook!'

Bliss tried to read what she could see of his face and it seemed quite free of guile, so she gave up and turned her full attention to her driving.

About ten miles east of Totteringham they came to the junction with the main road to the north coast. Palanga indicted they should turn north. A few miles further on and they found themselves in a tailback of slow moving traffic approaching a roundabout.

'What sort of attraction *is this*?' asked Bliss. 'An animal-petting farm?'

Cornelia let out a groan at the thought.

Palanga was preoccupied, consulting a set of instructions he had obviously prepared with some care beforehand. 'Nearly there,' was all he would say.

'Oh, hell! Do tell!' demanded Cornelia. 'It's not shire horses, is it?'

With a show of reluctance he produced from his pocket a page torn from the Emsbury & District Advertiser. "Tinmouth Farm Boot Sale. The biggest and best in the County", read the headline of the largest display ad.

'*A boot sale!*' said Cornelia indignantly.

'How interesting!' said Bliss. 'I didn't know there was such a thing around here. Never been to a boot sale in all my life!'

Lovage held out his hand for the ad and examined it closely with the look of one equally unfamiliar with the concept.

'Charity stalls, homemade jam, unwanted second-hand household stuff sold out of the backs of cars,' Bliss informed him.

'Quaint!' was Palanga's only comment.

The boot sale was a tumultuous scene of commerce, filled with straggling rows of vehicles, their contents piled on tables or scattered across the grass. The trades of many of the sellers could be identified from the signs on the sides of their vans: plumbers, Sky satellite dish fitters, civil engineering support staff, glaziers, carpenters, carpet fitters, pet supplies merchants, motor engineers... Their merchandise was the wreckage of domesticity; the stink of obsolescence was everywhere. There were unsellable videocassettes in profusion and thirty-year-old LP records, paperbacks with gold embossed titles by authors only Palanga had ever heard of, piles of second-hand clothes and the last dregs of the estates of deceased parents. Second-hand tools and plumbing fittings were laid out in rows on old carpet or polythene sheeting, surrounded by pushchairs and keep fit aids still in their boxes. Ceramics, particularly novelty teapots, and unwanted Christmas decorations were common stock-in-trade, as were bowls brimming with McDonald's Happy Meal toys. Throngs of buyers snaked between the rows of sellers and at the top of the field a line of inflatable slides and bouncy castles was vying for trade from those encumbered with children.

'Long live distinctive working-class institutions!' said Palanga. 'Boot fairs are a mainstay of the unofficial economy. Look closely and you will see multi-cultural Britain purchasing its needs: eastern Europeans buying tools, Nigerians buying anything and everything.'

Bliss smiled, seeing in him the streetwise sociology undergraduate who speaks with the pride of one who knows about such things. But what he said was true: the crowd was polyglot in a way the holidaying crowds in Emsbury weren't.

'Okay, you're right: immigrants,' she agreed. 'Where are the illegal ones.'

'Wait and see.'

Bliss plunged into the crowd and came back swinging a walking stick with a carved handle, and for two pounds Cornelia bought a pair of sunglasses with pink, heart-shaped frames that made her look like a loutish Lolita. They walked the straggling rows, Palanga unmoved by everything and constantly rounding them up and pushing them on. Bliss noticed that he was growing increasingly disconsolate.

'*Well?*' she said, growing weary of examining the endless unlovely objects.

'I don't see what I'm looking for. If this was anywhere near London...'

'Dear boy, it isn't,' she said a little tartly. 'What exactly *is it* we're looking for?'

Palanga stopped and bashed his head. 'Counterfeit DVDs. People from South East Asia selling counterfeit DVDs of pre-release movies.'

Bliss was underwhelmed by his explanation. She and Lovage exchanged glances. 'And this is what you brought us here to see?'

Palanga nodded.

'Doesn't sound very deep,' she said, 'as far as plots go.'

'Would you mind explaining what *the hell* we are doing?' complained Cornelia.

'Okay, I can't see any here. I was assured they are usually here. And don't doubt it's big money! The gangs have copying facilities somewhere. God knows what the quality's like, but most people take a punt 'cause they're only a pound apiece and they're all new releases they haven't seen yet.'

'*Fine!*' was Cornelia's unfeeling comment. 'I don't know why this is any of our business, but can we go on shopping now?'

The four sleuths walked almost the whole field, and all – apart from Palanga – became burdened with sundry purchases. They went on a little further before they sat down on the grass. The boot sale was beginning to change.

The car park was thinning out, and, here and there, sellers were clearing their pitches and looked eager to be gone.

Palanga checked his watch. 'It's gone twelve. Soon everyone will be shutting up shop. If they were here the gangmaster would be pulling them out.'

'All very fine,' said Bliss, speaking for them all, 'but we haven't seen anything to support your story.'

Palanga held up the only purchase he'd made all morning. 'I bought this from a stall. It's of a movie that's not on general release yet. It's in a flimsy because it's bootlegged. Probably copied by a projectionist, or some such. The bloke I bought it from picked it up at a boot fair a couple of weeks ago. I didn't ask but it's probably rubbish. I paid 50p for it.'

This statement raised hardly a spark of interest. They were all ready to go and there was nothing for it but to return home. When they arrived Bliss opened the boot of the car and felt faintly disgusted by their purchases in their used plastic bags. They had coffee on the lawn in near silence. To the surprise of the others, it seemed that Palanga thought their trip had brought matters to a conclusion. He drained his cup, looked at his watch and said he was late. He was in such a whirl to be gone there was no opportunity for a post-mortem.

'See: plenty of illegal immigrants around here,' was his parting shot, 'and look how they disappear... just like that!' He rose to leave, giving them a broad grin.

'That's a second time he's rushed off leaving us frazzled,' said Bliss, after he had gone.

'I suppose,' decided Lovage rather dismissively, 'it's another leg of his big-time exposé. He's afraid of losing it; that's what all the secrecy is about.'

'Whatever it is, the police don't want it published. You remember: Wriggley put the hex on him when he carted him off.'

'He'll have to bide his time, then, won't he? I'd leave him to get on with it, if I were you.'

Bliss was ready to agree, but something still rankled. It seemed as though the morning had been nothing more than an opportunity for Palanga to demonstrate his man-of-the-world credentials. If anything, her suspicion had strengthened that his enquiries had taken a new direction, and his interest in Daguerre had changed, although in what way she could not define. Again she found herself wondering, how trustworthy was this Jack Palanga? He had already confessed he was really Matt Fernyhaugh, and now she wondered, why had Mr Fernyhaugh gone to London, and so speedily returned?

THIRTY FIVE

Daguerre had hardly been seen since the arrival of the curators on Thursday afternoon. He had declared the West Studio out of bounds and only Mortimer was admitted. An air of gloom descended on Terpsichore Manor, as it always did when works was not going well. Belatedly, Mortimer left for the weekend at lunchtime on Saturday, tight-lipped about what was happening with the stampede of furniture. Despite his reputation for stoical calm, he looked more than a little out of sorts as he bid Carrie goodbye.

'Everything'll right itself next week,' was all he would say as he put is bag in the boot of his car.

Rita was left to fend off the press and entertain Daguerre's visitors. Despite the attentions of a masseuse and a manicurist whom she had acquired from Emsbury with the help of Carrie, she found the weekend wearing. Inevitably, a story about the Meade Daguerre's vandalised yacht had appeared in the dailies, but not unduly prominent. After her disastrous press conference, Rita had decided to issue bulletins, but when Carrie took her first effort to the gate to distribute it she found that the waiting journalists had drifted off. That is, but for one disgruntled-looking youth who treated it with contempt. Rita had more success with the curators.

They were effusive in their admiration of everything about Terpsichore Manor and did not appear to find their host's disappearance strange; her explanation that he was on a working jag more than satisfied them. They announced they were collaborating on a text about Daguerre and had taken on the dreamy demeanour of holidaymakers; an early return to London was clearly not part of their thinking. After breakfast on Monday the "Do not disturb" sign taped to the West Studio door disappeared and Rita received a text from Daguerre inviting her to join him. She rushed over to the studio. Daguerre was alone and looked as if he had been there all night. He had two days of stubble and his clothes seemed to be hanging off him. But what surprised her most was the extent of the change that the stampede of furniture had undergone. In fact, it was in turmoil. When she had last seen it in the company of the curators she had assumed it was nearly finished, but now the allusion to animals had completely disappeared and it had become a pile. The change was so complete it made her wonder if Daguerre knew what he was doing.

'Any news from the police?' he enquired wearily.

She shook her head. 'Still no crew. Carrie's getting the yacht cleaned.'

He seemed not to have heard her. 'It needed some elevation,' he explained, flapping an arm in the direction of the pile.

'It's lost something of its animalistic flavour,' she ventured, choosing her words with care.

'True.' All weekend he had been rehearsing an idea and now was the moment to try it out. 'I decided I wanted to make it clear I'm not a figurative artist; to make it explicit that figuration is only a means to an end. This piece is a flow. It starts over there and comes up in a blossoming...' He felt himself losing momentum. '... Or some such crap.'

Rita knew that this was a moment to avoid saying anything that sounded pandering or inflated. 'Meade, it's monumental! No need to be so hard on yourself, I think it works... *really well*!'

'So, you like it better now it's not a stampede? You prefer it to the Afghan idea?'

'It's... developed. I haven't seen the Afghan piece, have I? Be fair!'

'Rita,' Daguerre said, staring hard at the pile. The thing that was really burdening him had finally come to the fore. 'You know Avery Audley?'

'Of course,' she said without much enthusiasm. 'What about him? When I hear his name I always think of the disagreeable nuisance he used to make of himself at private views.'

'Yes, well,' Daguerre was somewhat discomforted by the knowledge that it was he who had been responsible for Audley's attendance at the gallery's private views during the early years of his success; a responsibility blackened by the memory of several impromptu "performances" by Audley. In one of the more intoxicated he had been dressed as a giant pink and black panda, and proceedings had ended with some unintended nudity by a young female Arts Council administrator, 'he never did fulfil his potential; his career has taken a few unfortunate turns.'

'Anyway...?' she prompted.

'Ah! Oh, well... matter of confidence in the Afghan piece. You know, what I told you in the restaurant.'

'Yes,' she agreed, brightening at the thought of further news about the Afghan piece and clearly unsuspecting of the reason they were discussing Avery Audley, 'your installation with knobs on.'

He looked pained. 'Rita, I don't think moving the Afghans to Parliament Square quite constitutes "knobs", does it?'

'No, no, sorry... reached for the first phrase that came to mind. Bit distracted with all this stuff. You know, the curators... Dealing with reporters... Well, the innuendos, Meade, the downright fabrications, you would not believe!'

'Anyway,' he said, determined to press on. 'Avery seems to have heard you think it stinks.'

'Stinks? Dealing with reporters?'

'No, the Afghan idea. You think it stinks.'

'You mean Avery thinks that, surely? He's the sort of silly man who'd think it should be Martians, not Afghans.'

'No, I—'

'Remember that panda stunt he pulled in the gallery? The bare bottom business?'

'Those public sector harridans get what they deserve,' Daguerre retorted defensively. 'Anyway, isn't there something you need to say to me about the Afghans?'

'No, not particularly; I'm generally concerned about how your show goes off, you know. Rupert rang this morning and told me two more of your works have been consigned to the autumn's "Modern and Contemporary" auction at Christies.'

'Two more! You mean four in all?'

Rita made a steadying gesture with her hands. 'I know, pieces up for auction is always a delicate time. Don't worry, your prices are solid.'

'But four!' The thought of that many works being consigned to the same auction made his gonads contract with fear. 'Jesus!' He gazed at the pile of furniture despairingly. 'Avery says you've been spreading the word that you think—'

'That boy makes things up; gossip's the only creative outlet he's had since he turned twenty.'

'Rita, the only person I've told about the Afghans is *you*. How come within a day of me telling you, Avery's hearing you're nervous about the Afghans from that pea-brained Siegfried?'

There was a pause.

'Christ, *Orlando*! Quite right,' she confessed, her voice suddenly breaking. 'Sorry, I may have committed an indiscretion. If I did it was a mistake. I've been dealing with the press and they say such nonsense – sheer slander, you know. This yacht thing... It's difficult not to be twitchy about everything! Look, declare a truce and,' she clenched her eyes shut and suddenly looked on the verge of tears, 'we'll get things back on an even keel.'

As she finished speaking, Carrie poked her head round the door, a mobile clasped to her bosom. 'The journalists are back,' she announced. 'Rita, a couple are waiting at the gates and won't get off the intercom. They say you promised to give them some local colour on Meade's life in the country, or some such.'

Taken aback by her distress, Daguerre couldn't take his eyes off Rita. She was staring into a corner of the studio's roof, her expression quite woebegone. It was a disconcerting picture of a normally resolute woman. That, and the news of his works up for auction, made him wonder if his affairs were in an even worse state than he had imagined, but before he could say anything further she turned to go, raising a hand in acknowledgement of Carrie's call. 'I'll be back,' she promised him. 'Just let me deal with this first.'

'Yes, go,' he agreed. 'Afghans are topical as hell, Rita. And I need topicality!' He mimed her exit with a sweep of his hand, thinking with a sinking feeling that what he needed most was more furniture.

Still at the door, Carrie motioned with the mobile, indicating that she had a call for him.

For a moment he resisted the idea of taking it, then he mouthed, 'Who is it?'

She held up her clipboard on which she had scrawled "Lara Bliss".

He signalled for her to pass him the mobile. 'Lara, what gives?'

'Hello, Meade. I've been painting all morning, and I'm feeling dissatisfied with progress, so I'm just about to open a bottle of a very decent white wine. Fancy coming over and giving me a crit? You promised you'd come and see what I was doing.'

'Oh! Yes, I'm sorry about that.' He found himself gazing despondently at the pile. 'Sounds rather a nice offer. I've got some issues of my own, so if you don't mind I think I'll come and let you give *me* a crit. I'm still besieged so I'll have to make a run for it. Keep that wine on ice and I'll see what I can do.' He threw the mobile back to Carrie.

'Mortimer!' he yelled. 'Where the hell are you, Mort?'

It was Celeste who appeared from the workshop end of the studio. She was chewing gum. 'He's not back yet.'

'Oh, yes, of course. Have you seen any new chairs?'

She shook her head. 'I'm in the darkroom, montaging John Lennon's head onto his body.'

He looked puzzled. 'What the hell for? Wasn't it there already?'

She shook her head. 'It was, but you didn't like it. You asked me to find him a better body.'

'Oh, yes!' He nodded animatedly. '*A better body.* Good!' For a moment he felt vaguely gratified but then his expression clouded as his attention returned to the pile of furniture.

THIRTY SIX

It was late morning before Bliss heard the crunch of Daguerre's Range Rover on her drive. She went out to meet him.

'Meade! Got away then!'

'With extreme difficulty. I sneaked out the back way and I'm not sure I wasn't followed.' He kissed her on both cheeks.

'Well, thank you for coming.' For a moment she felt impressed with herself for having secured Meade Daguerre to discuss painting with, but a second look at him dispelled the thought. 'You look tired,' she decided, in a concerned voice. 'Well, actually, *dishevelled and out of sorts*!' It was the first time she had seen him since together they had discovered the terrible scene on his yacht and she was full of sympathy for him.

He nodded. 'I'm not sleeping... the press... *work*!'

'Have those horrid policemen decided to leave you alone?'

'Have you heard: it was pig's blood?'

She stared at him, uncertain she understood him correctly. 'In the yacht?'

'Yes.'

'Good Lord!' Her brow cleared. 'No murder then; just vandalism.'

'It seems somebody was trying to make a point. I'm just not at all certain what the point was, or who it was aimed at.'

For a moment she put a commiserating hand on his sleeve. 'The crew, I suppose. Have they found them yet?'

'God help us, *no*! I believe they've been chasing all over the county looking for them. It seems the silly buggers abandoned their stuff somewhere down the coast and went on the run.'

'Yes, I've been down there; saw they'd left everything,' admitted Lara.

'You did! Why?'

'Oh, Jack Palanga had a hunch they were there; he'd decided they were landboarding.'

'Really? I can see why that man might attach himself to you, Lara, but why you him?'

'Actually, it started when I heard he was after a story about you. I thought he might be making trouble. I have interests in the town and I don't much care for snoopers invading people's privacy!'

'Huh! I thought you and he were friends.'

'Well, travelling companions about covers it. He's still pursuing some farrago; God knows what! Anyway, that ghastly Wriggley hauled him in for some sort of telling off and I went to Foreland without him. They'd already scarpered when I got there.'

'It's a mystery how they could have disappeared so completely; nearly a week now. The journos were back again this morning. It's spooky the way they're waiting for something to happen. Maybe they think all hell will break loose when – if – the crew turns up.' He stopped himself. 'Have the press been here?'

Bliss laughed. 'No, but I'm not newsworthy.'

'Lucky you! Where are we going?'

'The studio's across there.' She led the way, thinking there was something a trifle condescending in his tacit acceptance of her opinion of herself as not newsworthy.

'It's no joke,' he complained as they crossed the lawn. 'They've started photographing everybody as they come and go.' He waved the thought away as he reached the open door. 'This looks a very nice studio.'

They entered. Bliss had cleared away Lovage's bed and brought down the half-finished painting from her bedroom. It was leaning in a corner where Daguerre failed to notice it.

'It's a bit of a mess, actually,' she said. 'One of the archaeologists from the dig is staying here. I've been trying to help him find out who the nighthawks are.'

'Oh yeah, the dig. Is it still causing controversy?'

'Haven't you been to see it? It's on your land, after all.'

He gave her a look she interpreted as meaning that that was the least of his concerns, but then his expression changed and he put his hand to his brow as though recollecting something. 'Actually, I seem to remember that on the night we found the yacht trashed, Mortimer told me he thought one of my fabricators might have a metal detector.'

'I remember him saying something rather vague about that in the pub. Didn't amount to much though, did it?'

'No, later in the car he was a bit more fulsome. I'd forgotten about it.'

'Really? Did he say who?' She poured him a glass of wine.

'No, he didn't. I wasn't in the mood for complications.' He shook his head and took a sip of the wine. 'Excellent! We should ask him when he's back. He's away for the weekend.'

She frowned, making a mental note to tell Lovage. 'Have you heard my news: it turns out at least one member of the League was connected with the nighthawks?'

'Really? One of Emsbury's own?'

She nodded. 'It seems the police found him with some things that might have come from the site. He'd had an accident... rather disgraceful... and fatal. Nevertheless...'

'Sounds grim.' Daguerre had walked on a few steps and was pointing at the storage rack along the far wall of the studio. 'You going to show me a picture? I see you have your stretchers made by John Jones.'

'You interested in the technical business of painting?'

'Of course.'

'Who was it said he painted with his penis?'

'I have no idea,' he replied with a grin.

'Nice honest sentiment, I suppose... from a man!'

'I suppose.'

'Well, I paint with my tush.'

Daguerre laughed. 'Can't wait to see the results of such an esoteric technique!'

She went to the far end of the storage rack and drew out a large canvas wrapped in black polythene. She hung it on two nails driven into the long empty wall beneath the skylight and pulled back the plastic. The painting depicted a languorous mermaid in the arms of a naked Jack Tar. They were posed on a rock amidst billowing waves. In the distance was a faithful rendition of Emsbury nestling beneath the wooded hillside. The scene was unified by an equally faithful rendition of the fading light of evening, suffusing the limbs of the mermaid and her lover with deep, glowing shades of pink.

She watched Daguerre examine the painting.

'I hadn't expected anything so ambitious,' he confessed. 'There's real delicacy in the detail.'

'I thought you might find it folksy... Hopelessly anachronistic.'

'No, extraordinary! Really! Excellent atmospherics! I love the way it glows!'

'Ah!' she said, 'I do love rose madder genuine!' She was delighted that his taste was broad enough to allow him to admire the painting – so different from his own work – without, apparently, being driven to flattery.

'How long have you been painting?' he wanted to know, his eyes still fixed on the picture.

She had thought he might be playful, even flirtatious, but now they were touching on professional matters he seemed inclined to treat her as an equal. 'Since forever. I designed textiles for a while but I had an epiphany.'

'Epiphany?'

'Yes, my husband died unexpectedly and I decided I needed to focus.'

'I'm sorry.'

'He was a soldier. Afghanistan.'

'Oh!' He gave an involuntary wince. 'That's awful.'

'Yes, it was a terrible shock. He was such a strapping man. But let's talk about painting, Meade. No dwelling!' She looked at him, willing him to stay with her work, but she sensed some indefinable change had occurred. It was, she thought, as though something about the course of their conversation had disturbed his equilibrium.

'What… erm… what are you doing now?' he asked, clearing his throat awkwardly.

'I'm doing something very similar,' she replied, thinking how cosy that sounded.

'Oh,' was all the reply he could muster.

She read his silence as a failure on her part to hold his interest and, recalling the ever-changing panorama of his work, decided that her answer must have been a disappointment. She could not bring herself to direct his attention to the painting she had brought down from her bedroom. Instead she felt tempted to confess to her struggles, something she knew her paintings' innocent charms belied. 'We're ideological creatures, aren't we Meade?' she said.

He looked uncomprehending. 'I suppose so. Why do you say that?'

'You and I, both calling ourselves artists, have nothing in common, do we? I believe in the goodness of rum truffles.'

He laughed, despite himself. 'I suppose not, not ideologically. But you're a genuine artist in my book, Lara.'

It was her turn to laugh. 'I'm not so sure about you.'

'Don't get me being philosophical; at the moment I'm inclined to agree – it feels like breaking stones.'

'It's modern times that do the damage. We try to avoid them down here.'

'So you say! But be warned, Lara, I'm always looking for ideas. I could start painting mermaids!'

'And we could row out on the estuary when the moon's up and see if we can find some.'

He took another sip of wine, his face somewhat melancholic. 'If we did I'd only cut them to ribbons with the outboard motor. A fish and monkey sewn together.'

'What's that?'

'The fake mermaid in the British Museum.'

'A fish and a monkey! I've not heard of that.'

He shrugged. 'I've seen it. It gave me a shock when I saw it; it rather reminded me of what I do.' He turned to take another look at her painting. 'As far as mermaids go, it isn't a patch on yours.'

'Mine aren't fake. Painted from life, mine are.'

'It shows.'

She was about to romance her sightings of mermaids, but before she could she was cut off by the ring tone of his mobile. He took it out of his pocket and looked who was calling. 'Would you excuse me, Lara, it's Carrie.' He went to the open door and stood on the threshold while he took the call. Lara could hear what he was saying.

'*What!* Fuck! – All five? – Who's not there? – Where's he? – Do the police know?' His voice turned incredulous. 'What the fuck? The Atlantic Splash! *Since Wednesday?* – Okay. Thanks.' He terminated the call and gazed at the floor, lost in thought.

At last Bliss could restrain her curiosity no longer. 'Do I gather your crew's turned up?'

'Four of them,' he said bitterly. 'No Henry Balfour. They've been at a bloody music festival.'

'And now they're back?'

He nodded. 'At Foreland. You know where that is, don't you?'

'I'll show you, if you like. I'd be fascinated to hear what they've got to say for themselves.'

THIRTY SEVEN

'I wonder who was headlining,' mused Daguerre as they bumped along the track beside Foreland Water. 'Now I think about it, the Atlantic Splash is exactly the sort of place they would fuck off to.'

'So, what do you make of them now?'

He gave a wry snort. 'They never were likely to be involved in violence, you know, but God knows what else they were up to. They're so bloody...'

'What?'

'It's difficult to explain... I like young people; they're not stuffy, you know... and this lot are bright, very bright. They're charming, actually. Do you think they took me for a fool?' He looked at her anxiously.

'Good grief, no!' Bliss assured him.

'They were fun and I felt they were in touch with... well, I suppose you'd call it "youth culture"; they knew things I wanted to know... They knew a lot of people: "bright young things", I suppose. You should see them sail my yacht; they trimmed it that taut it sang. Nothing seems impossible when you're with them. I found that relaxing. Yes, I liked that. I thought Henry was keeping them in order, but it seems not. I have a pretty good manager up at the studio in Mortimer but they... They were off on their own too much. Anyway...' his voice trailed away '...they've ruined things.'

When they reached the spot where Bliss had pulled over the Astra on her previous visit, she pointed out that the VW campervan was still parked where it had been then, but now a second, similar vehicle – newer – was parked beside it.

'So, they've got visitors,' said Daguerre. He pushed on, undeterred by the state of the track. The campervans showed no sign of life, but as he brought the Range Rover to a halt some way short of them he could see that nearby, amongst what looked like luggage and equipment, there were three sleeping bags shaped by sleeping figures. The slam of his door made no impression on their slumber. He went straight to the nearest sleeping bag and prodded it with his foot.

'You awake, buddy?'

The figure turned onto its back and a befuddled face peered up at him.

'Hello, Michael Ditzel! Welcome back!' Daguerre crouched down and smiled in a grim parody of welcome. 'You guys...' He gulped back his fury. 'Are you aware of the trouble you've caused? What happened on my yacht?'

The fuzzy-headed sleeper sat up with a sudden sense of alarm.

'Meade, man, sorry! What's up?'

Daguerre straightened up and went to rouse the other bundles. 'Wake up, you sleepy heads!' he bellowed.

In a few moments he had all three awake. The side door of the older of the two minibuses slid open revealing a fourth young man, Cosmo Fairweather. He was pulling his clothes on as he stepped down, as was the young woman who followed him.

'Glad to see you're here... With company too!' Daguerre considered them collectively. 'Well, you sorry, dishevelled cretins,' he said scornfully, 'anybody got anything to say?'

Realisation was dawning on them that something had gone seriously awry.

'Sorry, man, we thought we weren't needed,' said Fairweather. 'What's happened?'

'You haven't heard?'

'Henry told us we weren't needed,' he said finally. 'So we came out here. We met Margie, and decided...' He made a vague motion in the direction of the second minibus where a second, younger woman, slight and radiant, had appeared.

'I get it,' said Daguerre dismissively. 'Atlantic Splash. Right?'

'Can we—'

'Last Monday, night, my yacht, trashed. Blood everywhere, like an atrocity. Pig's blood for Christ's sake! Who did it and why?'

Fairweather shook his head as though he wasn't hearing right. The first man Daguerre had aroused – Michael Ditzel – went over to the radiant young woman and led her away over the ruined dune as though to shield her from what was none of her concern. Nobody moved to stop him.

'Say again?' said Fairweather when they were out of hearing. 'Trashed?'

'That's it.'

'That's terrible!'

Daguerre was in no mood to explain. 'Just tell me about Henry.'

'He stayed in Emsbury. He said we should go.'

'Oh! So what the fuck you've been doing with my yacht!'

'*Hey!*' intervened Margie, looking riled. 'They've been with us, listening to music. So cut the crap!'

'You look like one of my mermaids,' said Bliss, unexpectedly.

'Yeah, *and my sister*! So what of it?' countered Margie.

To judge from her indulgent smile, Bliss was enchanted by her brusque manner; her voice indicated otherwise. 'Look, rabbit, we thought there'd been a murder! We happened on this bloody vandalism and it wasn't nice. The police have been looking for these boys ever since. Why? Because they're halfway to being the main suspects in a murder enquiry. It's still likely the police are going to be all over them once they know they've turned up because nobody knows where Balfour is, so they need to shape up. If I were you, I'd encourage them to go see the police first thing, and be nice!' She gave Margie a wink and switched her gaze to the men to check that they were following what she was saying. 'Meanwhile we'd like an inside line on what's been going on: Mr Balfour, Mr Daguerre's yacht.'

'That's right!' agreed Daguerre, his arms folded.

'We're out of the loop, man,' said Quartermain, the youngest man, who was still not fully out of his sleeping bag. He shrugged. 'Henry didn't tell us anything. Cosmo and he could sail that thing without us, and they did.'

'He was in deep, you know?' added Cosmo Fairweather. 'I wouldn't be surprised he's got on the wrong side of someone. That's all I've got to say.'

'You'll need to be a wee bit more fulsome than that with the police!' decided Bliss.

Contrary to her advice, Fairweather seemed to be shrinking in on himself. 'It's nothing to do with any of us. I wasn't involved. If you want to know more, speak to Willy Basington.'

Bliss was nonplussed. 'Did you say *Willy Basington?*'

Daguerre, too, was taken aback at the mention of his name and he jumped in. 'What's Basington to do with it?'

Fairweather laughed weakly. 'Henry wasn't just working for you, Meade. He was working for Willy Basington as well.'

'Really?' Daguerre was astonished. 'Didn't know we had a timeshare! How did that work? What was he doing for him?'

'He ran errands for him when you weren't around.'

Daguerre was so scandalised he was lost for words.

Bliss pointed an accusing finger. 'You went along for the ride when Balfour was running errands, didn't you? So, you know what he was mixed up in, don't you?'

Fairweather stared at the ground with a stubborn, goatish air. In a gesture of solidarity, Margie put a hand on his shoulder and glared at Bliss. 'Henry had a habit of disturbing things best left undisturbed,' she said fiercely. 'I guess he just went too far.'

Daguerre was finished with them and he walked away in disgust.

Bliss gave Margie a winning smile. 'Who was headlining?'

'Some old fart,' was the insolent reply.

Bliss had to restrain the desire to tear into her. She squeezed her lower lip between her thumb and forefinger. 'This has *nothing* to do with smuggling, has it?' she said in a voice touched with sarcasm. She got no response and decided to leave them to mull over the news she and Daguerre had brought. She gave them a regretful shrug and followed after him. They were well out of earshot by the time she caught up with him.

'Well, what are you going to do now?' she asked.

'You tell me.' He gave a wry laugh. 'Sack them?'

She looked back to size up Fairweather. 'He knows more than he's saying.'

'Oh, sure! The police can sort it out. They'll prise it out of him soon enough.'

'What about Willy Basington? That was a surprise.'

'Yeah, what the fuck?'

'Do you know him?'

'No, but I bumped into him at The Estuary the other night. Very pally, he was. My wife's done some charity thing with him.' He stopped and stared off into the distance. 'Could *he* be involved in all this stuff?'

'Goodness, no!' Bliss laughed. 'He's a gentleman. Collects steam engines. Has a reputation to uphold in these parts. Mind you, he seems to have his thumbs in a lot of pies.'

Daguerre gave her a frowning look. 'What does that mean?'

'Well, funnily enough his name has come up in relation to the nighthawks' conspiracy. It seems there's been some rather odd transactions going on with members of the League. And now here he is *again* in connection with Henry Balfour! I don't know what to think,' she decided, rather deflated.

'Whatever,' he said, reconciled to letting someone else sort things out while he focused on what was important: his struggle with the work in his studio.

They had reached the Range Rover and he unlocked it. She, meanwhile, had been struck by an idea that she was not sure she wanted to share with him. It concerned Jack Palanga. She had spent a great deal of time pondering his motives since their visit to the boot fair. Now a new realisation darkened her thoughts.

'How does a man who prides himself on his investigative skills not know about Willy Basington?' she demanded of the dismal sky.

'Who you talking about?'

'Jack Palanga.'

'Hah! Because he's fixated on getting something on me,' said Daguerre, not without a touch of self-satisfaction. 'Wait a minute!' He'd had a sudden realisation. 'It was he who was having dinner with Basington at The Estuary!'

This news roused Bliss from her reverie. '*What*, Palanga and Basington together? When?'

'Oh, last week. Wednesday.'

Bliss made a quick calculation and realised Palanga had left her house and gone more or less directly to meet Basington. She was not pleased. 'Good grief! That was just before the conniving so-and-so went off to London. Look, Meade, you know this theory that your yacht's been used for smuggling?'

'Yeah. Lot of rot, isn't it?' he said doubtfully.

'Well, Balfour wasn't distributing circulars for Willy, that's for sure.' She gestured back to where Fairweather and the others were beginning to pack up. 'Are you aware Palanga's got hold of some story about meeting merchant ships out in the channel; evading border controls?'

Daguerre was shocked. 'No!'

'Circumstantial guff, maybe, but he thinks it's got mileage. What if it was Willy Basington who was paying for your crew to bring them in, when you weren't around?'

'Them! What *them,* for Christ's sake?'

'Illegal immigrants.'

'Illegal—' In an instant Daguerre's view of Henry Balfour and what he had been doing while he was away underwent a very unpleasant and unwelcome turn. He made his way to a nearby hump of grass and sat down as though his legs had gone. He was grey and stricken. 'Not illegal immigrants!'

'Don't tell me you'd rather it was drugs!' she said, unheeding of the lineaments of despair the news had drawn on his face. 'It could be very tricky. He's a patron of the League, you know!'

'Who is?' he asked weakly.

'Willy, of course. He supports the League.'

'Is Palanga about to publish this stuff, or not?'

'I told you, that policeman – *Wriggley* – warned him off. There's a bigger picture, apparently.'

Daguerre got to his feet, as though in a trance, almost falling. 'Lara, we must be going. I have terribly important matters to see to, and if we don't go now I shall positively explode!'

'I wouldn't worry, Palanga can't do anything for the time being.'

He raised his hands in supplication to the heavens. The thought of explaining what was running through his mind filled him with dismay. Faced by a woman whose husband had been killed in a purposeless military adventure in a distant land, he could not bring himself to confess. Confronted by bereavement, "Vehiculating Voicelessness" seemed a frivolous catchphrase. Even worse, he now found himself wondering if behind Henry Balfour's actions lay an idealism missing from his own. He felt the hot prick of shame. A second blow to his artistic plans, coming so soon after the first, was almost too much to bear.

'I'm sorry; I had an idea... an idea for a... an installation,' he stammered. 'I thought I was a good move, though maybe my judgement's awry. It seems Henry Balfour's entrepreneurial spirit has done for me – and the idea!'

'How come?'

'Lara, I'm really sorry, but I don't want to go into it. Let's say I'm double fucked and leave it at that!' He turned to go. 'I didn't realise your husband...'

'What?'

'Was – *you know* – killed in Afghanistan.'

She waved the idea away with a pained expression. 'He wasn't. He was in stores. He had a massive brain haemorrhage in Aldershot, coming home on leave.'

The news should have lightened Daguerre's mood, but it didn't. Silently they climbed into the Range Rover. They had shared a moment of intimacy in Bliss's studio, but now, beset by cares, he was carried away on the rip tide of his celebrity.

THIRTY EIGHT

In Daguerre's rush to get back to Terpsichore Manor he dropped Bliss off at the end of the lane leading to Seaview. As she walked towards her house she mulled over what she had witnessed at Foreland. It vexed her to find her thoughts monopolised by Daguerre's problems. She had no way of understanding what had happened to him once fame had entered his life, but she recognised that it had marked him out as different, and made demands on him that she had never experienced. On the journey, despite his best intentions, she had wheedled out of him the outline of his plan to turn a ragbag of humanity into an artwork (although he had kept from her his intention to use Afghans). Nevertheless, what he had told her was enough to wake a vein of cynicism in her nature she did not welcome. She knew enough about his career not to expect him to use conventional art materials, but using real, living human beings seemed to her a step too far. Could it rise above street theatre of the most banal kind? Of course his intention, she acknowledged, was that they should embody a genuine plight, and were not to be seen as actors, but wasn't art about some artifice on the artist's part intended to impress and delight with its creative invention? That's what she believed, anyway.

It pained her to think this, because it went against her open, accepting nature, but to her it seemed that the idea's currency, its claim to profundity, came only from the difficulties in realising it. Only Daguerre amongst his contemporaries had the resources and cultural cache to do so. In every other way it was – and he too seemed suddenly to have come to this understanding – an extravagant commonplace. It was very clear to her that his work was not going well. She could see plainly enough that he was playing for very high stakes, and she was repelled by the anguish that had welled up from beneath his veneer of charm. She was glad it was he, not she, the press were hunting.

When she reached the gate Bliss could hear the sound of music coming from the open door of the studio and she crossed the lawn to find Lovage sitting in the shade amongst the flowerpots, daydreaming over a glass of wine. Before he could say a word she poured out the story of Daguerre's visit to her studio and their trip to Foreland. As she concluded she had a sudden recollection.

'Here's another thing: he told me he'd heard one of his studio assistants might have a metal detector.'

Lovage was indignant. 'That sounds rather important. Who was it?'

'He only said *"might"*, and he doesn't know who. Apparently, Mortimer, the chap who runs his studio, said something about it.'

Lovage mimed putting a mobile to his ear.

'I can't go pestering again; Meade's definitely not going to like it, things being as they are. Anyway, Mortimer's not there.' Bliss ducked her head. 'He'll be back soon and I promise I'll find out who it was.' Finally, changing the subject, she said, 'you packed up early today.'

He hardly stirred as she picked up the bottle and looked around vaguely for a glass.

'Lara, I have to go back to London. Seems there's been an outbreak of nighthawks at a site in Suffolk.'

'Oh dear! You will be coming back, won't you?'

'I don't know. I'll have to let you know.'

'Good grief, Lovage, isn't your work here important?'

'They still won't let us dig in the wood.'

'But still...' She put down the bottle and looked him over, trying to make out his mood. 'Never mind the botanicals, come and have a drop of chemical in the house. Suddenly I've seen the blindingly obvious and I need you to trample it into the ground, good and proper!' She got him to his feet and together they headed towards the house. 'We'll miss you! You're practically one of the family. Cornelia will be devastated.'

Lovage laughed. 'I doubt that, Lara. I think she's fully occupied with the dinghy now she's got that outboard motor. It's been a lovely interlude, but I've scarcely been pulling my weight, have I? The locals haven't exactly made me welcome.'

'I thought you were on the verge of a conquest.'

He gave an embarrassed laugh and shook his head. 'Ah, you mean Judith! I go as I came. I did have a moment, but I overshot.'

'Overshot! Good grief, man, I doubt that. We all love a wild man your side of thirty. You should come back and... and *effloresce*!'

'I'm not sure that would be me!'

There was about him an air of deflation and Bliss had an urge to put an arm round him and put things right, but her practical self restrained her, knowing that the delicate flower that was Lovage was best taking care of itself.

'So,' he continued, determined to redirect the course of their conversation, 'what's blindingly obvious?'

They had entered the house.

'Jack Palanga, Master Newshound,' she said as she set about preparing their gin and tonics. 'He turns up here and charms me with his eager sleuthing. Took us to a boot fair yesterday, shows us nothing conclusive and then shoots off like the whole thing's done with.' She handed him his drink and took a sip of hers with the expression of one taking medicine. 'Where does this man come from? Done a check? Yes, there's a column called Celebrities' Confidant written by a Jack Palanga, but we know that's just a pseudonym. There's another journalist goes by the same name. Remember, he told us?'

'Yes, Farthing.'

'Correct. Anyway names don't matter just now. Concentrate! Imagine employing a gardener with references. He cuts down the plants with the weeds and makes a hell of a mess before he's rumbled. Fake references! Apparently Jack Palanga hasn't heard of Willy Basington. In all his speculation about people smuggling and what the crew of Daguerre's yacht were up to, he's never so much as whispered the name "Willy Basington", but before Daguerre put him in the shade with his Bond Street glamour Willy Basington was our big local celebrity.'

'Okay, he missed Willy, but so what?'

'What if he knows all about Willy and is deliberately keeping him out of the picture?'

'You spout words, Lara, but I've no idea what you're driving at!'

'Smashing up the yacht and the pig's blood was meant to terrify Daguerre's crew; to make them do something.'

'Or stop doing something.'

'Quite. But the only one who could have seen the mess was Henry Balfour, and he's done a bunk. The others are as shifty as hell and one of them – name of Fairweather – is saying that Balfour was moonlighting for Willy; seems he'd been doing "errands" for him. Incidentally, Meade went white as a piece of haddock when I told him they could have been landing illegal immigrants. Reality is trampling all over his artistic plans, apparently. He rushed off to Terpsichore Manor in a hell of a state.'

'What errands? Did he mean bringing in illegal immigrants for Basington?' He was getting impatient. 'What did Fairweather say?'

'Not much. They all clammed up sharpish when they heard about the yacht. They looked genuinely shocked though. Here's another thing: I've had a lot of dealings with Willy over the years; he donates the rent of the town hall for the League's annual exhibition. Nice philanthropic gesture! I walk him round the exhibition before it opens and he's never given me the least indication he's been buying Jayne Wilson's ceramics. I can't get it out of my mind.'

'The aberrant taste or the silence?'

She gave him the evil eye.

'Well,' he added hastily, 'we do certainly seem to keep bumping into him, so to speak.'

'Why has Palanga never mentioned Willy Basington to us? Willy is newsworthy, TV celebrity and all that. He may not provoke quite the passion that Meade does, but it would be a scoop for any journalist who could show he was doing something scandalous. Now, here's the clincher: Meade told me that on the day of Palanga's set-to with the police he saw Palanga having dinner with Willy at The Estuary!'

'Now, that's *really* odd! I thought Basington was difficult to get to.'

'Too true! And the next day he clears off to London.' She took a meditative draught of her gin. 'The police might have him under their thumb for the time being, but that's no reason to keep things from us, is it? The question is: what devious game is Mr Palanga-stroke-Fernyhaugh playing? He's certainly not playing with a straight bat, even for a journalist!'

'Maybe he's just dumb.'

'No, no, not he! What would you do, in the circumstances?'

'Follow your line: barge straight in and ask the dope what's going on.'

She attempted to laugh through her sip of gin and almost choked. 'You're right!' She looked at her watch. 'Supposedly, he holds court at the King's Reach Hotel.'

'Well, I'm at a loose end. Not too late to get him to buy us a cup of tea. Let's take the ferry.'

Bliss was greatly encouraged by Lovage's willingness to confront Palanga; in the past he had always seemed disinclined to take him to task. 'Better still, Cornelia can take us in the dinghy.'

They fetched their coats and went down to the water where they found Cornelia staring out over the roadstead, whistling tunelessly.

'What's going on?' asked Lovage.

'That steam launch again,' she replied. 'Still playing hide and seek.'

Bliss and Lovage gazed out over the estuary, which was a set piece of high-season bustle, but couldn't spot her.

'That's our Willy!' said Bliss. 'Whatever way we look he comes swimming into view like a grand old pike patrolling his patch.'

Lovage gave a grunt of agreement and made for the beached dinghy. 'Come on, Cornelia, take us across to Emsbury. Lara wants to go for a spin.'

They set off, the rigmarole of starting the outboard motor lending their departure from the shore the spirit of drama that oars had not. The estuary was a smooth, lustrous dark green. Somewhere towards the middle of their crossing, Cornelia, who was sitting at the bow acting as lookout, gave a sudden yip.

'There's the swinish thing!'

'Where?' Bliss found herself recalling Lovage's story of the last time they had crossed the path of the steam launch. As before, it was coming upstream through a flotilla of small craft, but this time it was not blithe indifference that put them on a collision course. A powerboat cutting across her path suddenly stalled and the steam launch had no alternative but to swing to starboard to avoid the wallowing obstacle.

'Christ!' cried Lovage. He cut the engine and turned the dinghy to meet the bow wave head on.

The steam launch swung back to port, but swept past so close that beneath the thump of the pistons they could hear the throaty roar of the fire in the smoke stack. Bliss caught a glimpse of a tall, distinguished-looking man in a pale blue suit standing in the shadow under the awning. He waved and she could have sworn there was a grin on his face. The wake slapped into them full force, the water hard and unforgiving. Lovage's manoeuvre meant that it struck the bow first, saving the dinghy from the danger of capsizing but causing it to buck up at such an angle that Cornelia was nearly thrown overboard. Wet through, she gave an ironic cheer.

Bliss too had taken a good soaking. 'Grief, I do believe that was Willy Basington!' she said, gripping the gunwale tightly as the dinghy's violent rocking motion subsided.

'That was on purpose,' laughed Cornelia. She waved her fist. *'Vengeance is mine!'*

The powerboat was even more swamped than the dinghy and a surly-looking man was bailing furiously and bawling at one of the boys with him, evidently the culprit who had stalled the motor.

Lovage was scandalised. 'Was that really Basington? That was an incredible manoeuvre!'

Bliss made a lady-like attempt to tidy her hair and put her clothes to some sort of rights. 'That was him, all right. *Onward!*' she declared. 'On no account shall we be deflected from our purpose.'

The rest of the crossing was uneventful and they moored the dinghy at one of the floating jetties not far from the *May Queen*. From Emsbury's quayside they took the road that skirted the estuary in the direction of the sea. There was only an occasional building on the seaward side of the road, most notably – towards the outskirts of Emsbury – the King's Reach Hotel, which stood on a rocky outcrop where the road looped away from the shore. It was a large, rambling building of white stucco, with a verandah snaking along the facade overlooking the estuary. At the far end there was a terrace with Pernod umbrellas overlooking a maze of hedges surrounding the alleys of a miniature golf course.

They reached an elevated vantage point on the road and Lovage stopped to peer over the boundary wall, his eyes drawn by the animated scene on the terrace. Bliss and Cornelia, who were a few steps behind him, came to a halt too, their brows furrowed against the afternoon sun.

'I do believe that's Palanga,' Lovage declared. 'At that table with two other men!'

'So it is!' exclaimed Bliss, her face a picture of outrage.

'And I recognise that man in the shorts sitting on his right! He was the lout ogling the girls at the archaeological dig a couple of days ago. Who do you think he is?'

'I don't know, but I certainly know the other!' she said in a whisper, taking cover behind the wall. 'That's Barnstable Bennett, Silas's son. He's a bad lot too: bit of a spiv. What a threesome!'

He sidled back to where she was crouching. 'What do we do now?'

'Wait till the others have gone and have a chat with Mr Palanga,' was the reply.

The three spies established themselves a little further along the road on a municipal bench from which they could monitor developments in comfort, and soon enough they saw Barnstable Bennett and the peeping Tom say their goodbyes and leave the terrace. They waited a while longer and were rewarded by a down-at-heel red Porsche puttering past. They caught a glimpse of Barnstable behind the wheel, and with him, in the passenger seat, Lovage's peeping Tom. Their laughter was so uproarious they could hear it above the noise of the engine.

'What was amusing them, I wonder?' said Bliss as the car rounded the bend.

'Their evil plots,' said Cornelia, glaring after them, even though they had long disappeared from sight.

'Time to go and talk to Mr Palanga?'

'Your party,' said Lovage, wilting a little now that conflict and embarrassment seemed imminent.

Bliss led the way. She showed an excellent grasp of the field of action, leading the advance at a fast clip. They rounded the wall at the entrance to the car park and slipped unnoticed into one of the alleys of the miniature golf course that led to the terrace. She was first onto the decking and stood there, momentarily statuesque against the deep hue of the estuary.

'Hello, Jack,' she said, 'keeping company, I see.'

Palanga started. There was a notebook open on the table before him and he closed it with a snap. He did not speak at once but when he did he had a cold, blank look to his face she hadn't seen before. 'Lara! Go away, you don't want to get involved in this.'

'Working for MI6, are you?' she wondered with a humourless smile. 'Undercover agent Jack Palanga, mixing it with crooks and riffraff.'

'I've nothing to say, Lara,' he continued in an even, insistent tone of voice. 'I'll gladly share reminiscences with you at a later date.'

At that moment Lovage stepped up onto the terrace with Cornelia at his heels.

'Oh, you here too! Look, I'm up to my neck with things just now, so if you'd all please leave, I'm working.' He stood up, apparently prepared to quit the terrace to avoid their company, even though it was he who was on home territory.

'What happened at the boot fair yesterday, eh, Jack? Were you nicely wrapping things up for us?' demanded Bliss. 'You're a different animal on your own turf, aren't you? Comfortable with the way things are panning out?' She stopped abruptly, conscious in the corner of her eye of a disturbance in the doorway to the hotel. Glancing round, she was amazed to see Willy Basington standing there, dressed in his immaculate pale blue suit, open shirt and loafers.

'My God!' she exclaimed, her jaw dropping. 'Look who's here! It's Willy! Now the cat's in with the canaries!'

Basington adjusted the fall of his jacket and came straight towards them, exuding charm.

'Ah, Lara! Pleasant surprise. Afternoon, Palanga!' He turned back to Bliss with the air of a man sharing a confidence. 'I'm here to meet Mr Palanga in a vain attempt to advertise the next series of my TV programme. So difficult to get noticed these days!' He gave her a satirical wink that told her the programme was not in the least in need of publicity, and he was merely honouring his contractual obligation to garner publicity wherever he could.

'It's hard work getting anything out of Mr Palanga, that's for sure,' she responded as Basington kissed her ceremoniously on each cheek.

'It is!' he agreed with a laugh that he shared with the company. 'A hard man to please. With friends, I see. Your niece? Charming!' He scrutinised Cornelia closely, particularly the lifejacket she was wearing and, with a look of realisation on his face, turned back to Bliss. 'So, Lara, it *was* you in the dinghy! Nothing quite as dangerous as a grockle in a speedboat! No harm done, though.' He laughed richly.

'You nearly swamped us!' said Cornelia.

'Come, come, young lady, you have my most abject apology!' He made a little bow in her direction. 'And how's the art, Lara? Still doing good things?'

'It seems to be all distractions at the moment, Willy, much to my regret.'

'Is that so!' He turned to Lovage and Cornelia with a cluck of disapproval, holding them responsible for Bliss's distracted state. Their faces fell and he roared with laughter.

'This is Doctor Lovage from the British Museum,' said Bliss quickly to head off any further sallies.

'You've a lovely boat,' said Lovage politely, as they shook hands.

'Ah, yes, quite a rarity, my little *Bella*!'

'Doctor Lovage is staying with me and keeping an eye on the archaeological dig over on my side of the estuary.'

'Ah! That's *very* interesting! News had reached us. Isn't there trouble over there?' He gazed at Lovage – this was a TV trick of his – with an intense air of expectancy.

Lovage nodded. 'With metal detectionists.'

'That's it! Yes! We make those blessed things!' The thought made him laugh some more, although he was careful to embrace them all with his expansive good humour. 'They been running amok?'

'Seems so. Finds keep turning up all over.' Lovage's smile was bland, as if to say he had no particular culprits in mind.

'Gold and treasure has been stolen,' Cornelia reminded them, her voice full of righteous indignation. 'The destruction of archaeological insights has occurred!'

'Indeed, that *is* a shame!' Basington's face clouded with concern. 'Though I'm sure the British Museum is perfectly capable of protecting our archaeological heritage, eh, Doc?' He smiled somewhat wolfishly, and turned back to Palanga. 'Are we ready for the in-depth probing?'

Palanga got to his feet. 'There's a spot in the lounge where we won't disturb anyone.'

Basington made his goodbyes, with Palanga taking refuge behind his shining presence, and then the two of them were gone into the hotel, leaving Bliss, Lovage and Cornelia sitting at the table like conspirators who had been comprehensively outmanoeuvred.

'I'm not sure I can trust myself to speak,' observed Bliss, when silence no longer sufficed to express their common sense of outrage. 'That's quite a gang we've seen here this afternoon. What d'you make of it?'

'Not the foggiest!' said Lovage.

Cornelia was in no doubt about what she thought. 'They're all in it together, like a bunch of toads.'

'In what, though? Just because Palanga's with them doesn't mean he's one of them,' said Lovage reasonably.

'I'm ordering tea and cakes,' decided Bliss, signalling to a slouching youth in a white jacket.

'The point is,' said Lovage, 'Palanga, being Palanga, doesn't want anyone to know what he's up to... Wants all the glory for himself. He's been like that all along. He's never mentioned Basington and now it turns out *he's writing about him for his column*!'

'Understandable, if he thinks he's protecting a juicy story, although half of me thinks he's in with them somehow,' said Bliss. 'If we can't rely on Palanga, we have to sort out the mystery for ourselves.'

'Mysteries,' corrected Lovage. 'Nighthawks might be my thing, but let's not forget about the smuggling business! I bet Palanga hasn't! Just look at this.' He reached for the tea menu and, turning it over, began to write down a list of possible nighthawk conspirators. 'Willy Basington, both the Bennetts, the peeping Tom, Jayne what's-her-name, her mate Toby Griffin, Cosmo Fairweather and the rest of the crew of the *May Queen*... Er, who else?'

'Anybody and everybody employed by Meade Daguerre,' added Bliss.

'And Bolshoi Bertie,' said Cornelia, with a pert shudder.

Lovage started to write his name, then decided that her suggestion lacked merit and crossed it out. 'And others unknown,' he decided, throwing his pen down on the table. 'Impossible: it's nearly all of Emsbury!'

'Well,' insisted Cornelia, 'I told you they're all in it together!' And having made her sense of conviction plain she turned her attention to the cakes, which the slouching youth had produced with surprising alacrity.

'Do we have any clues, lines of enquiry?' Bliss wondered.

'No, just suspicions and circumstantial guff,' replied Lovage. 'What are the facts? We have two mysteries – one, the business around Daguerre's yacht, the other, the looting of the archaeological site – that seem in some way connected.'

'Even if there isn't a link, I'm damned if they both don't get solved!'

'Green sock,' said Lovage. 'We found a green sock in the wood after I was attacked.'

'Um, and what does that crook use his steam launch for?' added Cornelia. 'And why did his gang try to shoot me?'

'Shoot you?' Bliss eyed her niece and decided she was embroidering again.

'Since I'm now free,' Lovage continued, 'how about if tomorrow we do what I've been wanting to do since before you got sidetracked into the Henry Balfour business?' He wagged the menu card. 'This list's nothing but suspicions; it's always the same. What I want to do is walk Pilgrim's Way; I want to know how the nighthawks actually got to the site. The reason is—'

Bliss held up her hands in surrender. 'Yes, yes, I know – because you think that somehow it will lead you to who they are. Well, it's the least I can do, last throw of the dice.' She turned to Cornelia. 'Lovage is going back to London on Wednesday.'

'London?' Cornelia looked at him sharply.

He nodded.

Cornelia didn't speak, but her glare said the news was a betrayal.

He registered her look and felt guilty, though for the life of him he couldn't think why.

Bliss was consulting her watch. 'Didn't I tell you she'd be devastated?'

'I'm not devastated,' Cornelia retorted. 'He can run out on us if he must. I don't care what anyone does.'

'Don't be contrary!'

'I am and I will be,' she said crossly.

Lovage had raised his eyes heavenwards. 'She thinks I'm running out on *what*?'

'Forget it, you've never had the heart for finding out who's been stealing from that dig.'

Before Lovage could respond Bliss cut him off with a hand on his arm. 'Ignore her, Lovage, she exaggerates, as usual. Tomorrow it's Pilgrim's Way, and that means you, Cornelia! But before we go, there's someone's brains I need to pick.' She reached for a fancy iced cake from the cake stand and decapitated it with a bite.

'Then I'm coming with you,' said Cornelia.

'Certainly not! I don't want you frightening my informants with your moral certitude.' She looked up at the sky with a frown. 'It looks like rain. We're going to get wet on the way back.'

THIRTY NINE

It was some time after Daguerre had arrived back at Terpsichore Manor before he could bring himself to face Rita. He found her reading in the conservatory on the south side of the house.

'*Meade!*'

Daguerre could see she was taken aback to find him looking for her, no doubt because she still thought of herself as in disgrace for the reservations she had expressed to Orlando about the Afghan piece. 'I'm sorry about this morning,' he blurted out, throwing himself down on an empty recliner. 'I've decided you're right about the Afghan idea.'

She looked at him hard. 'What do you mean? Listen, this is all a dreadful misunderstanding. It's me that should apologise. I know you think I betrayed you, but Orlando convinced me I was wrong and he was right. Fine, I expressed doubts to him, but he made me realise I was being a bit conservative – thinking stuck in tramlines, in my usual way. After I'd talked it through with him I knew I have to have a personal revolution every bit as radical as Mitsy Rothchild-Breitling's. Her Klees – with no presence at all – *have got to go!*' She scrutinized his face, the blank look of which suggested he had not grasped what she was saying.

For a long time he said nothing. 'I think... Er, it seems,' he stammered at last, 'I think we've just passed one another, going in opposite directions.'

She arched an eyebrow and looked at him quizzically. 'You mean...? Meade, what are you trying to say?'

'Art has been overtaken by life,' he laughed. 'The Afghans seemed to have come home to roost. I've lost the thread in the dark and I'm struggling to find it again.'

Rita was bewildered. She had thought their mutual apologies would be more than enough to clear the air, but now hers seemed to have been in vain. 'You're talking in impenetrable clichés, Meade. Can't you be more explicit? I'm not clear what you're trying to say.'

Daguerre made an effort to pull himself together and shake off his despondency. 'You want me to convince Mitsy Rothchild-Breitling she should sell her Klees. Is that right?'

'Well, ship them to her other place. She'll listen to you. Orlando says they look ridiculous with his new interiors. The finishes are all wrong for tiny little pictures with no presence at all.'

'Okay Rita, let's do a deal. I'll talk to Mitsy if you forget about the Afghans. Believe me, it's not going to work. It's gone sour on me, and stuff's going to come out about Henry that'll put the idea off-limits. I can't have art and life getting mixed up.'

'Really? What's he been—?'

'It's all too close to the bone.'

'*Henry!* There's always been an unreliable streak about that boy. Gets it from his mother's side: they're all flighty. Pity he isn't more like his father. What will you do instead?'

'Good question. The Titanic piece is on hold until Mortimer gets the figures back from that Justin creep. Everything else has gone stale on me. I suppose I'll have to start again.'

Daguerre would later realise that here, now, in this, the moment of silence that followed, he had reached an unspoken understanding with Rita, an understanding that would smooth his path for the next few months, months that would try them both to the limit, but mark new, glittering heights in his career. Nothing further needed to be said between them, which was all to the good because at that moment Mrs Ikeda stuck her head round the door.

'Oh, most fortunate!' she exclaimed with a twinkle that suggested she had caught them in some naughtiness. 'Discussion of art strategy, I anticipate. Time to go see cultural excavation?' She gazed at Rita expectantly.

The gaze was of such intensity, Daguerre looked at her too.

'I said I'd take Mrs Ikeda and Magnussen to see the archaeological dig,' she explained. 'I hear it's quite interesting.'

He gave an appreciative nod, grateful that the curators were being entertained. 'Good idea. I've been meaning to go and have a look myself.'

'Carrie spoke to somebody at the county's Heritage Services. Apparently we need to contact a Dr Middleditch when we get there.'

'You mean Dr Lovage, don't you? He's staying with Lara Bliss. Give me a moment; I'll meet you at the car.' Daguerre shooed Rita and Mrs Ikeda out of the studio. He took his new mobile from his pocket and called Carrie. 'Carrie, any sign of Mortimer?'

'Yes, he's just arrived.'

'Good, can you find him for me? I need him.'

In no time at all Mortimer entered the studio as though summoned by bells. 'You wanted me, boss?'

'Ah, Mort, glad you're back!' Daguerre threw his arm around his shoulder. 'I've been thinking, this thing,' he indicated the pile of furniture, 'this thing isn't complicated enough... not big enough. And another thought is that I'm on the wrong track; that what it needs is not *more materiality*, but *the illusion of materiality*. You know those mirror tiles in the container!'

Mortimer nodded, recalling the boxes of foot square mirrors that Daguerre had bought in a surplus store.

'I want you to insert those tiles into the pile. They've got to cut through the furniture like they've been shot from a gun. Know what I mean?'

'Like what, slicing through everything?'

'Yes, little pools of reflection to make the pile seem more dense and self-referential. They must swim in and out of consciousness when someone looks at the pile. Not too visible, not too much illusion. They should be horizontal, rather than vertical, and mingle in seamlessly. Yeah, *seamlessly.*' He looked pleased with the picture he had painted. 'Think you can do that, Mort, while I'm away?'

'Horizontal... and seamless,' repeated Mortimer doubtfully.

'Yes.' Daguerre gave him a hug. 'Meanwhile I'm going to look at the archaeology.'

Rita and Mrs Ikeda had found Olsen reading Umberto Eco on the lawn.

'There's rain in the air,' he said as he packed away his book.

To the west, a distant black cloud peeped over the chestnut trees. Collectively, and without comment, they stared in that direction. Then Rita, who had picked up a set of keys from Carrie, led the way to the Range Rover. Daguerre joined them as she was unlocking the car. He held out his hand.

'I'll drive. We can avoid the press by cutting across the fields. It's half the distance.'

Once they had moved off Olsen cleared his throat, the sign he was about to launch into one of the monologues for which he had gained a certain notoriety over the past few days. 'Ya! – we are all, I mean *all*, educationists now; for skills acquisition this is the new frontier. Our next conference at the Post-Family Art Foundation will focus on a discussion of key problematic issues to critique how curatorial practice is especially susceptible to instrumentalisation by various hegemonic forces to produce determined "socially beneficial" goals – ya! The first step will be to explore how new organising principles for curatorial practice might be made manifest that seek to de-privilege the production of a subject-centred individual private subjecthood. The second – ya! – will be to propose urgently how curatorial practice could avoid agency as an instrument of the State (i.e. avoid complicity with weak naïve Liberal or stronger cynical Neo-Liberal political modalities) and avoid banal assimilation and desublimation into the mill of commodity exchange (i.e. avoid being a pawn in, or avoid producing, new market paradigms).'

'Really?' said Daguerre. While the monologue had been proceeding he had jolted and jerked them across the first field, steering through the deepest ruts he could find.

It was, he reflected, the most fun he had had since he had arrived at Terpsichore Manor. Their route required them to cross Pilgrim's Way. The track was a quagmire and Daguerre forced Olsen out of the car to open and close the gates on either side.

'Dr Nugent – ya? – of the University of Caracas will be our keynote speaker,' Olsen informed them once they were on the move again. 'He has written texts on the various "economies of scope" of Post-Fordist Capitalism trajectories for a Post-Everything Culture and produced most interesting prototypes for an Advanced Outdoor Visual Culture.'

Daguerre caught Rita's eye in the rear-view mirror and allowed himself a fleeting smile.

Eventually, after several more fields, they passed through a hedge and out onto an open hillside. The black cloud they had dismissed as inconsequential before setting out had become threatening and immense, in keeping with the scale of the landscape they were now crossing. They went up over the crest and found themselves looking down into the amphitheatre hanging over the valley of the Em estuary where the dig was located. From the back of the car Mrs Ikeda squeaked excitedly when she caught her first sight of the trenches and the encampment above them. The Range Rover had hardly come to a halt by the burnt-out wreck of the minibus before the rain came in a sudden squall, lashing down on the roof. Daguerre looked round at his passengers.

'You're not expecting us to wander round a field in this, are you?' said Rita in a mutinous voice.

'No, but I'm going.'

'I'd love to see,' said Mrs Ikeda, and searching her plaid bag, she drew forth a Pac-a-Mac, which she began to unfold.

'I think – ya! – I will stay here with Rita until it stops,' announced Olsen, looking doubtfully into the teeth of the squall.

Daguerre climbed out. He hastened round to the rear door and pulled out a golfing umbrella. As he snapped it open Bolshoi Bertie came bustling up dressed in an old-fashioned yellow cycling cape. His bare legs – ending in walking boots – protruded from beneath the cape, oddly suggestive of the possibility that the cape was the only article of clothing he was wearing.

'Can I help you?' he yelled, straining to make himself heard. 'I'm Bertram Middleditch, Heritage Services.'

Daguerre heard Bertie's introduction, but distracted by the drumbeat of rain on his umbrella and Mrs Ikeda's struggle to open her door of the Range Rover, the words failed to sink in. 'I'm sorry,' he said, suddenly feeling quite drained, 'did you say you're Dr Lovage?'

'No. I'm—'

'I was expecting Dr Lovage. Isn't he here?' Daguerre looked perplexed, unwilling to believe his information was faulty. 'I'm Meade Daguerre. I own the land so... I understand from Lara you're staying at her house while this excavation is going on.'

'No, that's *him*. He's here on behalf of the British Museum. I'm camping here.'

Such was the disordered state of his mind that Daguerre was still reluctant to give up on Lovage. 'Then must be *he* who knows Roger Pusey.'

'Isn't he the Anglo-Saxon expert at the British Museum?'

'That's him! I did an intervention in his section. It was a little thing with pots. Mind you, it caught the royal attention. I received an invitation to Gloucestershire on the back of that.' Daguerre had angled his umbrella forward in an attempt to shelter Bertie while they spoke, at the expense of the rain pelting the back of his neck and soaking his shirt. 'Dr Lovage is well off his normal beat, isn't he?'

'I suppose.'

Daguerre sensed something truculent about Bertie's demeanour. It struck him that beneath the cape a deferential civil servant was doing battle with a stroppy Marxist.

'Protocol being what it is, the British Museum has a watching brief in circumstances like these: treasure, hoards of gold, that sort of thing.'

'Ah, yes! I hear you've been having trouble with tomb raiders. Owning the land, I… so I thought…'

'Yes? What… exactly?'

'I wanted to take a look at what's causing all the excitement. Owning the land I thought I should… well, I'm curious, you know.'

'Yes, of course. Well – ah – we are obliged to you for your cooperation…'

Daguerre saw that, defeated by the strange mixture of his celebrity, the wealth implied by his mention of ownership of the land, and a certain hesitancy of manner – a combination he often deployed to get what he wanted – the stroppy Marxist had taken himself off.

'Would you care for a guided tour?'

'Could we get out of the rain? In that marquee down there?'

'Of course. Shall we?'

Mrs Ikeda had finally freed herself from her safety belt and emerged from the Range Rover in her Pac-a-Mac and matching bonnet. The change in atmospherics had fogged the lenses of her glasses and she struggled to wipe them. 'Others stay, but I wish to see your lovely earthworks,' she said to Bertie with reverence, her voice elevated against the noise of the downpour.

Daguerre made a hasty introduction and they set off down the hillside.

'I base a lot of my work on obscure technical vocations,' he explained to Bertie as they went. 'They have their own vocabulary, their own tools and so on. I find these strange corners of expertise incredibly illuminating. I'm sure archaeologists have all sorts of arcane skill sets... Or does that sound a bit dotty?'

Bertie laughed good-naturedly. 'No, no, not at all. I see you're one of those artists who absorbs everything and anything, and turns them to good use. Hello, are they filming us?' He pointed back up the hill to where, some way above the parked Range Rover, a film crew was at work, draped in polythene. His first glimpse had suggested that the camera was pointing in their direction, but now he looked again it was clear the cameraman was panning across the dig. 'Must be the university making a video diary,' he decided.

'What, in this rain?' Daguerre stared, a doubtful frown on his face. 'There's always cameras, everywhere I go!'

'The video diary,' said Bertie, missing the existential gloom in Daguerre's remark, 'is one of archaeology's newer tools. So, you've heard about the nighthawks?'

'Yes, there's some who think it's my people.'

'Well, there's been a development there. The police have found some things in the possession of a local artist that could well have come from this excavation.'

'Yes, I heard. What were they?'

'Some little gold figurines, Roman. Probably votive offerings.'

'Lara Bliss told me there'd been an accident... fatal. Did you know him?'

'No. His name was Toby Griffin.'

Daguerre almost tripped over himself in his surprise. 'Toby Griffin! But he *does* work for me! I can't believe it! He does bookkeeping; been looking after the studio accounts since the spring!'

'Really? What a coincidence! Did you know he was an artist?'

Daguerre put his hand to his head in confusion. 'Probably. I only met him once or twice. Everybody who works for me is an artist, one way or another. It's something I tend to discount; being an artist is a condition of modernity.' He gave a wry laugh, as though he'd coined a disquieting truism.

Mrs Ikeda had come scurrying alongside, the crinkling noise of her Pac-a-Mac even louder than the rain.

'Mr Daguerre correct,' she said. 'We all artists once we understand life's true meaning: artist-surgeons, artist-politicians, artist-chefs—'

'Artist-undertakers,' suggested Daguerre, still put out by the news about Toby Griffin.

'—But some speak from heart in ways that move us. We will have museums still to immortalise them!'

'And artist-curators to curate them.'

The rain abated as suddenly as it had started. All three came to a halt, suspecting a trick. They gazed at the leaden sky before hurrying on to the marquee.

Once under cover Daguerre lowered his umbrella with a sigh of relief. His socks were sodden and he realised he was wearing the wrong shoes. He was still digesting the news of Toby Griffin's death. 'I can't believe that guy's dead! He kept a very orderly book, so Mortimer tells me.'

Bolshoi Bertie pulled a face that suggested he was conveying information of a saucy nature. 'Apparently a man of many parts. Self-strangulation.'

Daguerre pondered this last piece of information. It came to him that, in her hunt for the nighthawks, Lara Bliss would see a connection between the news that Toby Griffin worked at Terpsichore Manor and Mortimer's suggestion that someone there had a metal detector. 'It's certain it wasn't murder?'

Bertie smirked. 'No, an accident.'

'I see. I'm glad.' Bliss hadn't thought to tell him it was Toby Griffin who had been found with looted figurines. If she had, he thought, with a vague feeling of guilt, he would have pursued the matter of the metal detector with Mortimer days ago. He reached in his pocket for his mobile, meaning to call Bliss, and then he remembered it was a replacement for the one he had flung at Carrie; it had only Carrie's number in its directory. 'She's hunting nighthawks, you know,' he said.

'Who is?'

'Lara Bliss.'

'I expect it'll come to nothing,' said Bertie dismissively.

Daguerre had brightened at the thought of Bliss on a mission. 'Oh, I'm not so sure!' he decided, making a silent vow to call her. He looked around the interior of the marquee. 'Where is everyone?'

'They're playing cricket against the county's branch librarians' eleven,' replied Bertie, 'if rain hasn't stopped play.'

Daguerre's opinion of Bertie took a fall as he saw his face brightened at the prospect that at that very moment the game was being rained off. Meanwhile Mrs Ikeda was a picture of impatience, trampling her feet in her anxiety to get to the trenches.

'The way trenches are placed has much meaning!' she said excitedly. 'They become negative sculptures defining way we go to understand past. The rain is magnificent. I have not seen such rain since I depart Japan!'

Daguerre gave her a vaguely hostile look. 'It's stopped,' he reminded her.

She was gazing up at the sky with mystical intensity from the edge of the marquee. 'It will resume.'

'Shall we get on while the rain holds off?'

'Before we do, can I point out the main features of the site?' said Bertie. 'You can see them rather well from up here. We've opened eight trenches, which is rather a lot, but we're having some difficulty understanding the relationship between the lengths of foundation we've uncovered. There was a peak of activity here in the fourth century AD, although we're pretty sure...'

Daguerre had already stepped out of the marquee.

Bertie pointed hopefully at one of the tables occupied by a cocoon of plastic. 'We found a Roman burial off the site: a rather good lead coffin. Would you like to see it?'

'Perhaps later,' said Daguerre. The rain had resumed and he started off down the hillside, leisurely raising his umbrella. 'I would like to do something with archaeology,' he confided to Bertie when he saw he had caught up with him. 'Most of what you find is rubbish, isn't it? I mean, stuff people have thrown out. I think framing the remains of discarded, everyday objects with modern forensic technology might be rich in visual possibilities. It suggests lots of fascinating forms of presentation. Maybe... maybe I could invert the relationship in some w—'

Daguerre had pulled up in mid-stride. In her eagerness to reach the excavations, Mrs Ikeda had trotted on ahead. She now seemed to be fleeing before the rain, which flung itself down with increasing fury; she was rushing headlong, caught in the heart of the tempest. Everything around her had turned into a grey, misty version of itself. In full flight she reached the nearest trench and disappeared.

'Did you see that?'

Bertie looked at him enquiringly.

'She fell in the hole! She just ran straight into it!'

Bertie scanned the lower part of the hillside and realised that Mrs Ikeda had, indeed, disappeared. Daguerre was hurrying down the hillside and he followed in his wake. The wind caught Daguerre's umbrella creating an air dam effect, braking his progress so suddenly that Bertie nearly ran him down.

'I'm telling you,' Daguerre insisted, clutching at him, 'she just ran straight into that hole.'

'That's trench B,' Bertie advised breathlessly. 'There are eight trenches... eight trenches in all... and we give each a letter.'

They reached the lip of trench B to find Mrs Ikeda laid out on its floor. Her glasses had disappeared. She appeared to be asleep and her head was pillowed on a stretch of excavated foundation.

Daguerre reached for his mobile. 'Carrie,' he said in as calm a voice as he could muster, 'call an ambulance: there's been an accident. Mrs Ikeda's fallen in a trench and hit her head on the archaeology.'

FORTY

The rain had blown away to the east and the evening sunlight threw the hedge alongside the track into stark relief against the receding storm clouds. Bliss drove across several down-at-heel pastures before buildings came into view: a pretty cottage nestling amongst a group of unprepossessing farm buildings of corrugated iron. The expanse of yard at their centre was of concrete, but on all sides a creeping mat of vegetation was taking over. Bliss announced her presence with a few pips of the Astra's horn and Miles Sleight came stumbling out of the largest shed wearing a full face mask. She saluted him, temporarily struck deaf and dumb by the racket of a nearby compressor. Miles pulled off the mask.

'Hard at work?' she yelled as the compressor clattered to a halt.

'Bliss, what an unexpected pleasure!' He beckoned her to follow him back into the shed where a number of rocky shapes reared up in the gloom. He took out a packet of cigarettes and lit one with an amiable nod. 'Rock drill,' he explained, indicating the hefty appliance lying on the floor. 'Cheaper than a studio assistant.'

They both gazed up at the block of stone he was standing beneath.

'What is it?'

'Financial Prudence,' he said, expelling his first drag on the cigarette, 'the new spirit of the City of London. Commissioned by the second largest hedge fund incorporated in Bermuda. Long, short, short-short-short. Apparently, it's an immensely lucrative strategy. They've got an atrium. Plonked down in there it's going to look rather grand. Same sandstone as Coventry cathedral.'

Bliss strained to make out the detail of the carving in the gloom. 'Is that a woman's face?'

'Yes, of course! That *is* Prudence!'

'It's monumental!'

'As you'd expect,' he agreed, with a melancholy smile.

It struck Bliss that she had always thought of Miles as somewhat infirm, but here he was wielding a heavy piece of industrial equipment.

'Drink?' he offered. An open bottle of red wine stood amidst the masonry tools on a second block of stone. 'Intimations of mortality comes like sirens at the wane of day, and I've taken to saying farewell to the final shafts in the company of Bacchus.'

'Ah, cocktail hour!' said Bliss, unclear whether the manner of his invitation was flippant or bathetic, and since she still hadn't entirely forgiven him for his behaviour at their lunch with Meade Daguerre – or following the death of Toby Griffin – she wasn't certain she was bothered which. 'In the absence of the chemical, I'd be happy to join you.' She nodded towards the wooded slopes beyond the farmyard. 'Willy Basington's a neighbour of yours, isn't he, Miles?'

Miles coughed a lungful of smoke through his clenched fist. He sniffed, blinked, his eyes momentarily watery. 'He keeps on buying up the farms whenever he can. A befriender of widows, he is. I'm next, apparently.'

'Didn't the Masseys own that woodland?'

'They did. Old man Massey's gone to Spain for his knees.'

'You're not thinking of selling up, are you?'

Miles shook his head. 'Not likely!' He gestured at the pneumatic rock drill with his cigarette. 'Not while I can wield that beast.'

'Hear about the produce business Willy's financing? I'm told there's a depot somewhere hereabouts.'

He passed her a Tesco's plastic party cup brimming with wine. 'Why the interest in Willy Basington?' he asked, a shrewd look on his face.

'His name keeps coming up.'

He gave a laugh. 'So does Meade Daguerre's; you're not asking about him.'

'No, but Meade's as transparent as a baby; Willy's positively stygian.'

Miles took a final drag on his cigarette and flicked it away into the weeds in a way that suggested he was dismissing her comparison. 'I'm not sure I approve of your flirtation with Daguerre. Willy's a local, after all.'

'We should be more welcoming, Miles. Your behaviour in The Estuary was positively atrocious!'

He laughed and lit up another cigarette. 'Ten years, and upstarts and whelps of his ilk will have taken over the Royal Academy.'

'True. We're all doomed.'

'And my Prudence will have been consigned to some public sector horticulture scheme in Balham.'

'Never!'

'I sometimes think I shouldn't have given up on the fibreglass.'

This time Bliss sensed that the bathos was tinged with palpable regret, as if in turning to stone he had betrayed his muse.

'Anyway, since you've got the bloodhounds out… Willy Basington. Ah, yes! Aren't conventionally handsome men tedious? Lord knows what he's up to! I've seen them come and go, the people Willy employs. All freelance, of course. Here today and gone you know when. Recall Arthur Peddleton, the watercolourist? He lives over Smeltertown way. Paints zebras. Know who I mean?'

Bliss gave a slight nod, not wanting to interrupt his reminiscing.

'Arthur says Willy has a new warehouse over there. Arthur says they're packing seafood. They must be landing it on the creek.'

'Wait a minute, I thought the packing business was on Willy's land, this side of the estuary.'

'True enough, there's one over this side devoted to produce of the land – a beets to beef sort of thing – but apparently there's a spanking new warehouse down in Smeltertown devoted to seafood. I haven't seen it myself, but Arthur says it's imposing.'

'*Imposing!* Sounds like a war memorial!' She sketched a line in the air with her finger, trying to find the words for something. 'Isn't that what Barney Bennett went to prison for?'

Miles looked uncomprehending.

'Wasn't he banged up for taking liberties with the crustacea? I seem to recall he was caught red-handed rifling other people's pots.'

'My dear lady, Barney Bennett might seem a likely supplier to any dubious enterprise you'd care to mention, but I doubt the needs of one of Willy's businesses could be supplied by poaching, even on Barney's ambitious scale! Mind you, Barney's been tooling about in a red sports car.'

'Yes, I've seen it. So, there's a seafood packing business over Smeltertown way in a new warehouse belonging to Willy Basington. But is it his business, or what?'

'Well, dear old Willy runs everything at arm's length, doesn't he? It's supposedly run by someone Willy's backing because of his telly programme.'

'Strange I've not come across him.'

'No, it's not surprising because nobody's seen him, and the workers are bussed in.'

'Really?'

'All out-of-towners, apparently. If you're so curious about what's going on over there why not go and take a look?'

'I will, Miles, I will.' She took a sip of the wine and put down the cup. 'Thank you; as usual, you're a font. I've been meaning to go over that way for a while now on another bit of business, and I've never dropped in on Arthur. Give him your best, shall I?'

Miles nodded and the stub of his cigarette followed the first into the weeds. 'Do that, and mind what you put your foot in.' He gave her a meaningful look that suggested she was meddling in something best left alone. 'Always got your eyes on the sunlit uplands, eh Bliss? Me? When the hunt's out my sympathies lie with the local fauna. Now, if you don't mind, I ought to get back to my labour of love.' He limped over to the drill and picked it up. It was hardly in his hands before the compressor clattered back into life. He held up the drill in salutation and began to climb the scaffolding tower anchored alongside the block of stone.

Slowly Bliss made her way back to her car, reflecting that Miles probably knew a great deal more about Willy Basington's affairs than he was letting on. He had always been closer than she to the Emsbury saloon bar crowd where unofficial news circulated, and his social habits encouraged the confidences of others. She took one more look around the farmyard, recognising in its neglect a sign that he had taken root, and become more of a local than she would ever be.

FORTY ONE

Meade Daguerre was at a loose end in Emsbury, waiting for Mrs Ikeda to be released from the district's A&E. A taxi had been hired to bring her and Carrie back to The Estuary. He had a drink there and chatted with Terence until it got busy. He decided not to eat and, instead, wait until he got Mrs Ikeda back to Terpsichore Manor. Now it was eight thirty and he had wandered down to the marina where the *May Queen* was moored. He was wondering what kind of job had been made of cleaning the yacht's cabin, but hadn't yet decided whether he was going to take a look. He found it difficult to believe that the stink would have gone, and he had a horror of finding remnants of congealed blood in the crevices and corners. By the time he reached the jetty he had almost decided to get rid of the yacht, anything to avoid being reminded of the past week's events. It was then he saw that a dinghy was moored alongside the *May Queen*, and a blond-haired girl was sitting on the starboard deck, her legs dangling over the side. Daguerre approached with a certain caution, as though approaching some species of wildlife that might bolt if alarmed. What struck him most about her was that she was barefooted, and her feet were long and narrow and elegant.

'Hello,' he ventured, sticking his hands away in his pockets as though they were offensive weapons. '*You are?*'

'Cornelia,' she said reluctantly, as though divulging secret information. 'I've come to see your yacht. Lara Bliss is my aunt. She told me about the bloodbath.'

Daguerre laughed uneasily. 'I see. So, you're Cornelia! I wouldn't say it was that bad.'

'My word: bloodbath. I like dramatic effects.' She gave him a sudden penetrating stare from under her mop of blond hair.

'Well, it *is* – very dramatic. Much too dramatic for a place like this.' With a gesture he took in the tranquil expanse of the estuary and the long wooded slopes.

'Also,' she added, as though it were an important afterthought, 'I'm following a steam launch that's up to no good.'

'I see. Is it moored here?'

'No, it's not *that* easy.'

'No, I suppose not. If it was that easy it wouldn't be worth doing.'

'Exactly!' She felt in the pocket of her shorts for the page she had torn from Bliss's July copy of Vogue. She unfolded it and held it out for him to see. 'This is you, isn't it?'

Daguerre approached closer to see what it was. 'Ah, yes, that's me. And that's my wife.'

'She's terrifically beautiful, like a princess in a tower, or sent to sleep for a thousand years, then kissed by a frog.'

'Ah, well, perhaps pictures exaggerate.'

Cornelia grimaced as she considered the idea. 'No, I think not.' She examined the photograph once more before putting it away. 'I have a painting in my bedroom. I see things in it. It's a magic painting.'

'A magic painting? You mean at Lara's house.'

'Yes, opposite the end of my bed. I look at it every night before I go to sleep. There are flowers of all kinds, and fruit too. There are little drops of water on the petals of the flowers, and insects that look like they've just landed, and grapes that look like you can eat them. Do you do things like that?'

Daguerre laughed. 'No, I don't do things like that. It sounds like a Dutch still life painting. Is it dark and mysterious?'

'Yes, some of it is very dark and mysterious. But there is also a view through a window, looking out over a town, with gardens and houses, and then a river going into the distance, getting smaller and smaller. You can see every detail for miles.'

'Is that the magic part?'

She examined him as though she was considering whether to confide further. 'There's a sailing ship on the river, and sometimes it is burning. Could it be a fireship?'

'Are there any other ships on the river?'

'Only some little boats with men fishing.'

'Then no, I don't think it's a fireship.'

'And there are some men near the town, very small, down by the river. There is another man on the ground and I've seen them stabbing him.'

'You mean...?' Daguerre was a bit nonplussed. 'You mean sometimes they're *not* stabbing him?'

She considered his question carefully. 'Yes, I suppose I do.'

'But a painting doesn't change, you know. It's not like a movie, is it?' The word "delusional" crossed his mind, but there, in the advancing twilight, already heavy in the deep cleft of the estuary, it seemed a mean-spirited word. He gesticulated, searching for some way to bring the conversation back to common sense. 'You can't *sometimes* see something in a painting. Either it's there or it isn't. And a burning ship doesn't make sense.'

'What about the men stabbing another man?'

Daguerre laughed disconcertedly. 'How many times have you seen *that*?'

'Oh, when I look very hard, I suppose.'

Daguerre still wanted a rational explanation that satisfied his pragmatic self. 'Ah, I see, it's a painting teeming with details, so you see something different every time you look. I've seen paintings like that. Do you see any other unusual details?'

'Not really. I was wondering if the men stabbing the man lying on the ground were something to do with what happened on your yacht. That's why I wanted to see it.'

Daguerre realised he was becoming quite mesmerised by the self-possessed, blond girl he had discovered on his yacht, talking like a child mystic. But somewhere at the back of his mind he was thinking it might be as well to check the painting to see whether it was as she said. 'Are you okay?'

She shrugged. 'Yes, of course. I'm fine.'

'So, do you want to see in the cabin, where the bloodbath was? But, you do know, nobody was killed there, don't you?'

'Yes, obviously. Someone was killed nearby, between the river and the town.'

'I don't think so. That's a bit much! Maybe it's just over-active imagination; you seeing things when you're on the verge of sleep.'

'Is that what you think?' She looked at him in disgust. 'That's silly.'

He sighed. 'You're right, it's a bit prosaic, isn't it?'

'I don't know what that means,' she said dismissively.

Daguerre looked her in the face, a gaze she returned unflinchingly. It was, he thought, all childish fantasy, indulged in by someone somewhat older than was normal. But, *so what*? Wasn't that what artists did? He shifted his gaze to the shore, to where the narrow strip of flat ground where the boat owners parked their vehicles gave way to the steeply wooded slopes, now dark and forbidding, that climbed away from the estuary. 'Anyway, I suppose the police have searched the woodland around here,' he said in a voice clouded by doubt.

Cornelia stood up and straightened out her tee shirt. 'You're an artist, so you have insights. If I owned this yacht I wouldn't stop until I sailed off the edge of the world.'

Together they stepped into the cockpit and Daguerre unlocked the door of the cabin. 'After you,' he said to Cornelia, still unsure as to whether he wanted to enter himself.

'God, it stinks!' said Cornelia, drawing back.

It did stink too, the stringent stink of bleach.

'It wants airing. You should air it.'

He held out the key to her. 'Take it. Come tomorrow and air it. You can sail it off the edge of the world if you like.' At that moment he was overcome by an extraordinarily powerful desire to give her something scandalously generous. He felt like telling her she could have the yacht; that he didn't want it anymore; that it was hers to do with as she liked. It wasn't as if the temptation passed, it was rather that he decided to leave the matter moot. Soon, he thought, there might be a day when he *would* give it to her. She would say just the right thing and he wouldn't be able to resist the temptation to tell her, 'Keep it, it's yours'.

Holding out the key, smiling playfully, he said, 'Take it, it's yours. To keep as long as you need. If you get rid of the stink for me, I'll get Carrie to pay you. How about that?'

She looked at him shrewdly. 'I'll do it *if* you show me how to sail it.' She took the key from him, pulled the cabin door to and locked it. She slipped over the side of the yacht and into her dinghy while he stood by, somewhat bemused. Before he could say, or do, anything, she had spun the outboard motor into life and was pulling away. She regarded him gravely as she made her way out into the estuary.

Daguerre stayed there a little longer before turning back towards the shore. As he went he was conscious, for a moment, of a faint, almost indiscernible, sense of unease. Pondering this, he promised himself he would speak to Bliss and ask to view the curious painting that hung at the foot of Cornelia's bed.

FORTY TWO

It was the following morning and Lovage finally had his wish. He was full of enthusiasm for their expedition to walk the Pilgrim's Way. He flattened out the map of the Em estuary on the bonnet of the Astra, the better to show Cornelia what he had in mind. She was sprawled across the bonnet's other half.

'...There's the dig. Remember: when we first joined Pilgrim's Way, we debated which way to go? Pilgrim's Way is this dotted line that runs close by the dig, and all the way down to the river, where we saw Willy Basington's boathouse. If we'd gone the other way we'd have come to this fork.'

Bliss came out of the house, locking the door behind her. 'Are we ready?' she asked as she approached, equally eager to get their expedition under way.

Lovage waved a hand of acknowledgement without breaking off from his explanation. 'The left-hand fork follows the bank of the Em upstream to Totteringham; the other continues to rise, passing close to Terpsichore Manor.'

Bliss took a good look at the map. 'Yes, yes, and then it drops down to the creek at Smeltertown. We're going to drive to where it crosses the road to Totteringham and walk from there.'

Cornelia glowered at the map. 'Walk which way?'

There followed an immediate difference of opinion, because Lovage was all for going back towards Terpsichore Manor and the estuary, while Bliss, in truth, was equally as interested in getting a good look at Willy Basington's seafood business over at Smeltertown as in tracking nighthawks.

'Look,' said Bliss, 'is it grockles or locals we're after? They're two camps, two universes! I admit it's possible there's someone with a foot in both camps. If such a person exists and hangs out at Terpsichore Manor he – or she – should be the owner of that metal detector. We'll find out who that is soon enough, I promise you.'

'Whether locals or grockles,' said Lovage, shaking his head slowly, 'the best starting point for the dig is where Pilgrim's Way crosses the road to Totteringham… unless they live at Terpsichore Manor.'

Cornelia threw her hands in the air. 'Let's decide when we're there!' she said, as if to do so was the most obvious of things.

'Yes, Lovage, we're polishing potatoes,' agreed Bliss as she heaved herself into the driver's seat of the car. 'Let's get moving!'

Lovage collected up the map and off they set, Bliss humming along to selections from *South Pacific* playing on the Astra's ancient cassette player. They climbed out of Seaview and soon had passed the turning to the dig. A mile or so further on they came to a lay-by on the left-hand side of the road. Bliss slowed to a crawl and immediately following the lay-by, on the same side, under a thick growth of young trees, there was a gated entrance to a turning-off.

'That's it, Pilgrim's Way!' announced Bliss, bringing the car to a halt.

The width of the road did not permit parking so she reversed to the lay-by. They all climbed out and walked back to the turning. It gave onto a lane running away into woodland, densely enclosed by trees and undergrowth. The lane had the look of a right of way not much used, but still useable. It was barred by a gate, and next to it was a stile. Half hidden in the young sycamores stood a dilapidated National Trust signpost pointing west, It read, "Pilgrim's Way. Em Estuary Coastal Path".

'What now?' asked Bliss.

'We should walk back to the dig,' said Lovage.

'How far is it?'

'Mile. Mile and a half,' he replied.

'Notice anything new?'

'No,' said Lovage, glancing round.

'Shiny padlock! It's the gate. On the map Pilgrim's Way's marked as a bridle path. You can't take a horse through a locked gate. Nor vehicles.'

Hastily Lovage opened the map and saw that what she said was true. 'Who would do that?'

Bliss snapped her fingers. 'Give me that map a moment.' She gazed at it, brow furrowed. 'Pilgrim's Way doesn't cross any other roads between the estuary and Smeltertown, does it?'

'No, this is the only one.'

'I'm sure Meade told me he escaped the press by using a back route out of Terpsichore Manor. He must have used Pilgrim's Way! How could he do that, unless he has a key to the gate?'

'Another thing to ask Meade when you get round to speaking to him!' said Lovage accusingly. He was looking for the continuation of Pilgrim's Way towards Smeltertown on the other side of the road, but there was no equivalent gate, stile or sign, just a bank thickly topped with hedge.

'It's further on,' Bliss informed him with a nod. 'It follows the road for a while before branching off again.'

Led by Lovage, they walked along the road and, sure enough, they soon came to a gate, stile and sign on the other side of the road.

'This one's padlocked as well,' noted Bliss. She frowned, as though trying to recall something. 'Wasn't the lay-by back there where the dead Chinese man was found?'

'Really?' Lovage uttered this in a voice that said this was a complication too many.

The thought of the dead man disquieted Bliss and she barely nodded. 'Palanga says he drowned in the sea; he says Wriggley insists in a barrel of brine.'

'Look,' said Lovage, 'we agree, don't we, it's pretty certain Jayne and Toby were in on it.'

'Who's Toby?' demanded Cornelia.

Lovage ignored her. 'And they – with others – could have been selling some of their finds to Willy Basington. They could have parked back there in the lay-by and made their way to the dig.'

Bliss looked doubtful. 'Except neither owns a car!'

'Yes, rubbish, Lovage!' said Cornelia grimly. 'But *it is* all about Willy Basington, isn't it?'

Bliss was not to be deflected from her growing conviction that the nighthawks were locals. 'Who's got the heft to attack you with a lump of wood? Those two haven't. Who amongst the locals has the wherewithal to mastermind setting fire to a minibus? How about Barney Bennett and his mate? From the start Silas Bennett put the idea into our heads that the nighthawks were grockles. If Terpsichore Manor people were involved they might want the other gate locked, but why this one? This one being locked has Silas Bennett, and that son of his, written all over it. If Pilgrim's Way's so little used that nobody else is going to object, then they've got their own private road between Smeltertown and the estuary. And who rents the land where the dig is? Silas!'

Cornelia had no patience for further debate. 'I've told you already, they're all in it together, like a bunch of toads.'

'Fine!' Bliss raised her eyes to the heavens as if to say, "you insufferable child!". 'Why don't *you* choose which way we go?'

'I say we go this way.' She pointed across the fields to where the wooded slopes began that led down to Smeltertown.

'Lovage?'

'I don't know.' He had the map open again with his finger on a couple of tiny rectangles where Pilgrim's Way approached the creek at Smeltertown. 'I suppose that's Silas Bennett's farm. Perhaps it's as good a place as any to start out if the nighthawks are using vehicles.'

'What *are* we waiting for?' demanded Cornelia. 'There's nothing here but trees!' She climbed over the stile and stood waiting for the others.

'Nothing here but trees,' laughed Bliss as she prepared to follow a fretful Lovage into the lane.

Pilgrim's Way on this side of the road was more open than on the other, and ran straight across fields for a while, separated from them by stout hedges, but then it began to drop down quickly and went into woodland. The ground became muddier underfoot. Eventually Lovage called a halt and pointed to the ruts.

'These tracks look exactly like the ones we saw down by the estuary.'

Bliss's thoughts had turned to Palanga's grand conspiracy of people smugglers. 'Miles says that somewhere down here Willy Basington has a new warehouse where they're packing seafood. Perhaps he uses Pilgrim's Way as well. After all, his boathouse is just across from where you joined the estuary.'

Lovage gave her a sceptical look. 'So Daguerre and Basington and the Bennetts all have keys, do they?'

Bliss gave a wry laugh. 'No, it's nonsensical! Daguerre doesn't even know Basington; he told me so.'

They walked on, the track descending rapidly into dark, gloomy chines where the vaulting branches of giant trees blocked out the light. They heard the noise of machinery in the distance, echoing strangely. It came intermittently: the sound of a two-stroke petrol engine, as if someone were cutting timber with a chainsaw. More than once they thought they were approaching the source of the noise, but each time it proved to be an illusion. Bliss was growing restive. She called out to Lovage, who was some way ahead.

'We haven't seen a sign of Silas Bennett's place. I don't think we're anywhere near.'

Lovage too was uncertain where they were. They were meeting frequent forks in the track not marked on the map, both left and right, and he was no longer sure they were on Pilgrim's Way. 'It's confusing,' he replied, sharing her feeling of discouragement. 'But never mind; let's keep going.'

At last the track stopped descending and they came out of the trees and into sunlight.

Bliss was relieved. 'Perhaps *now* we can get our bearings.'

Before them was a reed bed. Beyond that there were glimpses of a stretch of open water and on the far side the trees climbed upwards on a hillside the mirror of the one they had just descended.

'This must be the Smeltertown creek,' she decided. 'I don't recognise where we are, but it looks like this: silted up and boggy. We must have missed Silas Bennett's place. What now?'

Lovage looked indecisive. 'We haven't passed a single building.' He made a gesture of hopelessness with the folded map.

Cornelia, who was beset by flies, piped up with a suggestion. 'I think we should go right. That must be the way to the sea, mustn't it?'

'Surely that's not the direction of Pilgrim's Way?' objected Lovage. 'It goes inland to cross the creek higher up.'

Nevertheless, led by Cornelia, right was the direction they went, back into the trees. Not very far on they came to a gateway in the gloom beneath a huge beech tree, and beyond there was the ascending curve of a road, the metalled surface of which was turning back to rubble. Set on a rise to the landward side of the lane was a white painted cottage gleaming with a preternatural brightness amongst the trees. It couldn't have been more forbidding had it been made of candy and cake.

'Is that Landward Ho?' wondered Bliss as she passed the others and headed towards it. 'I knew it! We've run the old codger to ground!'

Reluctantly, the other two trailed after her. Already she was climbing the dozen or so steps that led to the gate. As she did so a diminutive man of radiant countenance and wearing an extremely natty waistcoat appeared on the other side of the gate.

Bliss hailed him from midway up the flight. 'Hello, Arthur. Greetings from the Emsbury League of Artists!'

'My dear lady, welcome to my *humble*,' said Arthur Peddleton with a whimsical smile. 'Do come in and take a pot of tea. I shall settle the kettle on the metal and bid it to do its work. Been walking, I see. Come across any wildlife, liberated by do-gooders? No? Never mind!' He caught sight of the others. 'Hello, you've come with company! Not dangerous, are they?'

'These two or the wildlife? Much going on down here in Dingley Dell?'

'Usual rape and carnage.'

'We're looking for nighthawks. Raids on the archaeological site over the hill. Oh, this is Cornelia, my niece. And that's Dr Lovage of the British Museum.'

'Ah, a delightful young lady! And a man of scholarship in these parts is a rare treat!' He thrusted out a hand to shake theirs. 'I heard you archaeologists are having a spot of bother. There have been rumours about objects being dug up around here as long as I can remember.'

'Really?' Lovage's interest was piqued. 'What sort of things do you mean?'

Arthur ushered them into the cottage. 'You hear about the marble garden ornament?' he asked of Bliss. 'It came to light in Totteringham.' He turned to Lovage without waiting for a response. 'An agent for Bonham's came to see it; the next thing we hear it's fetched twenty five thousand at auction in London. Then there was the giant cog. That was rather mysterious. They never did find the mechanical wonder it came from.'

'But gold, Roman coins specifically?'

'Well, no, but there are rumours, you know. They say Totteringham was a Roman settlement, but otherwise...' His attention wandered and his expression went blank, but after a moment he perked up as another thought crossed his mind. 'The only thing of note down here is the new building.'

'Ah!' said Bliss cautiously, for without prompting he had alighted on the very topic she was hoping to quiz him about. 'We've been told it belongs to Willy Basington. Where is it, exactly?'

'Yes, Mr Basington: the chappie on the box. It's at the end of the lane; fork left at the junction, right on the water's edge. There used to be a repair yard down there. It was derelict and he had it cleared away. Progress, I suppose.' He didn't look convinced.

'What goes on there?'

He shrugged. 'There's a lot of coming and going with vehicles.'

'Vans and lorries?'

Arthur gave her a droll look that said all vehicles were the same to him.

'They use Pilgrim's Way perhaps?'

'Oh I wouldn't know about that. It goes quiet at low tide. I think they go out on the sands.'

'Doing what?'

The droll expression returned. 'Not truffle hunting.'

'Quite,' she agreed. 'So...?'

'At low tide there's a Sahara of sand out beyond Chancellor Island and some say you can harvest cockles there.'

'I expect they're stealing them,' decided Cornelia.

'I couldn't say,' said Arthur blandly. 'I expect somebody sold something to somebody and made a profit: a lease, a licence or some such. That's the way the world works, isn't it?'

'Surely that's old newspaper talk,' said Bliss.

'I wouldn't know. Newspapers don't reach down here.'

Bliss gave Lovage a meaningful look that said they needed to get on. They drank their cups of tea as quickly as was decent, admiring several watercolours of zebras as they did so. As with Jayne Wilson, Arthur was anxious to grace them with an introduction to his work. 'As a lad I was interested in modern art,' he began, 'but then I thought it seemed so silly – all -isms, ego, and no finesse. Painting zebras means I can combine a goodly dose of Op Art with my love of nature. May seem strange, but I discovered it's all a matter of framing. Exotic animal is the zebra – so much more fun than the horse. Both have tremendous rumps, of course. I'd like to paint butterflies, but I think it's best to have a theme and stick with it, don't you?'

They nodded their agreement and bid him a hasty farewell, full of superlatives. When they emerged the sun had gone and suddenly it felt autumnal.

'We're supposed to be investigating nighthawks but we're back on the trail of who trashed Daguerre's boat, aren't we?' demanded Lovage, once they were clear of the cottage. 'Am I expected to believe that some kind of seafood scam led to that scary mess?' He was on the verge of mutiny.

Bliss ignored his outburst. She was musing on the possibility of cockle picking in the Em estuary. 'The deepest part of the estuary is over towards the Emsbury side, west of Chancellor Island. This side's a maze of shifting sandbanks so boats give it a wide berth. Nobody sails close. If you were taking cockle pickers out to the sands from here you'd have to use a boat, wouldn't you? There's still some sort of a channel, but it's supposed to be silted up. What's more, the currents are treacherous when the tide's running. Perhaps it's possible to harvest cockles and bring them in here if you know the tides and have a boat with a shallow draft. If you did... Well, all-in-all no one's likely to get close enough to be curious about what you're doing, are they?'

Her musings somewhat undermined Lovage's indignation. 'So you're saying this is what Palanga's illegal immigrants do when they're not selling DVDs?' He laughed at what he took to be the dumb stupidity of such a scheme. 'I don't believe it. As you said to Arthur, it's just an old newspaper story.'

Bliss was unmoved. They walked on, Lovage falling behind as he struggled to fold the map with the seaward section of the estuary outermost. 'Where *exactly* are you taking us?' he demanded.

'We have to see this building of Willy's,' she insisted.

'To the sea,' said Cornelia stubbornly. 'If you think they're out on the sands let's go and take a look!'

Soon they came to the fork in the lane.

Bliss was adamant. 'Cornelia, we must take a look at the warehouse first.'

They took the left turn and found themselves walking between ancient hawthorn hedges. Shortly they came out into an open expanse of rank grass and weeds, and beyond stood the new warehouse, close to the creek. On the side nearest to them lay an apron of concrete, and on the furthest side it appeared as if a mooring ran along the water's edge, although there was no sign of a boat. There was a brutal clarity about the limits of the compound, accentuated by the wire-mesh fence, topped with razor wire. As they approached the fence there was a growing stink of rotting fish.

'Christ, it smells bad!' Lovage rattled the gates but they were chained and padlocked.

They began a circuit of the perimeter, looking for a way in. Downstream of the warehouse, where the undergrowth almost reached the fence, they found a hole freshly dug under the wire and a vixen and two cubs were sitting, sunning themselves on the concrete apron.

'Foxes do *love* fish,' said Lovage facetiously.

'Cornelia... crawl!' urged Bliss, indicating the hole the foxes had dug under the wire.

Cornelia looked doubtful, but Lovage enlarged the hole by heaving up the bottom of the wire and with some effort she wriggled through.

'Now what,' she said, brushing herself off uneasily.

'See if you can open the gates from the inside.'

She crossed the compound to the gates, holding her nose. The other two met her there. She was appalled. 'There's rotting fish and stuff everywhere!'

'Lift the bolts.' Through the steel mesh of the gates Lovage indicated the bolts that dropped into holes drilled in the concrete. She did as she was told and stood back. Lovage put his shoulder to the gates and they swung inwards until the chain fastening them ran out of slack. He tried another push and the gates opened a little further so that the gap between them was wide enough for him, and even for Bliss, to squeeze through.

What Cornelia had said was true. Everywhere there were plastic boxes containing the remnants of decaying seafood and, despite being newly built, an air of desolation hung over the place. They crossed the yard to the warehouse door. The smell of rotting fish intensified still further, like a physical thing, overwhelming their senses.

'I'm not going in there!' said Cornelia.

Lovage screwed up his face in disgust. 'This is grossly unhygienic, isn't it?'

'Fled!' exclaimed Cornelia with her air of absolute certitude.

'How long has it been abandoned?'

'Since about the time that yacht was trashed, I'd say,' decided Bliss.

'And isn't *that* a coincidence!' said Cornelia with a sardonic snort.

Bliss laughed grimly. 'What a mess to leave Willy Basington; it's a public health issue! Do you think he knows about it?'

'Weren't they working for him?'

'Apparently not. "Arm's length" according to Miles. We should inform the authorities.'

'They must know already, surely? Let's get out of this stink!' Lovage had given up on the warehouse and was again consulting the map as if it were one of his academic texts.

'What happens if we carry on towards the sea?' wondered Bliss, peering over his shoulder.

He looked round to check his bearings. 'It seems to rise to a headland, judging from the contour lines. There should be a view out over Chancellor Island and the *supposed* cockle-picking sands.'

One after another they squeezed back through the gate.

'What happens on that island, anyway?' he asked.

'Seabirds; it's a nature reserve. Nesting ground… and it's off-limits.'

'National Trust, then?'

'Actually, no, it's owned by Willy Basington. He keeps it private.'

Lovage came to a halt, open-mouthed. 'No! I don't believe it! You see, Willy Basington again!'

'No, no, it's not like that. It's been in his family for ages. Without Willy it would have been a holiday camp long ago. Nobody actually *goes* there.'

Lovage made a scoffing noise. 'Fine!' he exclaimed. 'Willy Basington owns the warehouse and he owns the island but he doesn't know what's going on.'

'I didn't say that!' said Bliss defensively.

'His gang uses that steam launch to keep people away,' said Cornelia with a fine sense of indignation. 'We need to see what's happening on that island, like the Famous Five!'

Lovage rested his hand on her shoulder. 'Me: I'll go to the headland, just to have a look, but no further.'

She pulled away as though he were a traitor.

They retraced their steps to the fork in the lane, Cornelia leading the way. They took the seaward turn and the lane quickly gave way to a footpath that threaded its way across a wooded hillside, the slopes of blue slipper clay tumbling away through the trees. They came upon large depressions in the ground filled with water that looked as though they had materialised overnight. After a while there was the sound of waves breaking on rocks. They were forced to climb higher to avoid crumbling cliffs, and the sound of the sea died away. The deciduous trees gave way to pine and in time the pine gave way to thorny thickets, their tops sculpted into aerodynamic shapes by the onshore winds. The thickets were dense and allowed only occasional glimpses of the sea's far expanses and, nearer to, the sandbanks that ran out towards Chancellor Island. As they approached the headland Cornelia thought she caught sight of a boat in one of the channels that criss-crossed the sandbanks and raced on ahead, hoping she might have a chance of getting a clear view of it, but by the time she reached the next break in the thorn bushes the channel was again empty.

'The trees are always in the way!' she said in a furious voice. 'We need to see what they're doing on that island! Willy Basington needs arresting! You agree, don't you?'

Bliss shook her head doubtfully.

'I'll take you out there in the dinghy,' Cornelia offered.

'This is a wild goose chase!' snapped Lovage. 'Let's go back.' He blocked the path, forcing the others to a halt. 'When we started out we were trying to find out who the nighthawks are but *no!* it always comes back to Meade Daguerre and his yacht. That's something the police should be handling and the story about illegal immigrants *and* counterfeit DVDs *and* Willy Basington *and* rotting fish should be Jack Palanga's.'

'Fair enough,' conceded Bliss, recognising that his forbearance at the way he had been led astray had finally run out, 'but we have an interest in all those things… and it was your suggestion we should climb up here.'

'And that's my limit! What's more, if you really want to know, I think the nighthawks have already dug out whatever treasure there was. It's all either already in the hands of the police or in London, gone. What do you say to that?'

Bliss looked at him without answering, taken aback by how greatly his commitment to their cause had diminished during their walk. She could see that his imminent departure was weighing on his mind.

He smacked the folded map against his palm. 'My work here's done.'

'You can't give up on Willy Basington!' protested Cornelia. 'He knows we're on his trail.'

'He doesn't because he doesn't have a care in the world.'

Bliss doubted Lovage was to be moved, but she saw that Cornelia's face had grown radiant and, seized by her passion for the pursuit, she had taken on a kind of grace. Lovage saw it too.

'Since first I set eyes on you that's something I've been hoping to see,' he said to Cornelia, with an air of regret. 'You keep on his tail till you get him. Me? I'll do more good in Suffolk.'

There was something of the tragic in the finality of his words that Bliss found disconcerting. 'Perhaps our teenage sleuth is over-eager. Why not?' she said with a certain protective defiance, smoothing Cornelia's tousled hair.

'He's tried to sink the dinghy three times!' Cornelia reminded Lovage, making a half-hearted attempt to kick him. 'I'm going out to that island, whatever you do.'

He gave her a wane smile, and without a word, turned and began to retrace his steps.

'You do that,' said Bliss to Cornelia with an excess of indulgence, thinking she might make a quite lovely mermaid in a few years' time. *'You do that!'* And on the whole, she decided, as they began to make their way back, it seemed quite providential that Lovage was being sent off to Suffolk.

FORTY THREE

The tents and other camping paraphernalia had been removed from the scoutmaster's office and the desk brought back from the stage in the hall. Posters extolling good scouting lined the walls. Chief Inspector Wriggley sat on one side of the desk and on the other sat Cosmo Fairweather. A silent, gloomy Brisley paced the floor behind Fairweather's chair, hands clasped behind his back.

'All things considered,' Wriggley was saying chattily, 'the weather's not been at all bad for July. It knows how to rain in July in these parts.' He gazed through the room's only window. 'But this year it's held off surprisingly well.'

Fairweather eyed him from beneath a lowered brow, waiting for the trial by questions to begin.

'Course we have simple weather here, not like the weather you lot have in a place like Cambridge. You have Oxbridge weather there: raining noughts and ones, when it's not pouring quantums. *Ah, scholars!* You've read Heidegger, I suppose? Unknown unknowns and all that German mental gymnastics? Learnt your pre-Socratic philosophers by rote when still in knickerbockers, no doubt.' He gazed into Fairweather's face with the smile of the expectant innocent. Brisley ceased his pacing as though he too were eager to hear Fairweather's response.

Fairweather grinned awkwardly as though trying to work out how to oblige his interrogator. 'You want to know about Henry Balfour, I suppose,' he said finally.

Brisley gave him a round of ironic applause.

'I mean, I knew him well enough, but I didn't know everything about what he was up to. He was connected in ways I'm not.'

'*Really!*' exclaimed Wriggley, incredulous at Fairweather's estimation of his lack of connectedness.

'Yep, he kept things to himself… you know? I have no idea what he was doing for Mr Basington. As a matter of fact,' he let out a nervous squeak of laughter, 'I don't know what he did for Meade Daguerre!'

The expectant smile returned to Wriggley's face, but no longer so innocent. 'You're dim and daft, aren't you? Do you think we're going to let you go until you've told us exactly what he did for Mr Basington and Mr Daguerre? *Do you?*'

With an air of one engaged in an act of secrecy, Brisley inserted a biro in Fairweather's left ear. Slowly he applied pressure, forcing him to bend sideways until his upper body was approaching the horizontal. Finally Fairweather had to reach out to the floor with his right hand to keep from toppling over. By now the biro had reached the perpendicular and Brisley began to twirl it between finger and thumb.

'La-de-dah!' said Wriggley. He peered over the edge of the table solicitously, as though commiserating with Fairweather's predicament.

'*All right!*' Fairweather whispered between gritted teeth. 'We went out to meet a Turkish merchantman carrying timber.'

Brisley removed the biro and yanked Fairweather upright by his collar.

Wriggley smiled winningly. 'When was this?'

'About three weeks ago.'

'Good, *better*! End of June?'

'Yes.'

'Date?'

'I can't... We took on board ten Chinese immigrants and sailed back to Emsbury.'

'Did one of them fall overboard by any chance?'

'No!' There was a sharp note of protest in Fairweather's voice. 'We landed them in a cove up the coast where we were met by a contact. He transferred them to a minibus; Henry gave him money. It was to cover expenses in setting them up – their living expenses and so on – until they found work.'

'How much did he give him?'

'Five thousand.'

'*Five thousand!* That'd pay for a lot of cheap digs! Then what?'

'They drove away, and we came back to the mooring here in Emsbury.'

'Where did the five thousand come from?'

'I don't know. Perhaps Willy Basington.'

'And Mr Basington knew what it was to be used for?'

'I suppose so, but he didn't bring it himself.'

'Who did?'

'A man. I don't know who he was. I only saw him with Henry a couple of times. I asked Henry about him, but—'

'He didn't say, I suppose.'

'No, he didn't, but he was given money more than once. He told me the man called it his "little private charity".'

'When did he receive this largess?'

'A couple of times in June that I know of.'

'You picked up immigrants both times?'

'I don't know. I only went the once.'

'This man said it was *his* "little private charity", but you think the money came from Mr Basington.'

Fairweather massaged his forehead. 'Henry told me both things. But this man didn't look like he had five thousand to give away. No way.'

'And at one time or another Mr Balfour told you the money came from Mr Basington?'

'He mentioned his name, yes.'

'Was this man oriental-looking?'

'No.'

'Was he called Mr Bennett, Mr Barnstable Bennett, by any chance?'

Fairweather shook his head. 'I don't know.'

'And you had no proof that the money came from Mr Basington?'

'No.' He thought for a little while. 'None, I suppose.'

'What happened then?'

'Things soured. I couldn't find out why; Henry clammed up. He started using different moorings, like he didn't want anyone to be sure where the yacht would be. He was sleeping on it too. Cut himself off. I began to think maybe he was taking it out by himself.'

'That's a big boat to manage by yourself.'

'Yeah. Maybe on the auxiliary…? He told us to go up to the north coast for a break. Said we weren't needed;

Meade was in London, then Germany. We weren't that keen on going, but we were just hanging about with Henry holed up in the yacht. It became really weird, and I didn't want to know any more.'

'Don't play the innocent with us!' said Brisley sharply. 'You were in on it all. We've seen the emails! *Global Migration Paradigm!*'

Fairweather looked down at his hands silently. It was not clear to his interrogators whether he was withholding something, or whether his anxiety to avoid saying something that would annoy them had rendered him tongue-tied.

'Detective Sergeant Brisley is right, you know,' decided Wriggley, 'it would be judicious to spill the beans. Our friends in East Anglia have provided us with a rich tapestry of material that puts you not very far from the epicentre of this Global Migration malarkey. It's no good trying to fade away as we approach the day you all took off. We're not particularly interested in pursuing you for people trafficking – we couldn't give a damn really – but we *are* looking for a gang of traffickers. We know you didn't leave Emsbury until Monday, the day the yacht was damaged.'

'I did see Henry that day.' Fairweather hesitated. 'He came by the cottage.'

'What for?'

'He picked up some things he said he needed.'

'Like?'

'A chainsaw, some tools.'

Brisley stopped his pacing.

'A chainsaw!' exclaimed Wriggley. 'Now there's a novelty. What did he want with a chainsaw?'

'I don't know. He sometimes carved lumps of tree trunk into staddle stones.'

'*Staddle stones in wood!* That doesn't make sense!'

'He sold them as garden ornaments. He always needed money and he wouldn't take it from his family. Apparently there's a market for that sort of thing.'

'Wooden staddle stones, eh? That's the sort of heritage stuff my colleague Detective Sergeant Brisley has a yen for.'

Brisley gave an impatient snort, nettled by the jibe. 'Was he taking the chainsaw to make staddle stones on that particular day?' he demanded.

Fairweather lifted his head and half turned in his chair. 'No, I don't believe so.'

Brisley slapped his hands together several times as though ridding them of dust. '*Thank you!*'

Wriggley had arranged himself in the pose of someone about to speculate. 'Oh, I know! He took it to cut through something. Or cut up something, perhaps something he wanted to dispose of. As a matter of interest, how can you be certain he didn't intend to make staddle stones?'

'Because he didn't take his boots.'

'His *boots?*'

'Yes. He was most particular about wearing boots with steel toecaps if he was going to use the chainsaw. He was afraid he might cut his toes off.'

Brisley guffawed.

'*Really!*' Fairweather insisted, again twisting in his chair.

'So, he took the chainsaw... for someone else to use. He was going to lend it to someone, perhaps?'

Momentarily Fairweather looked uncomfortable, and Wriggley pounced. 'Am I getting warm? Did he have a particular friend he might want to lend the chainsaw to?'

Brisley leaned over his shoulder. 'How do you know he didn't take his boots, anyway?'

'They were in the entrance. Still are.'

'Get back to the point, shall we?' urged Wriggley, irritated by Brisley's intervention. 'For whom was he taking the chainsaw?'

'I don't think he was taking it for anybody. I think he was going to sell it.'

'Ah, *sell it*! Did he need money?'

'As I said, he always did. That day he wanted some quick. He told me he'd been offered a job on a yacht somewhere in the Aegean. He seemed pretty certain about it.'

'Aegean! That sounds conveniently far away. Where would he sell a chainsaw in Emsbury?'

'Plenty of people in the boatyards will buy good second-hand tools for ready cash.'

'Okay… But why not borrow the money? He did ask, didn't he?'

For a moment Fairweather looked disconcerted at the extent to which Wriggley already had an understanding of the way Balfour operated. 'Because, if he was serious about flying off to the Aegean without telling his… his friends, I didn't want anything to do with it. *No!* Can you imagine what the others would have thought when they'd found out I'd known he was going, helping him to go without him saying anything to them?'

'Perhaps he was excessively frightened!'

'Excessively self-centred, as it happens.'

'Oh, *I see*: you disapproved!'

'It's like him to get in a mess with some scheme of his, and then cut and run when things get difficult.'

'Had a falling out, did we? Impetuous to a fault, our Henry,' mused Brisley from behind Fairweather's chair. 'Didn't I tell you they were boy anarchists?'

'You see,' said Wriggley, leaning closer to Fairweather, 'this is the stuff we like. Now I'm getting a whiff of the real Mr Balfour. His friends! His character! Not quite the sport he's made out to be, is he? This is all good stuff, isn't it, Cosmo?'

'If you say so. I don't know how it helps. I was in the cottage; he came in and collected a few things. I didn't really take that much notice.'

'But he asked you for money! How much?'

'Two hundred.'

'Were you alone?'

'Yes, the others had gone to the supermarket.'

'What time was it?'

'Mid-morning, about eleven.'

'You must have been packing up to leave.'

'We were; we'd decided to go to Foreland.'

'And was Mr Balfour in a vehicle?'

'Yes, I suppose he was. He came, went in and out twice, carrying stuff, so I suppose he put it in a vehicle.'

'But you didn't see it?'

'No.'

'He didn't own a vehicle, did he?'

'No.'

'But you do.'

'No. Michael Ditzel has an old VW.'

'So. Mr Balfour had someone else's vehicle, or someone was driving for him. You sure he was sleeping on the yacht?'

'Sure as I can be, without seeing him asleep.'

'Maybe he had a bivy somewhere? What about someone close to him: a girlfriend. A girlfriend with a... with a wood-burning stove?'

Fairweather started to laugh and Brisley slapped the back of his head.

Wriggley was stern. 'No girlfriend somewhere in the background we haven't heard about yet? What about the animal spirits?'

Fairweather had thrown back his head and rolled his eyes till his pupils almost disappeared. For a moment Wriggley thought Brisley's slap had induced a fit, but the spasm passed and Fairweather's composure returned.

'Henry made friends very easily... had a lot of friends. There were always people passing through, so, yes, he had girlfriends from time to time, but nothing especially intense, if you know what I mean.' He gave them a cryptic smile and hunched his shoulders, as if to indicate he had no more to say. Wriggley looked at him intently for a while. Then he glanced enquiringly at Brisley, who gave a shrug of indifference.

'I think that's all for now, young man. Go and wait in the hall.'

Fairweather sprang to his feet as though released from invisible bonds. 'Thank you, inspector. I appreciate the hard work you're putting into this investigation.'

Wriggley gazed at him, sensing an undercurrent of insolence in his thanks, but before he could take him to task Brisley was hurrying him out of the door. He was still turning this over in his mind when Brisley returned.

'So, boss, what do you make of that?'

'Eleven o'clock in the morning Mr Balfour leaves that prat's company with a chainsaw. Who was he with? And where did he go with a chainsaw?'

Brisley squeezed his lips between thumb and forefinger. 'Fairweather said he sold it.'

'Then we should be able to find it, shouldn't we?'

'You don't think he did?'

'No! Going abroad? Not a chance! He took it somewhere for someone to use. Yes, indeedy. And I think we'll see what Fairweather does next.'

'On bail?'

'What you going to charge him with? No, the smuggling is probably all there is and that looks like petty stuff. But he's a cleverclogs, he is; got Pont Street arrogance all over him. Trying to drag Mr Basington into the muck with him!'

'Scandalous!'

'Thinks we're slow as tortoises! Let him out. We'll keep a collar and lead on him though. Have him back in here for another session tomorrow, ask him the same questions – see if there's any more to his story. Meanwhile we'll follow the chainsaw; see where it takes us!'

FORTY FOUR

Another night devoted to the stampede of furniture. Meade Daguerre came out of the west studio into the sharp early morning light, bleary-eyed. He crossed the farmyard and went through the gate in the high wall that led to the lawned expanses at the front of Terpsichore Manor. Lara Bliss was standing by her car on his driveway.

'Good morning, Lara. Bright and early!'

'Morning, Meade. Still not sleeping, I see.'

He nodded. There was a distracted, feverish air about him. 'Everything seems to be happening to me. I've got a Japanese curator with a cracked skull.'

'I heard there'd been an accident. She all right?'

'Concussed. On the mend. I saw your niece, Cornelia, at the marina the other evening. Or was it yesterday? No, I'm losing track of time. Interesting young woman. You should keep an eye on her; she's something of a visionary. She was telling me about a painting.'

'Painting? Ah, yes, in her bedroom. It belonged to my grandmother.'

'I'd like to see that painting.'

'You shall.'

'I've been meaning to tell you something: Toby Griffin did some work here, bookkeeping.'

'Toby Griffin? *He worked for you?*'

'Yes, in a small way. Another appalling business.'

Bliss was flabbergasted. '*Someone with a foot in both camps!* Do you realise the police think he was a crook? And there were gold figurines at his house that could have come from the dig!'

Daguerre looked aghast. 'Oh, my God!'

'All this time we've been looking for a link between your grockles and locals. Here he is! What about the metal detector? Is it his?'

Daguerre shrugged. 'To tell you the truth, I still haven't asked Mortimer.'

She was now in state of high excitement, and not to be put off. 'Well, let's jolly-well get that cleared up, shall we?'

'I suppose.' He didn't seem entirely convinced. 'How did you get in without buzzing?'

'Oh, someone let me in; looked like a gardener. The press have gone.'

'*Have they?*' He brightened. 'That *is* a relief. The news moves on, I suppose. We're in the studio working on a piece. I've been doing purdah to try and sort it out.' He jerked his head to indicate she should follow and he led her round into the yard.

'Grief! This is more like a film studio than an artist's studio,' said Bliss, impressed by the scale of the buildings.

'Yes, they were part of the attraction when I bought the place. I need space. My studio in London is chocka. I do the monumental, you know.' He did a wry imitation of a big shot.

'Yes, of course, I remember the Wickerman.'

'And the Colossus of Rhodes.'

'Yes, and—' Bliss was silenced by the monstrous pile of furniture that confronted her as they entered the studio.

The piece had undergone many changes over the days of weary labour since Daguerre had returned from Germany. In its most recent phase it had grown enormously tall; the furniture was piled up so high it almost touched the steel trusses of the roof. The foot-square mirror tiles that had been inserted throughout the pile lent it a disconcertingly Cubist air, or at least, that was the thought that plagued Daguerre. Fabricators Seth and Taz were resting with mugs of tea in their hands, staring at the pile with an air of desolation.

'Where did all the furniture come from?' Bliss exclaimed, awed by the scale of the undertaking that had secured so much raw material for a work of art.

'I have containers of it in the field,' said Daguerre.

'It's stupendous!' she decided, moved by the sheer spectacle.

Daguerre acknowledged her praise with a slight dip of his head. He took several steps towards the pile and barked, 'Higher! High as you can, Mort!'

Mortimer was nowhere to be seen, but Bliss registered a quiver in the mountainous structure and a Windsor chair at its apex reared up.

'Is that any better?' came a muffled enquiry from the heart of the pile.

'Higher!'

The chair rose a further few inches.

'Yeah, that's better,' Daguerre decided without much enthusiasm. 'Can you fix it there?'

There was the whine of an electric drill followed by the sounds of struggle as Mortimer wormed his way back down. Eventually he emerged at the base of the pile, between two chests of drawers, bearing a Makita drill. He saw Bliss and gave her an amiable nod.

Daguerre signalled for Seth and Taz to leave. 'Have a break, guys, we need some space.'

The two fabricators stretched and grinned with relief at being allowed out.

'Mort,' Daguerre began, when the studio door had closed behind them, 'on the night we went down to the *May Queen* in Emsbury you were going on about somebody having a metal detector. You remember?'

Mortimer considered the question for a moment before replying. 'Was I going on? If I was, you didn't wanted to hear about it.'

'Yeah, sorry, I didn't mean you were in the wrong; I was a bit preoccupied, you know, about the yacht. Who was it you thought had one?'

'Henry mentioned—'

'*Henry Balfour?* Not Toby Griffin? The police think he was involved in this.'

'Yes, Henry. He said something about a metal detector once. I wasn't clear whether he meant he had one, or someone else. Then, when he came to help us with the furniture, while you were in Germany, he brought a box. Asked if I could store it for him.'

Daguerre shot a glance at Bliss. 'What did he say it was?'

'He didn't. It was sealed with tape so I didn't... couldn't look.'

'So?'

'Well, after I mentioned it to you – in the light of Henry disappearing – I thought I'd better take a look.'

'And?'

'It was what I suspected.'
'A metal detector?'
'Yes.'
'And where is it now?'
'It's still in the store.'
'In the material store?'
He nodded.
'Maybe we should take a look.'
'Fine.' He felt in his pocket for keys.

The material store was one of three shipping containers parked at the edge of the field immediately behind the studio. Mortimer undid the padlock and swung open the door. They entered. The interior was divided by racks into two aisles and the racks were piled high with plastic utensils, cases of Plastercine, boxes of tubes of paint, both oil- and water-based, the bleached skeletons of small animals, Airfix kits, plastic fruit of every description, pots of brushes and palette knives, fifteen lay figures of different sizes, a stack of prosthetic limbs and the rest of the humdrum raw material of art making. It reminded Bliss of the boot fair, but she put the thought aside as somehow irreverent. Mortimer led them to the end of the left-hand aisle and dragged a box clear of the lowest shelf.

'This is it.'
'Let's take it back to the studio,' said Daguerre.

He and Bliss backed up, and Mortimer hefted the box into the open. The label said originally it had contained a Dyson and it had been resealed with ducting tape. They returned to the studio where Mortimer placed it on a workbench. He went off to find a blade and while the other two waited in silence, Daguerre's eyes wandering over the pile of furniture.

'*How weird is that!*' he said in a voice of sudden revelation. 'I've built the Tower of Babel! I've cannibalised my own idea! I've made what I wanted my asylum seekers to make. It's *Vehiculating Voicelessness!*'

Bliss followed his gaze with a mystified smile, unsure how to respond.

Mortimer came back with the blade, too late to hear Daguerre's comment but something in Daguerre's face brought him to a halt. He looked from Daguerre to Bliss and back again, expecting one of them to speak. Instead Daguerre shook himself free of his thoughts – quite literally – and gestured for him to cut the tape. The box's contents were quickly laid bare.

'*One owner, top-of-the-range*, you might say,' observed Daguerre coolly.

'It's a good one, isn't it? Try it,' urged Bliss.

'Wouldn't know how. That's the "on" switch, I suppose.' He turned to Mortimer. 'Why did you seal it back up? Why not say something?'

Mortimer sighed. He spoke stoically. 'Like I said, I thought you didn't want it known that someone from here… you know.'

'But, since it was Henry…'

'Well,' said Bliss brightly, 'any idea where and why it was used, eh?'

'Can't help you there.' Mortimer shook his head. 'Ask the crew. They're the ones likely to know. They kept things to themselves… always did.'

Bliss didn't doubt it, and she nodded.

Daguerre had already given up on the metal detector and was trying to calculate the consequences of allowing the pile of furniture to be exhibited. 'I'm thinking of going back to London,' he announced abruptly, rather surprising himself since he hadn't intended the thought for anyone else. 'My time here has been a total waste.'

Bliss was dismayed. As they talked, Lovage was at her house, packing his things in his car, and now a second defection. 'What is it about Lon...? Why is everyone thinking of leaving?'

Daguerre gave her an opaque look. 'It's obvious, isn't it. It's impossible when distracted by so much... *greenery*!' He shook his fists at an imaginary landscape and did an enraged jig, only halting at the sight of Carrie hovering in the doorway. 'Did you know about this?' he demanded, brandishing the metal detector.

She came over, her eyes fixed on it. 'Henry was a bit mad at me because I was dating Taz.'

Daguerre was brusque. '*Oh, was he!* Did he use this, or was he keeping it for somebody else?'

'It was his,' she admitted tearfully.

'He was using it?'

'Yes, he was treasure hunting with it.'

Daguerre swore under his breath. 'Where?'

'I don't know.'

'Did you ever see him with a woman with blond-ish hair in braids?' asked Bliss suddenly.

Carrie was hesitant. 'Braids like Gitta, pinned up, or pigtails?'

'Her name's Jayne Wilson,' said Bliss. 'She's mixed up in this treasure hunting business.'

'I saw him with a woman in the Hampson Arms. She was called Jayne. They had some old coins.'

'When was that?'

'Maybe three, four weeks ago.'

'Did Henry meet Toby Griffin when he was working here?'

'We all knew him. Leery old bloke.' Carrie looked at Mortimer for confirmation.

Mortimer nodded. 'He looked after the studio's books. He checked orders against invoices and that sort of thing. He helped with the payroll too.'

'He came up the river by boat to the Hampson,' said Carrie. 'Henry sometimes came with him.'

'By boat?'

'Yes, he had a dinghy with an outboard motor.'

Bliss looked at Carrie with new interest. 'The crew drank at the Hampson as well as Meade's lads from here?'

'Sometimes. They came in Michael Ditzel's campervan.'

'Huh! Anything else we should know?'

She shook her head.

'How about an antiquities dealer from London called Selwyn?'

She shook her head again.

'You know this much, but that's it?' Bliss looked incredulous. 'Let me understand this little social scene. They were all meeting at the Hampson Arms, but you don't know what they were up to; what was going on between them?'

'No, not really. Just bits.' Her features seemed to be melting.

'They were just socialising,' added Mortimer sulkily.

Bliss gave a snort of disbelief. 'Oh, were they! They were conspiring to steal treasure trove from the archaeological site on Meade's land. Maybe it was

Henry Balfour who attacked Lovage when he was trying to protect the grave.'

Mortimer looked sceptical, but said nothing.

Daguerre was lost in thought, apparently deaf to Bliss's questioning of Mortimer, but now he stirred himself. 'So, who knows the rest of the story? Someone must know more.'

'Mermaids!' murmured Bliss. 'What were their names?'

'Who?'

'You know, the mermaids at Foreland. There were two of them: Margie and something! The young one! One of the crew took her away as you were breaking the news about the yacht. She was Henry's girlfriend, wasn't she? Where do we find her?'

Daguerre gave a hollow laugh. 'Lara, you cracked it; leave it be! Cosmo Fairweather to find Margie, Margie to find her, her to find Henry. The only problem is you're chasing shadows. Henry didn't have a girlfriend, did he Mort?'

Mortimer hunched his shoulders to signify his agreement.

'You mustn't go back to London,' Bliss urged Daguerre. 'She does exist, and we need to find her. I'm going to get it out of the crew if it kills me! I'll find her and then I'll find him.'

Daguerre's eyes had again returned to the pile of furniture and he had slipped beyond the reach of her pleas. 'Mort, this is a shambles,' he declared, 'a bloody shambles! It's gone over into the realm of disasters and, for the life of me, I can't see us getting it back. Carrie, go and fetch the Nikon. I want to photograph this monstrosity so I don't do it again!'

For Mortimer this was too much; his reserves of stoicism had reached an end. 'Last week it was too orderly and we've been working for days to make it more chaotic!'

'I know that; it's a shame.' Daguerre's expression of sympathy was dispassionate, as though he were commiserating over an unsolvable crossword clue.

'And the mirrors! What about the mirrors?'

'The mirrors are great,' he agreed, 'but it needs to have form and be chaotic simultaneously.' A new idea struck him. 'Or maybe it needs to flip backwards and forwards between the two… like traffic lights.'

'And how do we do that?' wondered Mortimer, drawing on the last dregs of his patience.

Daguerre threw up his hands in despair. 'I don't know! Maybe we put the mirrors on motorised swivels.'

They stared at the pile in silence; Mortimer's expression was glum. For a moment Bliss wondered if they might be on the verge of a serious row, but halting the pile's drift towards disaster had become a technical issue that had captured their attentions so completely they had lost sight of the fact that others were present. Carrie was happy to fetch the Nikon and wait, but not Lara; she needed to get back home to see Lovage off and she found herself in the uncomfortable position of reminding them of her presence by bidding them farewell. Their lack of interest in her going made it clear that she had no contribution to make to solving the conundrum their collaboration now faced. As for the matter of Balfour and the metal detector, it seemed that all of them were done with it. She had been meaning to ask Daguerre whether he had padlocked the gates on

Pilgrim's Way, but she saw that for now further pursuit of the nighthawks business would go down badly.

'The problem *is*,' she heard Daguerre announce, as she headed for the door, 'it's too wooden!'

FORTY FIVE

Bliss arrived home to find Lovage ready to leave. He seemed unmoved by her news about Balfour. When she started in on the detail he waved it away as though he had only thoughts for the drive back to London, and beyond that, Suffolk. 'I might have known it,' he said as he eased himself behind the wheel of his Renault. 'His kind are a total menace. Was Daguerre even surprised?'

'No, not greatly. Seems inclined to write it off. He's up to his neck, of course, but half of me doesn't wonder whether he thinks, since the land is his, anything found at the dig is kind of his.'

Lovage raised his eyebrows and gave a grunt of amusement. 'Until they changed the law it was. Let me know when you find Balfour. I'll come back... if I can.'

Bliss was sad to see him go and tears pricked her eyes as the car turned into the lane. Cornelia was nowhere to be seen.

'Farewell, you silly man,' she said fondly to herself.

She consoled herself with a chocolate biscuit and prepared to catch the ferry across to Emsbury. Once there, it did not take her long to find the turning off the High Street that led to Cider Cup Place. The crew's rented cottage was one of a row standing beyond a little fenced-in green. She knocked long and hard, determined to get answers. One of the crew she recognised from Foreland answered the door. She strained to remember his name.

'Hello, you're Michael, aren't you? Michael...?'

He nodded. 'Ditzel.'

'I was with Meade at Foreland.'

'I remember.'

'I'm looking for Cosmo Fairweather.'

'He's with the police. With them yesterday... been back today.' Ditzel grimaced and shifted his gaze to the long, low hut visible between the trees on the hillside above the houses.

Bliss followed the direction of his gaze. 'That's where they're based, is it?'

He nodded.

'Maybe I should go up there and talk to them myself,' she mused, her eyes fixed on the hut.

'Do you want to do that, really?' He sounded certain she didn't. 'What's your interest anyway? You a friend of the family?'

'No, I'm freelance.'

'Maybe I can help?'

'Well, actually, you might.' She switched her gaze back to him. 'How about the young woman you took off across the dunes when we were questioning Fairweather – *you know* – about Henry Balfour and the yacht?'

'What about her?' Suddenly he sounded guarded.

'The blond girl; who is she?'

He gave a resigned sigh. 'You mean Princess.'

'That her name?'

Ditzel nodded.

'She's Henry Balfour's girlfriend, isn't she?'

'No, she's his sister; his half-sister, actually.'

'Half-sister! I find that... *Really?* Are you trying to tell me he was in love with his half-sister?'

'No, I'm not saying that.'

'I'd like to talk to her. Where is she?'

He shook his head. 'She's gone.'

'Gone? Where to?'

'I don't know. Cosmo sent her away.'

'How old is she, anyway?'

'Fifteen.'

'Fifteen! That's incredible! Wasn't she driving that minibus?'

'She was.'

'Where did she come from? Tell me!' Bliss was momentarily baffled. 'If they're trafficking people I suppose it's easy enough for them to make a young girl disappear, isn't it?'

Ditzel shrugged, as though there was no way of knowing the extent of their powers.

'Why are you telling me this, when you know I could go straight to the police?'

'I don't think you'll find they're interested. I know I can't change anything, but that doesn't mean I think it's right. What's done is done, and not even the police can put things back as they were. She's gone, and you won't find her.'

Bliss was increasingly puzzled. 'What about the campervan she came in? What happened to that? That can't have simply disappeared.'

'Why not?'

'Because it can't!'

He pulled a wry face. 'There's a big market for scrap metal in China.'

'Oh, is there?' She laughed. 'So, I suppose snakeheads crushed it and turned it into scrap.'

'Something like that.' He looked at her insolently, willing her to push on with her questions.

She could not fathom the logic of his defiance and her sense of certainty began to ebb away. 'I suppose you know everything that's happened and is going to happen; nothing's a surprise to you.'

He shook his head with a little pout. 'No, just the past, not the future. What I do know is that when things disappear they disappear properly.'

'Meaning?'

'If a friend borrows a thing, or if a burglar comes to your house and takes something, then that something circulates in a kind of world where it's possible – if you're lucky – to get it back… one day. But here circumstances are different; Princess and the men who trashed the yacht have disappeared so you won't ever find them. Tell your friends I said so, if you like. I can't help them, that's for certain. I can only give you advice.'

'Advice?' Bliss was scornful. 'It sounds like cowardice to me. What about Jayne Wilson, Toby Griffin and the archaeological dig? You go treasure hunting up there with Henry Balfour's metal detector?'

'I know some of the others went. They made some money selling stuff. I didn't go myself.'

Bliss could see that although he wasn't prepared to lie, nor was he willing to volunteer information, especially about events he hadn't been involved in. 'But Balfour was a ringleader, wasn't he?'

'Probably. He usually was.'

'And were they selling to Willy Basington? Did you know about a seafood business over in Smeltertown? Was that where the illegals you brought in were working?'

He sighed. 'I don't know anything about that. You need to talk to whoever runs it.'

Bliss wanted to take him by the throat and throttle him. 'I'll find that girl if it takes me a year and a day.'

'Go ahead! She went that way.' He motioned scornfully to the exit from Cider Cup Place.

Bliss followed the direction of his gesture – it was a reflex – and in an instant understood his meaning and returned her gaze to his pallid, unshaven face. 'See a ghost, did you?' she said, her anger rising. 'Lost your nerve before the might of force?' She leant closer as though to tell a tale. 'Your indifference is sick, so go to hell and stuff it, *and stuff you*! And just think,' she scoffed, 'I thought it was all about deduction and following the clues!'

FORTY SIX

At about the same time that Bliss turned her back on Michael Ditzel, a post office van delivered the day's mail to Terpsichore Manor. Among the invitations on smart, embossed stationery was a scruffy, fat envelope addressed to "The Artist In Residence". It was so unlike the rest of the mail that Carrie opened it first. Inside, wrapped in tissue paper, she found a leg; a tiny little leg that at first she couldn't place. Then she realised what it was and hurried to the West Studio to find Daguerre. Without uttering a word she held out the nest of tissue paper for him to see its contents.

'*Fuck me!*' he exclaimed. 'Where did you get that?'

She showed him the envelope.

'*Mort!*' he roared. 'Come and look at this.'

Mortimer came over from the workshop area.

'See this,' said Daguerre indignantly, holding out Carrie's hand.

His eyes ran from Carrie's wrist up to her elbow and he didn't understand what he was being asked to look at.

'Look in the tissue, Mort,' said Daguerre impatiently.

Suddenly Mortimer saw what he was meant to see and his eyes popped out.

'It came in the post.'

'Justin! He's amputated it!' Mortimer exclaimed.

'Yes, *what do you know*, it's the leg of one of the passengers from the Titanic!'

'I told you he was holding them to ransom.'

'What, you mean he's going to cut limbs off and send them to me until I pay up, the sick weirdo?'

Mortimer shook his head in some confusion.

'I thought you were going to get them back!'

He looked helpless. 'I can if you give him a bonus… or something.'

'Fuck! A bonus?'

'I don't know… a severance payment, a goodwill gesture.'

'*Goodwill…!* Okay, a bonus!'

'And a copy of your latest catalogue, signed.'

'*Jesus!*'

'And a signed photo of Gitta.'

FORTY SEVEN

Lara Bliss loitered at the entrance to Cider Cup Place, unsure as to what to do next. Every so often she raised her eyes to the scout hut visible between the trees on the hillside. It seemed to hover like a sentinel watching over Emsbury. She thought about going there immediately and telling the police what she had learnt from Michael Ditzel. She imagined being received by Wriggley and Brisley, and dismissed the idea with a shudder. The only other possibility she could think of was to let Meade Daguerre know what Ditzel had said. She took out her mobile and tried his number. Carrie answered immediately.

'Yes, Lara, hello.'

'Is Meade there, Carrie? I need a word.'

There was a succession of fumbling noises before Meade came on. He sounded distant and morose. 'Hello, Lara, where are you?'

'Sorry to bother you, Meade. I'm in Emsbury. Things any better?'

He gave a hollow laugh. 'I'm seriously thinking of running this furniture piece through the wood chipping machine. What would you advise for advanced sclerosis of the brain?'

'Gin and tonic, Meade, every time. Can't fail. I'm sorry it's a bad time, but does Henry Balfour have a half-sister?'

'Don't think so. He's got an older brother: MP. That's it, as far as I know.'

'One of those lads from your boat who took off to the music festival with Margie—'

'You mean Cosmo Fairweather?'

'No, one of the others. The name's Michael Ditzel. I've just been having a chat with him and he's told me the other, younger girl they were with at Foreland is Henry's half-sister.'

'He's trying it on. That's not right.'

'I thought as much; he's a very disturbed young man. I feel certain she's Henry's girlfriend, but she's a minor and they've been trying to cover it up. And now she's disappeared.'

'I told you: Henry doesn't have a girlfriend, not to my knowledge. Why would he get mixed up with a minor? How old, for Christ's sake?'

'Fifteen.'

'And she's disappeared?'

'So we'll never find her, so he says. Her name's Princess.'

Daguerre's voice changed. 'Hello, that rings a bell! Ever hear of Durville Maxwell?'

'No. Who's he?'

'No, it's an artists' colony, bit hippy, bit alternative. I had a couple of helpers from there earlier in the year. There's a family there called King of Spain.'

'*King of Spain!* What, you mean that's the family name?'

'Yes, Mr and Mrs King of Spain. Memorable, isn't it? They have three daughters; the eldest is supposed to have a precocious talent as a tumbler. Some big shot sports trainer wants to take her to the next Olympics; reckons she's a star in the making.'

'Princess King of Spain!'

'Could be. The two guys I employed took Henry over there, I'm pretty sure.'

'Why?'

'I think Henry had a chainsaw; they borrowed it and he went with them.'

'A chainsaw? They must have been cutting timber.'

'I guess. They said Durville Maxwell is like a kibbutz. Ruskin's Guild of St George and all that stuff. It's somewhere in a big patch of woodland, and they grow their own food and spend their time arguing about how to build utopia.'

'Good grief and hallelujah!'

'Not your sort of thing? Well, as I said, it's a bit hippy!'

Bliss needed to think about what Daguerre had told her and decided to let him go. 'Meade, I *think* that's very helpful.'

He laughed. 'You don't sound so sure. Oh, Lara, look, I should have said something when you were here this morning, but I forgot. These curators I've got staying here.'

'Yes?'

'I have to offer them some hospitality. Could you join us for dinner at The Estuary tonight?'

'Love to. What time?'

'Eight sharp. Oh, and Lara, I've got a Picasso print I'm a bit sick of. How about sticking it in an auction and giving the proceeds to the League?'

'What was that, Meade? *Meade?*'

The line had gone dead and she wasn't quite sure what he had said. She was still speculating when a police car rounded the corner and entered Cider Cup Place. It came to a stop outside the crew's cottage. Cosmo Fairweather climbed out, and to her surprise looked very much at ease. He chatted to the driver through the passenger window for a minute and then the car moved off. Bliss slipped into a nearby front garden before the car could round the green. It passed by her hiding place and turned up the hill in the direction of the scout hut. She could see Fairweather had been watching the car too. As soon as it was lost to sight he turned and entered the cottage with what she could have sworn was a smug grin.

Her immediate impulse was to return to the cottage and attempt another doorstep interrogation, but she decided that Fairweather was likely to be even less helpful than Michael Ditzel, so she abandoned the idea. She turned to go and was surprised to see Jack Palanga on the other side of the street, watching her. Before she could move he crossed over to her, a scowl on his face.

'Why are you always under my feet, Lara?' he hissed, pulling her out of sight of the crew's cottage. 'I'm trying to do my job and you're always sticking your amateur dramatics' nose into things!'

Bliss pulled her arm free of his grip. 'Well, well, Mr Palanga, what *are* you up to?' She jabbed furiously at the ground at her feet. 'Why are you *here*?'

Palanga laughed. 'Why are *you* here?'

Bliss put her hand to her head as if dazed. 'Well, I've just beaten you to an interview with Michael Ditzel. He tried to frighten me off with a lot of fatalistic gobbledegook. I think there's a girl called Princess King of Spain who'll know where Henry Balfour is. I want to find her.'

'Princess *what?*'

'Princess King of Spain. Yes, I know! Meade seems to think we'll find this girl of Balfour's at a place called Durville Maxwell. Heard of it?'

'Can't say I have.'

'It's some kind of commune. Maybe Meade can tell us how to find it.'

Palanga gave a wry laugh. 'Well, why don't you ask him? You'd be so much more successful than me!'

She wasn't so sure she wanted to call Daguerre again. 'He's had a bit of a blow with his plans; his muse seems to be giving him rather a trying time.'

'This isn't about the burning Ferrari on the steps of the National Gallery, is it?'

'*Good God!* Who told you he was going to do that?'

'One of the journalists: he was camped outside Daguerre's front gate all day, drinking all night in the bar at the hotel.'

'Really? You always have the gossip, don't you?' She stamped her foot. 'Why are you *here?*'

'Same old thing as you: now Balfour's crew have reappeared I was hoping they'd tell me what was going on.' He nodded towards Cider Cup Place. 'One or more must have been working for the Chinese, don't you think? The Chinese man in the dark suit who was with Balfour when he turfed Daguerre's helpers off the yacht murdered Balfour, didn't he?'

'Why do you think one of them was… Wait a minute, Balfour murdered? He's not dead. It was pig's blood! You already knew it was pig's blood when we went to the boot fair on Sunday, didn't you? That's when you realised the damage to the yacht was meant to scare the crew and had nothing to do with Daguerre.'

He hunched his shoulders. 'Okay, yes, the pig's blood was meant to scare the hell out of the crew. Doesn't mean Balfour wasn't murdered. Not on the yacht; that would have been stupid. The rest of the crew were at Foreland when the yacht was trashed and Balfour murdered. My guess is one of them came back here and went to the yacht. He saw the mess and scuttled back to Foreland. He was scared; knew it was a warning. They thought it advisable to disappear for a few days. Where better than a large crowd? So they all went to the Atlantic Splash. Disappearing for just a few days says "guilty conscience"; it certainly doesn't make sense if one of them murdered Balfour.'

'That's all ridiculous, Jack. I saw those boys when they first reappeared and I'd swear they didn't know a thing about the yacht being trashed. Balfour hasn't been murdered either. *He* found the mess in the yacht and did a bunk. It was meant to scare him; that's why he hasn't turned up yet. It's just a matter of finding him.' Bliss had other things she was determined to have out with him. 'We caught you in conference with some pretty strange company the other day. And you didn't like it, did you? So, what's going on? Whose side are you really playing for? Who was that man with Barney Bennett in his Porsche? And how come you haven't been weaving Willy Basington into your tapestry of what's going on in Emsbury?'

Palanga gave an exasperated snort. He felt he had said more than enough and it was with reluctance that he gave ground further. 'Look, Lara, as Willy told you, I'm doing a profile on him. That's why I was with those men. They work for Willy. Bennett manages a warehouse for him.'

'And what goes on there?'

'They pack organic potatoes.'

'Potatoes?'

'Yes, and a few vegetables more. That sort of thing.'

'Is this in Smeltertown, by any chance?'

Palanga regarded her coolly. 'Actually, no, it's just outside Emsbury, not far from Willy Basington's place.'

'And what about the warehouse down in Smeltertown? They pack seafood there. And it's been abandoned. We were there yesterday and it's rank with rotting fish.'

She had hit on something that Palanga was less comfortable with. 'All right, I've heard about that. But it isn't a Willy Basington enterprise. It was more arm's-length than that.'

Bliss laughed sarcastically. '*Arm's-length!* I've heard that before! Does that imply some kind of deniability, or what?'

'Look, Willy Basington was suspicious about what was going on there and when the drowned Chinese man turned up in the lay-by he talked to the police. They weren't interested. Like you, they thought he came from Bristol.'

Bliss looked unimpressed. 'What I don't understand is why you've been in cahoots with Basington. I don't get it at all. Why have you been protecting him?'

Palanga was exasperated. 'I've not been protecting him. If you must know I've been working for him.'

'*Been working...!* You too? *This is incredible!*'

Palanga pulled a face; reluctantly he had decided to reveal all. 'This is between us: I'm helping him with his TV programme. I'm writing his lines; that stuff doesn't write itself, you know.'

'I don't believe you.'

'I've done the research. Willy doesn't have the time.'

'Research? Research on what?'

'On Meade Daguerre.'

Bliss found herself laughing. 'There's no end to the wickedness of the world, is there Jack?'

He didn't follow her meaning. 'Jack Palanga knows more about Meade Daguerre than Daguerre does. We're fans.'

'If you're fans,' she said, not hiding her disdain, 'I'm glad I'm not famous.'

'Maybe so, but the wraps are coming off as soon as Gitta Jensson gets back from Denmark. She's on her way now.'

'Meade's wife? What's she to do with it?'

'She's in on it with Willy. Everyone's in on it.'

'Not me!'

'Well, no, but you will be.'

'So is Meade in on it? Come on, *is he in on it?*'

'You know he's not, *definitely not*! That's the whole point: he's the one being tested against Willy Basington's "Five Tests of True Entrepreneurship". The programme's a tie-in: *Super Start-ups Celebrity Special*.'

'But he's *an artist*; one of the most successful artists of his generation!'

'Yes, that makes him the perfect guinea pig and he'll come through with a perfect five. It's creative entrepreneurship writ large!'

'And he doesn't know what's going on?'

'No.' Palanga shrugged.

'And when he finds out?'

'He'll feel flattered… or exploited. Who knows? Either way it's the price of celebrity! He's been put up for the Queen's Award for Enterprise Promotion. He's going to win… and probably one step away from a knighthood. Gitta will bring him round; put it to him that it's great TV. He could refuse, of course, but then…'

Bliss had heard enough. 'I'm going; you've brain-battered me! Frankly, I could do with a drop of the chemical. Poor Meade! I'm having dinner with him at The Estuary tonight; I'll ask him about Princess then.' She turned to go but Palanga held her back by her arm.

'Lara, don't you say anything to him about the show. Tonight is when they're recording the opening segment. Remember: *now* you're in on it!'

FORTY EIGHT

It was a glorious, balmy evening. The Riviera couldn't have offered a sight more picturesque than the estuary of the Em from the terrace of The Estuary. At eight o'clock Lara Bliss, quite transformed, wearing her only evening dress and a matching bolero jacket, was climbing the steps to the terrace. She heard her name called and stopped. Meade Daguerre had arrived in the company of Rita Carshalton in her Fendi, Magnussen Olsen from Oslo and Mrs Mikko Ikeda from Osaka, her head wrapped in a turban of bandage.

'Evening, Lara. You look very striking. That's a lovely velvet,' said Daguerre warmly. 'I'll introduce you.'

There was a crowd drinking on the terrace and the restaurant was already full. The old banking hall looked resplendent: the mahogany banking counters recycled as the long bar, and the coffered ceiling, recalled the prosperous days of the china clay trade out of Emsbury Quay. The noise was deafening. As Daguerre's party stepped through the door the reassuring figure of Terence was at hand, looking calm and in control of every detail of the front of house.

'Evening Meade. Busy tonight.'

'Evening. Running smoothly?'

'Baltasar's in his element. The kitchen's in top gear.'

'Glad to hear it.' He leaned closer. 'Still thinking of sacking him… unless he poisons me first.'

'He probably will. Willy Basington's here with a party.'

Daguerre stiffened. 'Fine. Get my table started with Moët. I must meet and greet.'

'They were filming again a while ago.'

'Where?'

'On the terrace. I think it was something to do with Mr Basington.'

'I'll see what's up when I drop by his table.'

Daguerre wove his way between the tables aware that he attracted stares and furtive glances in equal measure from every table he passed. His eyes were fixed on the elegant figure in the sand-coloured suit on the far side of the restaurant, but what he saw in his mind's eye was a gigantic pile of furniture with Max running round it, crying, "Light the bonfire, light the bonfire!". A pretty teenage girl rose from a table, blocking his way. She offered him the back of the day's specials to autograph. He drew a heart-shaped fish and signed it with a flourish. As he did so he found himself wondering how long it would be before it was in sale at Bonhams or Roseberys. She simpered alluringly, her breasts peeping out from her low-cut top, and he moved on with a grin. As he approached Basington's table, Basington caught sight of him and rose to his feet with an exclamation of delight.

'Mr Daguerre! What a pleasant surprise! Should I compliment you on the lobster?'

Daguerre shook the offered hand, gave a nod to the rest: the sly fox had a couple of rabbits and an old rooster at his table.

'Twice in a week, Willy! The chef must be doing something right. I hope Terence is looking after you?'

'Marvellous!' He nodded to one of his guests. 'Councillor Todd was just saying what a great debt the town owes you for bringing a bit of London sophistication to our dining scene.' He laughed his confident, pleasant laugh and clapped Daguerre on the shoulder. 'Take a glass with us before you join your party. I'll send over some champagne.'

Daguerre grinned. 'Terence is already seeing to it, but I'll put it on your tab with pleasure.' He was vaguely aware that a complicated shuffling of places was under way to allow him to take a seat. He leaned closer to Basington's ear. 'Willy, you're a local boy done good, aren't you?'

'I suppose so.'

'Well, fuck me, Willy, why did you have to get Henry Balfour mixed up in some dirty business with illegal immigrants? You don't have to do that to make a penny, do you? I thought Henry worked for me!'

Basington didn't look the least put out. He smiled contentedly, as though what he was expecting had come to pass. 'Henry thinks he's a pirate, Meade. Something went wrong with his upbringing. It's like he never grew up. Haul up the Jolly Roger and away we go! Wrong side of the law, fight for freedom, the lure of treasure. In his own sweet way he's a fanatic and he got himself introduced to some acquaintances of acquaintances I'd never dream of doing business with. He loves the whole thing: elicit everything. I can only applaud his nerve, but take responsibility for him? *Never!* He'll run away with anything you give him. Offer him a metal detector and he'll come back, panting like a golden retriever, with a super-sized stick in his mouth.'

'A stick?'

'Quite.'

Daguerre gazed into his bland expression as though in a trance.

'I hear work in the studio's not going too well.'

'I was just thinking, *you paid him*! Who told you that, anyway?'

Basington shrugged. 'Who told you I paid him?'

'One of the boys.'

'Emsbury's such a small place! The world's here and at play; enjoy the sea, the festive air of holidays! The blissful cries of small children! You should sail that yacht more. Work will wait. Fête champêtre at my place tomorrow.' He waved in the direction of Daguerre's table. 'Bring them all; we'll have a yodelling competition. And how about a picnic on my steam launch next week? I'll take you out to Chancellor Island. See some nature.' He held out a glass of champagne, which Daguerre took without demur. 'We've been talking about the cricket at Lords. Catch any today?'

They both looked at the other occupants of the table and laughed uproariously.

Across the room Bliss had reached Daguerre's table to find Miles Sleight already sitting there with a dry martini, mostly consumed, parked in front of him.

'Ah, Bliss, what a pleasure!' he murmured, as she sat down, 'I have to say, the word "promiscuous" comes to mind when I think of the company we keep these days.'

'Frankly, Miles, I'm rather surprised to find you invited after your last outing with Meade. I have a word *for you*,' she said tartly, 'it's "benevolence".'

'How went the search for the pointy-eared wood elf over Smeltertown way?'

'Meaning?' she said, warily.

'Arthur Peddleton, of course.'

'Well enough. Still painting zebras. How's Prudence?'

'Topping, Bliss, topping.'

To Miles's left Mrs Ikeda was taking her seat and, no doubt struck by the extravagant bandage, he turned to enquire what disaster had befallen her. To Bliss's right Rita was lowering herself into her seat, placing her mobile strategically in the centre of her place setting. Bliss was quick to discover she was sitting next to one of London's most important art dealers. It crossed her mind that she looked like a driven woman in need of relaxation therapy and sensible shoes. Hardly had they exchanged a few pleasantries before Detective Inspector Wriggley appeared at her elbow.

'Inspector!' She gazed into his face, thinking indignantly, *even he's in on it!* Unlike their previous meetings, she sensed she had him at a disadvantage.

'Sorry to interrupt; dining out with my colleague,' he explained. He leant closer and lowered his voice to a confidential whisper, nodding to the table where Detective Sergeant Brisley was seated. 'In other circumstances it would be very pleasant to share a crust and drink a toast or two.' He gave her a wistful smile that she considered just short of unctuous.

Her rebuff was kindly. 'Yes, in other circumstances.'

He grew professional, his eyes twinkled; there was something almost gay in his demeanour. 'You may recall that right at the start of our investigation we thought someone – possibly Mr Balfour – had been murdered on

Mr Daguerre's boat. Closer examination of the evidence has led us away from such a conclusion. I believe it might put your mind at rest to know we've come to the view that while engaged in the planning of a serious crime Mr Balfour was waylaid by an unknown assailant – not from Emsbury, very likely no longer in the country. No knowing what the outcome was… Naturally, I say this provisionally, awaiting developments… over the course of time.'

Bliss laughed. 'Goodness that sounds full of excuses.'

Wriggley looked faintly put out. 'I wouldn't say that. "Convenient" might be more to the point, and Emsbury is quite unspoilt, isn't it? Shame to wreck everyone's summer.'

'*Further,* inspector – wreck it *further*!'

'Indeed, wreck it further.'

Bliss was suddenly outraged by his condescension. 'So what happened? Tell me that.'

Wriggley's face took on a look of regret. 'We don't know the details, of course. Mr Balfour could be the fulcrum for great things; to make things happen is such a rare ability! But circumstances were against him. He is one of those men to whom dangers come. There was a meeting, a disagreement. Somebody thought him a nuisance, then a threat. Perhaps a trap was laid. Mr Balfour knew time was running out; over-confidence was his downfall. You're a painter, Ms Bliss, so when I speak of this being but a small part of a much larger canvas, I think you catch my drift. Things are afoot; bigger fish to fry.' His expression brightened. 'I'm sure you're pleased, Ms Bliss, that the respectable name of the Emsbury League of Artists has not been sullied by any unfortunate association.'

She gave a cynical laugh. 'Hasn't it? Well, it appears I underestimated Toby Griffin. And Jayne Wilson too. I understand they were both selling work to Willy Basington. Funny that; I don't think he actually has any.'

'He's across the room, talking to Mr Daguerre.' Wriggley pointed with his chin. 'Settling differences, I suspect.'

'About what?'

'Oh, I don't know.' Wriggley waved his hands vaguely. 'Daguerre's lads have been trampling his crops.'

'You don't say! Making crop circles to be seen from the air in hot air balloons, like mischievous boys. And I was thinking it was our Willy who'd been trampling all over Meade.'

'Great good fortune to have famous people living in the neighbourhood. Makes life a lot more interesting, don't you ag—'

'Inspector,' she interrupted, in a chiding voice, 'do you even know about the fish-packing warehouse in Smeltertown?'

'Ah, yes! We've had an eye on several such places for some months. That one was abandoned about the time our investigation of this business on Mr Daguerre's boat started. Scarpered. Fly-by-night. Typical.'

'Doesn't the timing suggest that someone connected with that warehouse knows something about Balfour's disappearance?'

'Might seem that way. Our investigation points to unpaid bills, fraudulent ordering of equipment and materials; stuff they never intended to pay for. Coincidence, in short.'

Bliss was gathering herself to doubt the likelihood of the two events being a coincidence when she saw that Daguerre was bearing down on them.

'Detective Inspector Wriggley!' Daguerre exclaimed. 'Nice to see you here. Enjoying dinner?' He grabbed his hand and shook it vigorously, and then turned to Bliss. 'What do you think, Lara? Everybody who's anybody seems to be here!'

'I was about to ask Detective Inspector Wriggley whether he's heard of Durville Maxwell.'

'Ah!' said Wriggley thoughtfully. 'We found a chainsaw there. It seems it might have belonged to Mr Balfour. The King of Spains: they're gone. Apparently people come and go there all the time. No forwarding addresses.'

'Well!' said Daguerre with exaggerated bonhomie, 'what can we do about that?'

'Order,' suggested Bliss, flapping her menu disgustedly.

Daguerre laughed, and went round the table to his place between the two curators. He picked up his own menu and gave Wriggley a carefree wave that said it was time he returned to his own table. Wriggley took the hint but seemed to be contemplating a parting shot. He stood gulping air and nothing came. Perhaps he thought better of it, but it seemed to Bliss there was something in the way he stood that suggested a begrudging regard for the lineaments of a sensibility he could not fathom and, for all his powers, had no jurisdiction over. Whatever the reason, he saluted Daguerre most respectfully, gave her a nod, and sidled off to join Brisley without a further word.

'So tell me, Maestro,' declared Olsen, the moment Daguerre was settled in his seat, 'the Ferrari you have in your studio – ya! – is it the one you're going to burn on the steps of the National Gallery?'

Bliss saw a tiny tremor shake Daguerre. He gripped the stem of his glass of champagne, newly poured by the ever-attentive Terence, as though it were a safety line over a dangerous chasm. 'What's this, Magnussen? You have some news I've not heard yet! That Ferrari cost me a hundred grand.'

'In name of art such an act become priceless,' said Mrs Ikeda, leaning in from the other side.

Solemnly Olsen made a gesture with his left hand. 'Commodity fetishism!' He held out the other hand, palm uppermost. 'Art and the institutions of culture!'

'Most witty,' agreed Mrs Ikeda, beaming from beneath her cockeyed bandage. 'As usual, Mr Daguerre, binary articulated with enormous wit. Particularisation of commodity and institutional setting perfection.'

Since Daguerre had joined the table Rita's attention had been taken by the texts on her mobile. Now, suddenly, in what Mrs Ikeda was saying, she recognised something she had heard mention of before. 'What *are* you talking about?' she demanded of Daguerre and the two curators.

'We're talking about the Ferrari artwork,' explained Olsen with great gravity.

'Ferrari artwork? I remember now, a journalist said something about a Ferrari the other day.' Rita levelled a finger at Daguerre. 'Is this something new?'

Daguerre raised his eyebrows in Olsen's direction in the hope that he might furnish her with an explanation.

Still beaming brightly, Mrs Ikeda was quick to slip in a thought. 'In Japan we say Mr Daguerre's ongoing commentary on commodity fetishism is most persuasive theme of his work.'

Olsen raised his palm to indicate he was about to make one of his ponderous pronouncements. 'In London they know how to mix spectacle and controversy in a way that's unique; it makes other European cities look flatfooted.' He shook his head as though marvelling at Londoners' collective talent for spectacle and controversy. 'This mix is, of course, as much about curatorial daring as it is anything. The risk-taking is just of a higher order. Meade has been an inspiration for that kind of approach to the public space ever since he brought *La Mascletá* from Valencia to the courtyard of Somerset House. His Gunpowder Concerto – ya! – was one of the highlights of my year in London. The final cannonade was *tremendous*! And now, a fitting encore: a flaming red Ferrari at the very doors of the National Gallery. Design, style – an engineering marvel! – immolated at the font of dead, white, middle-class artists!'

Rita was so attentive it looked as though she had developed eye strain. 'That... is very interesting,' she said weakly, 'although I hardly think Rubens counts as middle-class.' She turned her attention on Daguerre. 'For the last forty-eight hours I've been worrying about how you're going to replace Vehiculating Voicelessness and here's the answer!' She rolled her eyes at him reproachfully. 'I'm somewhat aggrieved.'

Bliss was not sure what was going on. It was seemed as though Daguerre's Latest Idea was gaining substance as it was told and retold round the table, with no reference to its supposed maker. Covertly she watched as Daguerre gazed back at Rita without a flicker, more enigmatic than the sphinx. Daguerre had something other than making art on his mind. She saw his eyes wander in the direction of Basington's table. The teenage girl with the low-cut dress who had asked him for an autograph was simpering over Willy Basington, offering him her menu to sign. From where Bliss was sitting it looked as though Basington had his hand somewhere up the back of her skirt. Daguerre turned back to the table when Terence came into his line of sight. Bliss's eyes met his and he pulled an expression, part exasperation, part weariness. Beside her, Rita had leaned forward in his direction.

'Much... better... than... the... Afghans,' she mouthed across the table, breaking into a smile of satisfaction.

'A toast!' Daguerre declared, suddenly animated. He signalled to Terence that he should replenish the champagne. 'To fads and fancies and the irresponsible borrowing of money.'

'*To fads and fancies and the irresponsible borrowing of money!*' they all cried.

Mrs Ikeda still held her brimming glass aloft. 'To flaming Ferraris,' she proposed with a mischievous twinkle.

'*Flaming Ferraris!*'

Bliss was lost in thought about Henry Balfour, Princess King of Spain and Durville Maxwell. She wondered whether Balfour's disappearance, if not exactly forgotten, had in some way been *disposed of*. She took a look at the two detectives, who were already hunched over their puddings, and decided it was probably so. Abstractedly, she shifted her gaze to Daguerre. It surprised her to discover that she regarded him with real affection. She felt a pang of sympathy for him too: he looked so beleaguered, but then she reasoned she had no cause; he was the successful one, the star with the glamorous wife, the celebrity lifestyle. Soon it would be autumn and he and the rest would pack up and move on. Holidaymakers, illegal immigrants, Daguerre and his entourage – all were grockles. She should keep her concern for herself; it had taken her the best part of a year to complete the painting she had shown him, and it was quite a success. As glasses were returned to the table, half-empty, she decided she was glad Lovage had vacated her studio and she could get back to painting seriously. Perhaps the muse of the Em estuary would be kind to her.

'I say, "Here's to mermaids"!' she declared as Terence once again topped up her glass.

'*Mermaids!*' they all cried.

'Flaming Ferraris!'

'*Flaming Ferraris!*'

Olsen leant forward, eager to top them all. 'And to art that succeeds!'

'No such thing!' objected Daguerre, laughing. He took his hand from inside his jacket, levelled his index finger, cocked his thumb, drew a bead on Willy Basington and fired. 'It's all decoration, my friends.'

Bliss hardly had time to apprehend Daguerre's mime before Basington had lurched to his feet. He threw out his arms in an exuberant gesture of greeting, directed to someone at the entrance of the restaurant.

'*Ladies and gentlemen, Super Start-ups Celebrity Special!*' boomed a great, disembodied voice that stilled the restaurant.

There, at the door, Bliss saw an elegant woman dressed in a sheath of pearlescent silk, her blond braids haloed by the glare of lights. And behind her, a film crew. Such a picture of shining beauty was it, her breath it quite took away.

FORTY NINE

At the mouth of the estuary, Cornelia had finally caught up with the steam launch, moored close to the shore of Chancellor Island. She stopped the outboard motor and rowed up to it with great caution. The launch's boiler hissed and groaned faintly in the night air. The crew had gone ashore and were nowhere to be seen. She tied up the dinghy and climbed onto the launch's deck. In her hand was a bottle of white spirits she had taken from her aunt's studio while Lovage had been packing. She set it down and untied the spare shirt from around her waist. The inviolable lore of the spooks, spirits and denizens of the Em estuary dictated that the shirt should be hers, and that she should have worn it all summer. Nothing less personal would do. She crouched down, soaked the shirt with the white spirit and stuffed it under the wooden bench that ran the length of the starboard side of the cockpit. In her pocket was the lighter she had taken from Bolshoi Bertie's tent. That the lighter was stolen was equally important to the lore of wilding. It meant in all respects she was fulfilling the lore's second commandment: that crime was fought with crime. Only thus, it was decreed, would her act be made righteous. She reached under the bench and lit the bundled-up shirt. It caught fire with a gentle "woof!". She watched it burn until she could tell the flames had taken hold. With a look of satisfaction she scrambled back into the dinghy. As she rowed off into the darkness of the estuary the blaze leapt up, catching the awning. She rested on her oars for a moment, the flames illuminating the diabolical grin on her face. Only by such *extremis* was the balance of the universe restored.